The QUEEN'S RIVALS

Books by Brandy Purdy

THE BOLEYN WIFE

THE TUDOR THRONE

THE QUEEN'S PLEASURE

THE QUEEN'S RIVALS

Published by Kensington Publishing Corporation

The QUEEN'S RIVALS

BRANDY PURDY

KENSINGTON BOOKS
www.kensingtonbooks.com

KENSINGTON BOOKS are published by

Kensington Publishing Corp.
119 West 40th Street
New York, NY 10018

All Kensington titles, imprints, and distributed lines are available at special quantity discounts for bulk purchases for sales promotion, premiums, fund-raising, and educational or institutional use.

Special book excerpts or customized printings can also be created to fit specific needs. For details, write or phone the office of the Kensington Special Sales Manager: Kensington Publishing Corp., 119 West 40th Street, New York, NY 10018. Attn. Special Sales Department. Phone: 1-800-221-2647.

ISBN-13: 978-0-7582-6599-9
ISBN-10: 0-7582-6599-9
First Kensington Trade Paperback Printing: July 2013

eISBN-13: 978-0-7582-8936-0
eISBN-10: 0-7582-8936-7
First Kensington Electronic Edition: July 2013

10 9 8 7 6 5 4 3 2 1

Printed in the United States of America

My God, why hast Thou forsaken me?

—Matthew 27:46

If you are not too long, I will wait here for you all my life.

—Oscar Wilde

While I Lived, Yours.

—The inscription engraved inside the ring Katherine Grey sent her husband from her deathbed

AUTHOR'S NOTE

This is a work of historical fiction inspired by the lives of the Grey sisters—Jane, Katherine, and Mary. Certain details, events, locations, and characters have been altered, condensed, or invented.

PROLOGUE

Lady Mary Grey

October 31, 1577
A small house in the parish of
St. Botolph's-Without-Aldgate, London

What a splendid study in contradictions I am! Inside as well as out. A grown woman, wizened and white-haired, old before her time, trapped in a stunted, child-sized body, with a soul dark and stormy lit by flashes of brilliance, just like the sodden black velvet night outside my window, where the lightning flits, flashes, and flies, like a swift silver needle over the sky's dark bodice, there again, then gone, in and out under a fluttering veil of frosty rain, and the thunder rumbles, grumbles, and booms just like a master tailor bellowing at his seamstresses to sew *faster, faster,* the gown *must* be finished in time. Though sage sits burning in a copper bowl upon my windowsill, an old custom to keep the ghosts away upon this night when the veil between the worlds of the living and the dead is said to shimmer gossamer-thin, moth-eaten and frayed with holes and gaps through which any spirit might seep or creep, and all the sane and sensible folk of London have shuttered their windows tight, I alone amongst my neighbors have boldly thrown the casements wide in welcome to all those I have loved and lost. The sage says, *"Stay away!"* but the open windows, like my heart, cry out, *"Come in!"* My mind conjures up a picture of Kate lovingly, indulgently, laughing at me, coppery ringlets shimmering and bobbing as she shakes her head, the stormy blue jewels of her eyes sparkling with glee, an amused smile traipsing merrily across her pink lips like a troupe of happy-go-lucky strolling players, as she bends to kiss my cheek and hug me tight, and, with mirth and a pinch of exasperation, in mock seriousness teasingly intones, "Mary, Mary, *so* contrary!" I can still smell her cinnamon rose perfume, as strong as if she were still holding me. And oh how I wish she were! I miss my pert, vivacious sister, so saucy and sweet, a lovely, lively girl; a contradiction herself like a cream-filled pastry with a spicy red pepper hidden inside, a girl with a song always in her heart who danced through life as though she wore a pair of enchanted slippers . . . before love weighed her down and made her so terribly sad that in the end she died of it.

Tears fill my eyes at this vivid vision of Kate, so *real,* achingly real, I can almost reach out and touch her, yet—another contradiction!—it almost makes me want to laugh, to throw back my head and cackle like a madwoman at my old, foolish self. And why should I not? After the life I've led, the sights I've seen, the secrets I've kept, the dangerous confidences that have been whispered into my ears, and the love I've had wrenched right out of my arms, consigned to the grave with my heart thudding down after like an anchor landing on the coffin lid, the memories that keep me wide awake in my bed at night, I think I've earned the right to squat down on my haunches and howl at the moon and give my neighbors cause to call me "Mad Mary" instead of "Crouchback Mary," "Crook-Spine Mary," "Devil-Damned and Twisted Mary," "Milady Gargoyle," or "The Goblin Lady." A mind, and heart, can only take so much, and once broken, nothing is ever as strong as it was before; the mended seams are always vulnerable and weak. And it doesn't really matter what they call me; I've heard all the names before. I've been hearing them since I was old enough to understand words.

The nursery maids spoke of me in fearful whispers as "the changeling" and "the goblin child," and speculated that God had sent me to curse the Greys for their overweening pride and grandiose ambitions. But none of that matters now; I learned early that I had to be practical and discreet in order to survive, that I would only waste my life if I spent it weeping for what could never be, and that even though the darkness of the shadows may be frightening, sometimes it's safer there, especially for someone little and strange like me.

By now I've become accustomed and numb, or at least indifferent, to it all. I cannot even imagine my life without the whispers, stares, gasps of horror, laughter, jests, and insults, fast-turned backs and swiveled heads, and pointing fingers, and the children who run alongside me and mock my wobble-waddle walk. The threats that if they don't obey their parents and eat their porridge, learn their hornbook, clean their teeth, or say their prayers at night they will grow up to look like me has rendered many an unruly child the model of docility and impeccable obedience. And I've heard the stories describing how, whilst carrying me, my mother was frightened by a monkey that climbed in through her open window as she lay sleeping one stormy night and burrowed beneath her bedclothes for warmth, and when she turned in her sleep, inadvertently startling the little beast, it bit her; some stories even crudely name the privy part into which it sank its teeth, prematurely bringing on her protracted and hellish labor and my deformity.

Of course it isn't true, as anyone who ever knew my lady-mother can readily attest. If a monkey had ever *dared* such a presumption, Frances Grey would have sat up and dealt him such a slap his eyes would have been forever crossed and he would have flown clear across the room and smashed into the wall and probably left half his brains there. But it makes a good story, and that's what people like. And mayhap I should be flattered; such stories are like little gifts of immortality, truth or lies; as long as the tales are told, the people they are about never *really* die. Though 'tis sad to be remembered as a figure of fun or fright, one of Mother Nature's mistakes.

Stubby, lumpy, and crooked, I stand no taller than a child of five, the age at which I stopped growing. Mangled but alive, I endure a life of pain,. with a hunched and twisted spine that pushes my right shoulder higher than the left, a constant grinding ache in my back, hips, and knees, as though each joint possesses a full mouth of blackened, rotten teeth, and the limp seems to worsen every year. If I were to lift my skirts and roll down my stockings, I would see the veins bulging from my aching legs like a swarm of blue and purple snakes, swollen and pulsing with pain that I must take a syrup of poppies to subdue. Now I walk with a cane, a regal little staff crowned with a luminous orb of moonstone my husband made for me, knowing I would someday have need of it when he might not be there to carry me. Though it wasn't always so. I used to be right sprightly in my youth and even danced on my wedding night.

It seems a century ago, though only a dozen years have actually passed since I, his "bumblebee bride," as my Thomas, my Mr. Keyes, fondly called his Mrs. Keyes, lifted the black and yellow striped skirt of my wedding gown to display my dancing feet, nimble and proud in their dainty golden slippers, and the black silk stockings I had embroidered with a flight of dainty bees rising from my ankles to my knees, and—for my good husband's eyes alone—raised my hems even higher to most brazenly reveal the sunny yellow satin bows of my garters. How he smiled and clapped delightedly as I danced a rollicking jig and the jolly pipers played. I kicked my limbs ever higher until I fell laughing on my bottom, well cushioned by taffeta and velvet and the padded bum roll tied around my hips underneath my petticoats. Then my Thomas paid the pipers and sent them on their way and lay down with me. That night when his lips followed the crooked path of my spine, going over and down the hump like taking a slow, meandering stroll down a hill, and he said it was like a perpetual question mark, an eternally beautiful mystery, and dotted it with a kiss on my sharply protruding tailbone, I stopped hating and cursing my malformed back. From that moment on whenever anyone made reference to it, whether in pity, malice, a mean spirit, or just a plain statement of fact, I always remembered his words, his lips tracing the question mark of my spine, and how very much he loved me. In his arms I discovered that ugliness is not always a curse. I knew I was well and truly loved only for myself, for the *me* inside my head and heart. If I had been a great beauty like Kate, I might have spent my whole life wondering if it was only my appearance that roused and stirred lust and tender regards in men's loins and hearts.

In truth, though one would never know it to look at me, I am not, as years are measured, a *very* old woman. Yet I feel *very* old and *so very* tired inside, and my mirror is no kind flatterer and so does nothing to dissuade me. So to my eyes, as well as in my soul, I am a wizened old crone who has lived far too long. I've outlived all the love I've ever known, and such a life is not *truly* living, merely existing, waiting for the Sands of Life in God's hourglass to run out. Inside I *feel* three hundred and fifty, though I've drawn breath only three-and-thirty years, and that's not even half a single century. I should feel young and vital, but I'm all worn out. Years I've found are just a number; a convenient, or, depending on the circumstances, a not so convenient, calculation. Except when it comes to legalities I think in truth they count for very little. We are what we are, and a number does not define the marks the marching feet of Time, whisper light, carefree, or leaden, worry-weighted, have left upon us. I only know, if asked to guess my age, none would ever think me still young enough to bleed and bear a child. My face hangs weary, pasty pale, sagging, and heavily lined so any shadows that fall upon my face show how deep the sadness bites. My muddy gray eyes that I always used to despise and wish were instead a keen, piercing sapphire until my Thomas told me they were "like a cunning silver fox mating with a wily red one" rest in dark, wrinkled nests of flesh, and more wrinkles pucker round these rouge-reddened lips that still *long* for a lover's kiss. And perched precariously atop my head sits my fashionable pearl-pinned wig of dark sable red curls, its color as close to my own as I could find, though I dearly wish these great masses and mounds of high-piled curls would go out of fashion; I was born with an inordinately large head that always seemed to totter on my neck, too big for my squat, little goblin body, and this extravagant coiffure emphasizes it all the more. Beneath this flame-lit ebony monstrosity my short-cropped hair is white as the moon itself. I hacked it all off with my sewing scissors to the horror of my jailer, who found me sitting shorn and weeping amidst the scattered ruins of my tresses, when my scalp began to shed as profusely as my eyes did tears after I lost my Thomas.

Sometimes, when I lift off my wig before bed, I catch a glimpse in the looking glass of those wild wisps of moonstone white sprouting from my head like tufts of dandelion fluff, looking as though if a great gust of wind came along it would blow me bald-headed, and I just *have* to laugh. I am the only one of the Grey sisters to live to grow old and gray. "The brilliant one" and "the beautiful one" are long gone to their graves; only "the beastly little one" remains, growing more bent and beastly with every year that passes.

If I were to see those beloved spirits, my sisters and my husband, flying in through my window this All Hallows' Eve, defying the sage burning there, would they even recognize me as their Mary? And if they came, I don't know which I would doubt more, their existence or my sanity, nor which would hurt my heart the more—their coming or their going away again. I've already grown accustomed to living without them, to thinking every time I let myself start to feel again, to let fondness and care take root within my heart, those first tender shoots that herald the flowering of love in any of its many forms are also the first dip of the quill in the silver inkwell to begin the first grandiose curlicue of the word *good-bye* to be writ slow or fast across the pulsing rosy parchment of my heart. And I know, if they were to come to me this night, the one time of year, if tradition be true, that they can, they would disappear come cock's crow, and I would be left all alone again missing them all the more. *Stay away! No! Come to me! Come! Go! Yes! No!* my contradictory heart cries, vying to be heard over the howl of the wind, the boom of the thunder, and the beat of the rain rapping like fingernails tapping on the glass windowpanes.

Beyond my window the dark hulk of the Tower of London looms like a monster in a child's nightmare. I used to tell my husband I wanted a quiet life, a simple life, no great, grand palaces for me, thank you, I'd had all that before—Bradgate Manor in Leicestershire, luxurious London town houses, and the Queen's many palaces—and love always meant far more than luxury to me. I only wanted him, my kind, sweet, gentle giant Thomas, and a little house of our own, with a room with a fine view to delight me while I sat and sewed. I had in mind a pretty garden with flowers and songbirds where I could watch my stepchildren and, God willing, the children born of our love, play, not see every day that morbid, frightening fortress where my eldest sister, Jane, went in a reluctant queen and died an innocent traitor. The place where my reckless, feckless father also died; to his very end he was a gambler who never knew when the game was lost and to hold on to what he had rather than risk losing all. And where my sister, Kate, birthed both her boys and made those cold stone walls burn with passion when her Ned, aided by a softhearted gaoler who thought it "a cryin' shame that a 'usband and 'is wife should be made to lie apart these cold and many nights," crept down the corridor into her bed. And my Thomas, my gentle giant, suffered his great, tall, broad form to be hunched and crammed, stuffed and squeezed into a tiny cell, and grew sick on rancid meat a dog wouldn't eat. Perhaps that's why I stay here? Though my love has never been inside this little house, all I have to do is look out my window and I can pretend he's still alive, that only stone and mortar, locks and bolts, and not life and death, keep us apart, and that someday he'll come back to me, that he didn't die because of me.

Sage may keep the ghosts away, but not the memories; they constantly haunt the halls of my heart and the long and twisting corridors of my memory, like ghosts moaning and rattling their chains, demanding to be heard, to just be remembered, or to impart some dire warning or precious pearl of wisdom, so that from them I have no rest. But I don't *really* mind. The memories, mementos, their letters and likenesses are all that are left to me now. They're how I keep the ones I love alive, tucked safe inside my heart so that they can never truly leave me.

I have but one likeness of my husband, my Thomas, my Mr. Keyes, a miniature of a giant that shows only his great head and massive shoulders, but that's all right; it's all I need. The whole of him I shall never, can never, forget, even if I were condemned to walk this earth, like the Wandering Jew, until Christ's return. Not even eternity could make me forget even one look, word, touch, or gesture of my Thomas; they are my greatest treasures, and I guard them as such.

My Thomas, he is—I suppose in all honesty I should say *was,* though in my heart he still lives, so when my heart is speaking I *must* say *is*—a lean, seven-foot-tall pillar of strength, broad in the shoulders and sturdy-limbed as Hercules, with a sprinkling of salt-and-pepper stubble hiding under his jaunty spring green velvet cap with the curling white plume and the brooch I gave him, a large silver lovers' knot set with a great, round, rough-hewn emerald, a Samson who kept his strength even after he was shorn, and in fact preferred the razor's smooth glide to watching the tide of his hairline recede with every passing year. Perky and sprightly he was, in bed and out, with a mischievous wink and cheery smile, and a love of flashy finery, his garments showy and bright as the most magical sunsets and the plumage of tropical birds. If ever a man loved vibrant, whimsical patterns upon his clothing, it was this man—his favorite garment was his gold-fringed, grass-green Noah's Ark cloak over which marched just about every beast and bird known to man through a shower of embroidered raindrops worked in that perennially popular shade of blue-tinged white known as milk-and-water, presided over by a white-bearded Noah holding a shepherd's crook, with the wooden ark embroidered across the back between the blades of my Thomas's broad shoulders. And he loved every shade of green God or the silk dyers ever created, from the palest jade to the deepest forest.

My Thomas was not the lumbering dull-witted dolt many at a glance judged him by his mammoth size to be; it never ceased to amaze me how many people equated his height with stupidity, as if they imagined a brain the size of a pea rattling about within the immense ivory confines of his skull. He was in truth a man with an unquenchable curiosity about the world, avid to know all he could of medicine, science, and nature; each new advance and discovery enthralled him, and he always wanted to know more, to understand how and why. He also possessed a nimble mathematical mind and a love of words. I often saw him look up, the crystal lenses of the spectacles he wore to ease his eyes when he read flashing in the firelight, as he sat back in his chair, hands clasped behind his head, a book lying open upon his lap, and a thoughtful, faraway gaze, sometimes even tears, in his eyes as he contemplated the sheer beauty of the words he had just read. Just by stringing words together, like beads to make a necklace, he would marvel, the writer could reach right inside and touch the reader's heart or give their mind a knock, set the gears a-turning, rouse curiosity, indignation, ire, or desire, or just make a body sit and ponder far into the night until the fire burned out and he was startled to hear the cock's crow heralding the dawn of a new day.

Of my eldest sister, Jane, "the nine days' queen," I have a great many likenesses. There are portraits, full figure, half-length, and miniatures, some clad in the plain garb she favored, some so stark they are nigh nunlike, others of such decadent jewel- and ermine-decked opulence they would have appalled and embarrassed my sister, painted on canvas, wood panels, porcelain, or ivory; there are crude woodcuts, exquisite pink and white carved cameos, elegant engravings, drawings of varying style and skill in rich or pallid paints, stark black ink, or charcoal pencil, their lines delicate or bold, and ornate illuminated manuscripts depicting Jane in a nimbus of radiant gold paint as if she were some kind of saint. All of them sent to me by well-wishers and admirers of my Protestant martyr sister, they form a whole beautiful beatified legion of Janes, most of them bearing little or no likeness to my sister except the approximate color of her hair—though never the *exact* fiery chestnut that often appeared a deceptively boring brown—and the lily-white pallor of her skin, usually shown flatteringly unmarred by freckles. And none of them have her changeable eyes, as though when God created her He had daubed their grayness with paintbrushes dipped in brown, blue, and green. I have enough of these Janes—even a black-haired, violet-eyed Jane gowned in royal purple, ermine, and pearls, and a flaxen, rosy-cheeked Jane, buxom as a barmaid, in rose brocade trimmed with rabbit fur—to cover all four walls of my bedchamber and spill out into the quaint little parlor that adjoins it.

And there are also tracts, illustrated poems, and books, all lauding her with praise and heaping golden glories upon this proud, pious, and brave Protestant maid, and copies of her letters, preserved like sacred treasures, including her precious Greek New Testament inside of which she inscribed her last letter to Kate. There is even a kerchief stained with her blood—martyr's blood, said to have the power to heal—a rather morbid memento sent to me when I was so ill after I had lost my Thomas. These are the relics of Lady Jane Grey.

The pictures I hang upon my wall; the rest I keep spread atop a table like offerings upon an altar. There is even a cloth weeping gold and bloodred fringe so that they touch silk instead of wood, with a scene depicting her last moments beautifully embroidered upon it, with silver gilt thread for the ax's gleaming head. I keep it covered, for truly, however skillfully embroidered it may be, I have no desire to look at it; such talent should not have been squandered on such a ghoulish scene, better fruits and flowers than a girl of sixteen about to have her head struck off.

Sometimes, I confess, though inappropriate it may seem coming from me, for I truly do mourn my murdered sister, nonetheless, a chuckle sometimes escapes me as I behold these artists' renderings. Some I think must be the work of lascivious old men hungry as starveling wolves for tender young flesh. For them the naked white neck and shoulders bare and white as milk above the black velvet gown are not enough, and they must go even further and strip Jane down to her stays and petticoats, as virginal and white as an innocent little lamb, and give the executioner a bulging codpiece, sometimes even painted a lusty red, nigh level with my sister's face, though the blindfold mercifully shields her eyes from such a lewd sight. There is a sensuality about some of these images that offends and distresses me; it is as though the artists think the execution of this nervous and frightened sixteen-year-old girl was in some way erotic. How can they be so cruel and perverse? And how can they, the people who send me such pictures, think that I would want to see my sister thus?

Even before she died, people were already romanticizing Jane, making her into a tragic heroine, and forgetting that there was a core of mule-stubborn steel inside the delicate, dewy-eyed damsel who virtuously proclaimed that books were her only pleasure. And the stormy gray green eyes with a daub of blue and just a hint of hazel that the sentimentally inclined always thought were dewy with tears were in fact glimmering with the bold, mad, implacable gleam of religious fanaticism, flinty and hard as swords that longed to strike a blow for the Reformed Religion.

Jane wanted to be the Protestants' Joan of Arc. Though young and fair, Jane was shrewd and canny; she wielded her formidable intellect like a sword, dazzling all with her fluent Latin and Greek, what she regarded as the more frivolous French, and the Hebrew she had been learning when she died, displaying as some women do their jewels her knowledge of Scripture and the ancient Greek philosophers. She laid the foundation for what was to come, aspiring to a kind of martyrdom even before the scaffold steps were in sight. Long before she achieved her royal destiny and tragic fame, she would heave doleful, heart-heavy sighs, raise her eyes to heaven, press a prayer book to her breast, and impart her tale of woe to any sympathetic and willing ear, so that the story of how she was most cruelly abused, pinched, slapped, and beaten by our lady-mother spread across Europe from one scholar to another as they imagined blood welling from her bare back and buttocks and scars tracing silvery white lines over her lily-white skin.

Once when I sat curled in a corner, having nodded off over my embroidery, I started awake when Jane and the esteemed scholar Roger Ascham came in. With my tiny form in its midnight blue velvet gown half hidden by curtains and shadows of a similarly dark hue, they did not see me and I was too shy to stir myself and alert them to my presence. Master Ascham said to Jane that there was more to life than books, and she should, as becomes a young lady of noble birth, go out into the world more. He gestured out the window, at the Great Park, where our parents were even then hosting a grand picnic after a vigorous day's hunting. But Jane only sighed and hung her white-coiffed head while a rosy blush suffused her cheeks as she hugged her book tight against her black velvet breast, like a beautiful young nun confessing impure thoughts to her confessor. Then, with downcast eyes, my sister sank down onto the window seat and laid her volume of Plato on the black velvet cushion of her skirt as though it were a holy relic. "All their sport is but a shadow to the pleasure I find in Plato. Alas, good folk, they never felt what pleasure *truly* means!"

Master Ascham cocked his brow and smiled and queried her in mock seriousness. "And how attained you, madame, this true knowledge of pleasure seeing that so few men and women have arrived at it?"

"I will tell you, sir," Jane confided, "and it is a truth perchance that you will *marvel* at. One of the greatest gifts that God ever gave me is that He sent me, with such sharp, severe parents, so gentle a schoolmaster as Master Aylmer. When I am in the presence of my parents I must, whether I speak, keep silent, sit, stand, or go, eat, drink, be merry, or sad, be sewing, playing, dancing, or doing anything else, I must do it *so perfectly* as God made the world, or else I am so sharply taunted, so cruelly threatened, and tormented, with slaps, pinches, nips, and blows and other chastisements—which I shall not name for the honor I bear my parents—that I think myself in Hell, till the time comes when I must go to Master Aylmer, who teaches me so gently, so pleasantly, with such fair allurements to learn, that I think all the time nothing while I am with him and am as a vessel to be filled with the knowledge he pours into me. And when I am called away from him, I fall to weeping, because whatever else I do but learning is full of great trouble and misliking for me. And thus my books have been so much my pleasure—nay, my *only* pleasure!—and all that others call pleasure is naught but trifles and troubles to me."

"Oh, my dear child!" Master Ascham cried and tenderly pressed her lily-pale hand to his lips and held it there for a very long time.

I saw the smallest flicker of a smile twitch Jane's lips, and at the time, being so young, I wondered if his long, curly beard was tickling her hand, or perhaps he was in love with her, and she like any other maid was preening over her conquest, but now, as a woman grown older and wiser, I suspect that it was his pity that gave her the greatest pleasure.

While it is true that Jane was beautiful—if she had smiled and radiated charm and winning ways, she would have rivaled Kate as the beauty of the family—she was *not* blessed with these gifts, nor did she make any effort to cultivate them. On the contrary, she disdained them and flaunted a frankness that bordered on insolence. Tolerance and tact eluded her. No matter how much we encouraged her or how hard our lady-mother tried to instill grace and charm through beatings and harsh punishments, Jane dug in her heels like a balky mule and refused to budge.

In matters of faith and fashion she was intractable, and over both, she waged many a battle, and even though she won many, I always, in my heart, felt that she always lost. As Kate always used to tell her, "You win more friends with smiles than with frowns, and honey catches far more flies than vinegar."

But for all her brilliance and book learning, Jane lacked the ability to make herself liked. All she had was her intelligence, learning, and religious zeal to win her applause, accolades, and admiration. And she knew it. So if she could not be loved, she decided she would be praised and venerated. She saw herself as a victim, and she would make sure others saw her the same way, and she would shackle this idea to her strong, unwavering Protestant faith to create an image that would never be forgotten, as memorable, powerful, and inspiring as the Maid of France.

In many ways, Jane created her own myth. I loved my sister, but I sometimes wonder if I would have loved her if she had not been my sister. She was dour and gloomy, the kind of dull, dreary, and pedantic person who rains on every picnic. But as much as Jane scorned love, and urged us to turn away from the flesh and despise it and look to our souls instead, her need for it was all the greater, and she needed us—her sisters, who knew her best—to love her. She needed love in life more than she needed this posthumous fame and a glorious martyrdom. I wish she had lived long enough to find it. I *longed* to see Jane transfigured by love, *true* love, not just that tantalizing glimpse I caught of her in the dying throes of a girlish infatuation she once confided to us, or fighting furiously against and despising herself for her deep-buried and denied attraction to Guildford Dudley. I wanted to see her as a woman in love with all her sharp edges softened and beautifully blunted and blurred by bliss. But the allure of the victim, the sacrifice, the forever young and beautiful martyr, proved too strong, and Jane chose a remarkable and romanticized death, a potent and inspiring memory for posterity to glorify and cherish, over an ordinary life and the joy that can be found in the right pair of arms.

I have only two portraits of my sister Kate, my sunshine girl, along with the letters she wrote to me, tied up in bunches with silk ribbons the color of ripe raspberries, and a jeweled and enameled hand mirror shaped like a mermaid, a memento from her first marriage.

Sometimes I imagine I can see her laughing, happy face reflected in the oval of Venetian glass framed by the sea nymph's flowing golden tresses. How strange it is, it always strikes me when I contemplate these pictures, that in both of them Kate, who loved bright colors so, is dressed in black and white. Where are her favorite fire opals and flashing green emeralds? Neither portrait does justice to her great beauty of face and heart. Both are miniatures, round with azure grounds, the paint made from pulverized lapis lazuli, painted by Lavinia Teerlinc, a dainty, flaxen-haired Flemish woman. The first shows Kate at thirteen, her hair more golden than copper then beneath a gold-bordered white satin hood. It was painted when she was still new-married to her first husband, Lord Herbert, and trying to look grown up in a high-necked gown of black velvet edged with white rabbit fur and gold aglets all down the front and trimming the slashed sleeves, her chin sinking deep into the soft cushion of a gold-frilled ruff. Beneath these stark and severe matronly black-and-white trappings, her bubbly vivacity and charm are smothered so that if only this picture survives down through the ages none will ever know what she was *really* like. And that saddens me; I want everyone to know and love Kate as I did, before she became the tragic heroine, with "all for love" as her creed, living and dying for love.

In the second portrait she looks sad and sickly, or "heart-sore" as the poets might say, blessed with that peculiar kind of beauty that sorrow in some miraculous way enhances; for Kate, though her fame is far eclipsed by Jane's, is Love's martyr, not Faith's. This picture shows an older and sadder Kate at twenty-three, clad yet again in black velvet and white fur, a loose, flowing, sleeveless black surcoat through which her thin arms clad in tight-fitting white sleeves latticed with gold embroidery protrude like sticks, the bones and veins in the backs of her hands distressingly bold. In this likeness, Kate's bright hair is subdued and hidden beneath a plain white linen coif devoid of ornamentation, not a stitch of embroidery, not even a jeweled or gilt braid border or even a dainty frill of lace. And, though it doesn't show in this picture, her waist is thickening and her belly growing round again beneath the loose folds of black velvet with her second son, Thomas. Ned, the husband who held her heart in his hand, is with her in the form of a miniature worn on a black ribbon around her neck, and in the child they made together, the rosy-cheeked baby boy, named Edward after his sire. Kate holds her son up proudly, grandly garbed, like a little prince, in a black velvet gown I made for him, striped down the front with silver braid, and cloth-of-gold sleeves with white frills at his neck and wrists, his little black velvet cap twinkling with diamonds and trimmed with jaunty tawny and white plumes. He clutches a half-ripe apple, its flesh both rosy red and gold blurring into green, and one can almost imagine it represents the orb that is put in the sovereign's hand on their coronation day. Kate holds her son in such a way that the ring Ned put upon her finger on their wedding day is on display for all to see, the famous puzzle ring of five interlinked golden bands, as well as the pointed sky blue diamond betrothal ring, both declaring that this baby in her arms is not some baseborn bastard, an infant conceived in hot lust and shame, but a legitimately born heir with royal blood from both the Tudor and Plantagenet lines coursing through his veins like a scarlet snake that could someday rear up and strike down the Queen if those who oppose this petticoat rule of Elizabeth's ever dare to raise his banner and fight to take the throne in his name.

This picture looks like a warning in paint. If I were Elizabeth, or one of her counselors, that is certainly how I would see it. But I *know* my sister better than any. Kate *never* coveted a crown for her children or herself. She was there and saw what happened to Jane. Kate steadfastly refused to follow in Jane's footsteps, despite the urgings of others. Instead, she turned her back on the road of power and ambition and the golden throne that shone so bright it blinded the beholder to the scaffold lurking ominously in the shadows. The only ambition Kate ever harbored for herself, or her children, was to love and be loved. This is in truth a portrait of love, showing Kate with the three people she loved most—her husband, their firstborn son, and the one growing in the safe and loving warmth of her womb—and yet another example of my beautiful sister thinking with her heart instead of with her head.

And tucked inside my father's battered old comfit box, its sky blue and rosy pink enamel chipped and worn, flaking off in places, nestled inside a bag of warm burgundy velvet, is a cameo carved with the profile of the most *beautiful* boy I ever saw—Jane's husband, the vainglorious Guildford Dudley, when he was only sixteen and thought the world was an oyster poised to give up its precious pearl to him. That exquisitely carved profile is pure white, so I have only my memory to remind me of the gleaming brightness of his golden curls and the gooseberry green of his eyes. There was a grandiose portrait of Guildford clad head to toe in vibrant yellow and gold, but I don't know what ever became of it. 'Tis a pity; I would like to have it here with me, to once again behold Guildford, who now lives only in my memory. Guildford, the golden boy whose whole life truly was a masquerade; a boy who died tragically young, before he could throw the mask away and become the person he always meant to be, or at least try to be, though that would have probably ended in tragedy and bitter disappointment too. Also inside that dear, dented box is another treasure—an intricately woven rose I fashioned from three long hanks of coiled and plaited hair—chestnut hiding ruddy embers, the richest coppery gold, and sleek sable sheened with scarlet—there we three sisters are, entwined in a loving embrace forever—Jane, Kate, and Mary.

Hanging upon my parlor walls are three wedding portraits, each showing a husband and his wife shortly after their nuptials.

The first shows the grandparents I never knew. The beautiful and spirited "Tudor Rose," Mary Tudor, the youngest sister of Henry VIII. With her porcelain and roses complexion, blue eyes, and red-gold hair she reminds me of my sister Kate. She too dared all for love. When we were growing up how Kate used to beg to hear the story, told over and over again, of how our grandmother, who was as clever as she was beautiful, did not despair when she was forced to do her royal duty as every princess must and marry the ailing and decrepit King Louis XII of France, who had fifty-three years to her seventeen. Instead, she coaxed and wheedled and extracted a promise from her royal brother, Henry, who, like everyone else, adored her, that her second husband would be one solely of her own choosing. Oh what a merry dance she led gouty old Louis, bouncing out of bed at dawn and dancing until far past midnight! She wore him out within six months, and when he died, dwindled to a gaunt-faced shadow, exhausted from trying to keep up with his teenage bride, she married the man she had loved all along, her brother's best friend, Charles Brandon, the Duke of Suffolk. And they were *gloriously* happy until the day she died in 1533.

The portrait shows them in their wedding clothes, Mary, "The French Queen" as she would ever afterward be called, in chic black velvet embroidered with a fortune in pearls, some formed into exquisite rosettes, and rich golden roses set with sapphires to match her necklace. Her handsome, rusty-bearded bridegroom stands beside her, holding her hand, in sable-trimmed black velvet covered with silver piping with a row of silver-braided lovers' knots marching down his chest. In her other hand, the newly wed duchess holds an artichoke, a pun on the orb she would have carried as queen, to show that she had disdained another royal marriage for one of true love, and also as an emblem of ardent love and fertility. I like to think that perhaps she already knew her firstborn child, my lady-mother, was already growing in her womb, like the leaves of an artichoke unfurling as it ripens.

The second portrait shows my parents dressed for the hunt. Hunting and gambling being the two passions that endured throughout their marriage, it seems somehow most appropriate that they chose to don these clothes for their wedding portrait. And it is how I best remember them. My lady-mother never seemed to be without her riding crop, and if satin slippers ever peeked from beneath her hems instead of gold or silver spurred leather riding boots, I do not remember. My lady-mother, Frances, the Duchess of Suffolk, stands in a grand gold-embellished russet velvet riding habit gripping her horse's bridle in one leather-gloved hand and her riding crop in the other, a proud, fierce, willful, determined, voluptuous beauty, flesh already at war with the restraining influence of her corset, threatening to break out in open rebellion. She holds her head high, showing off her Tudor red hair, snared in a net of gold beneath her round feathered cap, and stares unwaveringly straight ahead with her shrewd ice-gray eyes, avaricious and calculating as a bird of prey eyeing a gentle, innocent sparrow with a wounded wing. There is something in the way she holds herself, her chin, firm and unyielding as chiseled granite, and the way she grips her riding crop that defines the words *dominance* and *control*. My father, Henry Grey, Hal to his wife and friends, stands beside her, auburn-bearded and handsome in a weak-chinned way in his white linen, brown velvet, and hunting leathers, with a hooded falcon on his wrist; he is a man awestruck, with the tentative smile and quizzical eyes of one who can't quite believe his good fortune.

The third, and most unfortunate, wedding portrait shows my fat and florid piggy-eyed, sausage-fingered mother with her second husband, our Master of the Horse, Adrian Stokes, the boy of not quite twenty-one she married a scant two weeks after Father lost his head on Tower Hill. Her eyes remain the same, flinty, cold, and hard, but the hair has darkened, and the strong chin is softened by the pads of pink flesh that swaddle the bones, pushed higher still by a tall, most unflattering chin ruff with a fortune in pearls edging its undulating frills. And beneath the rich pearl-embroidered black velvet of her gown it is obvious that flesh has won a great, bursting victory over restraint, her defeated corset remains only as a nominal presence, because no proper lady would ever be seen in public without one; it has become an obsolete ornamental necessity that serves no actual purpose except to add one more expensive, luxurious embroidered layer to my lady-mother's opulent person. She looks like she could devour the pale and slender black-haired boy standing beside her clutching his gloves as if they could save his life, and trying to look older than his twenty years, while showing off his grand gold and silver ermine-edged garments. Supported by a gold-laced ruff, his gaunt face always makes me think of the head of John the Baptist being offered to a most corpulent Salome, one who should keep her seven veils on instead of wantonly discarding them. Poor Master Stokes's dark eyes seem to say his is a life of hard bargains, and also to question whether it's really worth it—he's risen in the world by marrying a duchess, the niece of Henry VIII, and mother of the best-forgotten nine days' queen, but he doesn't relish what will come afterward when they are alone together behind the bedcurtains and everything but our lady-mother's riding boots comes off.

There is one more portrait in my parlor. A frosty, formal portrait of the cousin I was named for, the Tudor princess, and later queen, Mary, born of Henry VIII and his first wife, the proud and devout Spaniard, Catherine of Aragon. A plain and pious spinster, this Mary stands sunken-cheeked and stern-faced, severely gowned in high-necked black satin and velvet with a bloodred satin hood, petticoat, and full, padded under-sleeves; even the glimmer of the gold at her throat, breast, and wrists seems subdued and the jewels dulled amidst so much bloodred and black. Though it was painted years before people put "Bloody" before her name, at times I think it a prophecy in paint, a sign of things to come. Her hands are pure white and lovely, but I cannot look at them without seeing blood staining them.

Why do I keep it? Well . . . there was a time, many years ago, when my royal cousin and I shared a special kinship, something only the sad, hurt, lonely, passed over, and forgotten can truly understand. We both knew what it was like to live every day knowing that love, no matter how much we longed and dreamed of it, and needed it, was likely to pass us by and shower its blessings upon those pretty and fair. For us, even the royal blood in our veins might not be enough to tempt a husband. Cousin Mary had already dared to hope and been disappointed many times. With no husband or babies to give her time and love to, she would often come visit me, always bringing with her a basket filled with pretty scraps of material and bits of lace and gilt and gaudy trim she had been saving just for me, to fashion gowns for my doll, just as she had done for my other cousin, her half sister, the precocious, flame-haired Elizabeth, before Elizabeth, who was always old beyond her years, lost interest in dolls and turned her back on Mary and her sumptuous offerings, declaring them "a pastime fit only for babies."

We would sit and sew for hours. She was the very soul of kindness and patience, and taught me so much of stitches and styles, patterns and cuts, the dressmaker's craft and art. "Mayhap I flatter myself," she would often say, "but if I had to make my way in the world, I fancy I could make a comfortable life for myself as a dressmaker." It was true of Mary Tudor and equally true of me; my skill with the needle supplements my income and my embroidery is avidly sought after to this day. "There is magic in these fingers, little cousin," she would say, taking my hands and kissing my stubby little fingers when I showed her my latest creation.

When a rainbow of silken threads and materials pass through her hands, a dressmaker soon learns that there are many shades of gray between black and white, and of these two stark colors that stand like sentries at the ends of the spectrum there are variations as well—charcoal, ink, raven, shimmering jet hiding a dark rainbow, rusty black with its bloody undertones, and midnight blue black, and the white of eggshells, ivory, milk, snow, and the silvery white glimmer of a fish's belly, and the cream of custard and old lace. I cannot forgive Cousin Mary for taking Jane's life, yet I cannot forget the love and kindness she lavished on me, a lonely, ugly, deformed child best kept hidden away, consigned to the shadows of shame, and I cannot take back or kill the love I gave her either. Master Stokes's eyes speak truly, and his is not the only life filled with compromises and hard bargains.

And though I like not to look upon it, and keep it hanging,

shrouded in shadows, in a dark corner downstairs in my humble dining room, there is my own portrait, the only one I have; there was once a miniature painted by Lavinia Teerlinc, long ago when I was just a child, but I don't know where it is now, like so many other things, it has been lost. My Thomas wanted this portrait, so I sat for it to honor and please the one I loved most. Mercifully, it shows me only to my waist, so that those unaware of my stunted condition can gaze upon it without guessing that they are looking at a freak of nature. In a deep charcoal gray and black velvet gown discreetly embellished with silver embroidery and marching rows of shining bright buttons, with puffs of rose-kissed white satin protruding through my short, slashed over-sleeves, and a profusion of beautiful blackwork Spanish embroidery and gold wrist and neck frills decorating the delicate lawn of my under-sleeves and partlet, and ropes of blushing pearls layered at my throat, I stare warily out at the world, proudly displaying the gold ring set with the "mystic ruby" my husband put on my finger on our wedding day. He kissed my hand and said it would protect me always, even when he could not, and safeguard me from all poisons and plagues, explaining that this bloodred cabochon, so rich a hue that its light shines even through fine linen, was forged from the crystallized blood of a very old and wise unicorn that congealed when its horn was severed. And upon my little black velvet cap is a pink gillyflower, to tell all those who look upon my portrait that here is painted a loyal and loving wife. And arranged behind it, prophetically posed just above the pink gillyflower, is a silver pin from which teardrop pearls drip like a shower of tears. Yes, I still weep for my husband.

A scorching whiff suddenly reminds me of the cakes I have left baking in the ashes, thankfully before they burn. My rusty knees creak and pop in protest as I kneel to retrieve them—three warm, round, golden honey cakes, each decorated with red currants to spell out one dear initial—*J* for Jane, *K* for Kate, and *T* for Thomas—the three people I loved most. The red currants look like scabs of newly dried blood, and I shudder at the sight of them, thinking of the beloved blood that was spilled in vain. And as the wind howls outside my window, I think I can almost hear them calling my name as my mind journeys back to the long ago February day when our lives changed forever, when we three sisters found ourselves standing at a crossroads and realized that the moment had come when we must all take different paths. Solemn, sullen Jane, "the brilliant one," took the road to the scaffold and a martyr's fame, and saucy, carefree Kate, "the beautiful one," skipped along light and airy as a butterfly with jewel-colored stained glass wings, following her heart wherever it might lead, living, and dying, all for love, and I, "the beastly little one," thought I was destined to always walk alone, shrinking fearfully into the shadows to hide from those who passed me by lest they wound me with their words, laughter, blows, or even worse, the pity in their eyes. I thought for certain that Love, though he would surely stop for Kate and might even pause for Jane, if she let him, would pass me by.

❧ 1 ❧

Only a fool believes in Forever. Yet I was a fool, though I was only five years old at the time—take that as an excuse or not as you like—when my eldest sister, Jane, came home to Bradgate after the death of the much beloved Dowager Queen Catherine Parr, the sixth and final wife of our magnificent, fierce uncle, King Henry VIII. Jane had been the sixth queen's beloved ward and lived with Catherine and her new husband, the Lord Admiral Thomas Seymour, quietly pursuing her studies, until death and heartbreak brought her home to us. That was in September 1548, and Jane was a month shy of eleven, though her intelligence and quiet, solemn ways always made her seem much older than her actual years.

We would be constantly together in the years to come, we three sisters—Jane, Kate, and I, "the brilliant one, the beautiful one, and the beastly little one!" as we used to laughingly call ourselves as we stood together before the looking glass, poking fun at the way everyone saw us, like characters in a fairy tale. Rather than rage, pout, or weep, we had adopted it as our own and laughed about it instead. I didn't think then of marriage, of husbands, households, and babies, the responsibilities that would inevitably tear us apart, take us away from our home at dear rosy-bricked Bradgate in Leicestershire, and each other, and divide us from a trio of sisters into three separate lives. I thought we would go on forever, always together.

Jane was so sad when she came home that long ago September. Never before had I seen her so listless and full of sorrow. When she stepped down from the coach, she moved like one in weighted shoes, stunned by a heavy blow to the head, as though she were walking in her sleep, her swollen, red-rimmed eyes open but oblivious, even to Kate and me as we ran out with open arms and joyful, eager smiles to welcome her. But Jane didn't notice us. Even when Kate hurled herself at her, like a cannonball covered with bouncing copper curls, Jane absorbed the impact with barely a flicker. When I saw this, my smile and steps faltered and I hung back, feeling as though I were trespassing on my sister's sorrow, even though all I wanted to do was banish it.

She was still wearing the black velvet gown she had worn to the Dowager Queen's funeral, where she had acted as chief mourner, with her long, wavy chestnut hair still pinned tight and confined beneath a plain white coif, and her thin shoulders shivering under the little white silk capelet, both of which, coupled with the black gown, signified that the deceased had lost her own life bringing a new life into the world. With two black-gowned, white-coiffed, and caped maids bearing her long black train, Jane, carrying a lighted white taper clasped tight between her trembling hands, hoping her tears would not drip down and douse the flame, had led the grim and solemn procession into the chapel at Sudeley Castle.

Our always elegant lady-mother disembarked from the coach with a wave of rose perfume strong enough to knock any weak-stomached man or maid down, her leather stays creaking in violent complaint beneath the grandeur of her gold-embroidered green velvet gown and her favorite leopard skin cloak. Our father had given it to her when she, as a young bride, triumphantly announced that she was carrying a child that they were both confident would be a son, though it was in fact Jane in her womb as time would reveal. But our lady-mother kept and prized her leopard skin cloak just the same, even long after she had given up all hope of a son. *"I deserve it,"* I often heard her proclaim as she preened before her mirror with it draped about her broad shoulders. "After all that I have endured—*I deserve it!*" Though I never dared question her, I knew she meant us—Father's weak will and his body grown cushiony soft through unrestrained indulgence of his love for sweets; Jane's recalcitrant and willful ways that ran so contrary to our world's most cherished ideas of feminine beauty and charm; Kate's thinking with her heart instead of her head; my stunted, deformed body—a dwarf daughter is a daughter wasted, she can do no good for her family or herself; and the tiny baby boys born blue and dead with limp little phalluses that waggled mockingly, reminding our parents of the son, the star of the Grey family, the hope of the future, they would never watch grow to strong and lusty manhood and carry on our proud and noble lineage.

Jane blindly followed our lady-mother toward the house, meek and docile in her grief, her long train trailing forgotten over the dusty flagstones behind her. Her mind shrouded in black velvet sorrow, Jane didn't feel its weight or hear the rustling whisper that tried to remind her, like a little voice urgently hissing, *Pick me up! Pick me up!* Sudden as a serpent striking, our lady-mother swung around and dealt Jane's face a sharp leather-gloved slap that almost knocked her down. *"Pick up that train!"* she snapped, though we all knew it was a gown Jane would never wear again, for every stitch of that hastily sewn frock was full of sorrow.

Jane staggered and stumbled backward, a livid pinkness marring the milky, cinnamon-freckled pallor of her cheek and a drop of blood falling like a ruby tear from her nose to stain her white silk capelet. Seeing it, our lady-mother snorted like a horse, blowing hot fury, before she shook her head in a way that seemed to say to Jane, *You're hopeless!* and spun on her leather-booted heel and flounced into the house, the feathers on her hat bobbing with every step as she nimbly plucked the gloves from her fingertips, tossed them to a maid, and untied her cloak strings, as she called for wine and demanded the whereabouts of her husband. As soon as the door closed behind her, Kate ran to gather up Jane's train, bunching up the dusty velvet, wadding it against her chest as best she could, being quite daintily built and only eight. And I took Jane's hand and gave a gentle tug to get her moving and led her inside and upstairs to her chamber.

Jane never said a word as her nurse, Mrs. Ellen, ordered her to sit, and then, with an efficiency born of familiarity, silently bathed Jane's face and pressed a cold cloth to her nose to staunch the bleeding while Kate and I knelt beside her chair and held and rubbed our sister's hands. As soon as a servant appeared bearing Jane's trunk, she sprang up and ran to open it. From inside she took a portrait, which she had wrapped in petticoats to protect it on the journey. She unswaddled it tenderly as a mother would her child, as Catherine Parr would never have the chance to do for her own infant daughter, then propped it on a chair and sat back on her heels before it.

It was a portrait of the late Dowager Queen, gowned in sumptuous claret satin, her bodice and sleeves elegantly embellished with gold-embroidered black bands. Her auburn head was covered by a round, flat black velvet cap adorned with fanciful gold and pearl buttons and brooches. With its jaunty, curling white plume, the hat looked far more cheerful than the pensive pearl-pale face unsmilingly framed by the pearl-bordered white coif she wore beneath it. In the hollow of her pale throat I noticed was a pendant I had seen on portraits of our uncle's previous queens, all now deceased, their lives bled out in childbed or on the scaffold, a great cabochon ruby resting in a nest of gold acanthus leaves with a smaller emerald set above it and an enormous milky teardrop of a pearl dangling beneath.

I had never met Queen Catherine, but Jane had told me so much about her I felt I knew her: the book she had written, *The Lamentation of a Sinner,* a labor of love boldly espousing woman's equality to man, emphasizing femininity's Christlike virtues, such as meekness and humility; the finely arched brows she plucked with silver tweezers; the discreet henna rinses she applied to her hair when her husband was absent; and the quick pinches she gave her cheeks, to give them color, before she came into his presence; the milk baths she soaked in to keep her skin soft and fair; the vigorous scrubbings with lemons to fade and discourage freckles; the rose perfume she distilled herself from her own mother's recipe; the cinnamon lozenges her cook prepared in plentiful batches to keep her breath sweet; and the red, gold, and silver dresses her dressmaker made to show off the still slender figure of an aging woman who kept her waist trim by exerting steely self-discipline at the dining table, shunning the rich, decadent fare laid before her on gold and silver plates, and, to her great sorrow, by never having borne a child. All to keep a man who wasn't worth keeping, an ambitious scoundrel who lusted after a crown and was hell-bent on seducing her own stepdaughter—the flaming, vital, young Princess Elizabeth who stood just two steps down from the throne her brother sat upon. Only her sister, the Catholic spinster Mary, stood above her in the line of succession, and she had already rebuffed the Lord Admiral's passionate overtures.

Kate and Mrs. Ellen each bent and took Jane by the arm and raised her. As we undressed her, Jane never said a word or took her eyes off Catherine Parr's face.

Later, when the house was still, and the yawning, sleepy-eyed servants had climbed the stairs to their attic cots, and our own nurses lay snoring on the trundle beds, Kate and I crept on bare toes back to Jane's bedchamber, hugging our velvet-faced damask dressing gowns tight over our lawn night shifts lest their rustling betray us. Jane lay white-faced and still behind the moss green and gold brocade bedcurtains with the covers drawn up to her chin. The cups of mulled wine Mrs. Ellen had given her had eased her, warmed her inside, and loosened her usually cautious tongue. We roused her and, to our delight, found she was no longer a walking wraith and once again our dear, difficult, but much beloved sister. And as we huddled beneath the bedcovers, close as three peas in a pod, Kate still in her green velvet dressing gown and I in my plum one, Jane shared with us the strawberries, pears, apples, and walnuts sympathetic common folk, who also mourned the Dowager Queen's passing, had given her whenever the carriage stopped so that the horses could be changed or watered. "They were all so kind," Jane said in an awed little whisper as though human kindness was something strange and marvelous she was unaccustomed to behold.

It was then, as we munched our treats and sipped the now tepid wine Mrs. Ellen had left behind, that our sister confided all. And what tales she had to tell! Had it been anyone other than our plain-spoken Jane I would have suspected some fanciful embroidering. She told us all about the lewd, wanton romps that had astonished and titillated all of England when they heard how the Lord Admiral had made it his custom to creep into Princess Elizabeth's bedchamber early each morning to rouse her with tickling and kisses, handling her person in a most familiar and intimate fashion, and how the two had been surprised in an embrace by his wife, with the guilty fellow's hand roving beneath the princess's petticoats, which had resulted in Elizabeth being sent away, and had spoiled Catherine's joy in at long last finding herself with child. In the delirium of the fever that followed the birth of her daughter, Catherine's tongue had scourged her husband and stepdaughter like a metal-barbed whip; she accused the Lord Admiral of wanting her dead so he would be free to marry Elizabeth, his little wanton strumpet of a stepping stone leading straight to the throne. And Jane had with her own eyes seen him pour a white powder into a goblet of wine and press it to Catherine's lips, forcing her to drink, tightening his grip and pressing the golden rim harder against her lips when she shook her head and tried to pull away, and afterward holding his hand over her mouth to make her swallow when he thought she might attempt to spit it out. She died with small, round, livid purple-red bruises from his fingertips marring her cheeks and jaw. When the time came to bathe and clothe her corpse, her favorite lady-in-waiting, a stepdaughter from Catherine Parr's first marriage, Lady Tyrwhit, had painted over them with a paste of white lead and powdered alabaster to restore her complexion to pearly consistency.

Before Catherine died, a lawyer was summoned—Jane herself opened the bedchamber door to let him in—and the Lord Admiral prompted his fading wife to dictate a new will leaving all her worldly goods to him, thus making him a *very* rich man. He even gripped her hand and guided it across the parchment to sign her name, leaving bruises upon her knuckles that Lady Tyrwhit would also lovingly conceal. It disturbed Jane to recall how hard he had held her hand, hard enough to make the bones crackle and grate as if his bride's very bones protested his cruel, duplicitous ways. "There was naught of love in his touch, no tenderness, only cruelty and a determination to have his will," Jane said. "I wanted to do something, I wanted to stop it, but I was as helpless and powerless as the Dowager Queen was in the end. He as her husband had all the power."

But there was more, *much* more—the kinds of secrets that weigh so heavily upon a young girl's heart.

"I too sinned against the Dowager Queen," Jane, in a voice suffused with shame, confided. "She was more like a mother to me than our own—patient, loving, encouraging, and kind, so very kind—and I wronged her just as Elizabeth did, only she never knew it; I was not found out."

She went on to tell us how Thomas Seymour had fanned the flames of our parents' ambition by concocting a grand scheme to marry her to the young King Edward. Outwardly it seemed a perfect match, Jane and Edward both being the same age, English, and devout Protestants, of serious rather than merry mind, and Jane had been named in honor of the King's mother, Jane Seymour, the third and most beloved of Henry VIII's six wives. Though the young king, who was after all only a pale, frail boy trying hard to ape his splendid sire, in padded shoulders and plumed hats, posing with fists on hips and feet in slashed velvet duckbill slippers planted wide apart, pompously proclaimed that he wanted a "well-stuffed and jeweled bride" for himself, his "jolly Uncle Tom," who provided the young monarch with pocket money to earn his favor and gratitude, was certain he could persuade him that "what England needs most is a homegrown Protestant queen, a *true* English rose, like the Lady Jane Grey, who will uphold the Reformed Faith, not a French Catholic princess hung with jeweled crucifixes, dripping pearl rosaries, kneeling on an embroidered prie-dieu, and throwing boons to her pet cardinals and confessors." Brash Tom Seymour had so much confidence in his own schemes he "could sell fire and brimstone to the Devil," our lady-mother used to say as she toed a cautious line while our father wholeheartedly embraced the dream of seeing his firstborn daughter crowned queen.

But no one asked or cared how Jane herself felt about the future that was being planned for her. She did not want to marry Edward; she felt the coldness emanating from him like a great blast of icy air so that even in summer she shivered and longed for her furs whenever she was in his presence, and she saw cruelty glinting in his eyes, and that made her tremble and fear the man he would grow up to become. And she didn't want to be queen either. All Jane wanted—or thought she wanted—was her books, to spend her life quietly engaged in study.

Like a nun taking the veil and becoming the bride of Christ, Jane wanted to dedicate herself to the Reformed Faith; she wanted no man or marriage to interfere and had no time or patience for romance and even turned up her nose and scoffed derisively at the very idea. Many a time I heard her chastising Kate for being more avid for love than learning and urging her to "despise the flesh." Jane thought carnality was a vile, evil, disgusting thing and didn't want it to sully her life in any way, not even in songs or stories; anyone she caught indulging in either she told to their faces that they should be singing hymns and reading Scripture instead. Rather fanatical upon this subject, she urged everyone to "despise the flesh" and resented *any* carnal intrusion into her life, even if it were only by accident.

I remember once when we were going riding and walked in on one of the stable boys coupling with a wench on a bed of straw in a horse stall, Jane turned right around, strode straight back into the house, even as the boy and girl ran after her, half dressed, pleading for mercy, that they were in love and planned to be married soon, and reported the incident to our lady-mother and had them both dismissed from our service. And another time when she caught Kate sighing dreamily over a pretty picture of lovers kissing in a garden, Jane snatched the book from her, tore and broke its binding, and flung the whole thing into the fire and ran to wash her hands in scalding water, claiming they were as soiled as though she had just fondled manure.

Such heated reactions were all too typical of Jane, and our lady-mother said she pitied the man who would one day marry her as he would no doubt find Jane a very cold bride with "a cunny like ice." Then Thomas Seymour came along like a whirlwind, sending books, papers, pens, and Jane's own thoughts flying every which way in wild disarray, leaving all so disordered she didn't know which way to turn or how to begin to put it all right again.

It all began with a walk in the garden at Chelsea, Catherine Parr's redbrick Thames-side manor, a talk about self-sacrifice and destiny, and one perfect pink rose. Catherine was busy with the dressmaker, having extra panels and plackets sewn into her bodices and skirts to better accommodate the child growing inside her, and she had asked Elizabeth to bear her company and help in the selection of materials for some new gowns she had impulsively decided to have made, complimenting her stepdaughter's sense of style and color, the bold choices she made that another woman with ruddy-hued hair might shy away from. "I need to borrow a little of your bravery, my dear," Jane heard her say softly as she reached out a hand for Elizabeth's. Perhaps it was only a charade to keep her stepdaughter in her sight and away from her husband, but sincere or feigned diversion, either way Elizabeth couldn't say no without appearing impolite and ungrateful to her stepmother and hostess.

So Jane, who had no interest in such fripperies and believed that "plain garb best becomes a Protestant maid," was left to amuse herself and nurse the still healing bruises from a recent visit to Suffolk House in London where she had dared show herself "balky and sulky" at the prospect of becoming King Edward's bride, boldly proclaiming that she didn't want to marry at all, but to remain a lifelong virgin and give all the devotion a girl is expected to give her husband and children to the Reformed Faith instead.

Our lady-mother had worn out her arm and painfully pulled a muscle trying to horsewhip such "nonsense" out of Jane and had to have the doctor in to poultice and bind it. She was angry as a baited bear for a week afterward since her injury forced her to stay home and forgo the pleasure of several hunting parties. And without her restraining presence, Father had gained several pounds at the picnics and banquets that attended these events and had to have most of his clothes let out.

When our lady-mother heard that he had devoured the entire antlered head of a marzipan stag at the banquet following a royal hunt, she nearly screamed the house down and yanked several of his hunting trophies, his treasured collection of heads and antlers, from the wall and hurled them downstairs. Poor Father only narrowly avoided being impaled by the magnificent antlers of the king stag he had slain at Bradgate. And whenever our father came home, cheeks ruddy from riding hard in the bracing wind, the blood of the kill staining his hunting clothes, in a high good humor ready to boast of his prowess, our lady-mother would send a goblet of wine or a platter of food flying at his head and sulk all the more because she had missed all the fun, the thrill of being in the lead herself, the knife clutched in her hand, seeing the blade glinting in the sun, the scent of blood hovering like perfume in the air accompanied by the music of buzzing flies as she closed in for the kill, and woe to Jane, the cause of her missing her favorite pastime, if she happened to cross our lady-mother's path at such a time.

That day at Chelsea, the Lord Admiral had found Jane curled up in a window seat, extra petticoats beneath her plain gray gown cushioning her still tender buttocks and thighs, with an apple in her hand and a book open on her lap, brow furrowed intently beneath the plain gray crescent of her French hood as she pored over the pages, lips moving as she translated the ancient Greek of Plato's *Phaedo*.

"A pox upon Plato, it's too lovely a day, and you're too lovely a maid to squander on a musty old Greek!" he exclaimed, causing Jane to almost jump out of her skin as he snatched the book and flung it away, giving Mrs. Ellen quite a fright. The poor lady had fallen into a doze over her sewing and suddenly awakened to find her headdress knocked askew by a black-bound volume of ancient philosophy that had come flying at her like a bat.

"Come out and walk with me, Jane!" the Lord Admiral insisted. And, before she could demur, he already had hold of her hand and was pulling her out into the sunshine, even as she stumbled over her hems and glanced back helplessly and shrugged her shoulders at poor Mrs. Ellen.

When Mrs. Ellen regained her senses and ran after them, protesting that the Lady Jane must first put on a hat, to protect her complexion as she was prone to freckling, the Lord Admiral took the straw hat she held and sent it sailing across the rose garden where the breeze took it up and landed it upon the river, declaring that he loved freckles, and blushes too, as they lent character to faces that would otherwise be as pale and boring as marble statues, and that for every new freckle the Lady Jane acquired from their little walk he would give her, and Mrs. Ellen too—he paused to flash the nurse a saucy wink—three kisses. And that was the end of that. He gave Jane's hand a tug and set off along the garden path at a brisk pace, and Mrs. Ellen was left standing there alone, gaping after them, wringing her hands, feeling quite flustered, and wondering whether she should feel charmed by the Lord Admiral or insulted and go straight inside and complain to the Dowager Queen. The Lord Admiral tended to have that effect upon people.

He led Jane out, beyond the garden, into the Great Park, where a blanket was spread beneath the broad branches of one of the ancient and majestic oaks. And while Jane sat modestly arranging her skirts, eyeing with dismay the grass stains and tears upon the hem that had marked their hurried progress, the Lord Admiral took from a basket a plate of "still warm" golden honey cakes, a flagon of ale, two golden goblets wrought with true lovers' knots all around the rim, and a lute bedecked with gay silk ribbon streamers. And then he began to sing, slowing the jaunty, rollicking pace of the salacious tavern ditty to a sensual caress, like a velvet glove, lingering over, *savoring,* certain words, as his warm brown eyes met Jane's, and his fingers plucked the lute strings in such a brazen way that called to mind what they might do if given free rein to rove over a woman's body.

I gave her Cakes and I gave her Ale,
I gave her Sack and Sherry;
I kist her once and I kist her twice,
And we were wondrous merry!

I gave her Beads and Bracelets fine,
I gave her Gold down derry.
I thought she was afear'd till she stroked my Beard
And we were wondrous merry!

Merry my Heart, merry my Cock,
Merry my Spright.

Merry my hey down derry.
I kist her once and I kist her twice,
And we were wondrous merry!

At the end, as the last notes hovered in the air, he leaned forward and pressed his lips softly against Jane's.

"There now," he said, "whatever happens, I shall *always* be the first. Come what may, whether you are ever Queen of England or remain only Queen of My Heart, my darling Jane, I will *always* be the *first* man to kiss Lady Jane Grey, and no one can *ever* take that away from me; that honor—that very *great* honor—will be mine forever."

Jane sat back on her heels blinking and befuddled. "M-My L-Lord, wh-what . . . what are you saying?"

The words had scarcely left her lips before she found herself enfolded in Thomas Seymour's strong embrace, pressed suffocatingly tight against his hard, muscular chest in such a way that the pins holding her hood in place stabbed into her scalp like tiny knives, some of which Mrs. Ellen would later discover, when she helped Jane prepare for bed that night, had actually drawn blood.

"What am I saying?" he repeated. "Only that I love you, darling Jane, *I love you!* I love you! I love you! Can you not hear it in every breath I take, in every move I make, in every beat of my heart? I love you, Jane, I love you! You—*only* you!"

And then he let her go, so abruptly that Jane fell back onto her elbows and almost crushed the lute. With a resigned, defeated sigh, he sat back, but as he did so he deftly caught up her hand. With one last smoldering gaze and heart-tugging sigh, he took a moment to compose himself before he shut his eyes and then, reverently, bowed his head and pressed his lips chastely against the back of her trembling hand. "But, for England's sake, for the greater good, I must sacrifice my heart and let you go," he said with a crestfallen sigh. "You, my darling, were meant for far greater things than I can give you. You were meant to wear a crown and be the torch that leads the English people out of the Papist darkness into the light of the Reformed Faith! You, my darling, as much as it hurts me, must be Edward's helpmeet, not mine."

"But I don't want to marry Edward!" Jane protested, for the first time giving voice to her feelings. "He . . . he . . . frightens me! And I don't . . . I don't . . . love . . . him."

"I know you don't, my darling." Thomas Seymour enfolded her in his arms once again. "And I don't blame you. No one loves Edward, not *really!* He is my own nephew, the son my own beloved sister lost her life giving birth to, yet I cannot find it in my heart to love him and must in his presence result to playacting. He is as chilly as a fish, a frigid little prig who takes himself far too seriously. He has none of his great sire's charm or the common touch, and no sense of fun, and he knows *nothing* of love and warmth and has no desire to learn. But you *must* marry him, my love; it is your destiny to be Edward's godly and righteous, virtuous and learned queen; united together you will be the rulers of a new Jerusalem, the thunderbolt of terror to Papists everywhere; your reign will be the death blow to the Catholic faith in England! We must each sacrifice our own hearts, and deepest desires, for the greater good, for England, and the Reformed Faith, my darling. Our love shall be the martyr of duty!"

He pulled the hood from her head and plucked the pins from her hair and stroked it before drawing her close again and pressing his lips warmly, tenderly against her temple. "When you lie in his arms, think of me, darling Jane, think of me and how my heart beats only for you! We will always have our dreams to console us and the knowledge that they were sacrificed, selflessly, for the greater good. And as cold as Edward is, always remember, my love for you is pulsing hot, and it will keep you warm and give you the strength to go on and do your duty, as you must, indeed, as must we all.

"And when he enters you, close your eyes, my love, and think of all the good that you, our homegrown Protestant queen, can do for England, all the souls you will save, and the seed he plants in your womb is England's future, the son that will someday rule and keep us all safe from Papist enslavement, the Catholic shackles and chains that the Pope and Mary Tudor would fasten tight upon us! England needs you, Jane, and that claim, that need, must take precedence over my desire for you, and yours for me. For you do desire me, don't you, Jane?"

In that moment Jane suddenly realized, even as she was nodding her head and stammering it, that yes, indeed she did. How curious that she had never known it until the moment when she must renounce it. It was, she said, like never knowing you had an arm until the surgeon came to cut it off. The Lord Admiral really was the most persuasive and overwhelming man!

Jane was so overcome by the Lord Admiral's declaration of love that she couldn't eat a bite, only gulp nervously at the ale, and the honey cakes grew cold as her face and heart grew hotter. And when they walked back to the house, arm in arm, this time at a more leisurely pace, the Lord Admiral paused to pluck a pink rose and present it to Jane.

"Every morning when the dew appears upon the roses, always remember, my dearest, darling Jane, that they are weeping in envy because their color cannot compare with the pink in your cheeks . . ." And then he bent his head and pressed a last lingering kiss onto her cheek. "And lips . . ." And he kissed her, long and deep, and she tasted the cakes and ale still fresh upon his mouth.

When Jane ascended the stairs, she encountered Elizabeth upon the landing in a bold red gown that, coupled with the fiery unbound hair streaming down her back, made her look like a figure of flame. She was standing beside the window that overlooked the garden, idly tracing the *CP* and *TS* worked in red, gold, and green stained glass, moving her long, pale white finger in such a manner that, with a confident brush of her fingertip, the *C* acquired an extra appendage and became instead an *E* with a middle arm reaching out greedily for *TS*—Thomas Seymour. At Jane's approach, she abruptly turned around and gave Jane such a *blazing, burning* stare, the fire in her eyes as bright as her Tudor red hair, that Jane was certain that Elizabeth had seen what had just passed between the Lord Admiral and herself, that looking from a window above she had witnessed that tender kiss and imagined the words of love that accompanied it. Then Elizabeth turned on her heel, her loose hair flying out like a curtain of flame, almost slapping Jane in the face, and, with her nose in the air and a impertinent flounce of her harlot-scarlet skirts, flounced upstairs to her room and gave such a resounding slam to her door that it echoed throughout the manor.

The next morning, warm under the fringed velvet coverlet of her deep feather bed, Jane would smile to herself and wiggle her toes when she heard Tom Seymour creeping down the corridor and the door to Elizabeth's room creaking open, happy and secure in the knowledge that it was herself that the Lord Admiral *truly* loved, *not* the brazen and fiery tart Elizabeth.

"Elizabeth is just a toy, a peppery little tart to add spice to a man's life, a dalliance that means *nothing*." Thomas Seymour had shrugged when she dared to tentatively mention his seeming infatuation with the princess. "I am a man, with needs and urges, my darling," he explained, "and, since I cannot have you, as there cannot be *any* hint of unchaste behavior to sully the name of our future queen"—he lifted his handsome shoulders in a light, carefree shrug—"since I cannot have you . . . I amuse myself with Elizabeth, a little whore born of a great one, but I don't *love* her. How could I? When I love you, Jane, *only* you! I love you with enough nobility, respect, and honor to renounce you, to lay my own heart on the altar as a sacrifice and set you free, to serve a greater purpose. I cannot hold you back, my darling, for I love you far too much to think only of my greedy pleasure and deny England the queen it both deserves and needs."

In her bed at Bradgate, under the covers, safe in the loving arms of her sisters, Jane shook with sobs. "But I did not ask him about Catherine, his wife; I could not! I could not forget her. I could *never* forget her. She was so kind to me, but in those happy moments when he professed his love for me, I did not want to remember her either! He loved me! *Someone* loved me, *really loved me!* And that was enough! We knew we could not have each other, and I tried to tell myself that in truth we did no wrong, but we did, we did! The thoughts, the feelings, the desires were *real* and *true* and thus worse than what he did with Elizabeth, which was base and false and meant nothing! And now Queen Catherine is dead, and I cannot confess and beg her forgiveness. I shall have to live with the guilt for the rest of my life!" She sobbed and there was nothing we could say to comfort or console her; all we could do was hold her and let her cry herself to sleep.

After the Dowager Queen's death it all began to crumble. Her baby daughter died, yet another unloved, unwanted, and inconvenient little Mary. And without Catherine Parr's restraining hand to rein him in, the Lord Admiral cast off all caution and common sense and galloped headlong at full speed straight into the briar patch of disaster. His last flamboyant gamble cost him all when he crept into the King's bedchamber late one night and tried to steal the sleep-befuddled boy away to marry him secretly to Jane, hoping to see the marriage consummated and thus legally binding before the first light of dawn. In the morning light, he planned to return to the palace with the King and his new Queen, and replace his brother, Edward Seymour, as Lord Protector of the Realm.

But he had forgotten to factor a watchdog into his plans—upon spying an intruder, the King's pet spaniel barked. The Lord Admiral tried to distract the dog by snatching off one of his soft-soled velvet slippers—eminently more suitable for creeping about the palace after midnight than the Spanish leather boots he usually wore—and tossing it across the room, but Edward's vigilant pet showed no interest and instead ran at the intruder and lunged to bite. The Lord Admiral panicked and pulled out a pistol and shot the dog dead, and thus ruined any chance he had of charming his nephew into an act of royal clemency. The guards came rushing in as Edward howled and wept, his bare feet slipping in the loyal canine's rapidly cooling blood as he pummeled his formerly favorite uncle's chest.

Thomas Seymour spent the rest of his life in the Tower as, one by one, all his crimes came to light, his intrigues with pirates, a coin clipping scheme to embezzle money from the Royal Mint, the stockpiling of arms, and, most interesting of all to a public avid for royal scandal, the sordid details of his dalliance with Elizabeth. And that was the emphatic end to all plans to make a royal match for Jane as our parents hastily moved to distance themselves from Thomas Seymour and his foolhardy schemes.

Our lady-mother rushed in a state of feigned alarm to the Lord Protector and indignantly informed him that her eldest daughter was *not* a pawn in the Lord Admiral's game, and she resented and hotly contested all who tried to make it so. She slapped her palm flat and firmly down upon the King's proudest achievement, his *Book of Common Prayer* that was to grace every church in England.

"I *swear* it is *not* so and *never* was!" Jane, she firmly stated, had been the Dowager Queen Catherine's ward, and she had promised to arrange a suitable marriage for her; she had even hinted, our lady-mother with a demureness any who knew her would see through like the finest Venetian glass, that his own son, Edward Seymour the younger, had been one of the likely suitors Catherine had in mind, praising to the skies his wisdom, maturity, and charm, proclaiming him a promising young lad poised to follow in his father's footsteps. After all, with Catherine dead, there was no one to contradict her but the Lord Admiral, and his own brother knew better than any that if Thomas said the sky was blue it was best to glance upward just to be sure. And our lady-mother was canny enough to add that the Dowager Queen had told her in confidence that she herself had no quarrel with the Lord Protector and his wife, that the unpleasantness over the ownership of some jewels, whether they were Crown property or the Lady Catherine's, had been blown entirely out of proportion by the Lord Admiral; "knowing your brother as well as you do, my lord," our lady-mother added in a low voice accompanied by a sympathetic nod, which she reenacted for our father later, "I am sure you understand."

While the storm was bursting over Tom Seymour's head, Jane languished and moped around Bradgate. She tried to lose herself in the pages of her beloved books, to pound sense back into her head with Socrates and Scripture, struggling and fighting against her secret love for the Lord Admiral, now crushed like a flower under the hard boot heel of Truth, yet still stirring weakly with life, trying to revive itself even as Jane resisted. For all she disliked Elizabeth, many years later when I grew to know our sovereign lady better and witnessed personally her fight against her feelings for that charming, seductive scoundrel Robert Dudley, I would think that she and Jane had far more in common than either of them could ever have guessed.

Finally, our lady-mother, "sick unto death of Jane's sullenness and gloomy face," decided to accept Princess Mary's invitation to have us come spend Christmas and New Year with her at Beaulieu Manor in Essex.

Kate and I were unable to conceal or curtail our excitement, bobbing up and down on our toes and fidgeting enough to provoke some sharp words from our lady-mother, until at last we mounted our ponies and rode out with glad hearts, reveling in the warm softness of our winter furs, gold-fringed and embroidered leather gloves, and new velvet riding habits—cinnamon for Kate and black cherry for me.

Cousin Mary was always very kind to us, and a visit to, or from, her always meant lots of presents. She liked to pretend that we were the little girls, the daughters, she always longed for but never had and lavish us with the gifts she would have given them.

But Jane came out dragging her booted feet as though her severely cut ash-colored habit were made of lead instead of velvet, and the silver buckles on her boots iron shackles, letting the skirt drag until our lady-mother shouted at her to pick it up.

Jane mounted her horse with such a glum spirit I could almost see a dark rain cloud hovering over her, dripping icy rain onto her head. She despised our royal cousin's devotion to the Catholic faith she was raised in, and the rich ornaments, jeweled crucifixes, "the accoutrements of Papist luxury," with which she adorned her person and her chambers.

I had such a feeling inside me as we left the courtyard and passed through the gates, such a sick, fearful foreboding that I slowed my prancing pony to a walk and glanced back at Jane's scowling countenance. One look at her made me wish I had the power to tell her to turn back, but I was only a little girl, powerless to intervene or change anything. Our lady-mother, riding before us, looking grand as a queen, sitting straight in the saddle in her orange velvet, red fox furs and golden roses set with rubies, with her hair netted in gold beneath her feathered hat, had decreed that we would go, and she would make certain that I regretted it if I *dared* speak up about the fear that so suddenly and overwhelmingly possessed me. And I knew that if I tried to put it into words it would sound quite silly, just as I knew that the laughter that would burst from her lips would not ascend to her eyes; there I would see only derision and contempt. And that I did not like to see in my own mother's eyes, so I kept silent.

When we arrived at Beaulieu, Lady Anne Wharton, one of our royal cousin's ladies-in-waiting, came out to greet and escort us inside. As we passed the chapel, she paused before the open doorway and curtsied deeply to the altar upon which sat the golden monstrance containing the Host, the wafer of bread the Catholics believed would be miraculously transformed into the body of Our Lord when elevated by the priest during Mass.

Jane bristled, and I felt the icy prickle of fear down my back. I tugged at her sleeve, but she ignored me.

"Why do you curtsy?" my sister asked, in a voice sickly sweet, like rotten meat disguised beneath a thick coating of spices. "Is our cousin within?"

"No, my lady," Lady Wharton patiently explained, "I am curtsying to the Host—Him that made us all."

Jane brushed past her and made an exaggerated show of peering into the candlelit chapel, then turned back to face Lady Wharton with wide-eyed amazement. "Why, how can He be there that made us all when the baker made Him?"

My sister was fervently opposed to the Catholic belief in Transubstantiation and the Doctrine of the Real Presence. She had no tolerance at all for anyone who believed that during Mass the bread became Our Savior's body and the wine His precious blood. She scoffed and derided and venomously attacked this belief at every opportunity, insisting that it was an insult to common sense, faith, and intelligence.

At such times I was always glad I had never confided in Jane, the way I had Kate, that I believed in miracles and prayed every night that God would work one for me and make me grow up into a beautiful and shapely, slim-limbed young lady just like my sisters. Jane would have been so disappointed in me if she knew, and I cringed to think of the scathing sermons and lectures she would have bombarded my poor little ears with. But Kate and our father were always kind and quick to assure me that our family breeds diminutive and dainty women, our beefy, robust mother being the exception of course, but we always knew that I was different. Even though I used to sneak out into the forest surrounding Bradgate and climb a tree and tie to my feet the bricks I had stolen when the workmen came to build a new wall and hang from a limb, ignoring the bite of the bark into my tender palms and the awful, wrenching ache in my arms and shoulders, and in the small of my back, praying and concentrating with all my might, willing the weight of the bricks to straighten my spine and make my arms and legs stretch, I never grew another inch after my fifth birthday.

It was at that moment that our royal cousin appeared. Her sumptuous jewel-bright purple satin gown, gold brocade undersleeves and petticoat, and the elaborate jeweled hood perched like a crown atop her faded gray-streaked hair could not disguise the lines etched across her brow and framing her taut, thin-lipped mouth, her deep-sunken eyes, or the fact that she was pale and pinch-faced. A bulge in her cheek and a strong scent of cloves hovering about her, vying with the flowers of her perfume, told me that she was nursing a toothache. I saw the smile falter then die upon her lips, and her eyes were both fire and ice when she looked at Jane.

"I would lay my head on the block and gladly suffer death rather than sit through one of Edward's prayer book services!" she declared as she and Jane faced each other like enemies on a battlefield.

Thinking fast, I hurled myself at Cousin Mary, embracing her knees. She tottered and reeled backward, flailing her arms, and only our lady-mother's quick intervention kept her from falling. Drowning out our lady-mother's angry words with my tears, as soon as Cousin Mary had regained her footing and knelt to try and soothe me, I flung my arms around her neck and into her ear whispered a fervent plea that she not be angry with Jane. "She has been so sad since Queen Catherine died."

Cousin Mary gave a quick nod and said, "I understand." Then she rose and went to embrace first Kate, then our lady-mother, and lastly Jane, lingering as she held my sister's stiff-backed body in her arms and offering her condolences over the death of the Dowager Queen. I thought for certain Jane would challenge her when she said that Queen Catherine had been in her prayers, for Jane, as a Protestant, did not believe in saying masses for departed souls and prayers for the dead; the living had greater need of them. But Jane bit her tongue and smiled wanly when our royal cousin caressed her pale face and said she would pray for Jane too, for her "sadness to be lifted," and that happiness would again find her in this household. "I shall endeavor to make it so."

"I have a special gift for you, little cousin Jane—and for Katherine and Mary too," she added with a warm smile as she urged us to follow her upstairs. While our lady-mother, her patience sorely tried by Jane's, as well as my own, antics, claimed a headache and let Lady Wharton lead her to the room that had been prepared for her, Kate and I each took Cousin Mary by the hand and, with Jane trailing sullenly behind, followed eagerly to the room she had prepared especially for us.

In the great, grand pink and gold brocaded chamber we three sisters would share, sleeping in a giant canopied bed with gilded posters as round and thick as burly men, lovely gowns waited, spread out upon the bed for us to sigh over and admire. But first, three white-capped and aproned maids—one for each of us—stood by in readiness to undress and bathe us. There were three copper tubs lined up in a row before the massive carved stone fireplace, and the maids stood ready to pour in steaming pails of water and sprinkle dried rose petals on top. The baths would warm our flesh, and while we soaked, there would be cups of steaming, spicy hippocras to warm our insides as well. And then . . . the dresses!

For Jane there was a gown of palest sea green silk, a marvelous color that seemed to shift between blue and green as the shimmering folds, embroidered with silver, white-capped waves and exquisite little silver fishes, flowed like water over my sister's limbs, rippling as she moved. It was trimmed in pearly white embroidery, like the finest, most delicate filigree, punctuated with pearls, giving the illusion of white froth floating upon the sea. And for Kate, to complement her gleaming copper curls, there was a pale orange silk, not too delicate nor too bold, over which gold-embroidered butterflies fluttered, with frills of golden lace edging the square-cut bodice and encircling her dainty wrists. And for me, Cousin Mary, knowing that I preferred darker hues to clothe my person, had chosen a deep mulberry silk with a kirtle and sleeves of silver floral-figured crimson damask, with silver lace at the neck and wrists. And there were satin slippers to match each gown. With what loving care our royal cousin had chosen each gown and its accessories!

She had us line up in a row for her to admire, then walked behind us and around our necks, one by one, she fastened a necklace—pearls for Jane with a square spring-green emerald pendant hanging by one corner; a fiery orange stone suspended like a blazing fireball on a golden chain for Kate, a fire opal Cousin Mary said when I asked what it was called; and a long, braided rope of garnet and amethyst beads interspersed with silver roses for me. And then Cousin Mary, lamenting how faded and sparse her own lank, lackluster locks had grown despite the washes of saffron she had lately tried, recalling wistfully, with sighs and misty eyes, the happy golden days of her childhood when the people had called her "Princess Marigold" for the orangey gold glory that was her hair, had us each stand between her knees while she gave our tresses a hundred strokes each with a thick-bristled gold-backed brush, which she had us count aloud so that she might judge how well we knew our numbers.

Jane recited the numerals with a poor grace, making clear with her voice and manner that she considered this exercise an insult to her intelligence. But Cousin Mary chose to ignore it and smiled and nodded encouragingly throughout, then she kissed Jane's cheek and crowned her ruddy chestnut waves with a chaplet of pearls. For Kate's coppery ringlets there was a delicate cap of gold net latticed with peach-colored pearls, and for my stubborn sable red frizzy curls, a plum velvet hood with a garnet and silver rose border. Then, all smiles, she led us down to the Great Hall where another surprise awaited us.

Feigning a loving interest, our lady-mother, now apparently recovered from her headache, leapt up with a gasp and gushed, "Never before have I seen my daughters look lovelier!" But we were all more interested in Cousin Mary's next surprise. She clapped her hands, and two servants in the green and white Tudor livery came in carrying what I at first took to be a gilt-framed portrait of a beautifully jeweled and appareled lady. And it was, of sorts, but closer inspection, to our immense delight, revealed that this portrait was made *entirely* of sweets—shaped, colored, and gilded marzipan, sugar both artfully spun and colored, and crystals that shimmered like diamond dust, all sorts of sweetmeats and sugarplums, a glistening, tempting rainbow array of candied, sugared, dried, and glacéed fruits, comfits, lozenges, pastilles, suckets, wafers, sugared flowers, crystallized ginger, candied orange and lemon peel, and sugared and honeyed almonds both slivered and whole. The canvas it was created upon was crisp gingerbread, and the frame that bordered it was made of gilded marzipan. Father, who loved sweets so, would have been so delighted if he had seen it. When we told him about it, I knew his mouth would water and he would not be able to look at a portrait without imagining it made of sweet things to eat.

Cousin Mary beamed and clasped her hands at our delight, her toothache quite forgotten as she pinched a bit of candied orange peel from the candy lady's sleeve, and told us we might eat as much as we pleased, waving aside our lady-mother's protests that it would spoil our supper.

With an ill-mannered squeal of delight, Kate and I fell upon it greedily, like two little pigs, our eager little hands snatching up red and green candied cherries that masqueraded as rubies and emeralds.

But Jane would have none of it and turned her back upon our fun. She took from somewhere about her person a small black-bound book and sat down by the fire to read, ignoring the hurt in Cousin Mary's eyes and the anger in our lady-mother's. But that was Jane, true to her own self and no other, tactless in treading over others' feelings, heedless of whom she might hurt, even if in the end it would turn out to be herself that her insolence and insults injured most.

The whole visit passed in this manner, with Jane turning a cold back upon our royal cousin, snubbing and rebuffing her every act of warmth and kindness, disdaining her generosity, greeting with hostility and contempt her every attempt to befriend her. When Cousin Mary sat down to sew with us and tell us stories of the saints' lives, Jane would often claim a sudden upset stomach, an urgent need for the privy, sometimes even daring to loudly break wind to interrupt Cousin Mary's stories, a rude punctuation on some saint's work of wonder, before making her excuses and hastily leaving.

Another time, when Cousin Mary offered to teach us some exquisite embroidery stitches, Jane retorted that her skill would be better spent on plain straight stitches to make simple garments to clothe the poor. And when Cousin Mary introduced us to her confessor, Jane rudely turned her back on him and any other priest she encountered throughout our stay.

Every day she made a point of emptying her chamber pot from the window, onto the statue of the Virgin Mary in the rose garden below. And when Cousin Mary invited us to play cards, Jane stood up and preached a heated little sermon on the evils of gambling and swept the cards into the fire, denouncing them as the Devil's tools for ensnaring souls. When Kate admired a pink pearl rosary and Cousin Mary gave it to her, Jane promptly snatched it, breaking the strand and cutting Kate's hand so that it bled all over her new dress and gave her double the cause to weep. And, after that first night when Cousin Mary so lovingly dressed us, Jane refused to wear any of the finery our royal cousin had given her or any of the beautiful gowns our lady-mother had insisted that Mrs. Ellen pack either.

Throughout the Yuletide celebrations that marked the Twelve Days of Christmas and New Year's Day, when gifts were exchanged, Jane appeared constantly in severe, unadorned black velvet, and each time made a point of standing near Cousin Mary with a frown on her face and contempt in her eyes to show up the difference between "the plain, godly garb that best becomes a Protestant maiden and our sour, old maid spinster cousin's gaudy, overdecorated Papist fripperies." No matter how sharply our lady-mother scolded or how hard the pinches and slaps, Jane would not draw a veil over her contempt for our Catholic cousin.

Cousin Mary stoically endured it all and did her best to ignore my sister's insults and ingratitude, trying hard every time not to let the hurt show, smiling and behaving as though Jane's conduct were flawless in every respect, sweet as sugar instead of hostile as a hornet, but she would never forget it, and we would not be invited to visit her again nor would she ever again grace us with her presence at Bradgate.

In March, after we had returned to Bradgate, Thomas Seymour, his handsome rogue's smile long gone, laid his head upon the block and died, hoping to the last that his brother would send a messenger galloping up with a reprieve; even if it meant spending the rest of his life in prison, that was preferable to death. When our lady-mother, in her spice- and sweat-scented riding habit, swept in amongst a bevy of spotted hunting hounds, barking and howling with laughter as though she were one of them in human form, and repeated what Elizabeth had said when word of her paramour's death was brought to her—"Today died a man of much wit but very little judgment"—Jane forced herself to stay still and show no emotion, to pull the needle through the cloth and go on with her embroidery as though nothing were wrong, when all she wanted to do was cry.

"For all her Tudor fire," Jane said later when we were alone and it was safe for her to weep and show her grief, "Elizabeth's heart is cold as ice!" And when she heard that after he died and his corpse was undressed a letter to Elizabeth was discovered hidden in the sole of his velvet slipper, Jane wept, inconsolable; his last words on this earth, hastily writ in his final hour, had been addressed to Elizabeth, not her. He had sent nothing to Jane, the one he claimed was his true love, not one token, not even a single word.

But Jane had to soldier along bravely, pretending nothing was wrong, hiding her head, and her sorrow, in her books, letting time pass and her heart heal, forcing herself to forget that love for a mortal man had ever dared trespass on that sacred ground where there was room for only God and learning.

Another year passed, then another, followed swiftly by two more, lulling me into contentment and complacency, the false belief that life would always go on in this lovely, lazy, humdrum way at Bradgate with occasional visits to the city. Our parents divided their time between London and the court and hosting wild and libidinous hunting parties at Bradgate that sometimes lasted for weeks at a time and were known for the excessive drunkenness, debauchery, and gambling that our parents and their guests—neighbors from the surrounding countryside and nobles down from London—freely indulged in. There were always dancing girls clad only in high leather riding boots who spun and twirled and slashed the air with whips, and the serving wenches and lads wore headdresses of wood carved to emulate antlers strapped to their heads and were hunted, pursued, and preyed upon by the drunken and lusty guests who even sometimes chased them out into the surrounding forest to drag them to the ground and couple with them like wild beasts.

The parties at Bradgate were so salacious they were even deemed scandalous by London standards, and many notables eagerly vied and angled to procure an invitation. At one such party our lady-mother and the other female guests climbed up to stand upon the table and raised their skirts high to show their legs, even above their garters, so that some important gentleman from London could present a solid gold apple to the lady he judged to have the loveliest limbs. And at another party, where everyone was terribly drunk, they decided not to risk the contents of their purses and instead used their clothes and gems as stakes. By dawn when I peeked out, both our lady-mother and father, as well as many of their guests, were stark naked, and many were nearly so. There was hardly a lady present with her gown still on or a man who had not lost his breeches.

I was always kept out of sight and away from these goings-on, but standing on my toes high above in the musicians' gallery, I often peeked down into the Great Hall, curious to see what was going on. But Kate and Jane were often ordered to don their best and descend the stairs to entertain the guests with a musical recital, early in the evening of course, before the drunken lewdness was in full sway. Jane was a true prodigy and played the virginals, lute, harp, and cittern with great skill, but Katherine's playing was more passionate and that, coupled with her vivacious beauty and smiling countenance, won her much applause and kisses and caresses from our parents and their guests. After she finished, Father would always call her over to sit upon his lap and feed her sweetmeats and dainty cakes and pat her coppery curls, our lady-mother would lavish her with praise, and some of their guests were so charmed by her they would pluck a gem from their lavishly appareled person and present it to her. While Jane's air of pious disapproval, with which she regarded our parents' guests as she sat in morose and sulky silence after she finished playing, waiting to be dismissed, so she could rush back upstairs to shed her hated finery and return to her beloved books, earned her only angry words, slaps, and pinches.

There were occasional murmurs of marriage plans for Jane and the Lord Protector's eldest son and namesake, Edward Seymour the younger, the Earl of Hertford, whom everyone called Ned. He was a likeable lad of fifteen, soft-spoken and rather reserved, but handsome beyond words, tall, slender, and hazel-eyed, with gleaming waves of golden brown hair, and a somewhat shy, but oh *so* charming smile. And when he *truly* smiled, broad and wide, with laughter in his eyes, he could light up a room. He came to visit us once, bearing letters from his father, and stayed overnight. Jane exhibited a rude disinterest. She donned her dullest gowns, addressed as few words as possible to him, speaking mostly in mumbled monosyllables, and pointedly settled herself in the window seat with her nose buried in her Greek Testament, curled on her side so that her back was turned to him, and refused to budge. And on the sly she downed a purge, so that when our lady-mother stormed in that evening in all her finery to drag Jane down to supper, she found the room stinking and Jane with her shift bunched up about her waist crouched over her chamber pot with a volume of Cicero balanced on her bare thighs.

The next morning as Ned was descending the stairs to take his leave, he was waylaid by Kate, wringing her hands in a teary-eyed, trembling lipped tizzy. She seemed to come out of nowhere, springing from the shadows, her shimmering copper ringlets glowing like embers, a vibrant vision in a satin gown the exact same heavenly vibrant blue as a robin's egg.

Ned was thunderstruck, dazzled by her beauty, and all he could do was stand and stare as Kate grabbed hold of his arm and implored, "*Please*, sir, can you sing? *Please* say you can!" She was already dragging him after her, even before his lips could form an answer.

Her beloved cat, Marzipan, was birthing a litter of kittens and enduring a hellish long labor that Kate was convinced she could help make easier by singing. She had been up since before dawn singing herself hoarse. Now her voice needed a rest. She simply could not sing another note and needed to find someone who could, and my own voice she rightly deemed too shrill and reedy to soothe poor Marzipan. "Mary, I love you dearly, but I think your voice will only add to poor Marzipan's woes," she said, tempering her blunt honesty with a kiss and hug before we each set off in search of someone blessed with a more melodious voice. Thus,

Kate found her Ned; it was as if Fate pushed them together and struck the tinder that would ignite the first spark of love—if it ever truly was love, cynical me has to say—in both their hearts. And Ned spent the next two hours kneeling beside Marzipan's basket while Kate sucked mint lozenges to ease her aching throat and strummed a lute as Ned sang his heart out until the seventh and last kitten was birthed and Kate was all smiles again, hugging an armful of squirming, mewling kittens to her breast and lavishing kisses, praise, and loving pats upon dear Marzipan. She lingered long enough to kiss Ned's cheek and thank him yet again before she hastened to the kitchen to fetch a bowl of milk for Marzipan.

"That was the day I fell in love," both Kate and Ned would always say each time they fondly recalled their first meeting. But both were nobly born children, well-schooled in their duty, and they knew all too well that their hearts would not dictate who they married; their parents would make that decision. And Kate knew that Ned was supposed to be Jane's suitor, and Jane was her sister and as such had a prior claim upon Kate's heart. At eleven, almost twelve, with her head full of tales of chivalry and doomed love, like her favorite story of Guinevere and Lancelot, Kate saw exquisite beauty and true nobility of the heart and soul in making such a sacrifice for her sister's sake. She had yet to learn that life isn't like stories, and the things that sound beautiful and grand on the golden tongues of minstrels are in truth often full of pain that stabs deep into the heart and is bitter as gall.

But the dim and distant possibility that Ned *might someday* marry Jane was little more than a faint and gentle ripple upon the placid pond of our existence. He came and went, then his father, the Lord Protector, was disgraced, his head and fortune lost, and John Dudley, the Duke of Northumberland, stood in his stead, holding King Edward's weak, frail hand as it wielded the scepter of power, and not another word was said of Ned Seymour; he was now a person of no importance.

Then came the February day, in 1553, when our lives would change forever.

We were outdoors, frolicking in the snow that Kate said made rosy-bricked Bradgate look like a great mound of strawberries covered with cream, bundled against the cold in thick wool gowns and layers of petticoats, fur-lined velvet coats, boots, and gloves, with woolen scarves tied tight around our heads to keep our ears warm, as we three girls were from babes ever prone to ear pains. We had even persuaded Jane to forsake her beloved books and join us. A milk cow had gotten loose, and upon seeing it, Kate had instantly conceived the notion that we should have a treat.

"*A syllabub! We shall have a syllabub! A sweet, sweet syllabub!*" Her voice sang out like an angel's sweetest proclamation through a frosty cloud of breath as she danced in delight, her boots raising lively billows of powdery snow.

She sent me scurrying to the barn to fetch a pail. Jane, fifteen and more sullen than ever if that were possible, was left to mind the cow, under strictest orders not to let it stray from her sight or to let anyone take it away. And Kate ran quickly to the kitchen to charm the cook with her winning smile and wheedle a cup each of sugar, cinnamon, and honey, a long-handled spoon, and a bottle of wine.

Cook always used to tell us there was no need to add cinnamon and honey; wine and sugar alone were enough to make a tasty syllabub, but Kate always insisted it must be "sweeter than sweet" and "as sweet as can be," and she loved cinnamon best of all spices, so it must be a part of our special syllabub. And in the end, Cook threw up her hands and let her have her way.

Kate and cinnamon, to this day I cannot think of one without the other—she loved everything about it, its taste, color, and smell; she always delighted to suck on cinnamon sticks and candies, and when she was older, she even had it blended into her rose perfume to create a special aroma that was all Kate's own. Though other ladies tried to copy it, they could never get it quite right.

When Cook said she could not give the wine without our father or lady-mother's consent, Kate's blue gray eyes filled with tears and her pink lips pouted and quivered. Cook was no match against Kate's tears, and she quickly relented, with hands upon her broad hips, declaring that "neither God nor the Duke and Duchess of Suffolk can hold me accountable for what happens when my back is turned!" and pointedly turned away, giving her full attention to the pastry crust she was making, as Kate crept into the cellar to pilfer a bottle of our father's favorite red Gascony wine, the kind that is spicy and sweet all at the same time.

Kate concealed the bottle inside her coat as she passed back through the kitchen, smiling sweet and brazen, pausing only long enough to kiss the cook's cheek and whisper a promise that when she returned the cups and spoon she would bring her back some of our syllabub.

Everyone loved Kate, and no one could resist her; she was so saucy and vivacious, with a heart tender and loving as could be. She had a smile that made you feel like roses were growing around your feet, beautiful, sweet-smelling roses without the nasty thorns, just like my rosy, pink-cheeked, and smiling sister. She was thirteen then, glowing, and growing more beautiful every day, ripening into womanhood with rounded hips and pert little breasts of which she was very proud and longed to feel a lover's hand reach around to cup as he kissed the nape of her neck. Unlike Jane, who shrank from such "sordid speculations," and far preferred her ancient Greek, Latin, and Hebrew texts instead, Kate was avid for more fleshly knowledge, to learn all she could about carnal matters, and the "good and merry sport that happens between a man and his wife behind the bedcurtains at night." She was eager to be wedded and bedded and prayed that our parents wouldn't tarry too long over finding her a husband.

When Kate appeared at the kitchen door, I left the pail with Jane and the cow and ran to help relieve her of her sweet burden—the three full, brimming tin cups, wine bottle, and wooden spoon made a clumsy and precarious armful. Kate handed the rest to Jane and approached the cow. She rubbed her gloved hands together to warm them for the cow, she explained, for she would not like someone's icy fingers on her teats and didn't imagine the cow would either. Then, furrowing her brow in concentration—she had never milked a cow before—she gave the cow a pat, said, "Please pardon the presumption, My Lady Brown Eyes," squatted down, and began to gently pull at its cold pink teats, squirting the milk straight into the ice-cold pail I had brought from the barn. When the pail was full, we poured in the cinnamon, sugar, honey, and wine and took turns stirring vigorously, whipping it into a rich, creamy froth that we scooped into the now empty cups.

We sat back, sipping our syllabub, sprawled in a snowbank, as if it were a warm feather bed and not wet and cold, giggling and waving our arms and legs, making angels with flowing skirts and fluttering wings, laughing as the wine warmed us within, imagining the sugar, cinnamon, and wine blazing a zesty, spicy-sweet trail through our veins, racing to see which would be first to reach our heads and make us giddy. Jane started to expound on something she had read in a tedious medical tome, but neither Kate nor I was listening and she soon drifted back into glum silence again.

Suddenly Kate flung her cup aside and leapt up, pulling me and a most reluctant Jane after her, and we began to dance.

I was eight then, and my joints not yet so badly afflicted that I could not dance a joyful jig. Though in my bed that night I might ache and cry and beg Hetty, my nurse, to heat stones in the fire, then wrap and tuck them in against my back and hips or 'neath my knees, I was not thinking about that then; time enough for that when the pain held me in its grip, impossible to ignore, when all I wanted to do was sleep. I kicked up my heels, raising clouds of snow, like dainty, dwarfish blizzards, and gave myself wholeheartedly to the dance, laughing at the wet slap-flap my skirts made when I kicked my little legs as high as I could. With my sisters, I could dance, free and easy, giddy and gay, as I would never dare do before others.

When I was a little girl and first discovered the delight of twirling round and round, skipping, prancing, kicking, and leaping, I thought there could be *nothing* better than to be a dancing girl, but when my lady-mother overheard me prattling this dream to my nurse one evening, she seized me roughly by the arm, her fingernails biting hard enough to draw blood, and dragged me out into the gallery overlooking the Great Hall. There she swung me up, with a roughness that made the burly men who carted and carried sacks of grain seem tender, to stand upon a bench, and pointed down to where a troupe of dwarves clad in rainbow motley and tinkling bells capered and danced before my parents' guests seated around the banqueting table, rocking and howling with laughter and tossing coins, crusts of bread, fruit, and sweetmeats at them.

"Look!" she commanded. "Never forget, children like you are often put out to die, exposed to the elements if the wolves don't get them first! If you were not *my* daughter, with royal Tudor blood flowing through your veins, if you had been let to live, *that* would be *you* down there, puffing out your cheeks and boggling your eyes, cavorting and playing the fool for pennies and crusts from a nobleman's table! *Never* forget that, daughter! Only *my* blood saves you from being a fool in motley, no better than a performing monkey, and worse because you're no dumb animal and have the wit to understand what is said of you and feel the hurt of it!"

I understood at once. After that, though I never lost my joy in dancing, it became my secret. I never dared let any but my sisters and, many years later, the husband I thought I never would have, see me dance. When the dressmaker came the next day and unfurled her lengths of vivid, jewel-hued silks, I remembered the rainbow patchwork of the fool's motley the dancing dwarves had worn and burst into tears, fearing that my lady-mother had changed her mind and, as a punishment for my deformity and the shame it brought my family, had decided to clothe me thus and send me away to join their troupe. How I screamed and bawled in my terror, so incoherent with fear that I could not make its cause clearly understood. And though Kate and Jane were quick to comfort and shush me, before our lady-mother came storming in, and Hetty made excuses for me—"For the life of me, I do not know what has gotten into the child! She is usually so quiet and sweet. I am with her every day and night and I can assure you . . ."—I ever afterward, though my heart craved and cried out for bright colors, chose to clothe myself in darker, more somber, and subdued shades, the better to blend into the shadows and hide, lest I ever be mistaken by my bright, festive attire for a jester, some nobleman or lady's pet fool, instead of the Duke of Suffolk's youngest daughter, and someone hurl a penny at my feet and command, *"Dance, dwarf, dance!"*

Perhaps that was why I loved dressmaking so, especially for my beautiful Kate, and Jane when she let me. With Kate I could let my fancy fly free and unfettered and deck her peaches and cream and red gold, stormy-blue-eyed beauty with all the bright colors I longed to wear but didn't dare. For Kate I could stitch gold and green together, like the diamond-shaped panes in a window, and trim it with a double layer of green silk and gold tinsel fringe, to create the kind of gown I, with my dwarf's body, didn't dare wear. No one would ever mistake my beautiful Kate for a fool; they would only applaud her dazzling beauty. Kate was my living doll and I loved to dress her. And when she wore the dresses I made, I, vicariously, went out with her, and in those moments I was in the world and of the world, beautiful and brilliant, zesty as a pepper pot but sweet as cream, not hiding shy and nervous in the shadows. In those ruffles and frills, embroideries, cunningly cut bodices, and gracefully draped skirts, I was, through my glorious Kate, the center of attention, adored and admired.

When Jane pulled back, refusing to dance with us and complaining of the cold, Kate gaily insisted it was spring, *glorious* spring, the merry month of May, and began singing a rollicking May Day tune full of true love and new flowers, blue skies and bird song, kicking up her heels, as high as she could, seemingly light as air, even in her heavy boots and snow-sodden hems. That was my lively, lovely Kate; she brought sunshine to even the grayest winter day. When I looked at her I could well imagine her in a billowing white gown, with a wreath of May flowers and silk ribbon streamers on her unbound hair, dancing on the warm green grass in her bare feet. I laughed and sang along with her while Jane frowned and shook her head and pronounced decisively, "too much wine in the syllabub!" But Kate just threw back her head and laughed as she spun round and round before, at the end of her song, she flung wide her limbs and fell, flopping back in the snow again, and I tumbled down beside her, reaching out to pull Jane down so that we lay like three May flowers blooming in a row, and finally even Jane had to smile. And then she began to laugh along with us.

"Good-bye, Miss Glum and Serious!" Kate crowed and turned to plant a smacking kiss on our sister's laughter-flushed cheek.

It was thus we lay, wet, red-faced, and giggling uncontrollably in the snow, feeling high as the sky from the syllabub, when Mrs. Ellen came out to tell us that our father required our presence in the library; we must come in at once and change out of our wet clothes and make ourselves presentable for him "like proper young ladies, a duke's daughters, which is what you are, not silly peasant girls frolicking in the snow." As she walked away, I was tempted to hurl a snowball at her back, but Jane already had her arm raised, a ball of snow cupped in her gloved hand, poised to let it fly when Kate and I sprang on her and wrestled her back down into the snow. Sometimes Jane made it devilishly hard to like her with her constant frowns and moody and preachy Protestant airs, but she was our sister, and we *always* loved her and did not want to see her bring another punishment upon herself. No one ever knew what our lady-mother might do in her efforts to discipline and mold and shape Jane into her idea of a perfect young lady. It was easy for her to frighten Kate and me into good behavior—our lady-mother was more fearsome than any ogre or witch out of a fairy story—but with Jane it was a different story.

For a time, our lady-mother had been keen on devising punishments to fit the crime—when Jane turned up her nose at eating a certain dish, our lady-mother would insist that she be served no other fare, and for each meal have that same exact plate set before her even after what was upon it had grown quite putrid. Another time, when Jane was a tiny girl about to have her first proper gown, a grown lady's habiliments in miniature, replete with stays, layered petticoats, jeweled headdress, embroidered kirtle, and flowing sleeves with full, fur cuffs, and Jane had shown her willful side and rebelled against the gold and pearl embellished white velvet, clinging steadfast to her familiar old blue frock, our lady-mother made her go stark naked for a week, attending her lessons and sitting at the table thus, and even sewing in the parlor, and dancing in the Great Hall, while our lady-mother coolly explained to their guests why Jane was being punished in this manner, and slapping, pinching, yanking, and sharply rebuking Jane whenever she wept and tried to hide or cover herself, refusing even when she groveled at her feet and begged to be allowed to put on the new dress to cover her shameful nakedness. By the time the punishment was finished, Jane hated the white and gold dress even more, but she consented to wear it, and when she dribbled gravy on the bodice, she wept in terror at what our lady-mother would do to her.

Their quarrels over clothes lay dormant for a few years until Jane caught the fever of the Reformed Religion; only then would she dare reassert her disdain for ornate garb again, and by that time our lady-mother, sensing that Jane was incorrigible, and that thinking up suitable punishments for her was more trouble than it was worth, had long since contented herself with beatings and blows and fortnight long repasts of only salt fish, water, and boiled mutton bones that Jane licked and sucked ravenously as her belly grumbled and ached.

Though I did not know it at the time, that summons to the library would change our lives forever. Nothing would ever be the same again. Yet I felt not even a twinge of fear or foreboding then; instead I was smiling, swishing my midnight blue velvet skirts and humming a lively air, as I watched Kate skip lightheartedly ahead of us with a song on her lips to first keep her promise to Cook and give her the pail, still half filled with our wonderful, delicious syllabub, for her and the rest of the kitchen servants to share, before skipping upstairs to change into her green velvet gown and sunny yellow, quilted, pearl-dotted satin petticoat and matching undersleeves, the ones with the wide frills of golden point lace at the wrists that she was always fidgeting with, saying that she could not bear to have them cut off, they were so beautiful, but Lord how they made her wrists itch, like the Devil's own seamstress had made them just to torment her.

When we entered the library, Father laid down his quill and rose up from behind his desk. He was a tall, broad-shouldered, big-bellied man, handsome and rosy-cheeked with warm brown eyes, a luxuriant bushy auburn beard, and wild, ruddy hair that seemed ever wont to spring up in a riot of nervous panic, as though unsure of which way to run, it went every which way. That day he was dressed in the sedately elegant deep orange and brown velvet garments edged with golden braid that our lady-mother had chosen for him. With hands on hips, she often declared, "If Hal Grey were left to his own devices in matters of dress, he would come out of his room every morning looking like a sunlit rainbow, dazzling and gaudy enough to blind every beholder, and be mistaken by all for a fool in motley!"

At the sight of us he smiled and opened his arms wide. "My little girls!" he said fondly in a voice that conveyed, even though we were all girls, and none of us the son he longed for, he was nonetheless proud of us.

We cast a quick and wary glance around to ascertain our lady-mother was not present. She wasn't—that meant Father would be fun! And we ran into his arms and hugged him tight; even Jane forgot her solemn dignity and hurled herself into his arms. Kate settled herself on his lap, and he tousled and kissed her bright curls and took from the secret "sweet drawer" in his desk a special treat he had been saving to share with us. When he was last in London he had visited his favorite sweetshop and purchased a box of the most wonderful marzipan; the box was lined in blue silk, and each dainty, brightly colored piece was an exquisite replica of a creature from the sea—there were seashells, all manner of fishes, blue and green crabs, and bright red lobsters, oysters that opened to reveal candy pearls, sharks, dolphins, and whales, billowy branches of coral, undulating sea serpents, and even bare-breasted mermaids combing their flowing tresses or playing harps, and lusty, leering, blue-bearded mermen clutching tridents.

"Don't tell your lady-mother," he said with a slightly sad smile, his words only half jesting. "She thinks I overindulge in sweets, though I tell her that one can *never* have *too much* of a good thing. She says one day I'll get as big as old King Henry was and then she'll divorce me and find herself a lean, lusty lad to replace me." He lowered his voice to a whisper and confided, "I think she has her eye on our Master of the Horse, young Master Stokes."

"*No one* could *ever* replace *you,* Father!" Kate cried as she flung her arms around his neck and kissed his cheek. "And certainly not Master Stokes! He's only twenty—just five years older than Jane! Our lady-mother would *never* be so foolish!"

"Never!" Jane and I chorused, squeezing Kate so tight she squealed as we pressed to embrace Father and kiss the red-bristled sun-bronzed cheeks that bulged with marzipan.

He swallowed hard and smiled. "Now then, on to serious matters . . ."

And suddenly I felt the icy touch of fear upon my back, prickly as frozen needles. In that instant I just *knew* that he was about to speak the words that would set in motion actions that would shatter my world.

"My three little girls are about to leave me." Father shook his head and sighed dolefully. "How time flies! You're not little girls anymore; you're young *women*—young women about to become *wives*."

"Married?" Jane gasped and tottered back, tripping over her hems and stumbling hard against the desk. She leaned there looking white as a ghost, tugging hard at the high collar of her funereal black velvet gown as though it were a noose strangling her. And I was sorely afraid that she might faint.

"*Married!* I'm to be *married!*" Kate jumped up with a jubilant squeal, spinning around, hugging her clasped hands tight against her excitedly beating heart. "When? Will it be soon? Oh, Father, can I have a golden gown and golden slippers and a cake, a great big cinnamon spice cake, as tall as I am? No! *Taller!* And covered with gilded marzipan and inside filled with chunks of apples, walnuts, and golden and black raisins, and lots of cinnamon, lots and lots of cinnamon! And minstrels to play at my wedding clad from head to toe in silver since I shall be all in gold!"

"Aye, my love, my beautiful Katey, aye!" Father sat back in his chair and roared with laughter even as tears filled his eyes. "And, yes, it will be soon, in a month's time you'll be married and have left maidenhood behind. But as important as the cake and your dress and slippers and the minstrels are, don't you want to know *whom* you're going to marry?"

"Oh yes!" Kate stopped her giddy prancing and turned expectantly to Father. "Of course I do! Is he young and handsome? Do I know him? What's his name? Is his hair dark or fair? Does he have blue eyes or brown, gray or green? Shall we have a house in London and one in the country as well? Will he take me to court? Will we have our own barge? Shall I go to court to serve the Queen when Cousin Edward marries? Will he buy me jewels and gowns and puppies and kittens and pet monkeys and songbirds in gilded cages? Oh, Father, I do so *long* to have a pair of monkeys! I shall dress them in little suits and gowns just like babies! And parrots, *talking* parrots—I can teach them new words and feed them berries from my hand! And will my husband and I have lots of babies? I want a nursery *full* of babies! I want to be a little woman round and stout as a barrel with a baby always in my arms, filling out my belly, and a bunch of them tugging at my skirts calling me 'mother'! I want our home to be *filled* with joy and laughter!"

Father laughed heartily. "So many questions! You're curious as a cat, my Kate! Stop a moment and still your eager tongue, my lovely love, and let me answer! No, you've never met him. His name is Henry, Lord Herbert, he is the Earl of Pembroke's son, and a handsome, fair-haired youth not quite two years older than yourself, and I believe his eyes are blue. You'll like him. I'm as sure of it as I am that this marzipan is delicious!" He waved a hand at the nigh empty box on his desk. "As for the rest, all in good time, my pretty Kate, all in good time! Stop chomping at the bit, raring to be off, my fine filly; slow down and enjoy your life, without racing through it at breakneck speed. If you go too fast, it will all pass by you in a blur and you'll miss it all."

Nervously, I tugged at Father's sleeve to get his attention. "Me too?" I asked timidly. "*I* am to be married? Someone wants to marry *me?*"

"Aye, my little love." Father swooped me up to sit upon his lap. "Though being as you are only eight, you shall have to bide at home and content yourself with being betrothed a while, but, aye, my little Mary, you are to be a bride just like your sisters! And Time has a sneaky habit of flying by, and all too soon the dressmakers will be marching up the stairs to unfurl their banners of silk before you and make you a fine wedding gown of any cut and color you choose!"

"Who?" I asked in a dazed and breathless whisper. The man I was to marry was of far greater importance to me than any new gown, though honesty compels me to admit that a rich deep plum velvet and silver-flowered lavender damask trimmed with silver fox fur billowed briefly through my mind, and my inner eye caught a teasing, tantalizing glimpse of the fine wine sparkle of garnets and deep purple amethysts set in silver. *"Who* would want to marry *me?"*

"I've chosen someone *very special* for you, my little love." Father chucked my chin and kissed the tip of my nose. "Now he is a *wee* bit older than you are, five-and-forty, and a kinsman of mine. Mayhap you've heard tell of him, for he's a war hero, one of our greatest—my cousin William Grey, Lord Wilton."

Kate gave such a frightful shriek that I nearly toppled off Father's lap, and Jane momentarily forgot her own staggering surprise as horror, then pity, filled her eyes as she stared at me. Then both my sisters were there, crying and clinging tight to me, as though they could not bear to let me go. But all I could do was nod, my disappointment and hurt went too deep for tears, and there are times in a dwarf's tormented life when one feels all cried dry of tears.

The whole of England knew the story of Lord Wilton, and little boys fought to play him in their war games, their vying for this prized part often leaving them with bloodied lips and blackened eyes. He had been *hideously* wounded, his face grotesquely mutilated at the Battle of Pinkie Cleugh. A Scottish pike had smashed through the front of his helm, shattering several teeth as it stove in his mouth, and pierced through his tongue, knocking out even more teeth in its violent progress, and penetrated the roof of his mouth. At some point, his nose had also been broken and smashed in in a grotesque and bloody parody of one of those darling little dogs with the pushed-in noses that Kate adored so. To make matters worse, his helm had been quite destroyed by enemy blows, and the metal intended to protect his face had instead turned against him, biting deep, like jagged steel teeth, lacerating his flesh, and leaving behind ugly, jagged scars zigzagging like a violent lightning storm all over his face. The enemy pike had also cost him an eye. Some said he was merely blinded and wore a black leather patch to cover the hideous gray-clouded eyeball, though others claimed the eye was white and sightless as an egg, while others said that it concealed an empty hollow, that the Scottish warrior who took it had boasted he had plucked it out of its socket like an olive, though some rather ghoulishly insisted that he popped it in his mouth and swallowed it whole, and yet others insisted he had chewed it with great vigor and glee.

Regardless of which of these tales was the true one, Lord Wilton left the battlefield that day with a face that frightened children and now went about veiled like a lady in public lest his ears be assaulted by cries of "Dear God, what is that hideous thing?" and "Monster!" and the terrified wails of children, the screams of women, and the thud of their bodies falling down in a faint. I felt sorry for him; I, "Crouchback Mary," the "little gargoyle," the "goblin child," and "mashed-up little toad," could well understand his pain and torment. It must have been especially hard for him since he had once been accounted amongst the handsomest of men, whilst I had been born ugly and misshapen and had known no other form or face.

But empathy was not enough to make me want to marry him. Oh what a pair we would make! I could picture myself leading my half-blind and veiled husband around by the hand, my crooked spine straining and aching at the awful effort. People would think we were a couple of freaks loose from the fair or some nobleman's collection of Mother Nature's mistakes. Those who enjoyed such spectacles might even come up to us and offer us pennies to peer beneath my husband's veil or toss down their coins and cry, *"Dance, dwarf, dance!"*

"Nay, pet, look not so downhearted! You're frowning as if the world were about to end without your ever having tasted of all its pleasures! *Smile!*" Father cried, setting me down and with the tips of his fingers pushing the corners of my mouth up to form a smile that instantly disappeared the moment he removed them. "Lord Wilton is a *wonderful* man and a *great* hero! A husband you can be proud of! I myself have told him *all* about you, and he cannot wait to make you his bride. How impatient he is for his little Mary to grow up! He wants to be informed the moment you shed your first woman's blood! He *longs* for an understanding and intelligent young wife, a quiet, sensible girl whose head and heart will not be turned by a handsome face, one who is content to bide at home and sit by the fire and read to and converse with him, someone he can tell his stories to and relive his former glories with, someone like you, my little love, not some flighty little minx he is likely to find one day rolling in the straw with the stable boy between her knees! And, mind you, just because his face is ruined, doesn't mean that William is lacking in amorous skill, quite the contrary, but that is not a subject fit for your tender years. Suffice it to say that upon your wedding night you shall experience a heavenly rapture, and not of the spiritual kind, but a warm, quivering, panting, pulsing, throbbing ecstasy of the flesh! William has the tongue and fingers to rival the greatest musician in England; he plays a woman's body like an instrument! But forget I said that until you are old enough to remember! It's not a fit subject for a little maid like you to contemplate."

"But, Father!" Kate wailed. "He is *so* ugly! And *old!* I have seen him riding through London in his litter, his face covered by a thick veil, with a shawl about his shoulders, just like a hunched and shriveled-up old woman calling out to his bearers in a whining voice that they are going too fast, or too slow, or to watch out for that pig or that little girl or not to step in the street muck, and to turn here and turn there as though he laid the streets of London himself and knows them better than any!"

"Katherine!" Father barked sharply. "I am appalled and ashamed of you! Don't you realize, girl, that you are talking about a *great* war hero? The man who led the first charge against the enemy at the Battle of Pinkie Cleugh, mind you! I'll thank you to show some respect for your future brother-in-law! Everyone with a drop of English blood in them should go down on their knees and thank William Grey for sacrificing his looks, and his vanity, for their sake. And before he was injured, he had *much* to be vain of. He was as bold and brazen as a strutting cockerel! If you girls were boys, the stories I could tell you," he added with a wink. Then, hurtling over the obstacles that stood in the way of a good story, he went on as though our sex posed no barrier. "Why, when he was lying there with his face hanging from his skull in shreds and tatters all stitched up with crude thread and swathed in bloody rags, not knowing whether he was going to live or die, he called for a mirror though he was told it was best not to look, but look he did, he was that brave, then he defiantly flung the mirror away, and to prove himself still a man he called for women and more women and to keep them coming until he said, 'No more!' He wore out a dozen whores, by some counts as many as sixteen or thirty—everyone who tells the tale gives a different number—but I am sure, knowing my cousin

William, that it was at *least* a dozen wenches. But upon one point everyone agrees—those doxies staggered out of his tent nigh swooning with their knees trembling, complaining that they ached in their privy parts like just deflowered virgins; some of them even clamped rags over their cunnies to staunch the bleeding, saying his battering ram was that big and gave them such a powerful banging, and these were all seasoned camp followers, mind you, whores who had left maidenhood long behind them!" He guiltily clapped a hand over his mouth as though his own words surprised him. "But I shouldn't have told you that. You're just little girls, so forget every word! Your lady-mother would take a horsewhip to my buttocks if she knew I had been filling your heads with bawdy stories; the Good Lord above knows that she loves any excuse to do that! Let that be a lesson to you girls. *Never* marry a woman who lives in riding boots, for like as not she will wear them in bed as well, and the whip will never be far from her hand. Frances even wore them 'neath her bridal gown; I heard her golden spurs jingling as she walked up the aisle to take her place beside me. For the life of me, I could not figure out what that noise was, and when I bent to lift the hem of her skirt to see, she slapped my new feathered hat clean off my head right there at the altar in plain sight of everyone, and as I put the ring on her finger, I had a red and throbbing ear, the wedding guests sat there in the pews tittering as they watched it swell. But forget I told you that too!" he added hastily. "Your lady-mother wouldn't like it! Have some more candy, girls!"

He snatched up the box and offered it around to us. "Here's something more suitable for your ears and years that will help you understand, especially you, little Mary, what a grand match this courageous man is! Why, if I were a woman I would leap at the chance to wed Lord Wilton! But don't tell him I said that; William *deplores* anything he even thinks hints at sodomy, so he would not take my words as the sincere compliment I meant them to be, for I hold him in the *highest* esteem! But forget I said that too, the bit about sodomy I mean—you girls shouldn't even know that word or what it means! You don't, do you? *Please* say you don't and spare my hide your mother's riding crop!"

He gave a great sigh of relief and mopped the sweat from his brow with his velvet sleeve when we all nodded obediently. Then he proceeded to climb up onto the long polished table that spanned nearly the entire length of the library and, enthusiastic as a little boy, began a vigorous one-man reenactment of "the wounding of Lord Wilton at the Battle of Pinkie Cleugh," spiritedly wielding pantomime pikes and swords and playing all the various roles, the enemy Scots and the brave Englishmen, falling back, gurgling blood, clasping his throat, and gasping for air as my affianced husband was stricken, then rolling over on his side to quickly inform us how John Dudley, the Duke of Northumberland himself, or "the Earl of Warwick as he was then," had himself thrust his fingers down Lord Wilton's throat and brought up a handful of broken teeth to clear his airway so he could breathe, "thus saving his life."

Then the wounded warrior valiantly mounted his horse again—Father swung his leg over a pretend steed and began to mime a brisk canter, neighing as his boots went clip-clop over the varnished table—explaining in an aside how, with Northumberland at his side, Lord Wilton had ridden hard through the swarming bodies of armored Englishmen and kilted Scots, wielding clanging swords, swinging spiked maces, and thrusting and clashing pikes. "When suddenly Lord Wilton began to droop, overcome by the heat, dust, buzzing flies, pain, and loss of blood, and seemed poised to faint. 'Twas then that Northumberland grabbed a firkin of ale, tilted the swooning man's head back, and poured it over his head, and as much as he could down his throat, to revive him, thus saving his life yet again. And our brave kinsman finished the charge, a hero, though a trifle drunken with his face a torn and bloody ruin, he was a hero nonetheless, and for it by the Crown rewarded with a knighthood and the governorship of Berwick, and he was also made warden of the east marches and general of several of the northern!"

Our lady-mother walked in just as Father was reenacting the shower of ale, having first called to Kate to bring him the flagon from his desk. She stood, arms folded across her ample breasts, tapping the toe of her boot upon the polished oaken floor, and watched with us as, standing on the table, Father threw his head back and raised the flagon up high and poured a shower of ale down his throat and all over his chest, so caught up in the drama he was reenacting that he displayed a reckless disregard for his elegant new clothes.

"Hal, whatever are you doing?" our lady-mother demanded. "Get down off that table, you're making a perfect spectacle of yourself!"

"Well, at least he is doing it perfectly," Jane murmured tartly, making a not so veiled reference to our lady-mother's insistence on perfection.

Without even glancing at Jane, our lady-mother raised her hand and with the back of it dealt Jane's face a slap. "Sarcasm is not a becoming quality in a young lady, Jane, especially not a young lady about to be married. Or hasn't your father told you about that yet?"

Father dropped the flagon, and it fell onto the table with a loud clatter as he quickly clambered down, explaining that he had just been telling us the happy news.

"This required your standing on the table my mother left me, scratching it with your boots, pouring ale all over yourself, and ruining your new doublet?" she asked, arching one finely plucked brow in disbelief.

"I—I was just showing the girls how Lord Wilton was wounded at the Battle of Pinkie Cleugh," Father sheepishly explained as a blush flamed like a wildfire across his cheeks above his bushy auburn beard.

Poor Father! Mother always made him act like a mouse cornered by a cat. In her presence, he was forever fidgeting, stammering, and gnawing his nails, and tugging and twisting his hair, as a sweat broke out on his brow. Even when she was not there he was always starting at unexpected sounds and darting swift, nervous, and guilty glances around even when he was not partaking of the contents of his "sweet drawer."

"What in heaven's name for?" our lady-mother asked.

"I... I... The girls were... well I..." Father stammered, his eyes suddenly intent upon his toes. "It's quite understandable, my dear... you know he... he is not... pleasant... to look upon... and I-I wanted Mary to understand and... be proud that a war hero wants to marry her!"

Our lady-mother rolled her eyes. "Don't lie to her! Her mirror doesn't lie to her, and men's eyes won't either, only your foolish heart and tongue! You think you're being kind, but you're not. He's marrying her because *I* say she'll have him, and he's the only suitable man of rank and means willing to have her, and far better him for a husband than having the little gargoyle remain a spinster under our roof for the rest of her life since we can't very well send her to a nunnery since England is now Protestant instead of Papist, and she's too high born to be a fool in a great household. That would only shame and disgrace us! Her face will not make her fortune, like Kate's will," she added, her voice softening, growing tender, as she spoke my sister's name and turned to caress the bright curls and bend to press a kiss onto her cheek.

Her words stung me like a slap, and I could not bear the way she stamped all the fun out of Father, chastised him, and made him behave like a naughty schoolboy. And, I confess, it hurt me to witness the affection she showered on Kate, so I timorously piped out a question, never thinking that it might hurt Jane. "F-Father, who is Jane to marry? You did not say before."

Father flashed a grateful smile at me. *Anything* to divert our lady-mother. He too feared her sharp tongue that was like a metal-barbed whip, always criticizing and chastising us.

"Guildford Dudley," he answered promptly and proudly as though the boy whose name he had just pronounced was some great prize that he had won for his firstborn daughter. "The Earl of Northumberland's youngest son of marriageable age, and the only one of his brood with golden hair. All the others are dark," he added. "He is his mother's favorite and was christened with her maiden name—Guildford. It's rather different, don't you think?" he babbled on. "I mean when so many boys are named Henry, Edward, Robert, William, John, and Thomas, it stands out as wonderfully unique, don't you think?"

"Guildford Dudley!" We three sisters raised an incredulous chorus and clung together for comfort. I saw loathing and contempt in Jane's eyes, while Kate's and mine mirrored the pity we each felt for our scholarly sister to be wedded and bedded by such a conceited fool, a gilt-haired youth who made the proud peacocks that strutted across the royal gardens look dowdy and meek as sparrows in

comparison. Jane was fluent in Latin, Greek, and French, and was currently studying Hebrew to enhance her understanding of the Scriptures; she devoured the works of Cicero, Ovid, Plutarch, Livy, Juvenal, Demosthenes, Justin the Martyr, Plato, Aristotle, Socrates, and the New Testament written in Greek as other girls her age did chivalric romances and the rollicking, ribald tales of Boccaccio and Chaucer; she had even recently acquired a Latin translation of the Jewish Talmud. And now she was betrothed to a boy who thought books were merely decorative. *Poor Jane!*

Everyone knew that Guildford Dudley was vainer than any girl. His own family called him their gilded lily and their golden gillyflower and catered to his every whim, shamelessly pampering and indulging their petulant and decadent darling in every way imaginable. And he was such a fool, though he himself, and his adoring mother, who put him on a pedestal like a gilt idol, thought his brains as brilliant as his beauty. Everyone knew that all the Dudleys' servants were dark-haired, to make Guildford's own golden head shine all the brighter; Guildford, who washed his hair twice a week with a mixture of lemon juice and chamomile, was known to throw fierce tantrums if any boy with fair hair dared to stand within twenty paces of him. He was the only boy I ever knew who slept with his head in curl rags every night and insisted his hairdresser, standing ready to attend him, be the first person he saw when he opened his eyes each morning. That was Guildford Dudley—Jane's betrothed. *Oh my poor, poor sister!*

"I Will Not." One moment Jane was speaking, enunciating each word with hard, ironclad clarity, the next her skull was striking the floor and her feet flying up as our lady-mother felled her with one swift blow from her fist.

"You will," our lady-mother said with icy calmness.

Jane raised her throbbing head from the floor and locked eyes with our lady-mother. *"I will not,"* she repeated. "I will *not* marry Guildford Dudley."

There was an ominous quietness, wrapping us all like a shroud. We all knew what was about to happen; it had happened so many times before it would have been accounted a miracle if it hadn't. Jane would be taken upstairs to the Long Gallery outside our rooms, where we had always gathered by the fire and played on cold or rainy days. She would be stripped to her shift and made to wait, kneeling like a penitent, before a hard wooden bench. Then we would hear the determined tread of our lady-mother's leather-booted footsteps, the jingle-jangle of her spurs, and the slap of her riding crop against her palm as she approached. A few words would be exchanged, though to no profit, as Jane would not apologize for whatever offense she had committed. Then our lady-mother would point her whip at the bench and Jane would lift off her shift and position herself over it with her bare back and buttocks fully exposed to the merciless cascade of blows that were about to descend. She would bite her lips until they bled and silent tears would drip down onto the floor as she choked back her sobs and refused to cry out. She would not give our lady-mother the satisfaction of hearing her plead for mercy.

"To the Long Gallery," our lady-mother said, and briskly strode out without a backward glance.

"Oh, Jane!" we cried, huddling close around our sister, as if our love alone could protect her, but she brushed away our arms and walked stoically out after our lady-mother with her head held high and proud, just like a Christian martyr about to be thrown to the lions. There were times when I thought Jane actually relished the role, the sympathy her suffering stirred, and how it made her brilliance shine all the brighter, like a perfect diamond in a dull setting.

Father returned to munching his marzipan with a nervous vengeance, crying out once when he accidentally bit his own finger, and Kate and I stood helplessly holding hands staring worriedly after Jane, wincing inwardly at each imagined lash of the whip upon her vulnerable flesh.

In one day we had gone from being three little girls, a trio of sisters playing in the snow, growing drunk and giddy on syllabub, to three maids about to be married.

Later, when Jane lay upon her stomach, Kate and I knelt on the bed beside her, frowning over the blood-crusted slashes and livid red welts blooming like a riot of red roses all over her back, bottom, and thighs already crisscrossed with several silvery white scars from previous beatings. We cleansed them gently with a cloth dipped in a mixture of yarrow and comfrey followed by a comforting balm of lavender, which Kate also dabbed onto Jane's temples after she kissed them.

Finally I asked, "Why did you resist? You knew what would happen if you did, that you would be beaten, and in the end it would change nothing, nothing at all except you would be lying here like this." I brandished an angry hand over her wounded back, buttocks, and thighs. "None of us has the right to choose whom we will marry. We can only accept and try to make the best of it."

Jane didn't answer me. She lay there silent as a stone. Perhaps she was mulling it over in her mind, searching for an answer, or mayhap she was contemplating a day when the sorrowful tale of how Lady Jane Grey was beaten into submission and forced to marry a fool would be spread far and wide amongst Europe's most distinguished scholars. The laments that would be expressed when it became known that their bright star, the Reformed Faith's brightest candle, had been forced to douse her light and put away her books and accept a woman's lot of marriage and, eventually, motherhood. "What a waste that such a mind should be trapped in a woman's body!" they would say.

Though I never dared broach the subject with Jane, and perhaps my thinking is colored by what came after, I often suspected that though she despised the stories of the Catholic saints, and the suffering that made them martyrs, she secretly used them as her own personal embroidery pattern, envisioning a similar fate for herself. She never bit her tongue and humbly bowed her head and suffered in silence like most chastised and punished children did, nor did she ever school herself to adopt meek ways and avoid further beatings; instead she seemed to provoke and invite them. There were so many times when Jane could have saved herself, but she didn't. And afterward she *always* found a way—a sympathetic ear with a gossipy tongue—to tell the world. Jane felt her story *must* be told; she craved sympathy the way a drunkard does wine and praise as a glutton dreams of devouring a royal banquet.

"And at least Guildford Dudley is handsome, even if he is a fool," Kate added, "so it might not be so bad. Perhaps he will be kind? And failing that, he is always good for a laugh." She giggled.

"I once saw him in a shop in London; he bought a gray velvet cloak lined in pale blue silk and fringed and embroidered with silver flowers—it was a *very* beautiful cloak—because he had just the cat to wear it with. See, Jane?" She prodded her gently when the ghost of a smile twitched at Jane's lips. "You will always have a husband who will make you smile! And it could be far worse; poor Mary is stuck with Lord Wilton, and he has a face that gives little children nightmares." Kate made a sour face and shuddered.

All of a sudden I began to shake and shiver, and then the tears came, uncontrollably, though I did not wish to appear babyish before my sisters, especially after I had just been scolding Jane for resisting what could not be changed, but I could not help it.

"Mary, what is it?" Kate turned to me. "I am sorry for what I said about Lord Wilton, truly I am. I did not mean to make you cry. Oh *please* don't cry, or I will cry too!" And even as she spoke, tears began to trickle down my sister's lovely face.

"It's not that!" I blurted. "It's just . . . you are both going to leave me! In only a few weeks . . . I shall lose you both!"

"Oh, Mary!" Kate threw her arms about me, and Jane levered up her sore body and crawled over to put her arms around my waist and lay her head in my lap.

"Don't cry!" Kate pleaded. "I promise I shall have you visit me often, mayhap you can even come to live with me. I shall use my every charm to persuade Lord Herbert to allow it."

"And you shall visit me too," Jane promised, "as often as you can. Just think, soon you will be grumbling about all the time you spend on the road going from Kate's house to mine."

"R-really?" I blubbered hopefully.

"Really!" my sisters promised and hugged me tighter.

"We are sisters," Kate said, "and we shall never truly be parted, not even by time and distance."

"Even when we are apart, we will still be together—*always!*" Jane declared in a voice filled with unshakable confidence, as solid and strong as the bond between us.

And I felt better, with their words I truly felt the weight and strength of the invisible chain forged between us, a wonderful set of unbreakable shackles binding us together forever that not even marriage, motherhood, or death could sever.

The next morning, Kate and I helped Jane dress her stiff and aching body in a plain, high-necked black velvet gown and quilted dove gray petticoat and held her hands as she hobbled bent-backed between us out into the Long Gallery to enact the ritual we knew so well. Each time one of us was punished, the next morning we must crawl on our hands and knees the full length of the Long Gallery to where our parents sat waiting and humbly beg our lady-mother's pardon. By the time we reached them, our arms would be aching, our palms smarting and red from the hard stone floor, and our knees scraped raw despite our skirts and stockings. Sometimes our lady-mother would bestow her forgiveness right away, like a queen graciously granting a petitioner some bounty, and raise and kiss us once on each cheek; other times she would fold her arms across her chest, frown, and shake her head emphatically, and the ritual would have to be repeated each morning until she deigned to give it. There was no rhyme or reason to it. Sometimes she would instantly forgive the most grievous offense and deny it for the most trifling. I remember when I pilfered some bright yellow embroidery silk from our lady-mother's sewing basket, I had to crawl the length of that gallery seven mornings in a row, but when a curious Kate, at the time aged eight, charmed one of the kitchen boys into showing her his cock, and with an obliging smile returned the favor by lifting her skirts and displaying her cunny, our lady-mother instantly forgave her the first time she asked. And poor Jane, when she dribbled gravy on that white and gold gown, her first adult raiment, she was forced to crawl the Long Gallery and crave forgiveness a full five weeks—one for each stain that the laundress could not remove—before our lady-mother finally gave it.

This particular morning, seeing what pain our sister was in, Kate had "a brilliant idea" and ran back to her room and snatched two small cushions from the baskets where her puppies and kittens rested, and two lengths of wide satin ribbon from her sewing basket. She knelt before Jane and bade her hold her skirts up high and then with the ribbons bound a cushion around each of Jane's knees.

"There now"—she smiled up at Jane—"now it will not be so bad."

And at first it didn't seem to be. Kate and I held hands and watched anxiously as Jane crawled slowly down the gallery's great length to where our parents waited, our lady-mother clearly impatient to be off hunting, slapping her riding crop against her leather-gloved palm and dangling a leg so that the golden spurs on her leather boots jangled.

It seemed as though whole hours crept past, but at long last there she was, kneeling, a humble supplicant before our lady-mother.

Head bowed, she softly intoned the requisite words: "I most humbly crave your pardon, my lady-mother."

Compassion lighting his face like a candle within a gourd, Father whispered, "Dearest girl," and reached out a hand to stroke Jane's hair, but our lady-mother slapped it away with her riding crop. Poor Father started and snatched back his smarting fingers, raising them to his mouth to suck away the blood welling from his knuckles.

Supremely cool, our lady-mother lifted one finely plucked Tudor red brow. "Will you marry Guildford Dudley?" she asked.

There was a moment of lengthy tension in which I could feel the war raging within Jane, but at last she surrendered, and with head hung low and shoulders sagging in sad defeat, did what was expected of her and answered, "Yes, my lady-mother."

With a brisk nod and a smile of triumph upon her lips, our lady-mother reached out to clasp Jane's shoulders and bent to brush her lips against each of my sister's cheeks, then, sitting back, gestured with her riding crop for Jane to rise.

It was then that disaster struck. As Jane struggled sorely to her feet, the ribbons securing the cushions slipped. Jane stood there mortified, staring down at the plump little cushions of plum purple and cherry red puddled at her feet, and the pink and blue satin ribbons snaking out from beneath her skirts.

Our lady-mother's whip shot out, to whisk Jane's skirts up and reveal Kate's "brilliant idea."

With a nervous glance at our lady-mother, Father began to laugh and clap his hands, hoping against hope that his wife would see the humor of the situation rather than fly into a rage.

But our lady-mother was not amused. Two slaps, one to each of the cheeks she had just kissed, sent Jane toppling backward, barking her palms painfully against the floor when she tried to break her fall.

I tried to restrain her, but Kate broke away from me. "My lady-mother, no, *please* no, it was my idea!" Tearfully, she flung herself at our lady-mother's feet, bruising her own tender knees, and grabbed our lady-mother's hands and kissed and pressed them to her own tear-dampened cheeks, and said, "I most humbly crave your pardon, my lady-mother."

"This was *your* idea?" Our lady-mother flicked her riding crop at the cushions and ribbons lying in a guilty heap upon the floor. When Kate, still kneeling, nodded, a bright smile spread across our lady-mother's face and, beaming, she swept Kate up into her arms, nigh smothering her against her ample bosom. "My darling, you are almost as clever as you are beautiful! That kind of thinking will serve you far better at court than Plato ever will." She sneered at Jane. "Come, my love." She took Kate's hand. "Walk with me to the stables and you may pet the spotted hunting hounds and feed a carrot to my horse. Come, Hal!" she called back over her shoulder to Father, and he snatched up his feathered cap, gloves, and riding crop and ran after her, obedient as a dog himself.

I stood there, longing to run to Jane, but cowardly not daring to move lest I somehow incur my lady-mother's wrath. I stood there, staring after them, my heart beating as though it might at any moment burst through the wall of my chest. *Please, Lord, don't let our lady-mother turn round,* I prayed. *Let her forget about Jane.*

But it was not to be. In the doorway, our lady-mother paused and looked back.

"Mrs. Ellen!" she called to Jane's nurse, who through it all had stood back, an unobtrusive presence in her crow-black gown and hood, silently observing the scene. "Fetch some pins! You are to secure Lady Jane's skirts above her knees and then remove her shoes and stockings." Then she turned to Jane and directed sternly, "You are to crawl back and forth the entire length of this gallery on your *bare* hands and knees until we return from the hunt." Then she was gone, spurs jingling, the feathers on her hat bouncing, without waiting for an answer, confident as a queen that her will would be obeyed.

As soon as she was gone, I rushed to Jane, but she sat up and held out her hand to stay me. "No! Stay back, stay away, Mary, or she'll punish you too!"

All through the morning and long into the afternoon Kate and I sat, holding each other and sobbing, helplessly watching our sister, weeping all the harder when we saw the trails of blood that marked her slow progress up and down the Long Gallery as the day wore on. Kate pleaded for Jane to stop and rest a while, imploring Mrs. Ellen with tear-filled eyes to lie and say Jane had enacted her punishment exactly as described.

"My lady, I cannot, I dare not," Mrs. Ellen said sadly as she gently unclenched Kate's fists from the folds of her black skirt.

And Jane would not stop until, as the sky glowed orange through the windows, our lady-mother appeared in the doorway and spoke a single word: "Enough!" And Jane fell fainting, facedown, flat upon the floor.

If memory doesn't deceive me, it was the next day that we were called again to the library and the portraits, gifts from our betrotheds, were unveiled before us.

For me there was a lush, sable-bearded likeness of Lord Wilton in all his former glory, a big, handsome, burly bear of a man, towering and overpowering in a suit of satin-slashed buff brocade and golden breastplate and feathered helm, armed with a sword and shield like a war god. For the life of me, I couldn't rightly say whether I found him more frightening before or after his battle scars. He did not have the look of a kind or patient man, but the sort who would order his household with military precision. I only knew, in my heart, I didn't want him; he was not the man for me. But I also knew it was my duty to obey and futile to resist; no one cared what I thought; like all nobly born girls, I truly had no say in the matter. And so I praised the portrait, calling it "a handsome picture," and retreated into silence.

For Kate there was a miniature of Lord Herbert with a bail at the top of the round gold frame so that she might wear it upon a golden chain, jeweled necklace, or a rope of pearls. Lord Herbert had thoughtfully sent along a dozen of these as a betrothal gift so that no matter what gown she was wearing Kate would have something to suit and thus his likeness could always be with her until the day he took his place at her side, he gallantly explained in the accompanying letter. Kate squealed with delight. "How handsome he is!" she enthused again and again, dancing around the room as our lady-mother bent to examine the necklaces with the practiced eye of a pawnbroker, alert for any flaws or duplicity.

Her inspection done, and apparently satisfied with both the quality and workmanship, our lady-mother laid down a rope of pearls and ruby beads and smiled at her favorite daughter's girlish enthusiasm and pointed out that the miniature she was holding was ringed with diamonds. "Particularly fine diamonds, daughter; take note of them and measure any jewels that come after against them and you will always know *exactly* where you stand in your husband's affections. There are ways of managing a man," she added pointedly, "and the important thing is that you *never* wear anything that is not first-rate. Never settle for anything inferior, for once you do, he will never bring you the best again."

Kate clasped the picture to her bosom and breathed, "But he is *so* handsome; I am *certain* I would love him even if they were glass instead of diamonds!"

"Then you are a fool," our lady-mother stated simply, "a beautiful simpleton, nothing more, and you shall never amount to anything."

Kate gave a wounded little cry, and her lips began to tremble as her eyes filled with tears and she stared, hurt and uncomprehending, at our lady-mother.

"Now, now"—our lady-mother pulled her close—"it is good to see you so excited and eager to love your husband; you need only temper your exuberance with a little wisdom, daughter, and all shall be well."

"Yes, my lady-mother, yes, I promise, I will!" Kate vowed, all sunny smiles again. "I shall see to it that Lord Herbert gives me the best of everything, for I shall ensure that I am worth it by always giving my best to him!"

"That's my clever girl!" our lady-mother beamed and patted her cheek. "There are brains behind that beauty after all!"

Lastly, for Jane there was a full-sized portrait of Guildford Dudley. Its ornate frame of carved gilded gillyflowers and the Dudleys' heraldic bear and ragged staff was so heavy that it took two men to carry it in. When our lady-mother removed the gold-fringed yellow velvet that covered it, we all gasped and stepped back.

"My, my," Father said, patting his heart as he looked the painted likeness of his soon to be son-in-law up and down.

Head to toe, the spoiled and decadent darling of the Dudleys was like a gilded idol; all that was missing was a pedestal for him to stand upon and a throng of adoring minions kneeling at his feet. Each perfectly arranged golden curl adorning his head shone as though it had been sculpted by a master goldsmith, his lips were arranged in a perfect, petulant, pink rosebud pout, and his green eyes were the exact color of gooseberries; they made me shudder and think of snakes and pale emeralds all at the same time. His lavish yellow brocade vestments were woven thickly with golden threads in a pattern of gillyflowers accentuated with diamond brilliants and creamy gold pearls. His long, shapely limbs were encased in hose of vivid yellow silk, and he held one foot pointed just so that we could see the bouquet of golden gillyflowers embroidered over his ankle, and upon the toes of his yellow shoes, golden gillyflowers bloomed and twinkled with diamonds that made the ones that ringed Lord Herbert's portrait look paltry and dull in comparison. Even the rings on his fingers and the heavy golden chain about his neck were bejeweled golden gillyflowers; clearly Guildford considered this *his* flower. The artist had even painted a mass of them, yellow of course, blooming about his feet. Before our astonished eyes, this radiant young man held out his arms, golden wrist frills gleaming, as if to say to the world, "Here I am—worship and adore me!"

"With all those diamonds sewn upon the yellow, he makes me think of sugared lemons!" Father observed. "Mmmm . . . *sugared lemons!*" He shut his eyes and sighed. "So tart and yet . . . *so sweet!* It's like . . . love in contradiction!"

"Precisely"—our lady-mother nodded—"if he were entirely sweet, it would be much too decadent, too soft, and perhaps even effete, but that tartness beneath the sugar denotes strength and thus masculinity, though if one is not careful it can elude the eye. You don't know how fortunate you are, Jane; you are such a stubborn, ungrateful girl you can't see it. You know, Jane, I actually *envy* you! Look at him. He is a sugarplum for the eye, like a gilded marzipan subtlety come to life!"

"Yes, indeed he is! Mmmm . . . *marzipan . . . gilded marzipan!*" Father sighed rapturously, shutting his eyes again as his tongue savored the words as if the syllables themselves were sweets. "Guildford is just like *gilded* marzipan! So rich, so decadently delicious, as divine as a gift of sweetmeats straight from Our Lord's confectionary kitchen in Heaven served on golden plates by angels!"

Jane rolled her eyes and wondered sotto voce, "Where in the Bible does it say that the Lord has a confectionary kitchen in Heaven?"

"Ah well!" our lady-mother sighed. "One cannot have everything, and often carnality has to ride outside up beside the driver instead of inside the coach where the quality sits. Such are the cruel vagaries of life! But, no matter, I shall be this fine young man's mother-in-law, and he shall reap the *full* benefit of my advice; that is the important thing! He will go far; I shall make it my business to see to it."

"But I don't want to marry a sugared lemon or a piece of gilded marzipan either," Jane said softly.

I crept a little closer and reached up and squeezed her hand, and she gave me a grateful but oh so sad little smile.

"Mmmm . . . *sugared lemons!*" Father sighed again as a ribbon of drool trickled down his chin.

Our lady-mother rolled her eyes and with her own handkerchief wiped it away. "Enough of that, Hal, we shall plan the menu for the wedding banquet *later!* Naturally it shall include *both* sugared lemons *and* gilded marzipan as a tribute to our beautiful new son-in-law."

"Yes, dear." Father nodded and agreed as he continued to stare, rapt and transfixed, at the portrait of Guildford Dudley. "My God, I never saw anything so beautiful in my life!" I heard him murmur after our lady-mother had gone and only my sisters and I remained, but they were too caught up in their own thoughts to take note of Father's curious behavior, and besides we were all so accustomed to hearing him sigh rapturously over sweets . . . I tried to tell myself it was nothing, and that it was lewd to link it with Guildford's portrait, and yet . . . I couldn't quite convince myself.

After that the bustle never seemed to cease. From the break of dawn until we laid our weary heads down upon our pillows at night we were all caught up in a feverish mad maelstrom of wedding plans that had grown from an elegant double to an ostentatious triple event with the Greys and the Dudleys, though they would ostensibly be united by marriage, each vying to outshine the other. The Earl of Northumberland, Father informed us, also had a daughter named Catherine, aged twelve like our own Kate, but "a shy, sallow lass, nowhere near as pretty," he added, giving Kate's cheek a pat and popping a candied violet in her mouth. He then went on to explain that since the wedding was to be held at Durham House, the Dudleys' opulent London residence, Northumberland had decided to make it a triple affair and join their Catherine in wedlock with the young Lord Hastings.

Kate immediately began to fret, weeping and worrying that the Dudley girl's gown would be grander than her own. But Father was quick to assure her that even if it cost him the last coin in his coffers it would not be so. And with a kiss and another candy he sent her off to await the dressmaker's arrival, her head full of all the dreams that money *can* make come true, spinning rich, extravagant fantasies of cloth-of-gold, swirling, fantastically patterned cream and gold brocade, pearls and lace, and emeralds green as envy. That was our Kate; the storms never lasted long.

While Jane did her best to ignore it all, immersing herself even deeper in her studies, Kate drove our poor tutor, Master Aylmer, to frustration, ignoring the assignments he set her and instead filling page after page of her copybook with graceful, flourishing renditions of the name that would soon be hers—*Katherine, Lady Herbert,* and someday, upon her father-in-law's demise, *Katherine, Countess of Pembroke;* she even wrote it in the French style, *Katherine, Comtesse de Pembroke,* though as far as I knew she had no plans to cross the Channel and neither did Lord Herbert.

When Master Aylmer complained to Father, Kate pouted and said that since she was soon to be a married woman she didn't see why she still had need of a tutor; Master Aylmer really wasn't teaching her anything useful at all that pertained to court etiquette, housewifery, or, she added just to make him blush, amorous disport and what her husband would expect of her behind the bed-curtains, nor had he offered any sage advice pertaining to midwifery and child-rearing either. "And not all the Latin verbs in the world will save me when I am in the agonizing throes of childbirth."

At these words, Father smiled indulgently, patted Kate's bright curls, and said at least it was good practice of her penmanship, and turned to pacify Master Aylmer. "Be a good fellow and leave things be," he cajoled, offering him a sweet from his ever present comfit box, which he had taken the precaution of stocking with sugared and honeyed nuts beforehand knowing that they were Master Aylmer's favorite. "And I doubt very much that the future Lady Herbert will have much need for Greek or Latin," he added, "just a pretty bit of French and perhaps a dollop of Italian and a smattering of Spanish for songs and poetry and such." Whereupon he settled down beside Kate with his comfit box open between them on the table to admire the signatures that filled her copybook while I stood apart, watching my two sisters, swallowing down my tears, and keeping my fears to myself.

I could do nothing for Jane; she did not want my help, and I could do nothing without her willingness and cooperation, but she would not even meet me halfway or reach out a hand toward common sense. She would treat Guildford Dudley like an enemy until the day either she or he died, whichever came first, and by that time that is exactly what he would be—her enemy, when he might have been a fond, or even loving, husband with a little kindness and encouragement from Jane.

And Kate . . . Kate was *so* happy! And, truly, I didn't want to spoil it. But I was so afraid for her. She had already persuaded herself that she was in love with the bridegroom she had yet to meet, a man whose face she had beheld only in a miniature portrait—and who knew how accurate that likeness was? It has been commonplace since the art of portraiture began for the painters to flatter their patrons. Though she had never heard his voice, she could already hear him whispering sweet nothings in her ear and reciting poems about her beauty and comparing their love to an immortal flame. Every night, until she drifted off to sleep, Kate would lie abed whispering the names that filled her copybook over and over again like pearls on a rosary—*Katherine, Lady Herbert; Lady Katherine Herbert; Katherine, Countess of Pembroke; Katherine, Comtesse de Pembroke*—savoring them on her tongue as she dreamed of her husband's ardent kisses and bold caresses. She spoke with such confidence, such utter certainty, that it terrified me. What if Dame Fortune overheard and just to be cruel or contrary dealt my sister a different hand altogether? What if Lord Herbert, who was after all only fourteen, was *nothing* like Lancelot in his shining silver armor and white-feathered helm, riding hard and fast astride a white horse to sweep his ladylove up into his arms and carry her away to Joyous Garde to live in love forevermore? How could he be? Surely that was too much to expect of him. But it would break Kate's heart if he was anything but her dream of love come true. He *had* to be a hero right out of a storybook! He just *had* to be, for Kate's sake!

Yet every time I thought of the timidly smiling, slight-shouldered, pale-faced boy whose picture I had stolen a glance at by candlelight as Kate lay sleeping, my heart sank like a stone, and fear and worry gnawed unrelentingly at my stomach. Privately, I was convinced that my sister was in love with love, not with Lord Herbert, but I was only eight years old and didn't have the heart or the nerve to say so. I knew my sister well enough to know that she would deny it and answer me with peppery verve and heated words and demand what did I know of love and did I think my knowledge superior to hers. No, it was better, for both our sakes, that I keep silent and not invite a quarrel to come between us in the ever dwindling days that were left for us three sisters to spend together.

How envious she was when Guildford Dudley came to call on Jane. *Why has Lord Herbert not done the same?* she wept and stormed. But there was no time for tears then; Jane must be made ready to receive her betrothed. Our lady-mother and Kate made quite a fuss, dressing Jane in a gold trimmed and tasseled carnelian velvet gown, ignoring her heated protests, as they tugged it over her head and laced her in tight and fought to free her struggling hands from the voluminous over-sleeves that almost dragged on the floor, and the long-suffering Mrs. Ellen knelt to roll a pair of gold-embroidered orange stockings up Jane's limbs and thrust her unwilling feet into a pair of golden slippers with rosettes and rubies on the toes. They thrust rings onto her fingers, heedless of the stones' colors, as long as they were large and valuable, and hung gold and jeweled chains about her neck, and slapped down the pale, slender hands with their smattering of freckles when they rose in vain to try to protect her tightly pinned and plaited hair from the intrusive fingers that would determinedly pluck out the pins and brush it out into a mass of shining ruddy chestnut ripples that fell down to her waist.

As soon as our lady-mother had fastened the gold-flowered and fringed orange hood onto her head and smoothed the gold-veined white gossamer veil bordered with golden tassels down her back and Kate had pinned an amethyst brooch the size of a clenched fist—the biggest in our lady-mother's jewel coffer—onto her breast, Jane bunched up her skirts and bolted from the room to take shelter in the library. Mrs. Ellen was told to follow to provide discreet chaperonage to the couple and to make sure that Jane did not tear the tassels from her gown or the golden roses from her hood in protest of such adornment, and I tagged along, quietly following the trail of her crow-black skirt. When he arrived, Kate told me after, our parents explained to Guildford that Jane was "a modest and shy young woman, of a most retiring nature," and sent him into the library to meet her "in quietude without a crowd to unnerve her."

A little while later, Guildford strode in, dressed in gooseberry green velvet the exact same shade as his eyes, with puffs of silver-white tinsel cloth showing through his fashionably slashed sleeves. In his arms he carried a big, silky white cat, with a green silk ribbon tied round its neck in a most becoming bow with a gold-framed green stone pinned at its center. *Surely not an emerald on the cat,* I thought, shaking my head incredulously. He paused halfway across the room from Jane and doffed his peacock feathered cap and bowed low and grandly, pausing expectantly and looking around after as though he expected a round of applause from an invisible audience, but there was not a sound except the cat purring in his arms.

Then he came and stood before Jane, staring down at her, studying her as though she were a specimen in a glass cabinet, tapping his chin, and tilting his head from left to right. Through it all, Jane never looked up from her book or in any way acknowledged him, and I trembled for her knowing full well that our lady-mother would be certain to punish such rudeness. Nervously, I plucked at Mrs. Ellen's sleeve, and when she leaned down I whispered, "Please don't tell Mother; she will beat Jane." At last, Guildford took a step forward and plucked the musty, old, gray black bound copy of Virgil's *Aeneid* from Jane's hands and, with a fastidious grimace, flung it with a resounding thud into the room's darkest corner. Then he strode over to one of the bookcases that lined the walls, remarking as he did so that "books are so decorative," and selected a gilt-embellished volume bound in beautifully textured orange-red leather. "If you really *must* read then read this one instead; it matches your dress better," he said as he presented it to Jane.

He sat down beside her and introduced her to his cat, whose name he said was Fluff, and offered to let Jane pet him if her hands were clean as Fluff had just had a chamomile and lemon bath. "His eyes are the *exact* color of the finest jade," Guildford said proudly, pointing to the gem dangling from Fluff's ribbon.

Guildford made a valiant effort to engage my sister in conversation, starting with music, "my one *true* passion," and then moving on to food; like our father, Guildford loved sweets "like the Devil does stealing souls," but took great care not to overindulge and spoil his figure. He asked her if she had any pets, and when Jane didn't deign to answer, told her about his own. Besides Fluff, he had a white parrot with a great yellow crest atop its head that could catch the grapes and berries he tossed to it in its beak or claws.

After that he tried fashion, describing in detail the magnificent new wardrobe his tailor was making for him to start married life in. Next he tried beauty treatments, after snatching off the rather ostentatious, overdecorated hood and exclaiming, "Why do you attempt to hide such beauty?" as he rippled his fingers through the long fire-kissed brown waves. He went on to suggest several remedies to vanquish Jane's freckles and various washes for her hair—lemons and chamomile to lighten it, walnut juice to darken it, or henna to redden it and emphasize her Tudor heritage, any of which, he said, would be "a novel change," "striking," and "dramatic." He even brought up books and poetry, though he clearly fancied the more frivolous and flowery sort that Jane abhorred and turned her scholarly little nose up at. He even offered to let her kiss him. "We're to be married, so we might as well make the best of it and be friendly," he said, nearly knocking me off my chair as I had not expected such a wise and astute observation to come out of Guildford Dudley's pretty pink mouth.

But Jane only sat there sullenly staring at the pages of the book, though it was one of Father's cookery books containing a number of sweet recipes collected from various parts of the world that he was always begging our cook to try, and thus one my scholarly sister was ill-inclined to read.

In the end, Guildford had to admit defeat, declaring, "I've attended livelier funerals!" as he stormed out, slamming the door behind him hard enough to cause a bust of Caesar to fall from atop the shelf containing military tomes and chip his white marble nose upon the floor.

As soon as he was gone, I ran over to Jane and snatched the book from her to get her attention. "Why did you not talk to him?" I demanded. "He was trying to be friendly!"

"He's a fool!" Jane snorted contemptuously. "A vain, pompous, empty-headed, frivolous fool and I hate him and can't stand to have him near me!" She reached again for the book, but I threw it across the room rather than let her have it to hide behind.

"He's going to be your husband whether you like it or not," I reminded her, "so you might as well make the best of it and try to be friends; you'd do well to make amends with him before it is too late and the insult is beyond repair. Write him a letter, Jane, tell him nervousness and fear got the better of you and made you behave badly and you are sorry for it, tell him that you are accustomed to a quiet life of study, contemplation, and prayer, and fear the loss of all that is familiar and dear to you upon marriage and the responsibilities it will require you to assume. Tell him—"

"I don't need you to dictate my letters to me, Mary! And *no,* I will *not* write to him! I'd sooner strike off my own hand! What will be will be! I am a martyr to the fate our parents have decreed for me and soon the whole world shall know it! Being married to this popinjay is another trial, another punishment I must endure and overcome as best I can, God willing! And I didn't realize you were so smitten with him. Clearly his pretty face has charmed you; you're just like a magpie diving for a bit of shiny glass it has mistaken for a diamond hidden in the grass!" she added spitefully, angrily swiping the futile tears from her eyes as she ran past me.

"It doesn't have to be that way! You don't have to be a martyr to anyone or anything!" I shouted after her. "And I am not in the least bit enamored with Guildford Dudley, but even a blind man could see that he is trying to make the best of things, unlike you! It is you I am thinking of, Jane. You're my sister, and I love you well enough to tell you that if you scorn Love and turn your back on it, Love may turn its back and scorn you."

But it did no good; already I was speaking to an empty room. Jane had fled the library as though it were aflame. How I wished I could make her understand! Though many would laugh and wonder how someone like me could know so much about love, I knew better than most that it was the only prize truly worth winning. I wanted both my sisters to have that, even if I could not. Even though it would mean moments of the utmost sadness, a secret, yearning envy I harbored deep inside my soul that I could never reveal, I wanted to have that experience in the only way I could, vicariously, through my sisters.

With a heavy sigh and a shake of her weary head, Mrs. Ellen stood and followed her angry charge out. "For all her fancy, high-praised book learning, the poor chit hasn't a whit of sense when it comes to the *real* world," she grumbled as she went, and I had to agree with her.

Though my heart secretly wept, as my eyes did every night into my pillow, at the thought of relinquishing my sisters to husbands and new homes, nothing could diminish my delight during the hours we spent with the silk merchants and seamstresses. As the banners of silk unfurled before my eyes, I dreamed I was in heaven and that I could hear fanfares of trumpets and choirs of angels singing amongst the bright, billowing lengths laid out before us.

"Not another dreary dress the color of a mud puddle!" Kate cried, snatching a bolt of dung brown from out of Jane's hands.

"Ugh! Take it away! And not that one either. It's the color of wet moss and can't make up its mind whether it wants to be green or gray, but either way it's *hideous!* No, Jane, no!" She snatched and kicked away every drab shade our sister touched or even glanced at. "You should have pretty gowns in shades of gold, russet, and red, tawny, amber, yellow, and orange, colors that bring your hair to life and make the red in it glow like embers beneath the brown, colors that seem to dance and wave and cry out like a flirty maid, 'Look at me, look at me!' " As she spoke, Kate began to snatch up satins, silks, damasks, velvets, brocades, taffetas, and tinsels of the shades she had just named and wrap and wind and drape them all around Jane until she looked like an overgrown infant swaddled in a rainbow of autumn colors.

"Green and blue, in shades deep or delicate, are also good for Jane," I added, for I knew my sister deemed these brighter hues that Kate favored wanton and garish. I took up a length of lush green velvet and held it up, high as I could, against Jane. And after Kate had laughingly helped the seamstresses unwrap Jane from her rainbow cocoon, and she stood again, just like Kate, in her shift, I unwound a bolt of shimmering pale green silk sewn in silver with a pattern resembling fish scales and held it up against Jane's waist. "Wear this, Jane, and you will look like a mermaid who has dragged herself from the sea to marry the prince who has stolen her heart."

"What, damp and bedraggled?" Jane asked sullenly.

"Nay"—our lady-mother strode into the room and snatched the beautiful silk away from me—"with her sour countenance, since we cannot trust her to smile upon her wedding day, it will make her appear jaundiced. This will look better on Kate." She draped it around Kate's bare shoulders and brushed her lips against her cheek.

Her rebellious gaze aimed straight at our lady-mother, Jane pointed to a bolt of blue velvet so dark that only the brightest light would prove that it wasn't black. "That!" she said adamantly. "I will wear that. Make the collar high and the sleeves long and close about the wrists, with frills of white Holland cloth, edged in silver if you must, at the collar and cuffs, and a hood of the same velvet, but *no other adornments.*" She stressed each word as her eyes bored into the dressmaker's. "I shall wear my prayer book suspended from a silver chain about my waist; the word of God is the only adornment I want or need."

"For all your scholarly accomplishments, daughter, you really are a simpleton," our lady-mother declared, kicking the bolt of blue black velvet out the door to land where it would. "You cannot go to your own wedding looking like a nun at a ball! You must put aside your plain garb, and from now on dress to suit your station; you must be like a jewel in the crown of your husband and family. I will not allow you to embarrass and demean Guildford by appearing at his side dressed like a lowly little governess! I have given you a beautiful husband, and you must at all times endeavor to be worthy of him. You must adorn and adore him! Such is a wife's duty! Every time your father and I go out, everyone knows, whether they know my name or not, that they are looking at a person of importance; my jewels and my gowns, my regal bearing, and the proud way I carry myself, with my head high and my back straight, tells them so!"

"No!" Jane stamped her foot. "I shall not play the gaudy peacock! I am a godly and virtuous Protestant maid and mean to remain so, and plain dress is most pleasing to the eyes of the Lord! Even Princess Elizabeth has repented her wanton ways. Just as the harlot Mary Magdalene reformed and followed in the footsteps of Our Lord Jesus Christ, she has forsaken her jewels and put aside her finery, and clothes herself in pure white or plain black and *always* has an English prayer book about her person!"

"You little fool!" our lady-mother sneered. "And more the fool those who think you so brilliantly clever! At book learning, yes, but at life, the things that *really* matter, no! Princess Elizabeth has survived a scandal. She knows her good name has been tarnished and will do *anything* necessary to scrub it clean and make it shine again, even if it means putting aside her pretty clothes and giving up dancing and gambling, to curry favor with that insufferable little prig, King Edward, who like you takes these things to the utmost and most ridiculous extremes! But you mark my word, if the day ever comes when Elizabeth is crowned queen, she shall be as splendid as a peacock within the hour and never again shall a plain dress cover her back! And, I remind you, Jane, your dear Dowager Queen Catherine was a devout Protestant and she favored gold-

embroidered red satin—is that not the Magdalene's color? I'm not as well educated as you are! And her sister and their circle of learned ladies too! I knew many of them from girlhood, and I *never* saw a one of them without jewels and gilt embroidery; they were not the sackcloth and ashes sort, I assure you, not even for the sake of their souls!"

Jane hung her head and made no answer to that. Indeed, what could she say? It was true. But I could feel the anger seething inside her. I often thought that denying herself fine clothes was just another step along Jane's path to martyrdom, to make the world marvel at so beautiful a girl denying herself pretty things and praise her all the more for being spiritually above all things worldly and vain. Or perhaps Jane thought if she let her beauty shine people would take her scholarly accomplishments less seriously as beauty doth often blind the beholder?

"Enough of this!" Our lady-mother threw up her hands. "You shall do as I say, daughter, else you go to your marriage bed with your back flayed open and stain the sheets with your willful, disobedient blood as well as your maidenhead!"

Then our lady-mother took charge, and with her riding crop pointing the way, ushered the rainbow of rich materials out the door, to await preparations for Jane's and Kate's trousseaux, since they were proving too distracting, leaving behind only those in shades of white, cream, gold, and silver. They might have all the color they wished in their trousseaux, she said when Kate's eyes pooled with tears and her lips began to tremble, but the wedding gowns must be settled *first* as they were the most splendid and important gowns they would probably ever wear in their lives. In conference with the Duke of Northumberland, our lady-mother had decided that these hues of pallor and shimmer were the colors the three bridal couples would wear.

When I timidly tugged at her skirt and asked, "What about me?" she said my own wedding gown must wait; time was pressing, and I would not be married for a few years yet and fashions change, so it would be rather foolish to have it made now. "Besides," she added, "your own nuptials shall be a quiet, private affair, so there is no need for a gown as splendid as those your sisters shall wear."

At her words, my face fell, and the sight of my disappointment moved our lady-mother to one of her rare acts of kindness.

"The time is not ripe, my petite gargoyle, and neither are you, for wedlock, so leave the matter to rest for now. I promise that when the time comes you shall have a beautiful gown. And you shall have a fine new gown of fabric of your own choosing to wear to this wedding, though, of course, you shall not mingle with the other guests; they will be distracted and drunken and likely to mock and trample you. You must hold to your dignity, Mary, never let go, and remember that you are a Grey, and the cousin and niece of royalty. Your grandmother—my mother—was Queen of France, and there is Tudor blood flowing in your veins! Now, turn your eyes upon these woven and embroidered patterns"—she indicated the messy but luxurious heaps of partly unwound bolts of fabric piled haphazardly in the center of the room—"and help me choose the materials for your sisters' under-sleeves and kirtles."

I knelt down and let my eyes feast upon the fine array of figures woven with shimmering gold, silver, and pearly threads into the damasks and brocades and embroidered upon the silks, satins, taffetas, and velvets, caressing and feeling my way through the wonderful maze of arabesques, lattices, lovers' knots, hearts, braids, trellises, and vines, birds, butterflies, and bees, flowers, budding or in full bloom, fruit, cherubs, grandiose geometric intricacies as ambitious as they were beautiful, both marvelous and bewildering to the eye, swirls, loops, lozenges, crescents, mazes, stars, and scrolls until my eye fastened upon a lustrous creamy satin embroidered profusely with an intricate and opulent design of golden pomegranates nestled like babies in a womb amongst the crowded array of exquisitely embroidered blossoms, buds, and leaves, some of them whole and others sliced open to reveal their seeds, which were represented by pearls.

"This one!" I breathed, holding it up for our lady-mother to see. "It is *perfect* for Kate! It is the pomegranate, which symbolizes fertility. The late King Henry's first wife, the Spanish one, Catherine of Aragon, made it popular when she chose it as her personal emblem. I think it a fine, and mayhap even a lucky, choice for a young bride, especially one who is eager to become a mother," I added

with a knowing smile directed at Kate. With an exclamation of pleasure, she dropped the cloth-of-gold with which she had been draping herself and ran to embrace and smother me with kisses.

"A *perfect* choice," our lady-mother purred. "You have a fine eye for such things, Mary, though I think"—she turned to the dressmaker—"that we should put more pearls and some diamonds on it."

"Yes, m'lady"—the dressmaker bobbed an obedient curtsy—"it shall be *exactly* as you wish!"

"I know it will." Our lady-mother nodded, as though it had never even occurred to her to doubt it, and turned back to Kate. "For your gown, my darling, you shall have cloth-of-gold just as you have always dreamed of wearing on your wedding day, trimmed with diamonds and pearls of course—it is just foolish superstition that a bride should forsake them on her wedding day as they invite tears and sorrow—and the sleeves shall be furred in purest white, and you shall have a crown of gilded rosemary with pearl and jeweled flowers for your hair. And you may wear my emeralds—the *big* ones so green that grass would envy them," she added, laughing as Kate hurled herself into her arms, crying out her thanks. "I remember when you used to sneak into my room, you dear, naughty mite." She chuckled fondly, reaching down to caress Kate's curls. "You would creep in while I was out hunting and take out my gold gown, spilling crushed lavender all over the floor. Even though it was far too big for you, and you always stumbled and tripped and bruised your chin upon the floor, wear it you would, and parade solemnly up and down the Long Gallery, as though you were trying to wade through a sea of gold and in dire peril of drowning, so engulfed and overwhelmed were you by that great gold gown, pretending you were a bride upon your wedding day and that your father's suit of armor was your bridegroom waiting at the altar for you. Now, my beautiful little girl has grown up, and she will wear a wedding gown of gold and there shall be a handsome young man who is truly worthy of her waiting at the altar to make her his wife."

"My lady-mother, I am *so* happy!" Kate cried.

"As you deserve to be." Our lady-mother smiled. "Beauty such as yours should never know what sorrow means."

Jane gave a loud, derisive snort, and our lady-mother whipped around to impale her with a daggerlike stare. "Jane," she said severely, "you shall wear silver."

At those words, my heart sank. Our lady-mother was playing favorites again, and sending a silent message, giving Kate the full glory of gold and making Jane appear second best, and the lesser valued, in silver. Kate would be dazzling and radiant in gold, with her sunny, vivacious smile and laughing, loving jewel-bright eyes, and Jane standing glum and serious, sulky and silent, in silver beside her, with her downcast eyes and frowning mouth, would make a poor showing in comparison. With the gilded idol of Guildford Dudley as a bridegroom the effect would be even worse. They would all outshine Jane; even if they were naked, their smiles alone would do it! It wasn't fair!

Even worse, Jane didn't care, even though she should; she who would rather wear plain black, dung brown, or dull gray would *never* fight for gold. But Jane *needed* gold, she deserved it, just as much as Kate did! Gold would bring out the red and gold embers hiding in her brown hair, like coals glowing beneath wood and ashes, and make the green, blue, and hazel sparkle like jewels against dust and eclipse the harsh gray of her eyes. I had always associated gold with warmth, like sunshine, and silver with cold and ice, and even though Jane's personality was in truth better suited to chilly silver, and I had long ago given up my childish hope that if Jane wore gold these golden qualities would be magically and miraculously absorbed through her skin and she would smile and laugh and be merry just like Kate, I still longed to see her arrayed in gold on her wedding day. I wanted Jane herself to see when she stood before her looking glass that there was no sin in beauty, only in the vain attitude and condescending pride that often accompanied it, and that she could have her precious books and be beautiful too.

I swallowed down my tears and fears and steeled to do battle on Jane's behalf since she would never fight for a cloth-of-gold gown. Timidly, I gave a tug to the skirt of our lady-mother's crimson velvet riding habit.

"Please, my lady-mother, let Jane wear gold too. It is such a special day, and I would like to see both my sisters gowned in the full glory of gold on their wedding day. Let the Dudley girl wear silver if she will, but *please* garb *both* the Grey sisters, through your illustrious person kin to royalty, in gold."

"Your point is well taken, Mary; appearances are everything, and it is imperative that we present an image of importance, solidarity, and regal grandeur. Very well then, let it be gold for Jane as well as Katherine. And Jane can wear the ruby necklace Princess Mary so thoughtfully sent her for her birthday; that bloodred shall look *splendid* against the pallor of her skin and help coax out the red in her hair, and we shall wash it with my own mother's recipe for a saffron rinse with just a hint of henna the night before the wedding so the effect will be even more striking. Now, what pattern would you suggest for Jane's kirtle and sleeves? Thorns and acanthus leaves or thistles perhaps, to suit her unpleasantly sharp and prickly personality?"

"To symbolize pain, punishment, suffering, and humiliation, my lady-mother?" Jane retorted, her voice hard and her eyes cold as gray ice.

I felt the anger rising inside our lady-mother and the imminent rain of blows Jane was courting as I watched her hand curl tighter around the jeweled handle of her riding crop. Quickly, despite the jerking pain that shot up my spine, I ran and snatched up a bolt of ivory satin blooming all over with embroidered yellow gillyflowers amidst glorious swirls of green and gold foliage.

"This please, my lady-mother"—I held it up for her to see—"gillyflowers for marital devotion and fidelity. Since Guildford Dudley seems to favor this particular flower, and in yellow, he is *certain* to appreciate the gesture and take it as a compliment—a loving tribute from his bride, who has chosen to array herself in his special flower on their wedding day. It will bode well for the marriage, I think." Then, glancing at Jane's scowling countenance, I hastily amended, "I hope."

"A pretty choice as well as a diplomatic one." Our lady-mother smiled and reached down to give my head a pat. "So be it! Oh, Mary, my poor little gargoyle, had you not been born grotesque, squat, and twisted, you would have been such a credit to me! Though you lack Kate's beauty and Jane's scholarly brilliance, you have something even more important—tact and common sense; you know how to be pleasing and practical. I could have made so much of you! What a most *deplorable* waste!"

"What a waste indeed," I said softly, for in spite of our lady-mother's words, none regretted more than I all the chances that were lost to me because of my stunted and deformed body. The love I would never have, the babies I would never bear, a spine and limbs that didn't ache until old age beckoned, people who would smile and warmly embrace me rather than shrink away fearfully and avert their gaze, the good times I could never take part in, the bright parti-color gowns I could never wear without being mistaken for a fool in motley, to be able to dance without provoking laughter, and to be able to walk the London streets free from the fear of being snatched and sold into a troupe of performing dwarves or to a fair in need of a new attraction.

I was a small, shy creature meant to hide in the shadows, to live on the edge of the world, peeping out at it, not in the bright, frenetic center of it, never a participant and reveler, only an observer. But now was not the time to dwell on my misfortunes. My sisters needed me, so I forced myself to smile and, knowing that Jane detested Cousin Mary's "bloody necklace," I set about cajoling our lady-mother to send to the goldsmith and have a necklace of golden gillyflowers with emerald leaves crafted for Jane instead. "Perhaps a wreath of gilded rosemary with yellow gillyflowers for Jane's hair? It will look well beside Kate's."

But one cannot always win. Our lady-mother agreed that *both* the gillyflower necklace and wreath were splendid ideas, but she decided to order the new necklace to be made long, so that Jane might also wear the shorter ruby necklace with it. "After all, we do not want to offend Cousin Mary, and even though she is not invited, we want her to feel that she is in our thoughts and a part of this special day, don't we?"

"No," Jane pouted her lips and said in a sulky voice our lady-mother pretended not to hear.

"In this world anything can happen," our lady-mother continued, "and it is important never to offend anyone lest they someday be in a position to make you regret it."

* * *

Every day we were busy with the dressmaker, seamstresses, merchants from London displaying their fine fabrics and trinkets, the glovers, cobblers, gold and silver smiths, and stay-makers. Our parents had most generously decided that Kate and Jane would each have a dozen new dresses, with all the elegant accoutrements a lady required and desired—fans, headdresses, stockings, shifts, petticoats, ribbon garters, slippers, veils, pomander balls of precious jewels and metals, and the like—so there was much to be done and little time to do it in as every day brought us nearer to the wedding.

For Kate there were gowns the color of raspberries, cherries, and crushed strawberries, and the yellow of sunshine, egg yolks, and lemons—yellow was known as "the color of joy," and Kate could not get enough of it; she thought it a fortuitous omen for her marriage if her trousseau were rich in this sunny shade—honey gold, cinnamon, apricot, sage green, robin's egg blue, and the most delicate rose, like gray ashes that had drifted down over a pink rose without stifling or scorching its beauty.

For Jane, who tried in vain to push away the gaudy trimmings and vibrant colors and reach for the dreary spectrum of grays, browns, and blacks instead, I, with our lady-mother's approval, chose shades of garnet, damson plum, red wine, rich, regal violet, moss green, lion's mane tawny, midnight blue, deep forest green, vivid yellow, cinnamon, and the new fashionable color called "ruddy embers," and an extravagant gold-worked brocade of the delicate peachy pink flesh color known as "incarnadine."

For each there was also an array of exquisitely embroidered and patterned kirtles and under-sleeves of contrasting colors to match and vary with their new gowns.

Kate's favorite was a set of white silk worked with red roses in glorious full bloom and nascent buds, their thorny stems and leaves done in a style reminiscent of the Spanish blackwork embroidery that Catherine of Aragon had introduced to England and made so popular that for many a year afterward every woman had it bordering her shift and every man upon the collar and cuffs of his white lawn shirt. But Jane deplored the extravagance and complained about the great waste of silver and gold that had been used to create the gilt threads that adorned many of their new garments and said it would have been better spent to feed and clothe the poor and provide them with English prayer books.

Lastly, as a special surprise for each, gowns of cloth-of-gold and silver tinsel cloth with low square necklines and pointed stomachers edged in diamonds, and long, full, gracefully flowing sleeves that nearly brushed the floor as they belled over the full, puffed, and padded under-sleeves my sisters would wear with them. Then Father mentioned hunting and riding, and our lady-mother flew into a panic realizing she had neglected to instruct the tailor to furnish them with riding habits, so there were hurried selections of ginger velvet for Jane and Brassel red, a hue that was like a lively, lusty dance between brown and red, for Kate, and tall boots and soft gloves of brown and red Spanish leather. Then Mrs. Ellen burst in with a frantic cry of "nightgowns!" and there was a panicked flurry to equip them with embroidered lawn night shifts and caps, all calculated to delight a husband's amorous eye, soft velvet slippers, and robes of sumptuous fur-bordered velvets, flowered damasks, and quilted satins.

Through all the fittings Mrs. Leslie, our chief dressmaker, tried to coax a smile out of Jane, deeming it unnatural to see a bride "so downcast, melancholy, and brooding."

"Are you nervous, sweetheart?" she asked as Jane stood on a stool before her. " 'Tis only natural that you should be; I know, for I've dressed many a bride, but you'll see, once you're wedded and bedded, 'twill all turn out just fine, it will."

"No, it won't." Jane glowered. "I don't want to marry Guildford Dudley. I don't want to marry *anyone* at all!"

"But every maid wants to be married!" Mrs. Leslie laughed.

"*I* don't!" Jane insisted with mutinous conviction.

"Give it time, love," Mrs. Leslie smilingly advised. "You will. 'Tis unnatural for a maid not to want a man; women are meant to marry, to cleave to a husband and bear his babes. Your husband—and a handsome lad he is too!—will change your mind soon enough, I trow, and when you hold your firstborn in your arms and think back to this day, you'll laugh at the silly chit of a girl you used to be who thought she didn't want a husband. Why, this time next year you'll be looking at the man lying in bed next to you and wondering what you ever did without him, and how the sun would go right out of your life if he left you."

"No, I won't! I won't, I won't, I won't!" Jane stamped her foot and screamed, startling Mrs. Leslie so badly that she stabbed a needle into her thumb. Blood came spurting out, and it was only her quick thinking and a sudden swerve of her arm and an apprentice seamstress racing to staunch the blood with her apron that prevented the beautiful gold, yellow, and ivory gown from being stained.

After that, Mrs. Leslie sewed in silence and made no further attempts to cheer and enliven Jane, whom she eyed henceforth as warily as though she were outfitting a madwoman.

While his womenfolk fretted about fashion, Father was in his own heaven, planning the banquet, consulting with cooks and sampling the wares of various pastry chefs, comparing marzipans and fantasies of spun sugar, sucking on sweetmeats until our lady-mother declared that it would be a miracle if he had a tooth left in his head that was not black and rotted by the time the wedding was over. But Father merely smiled and went on dreaming of "a roast piggy with an apple in his mouth, mayhap even a gilded apple for my beautiful Katey," who of all his daughters was surest to appreciate the gesture, and a pair of roasted boar heads, one with the tusks gilded silver, the other golden, and a roast peacock with its plumage displayed in full glory, and a swan for Kate, "nay, *two* swans for Katey," a loving pair with their long necks entwined in a sweet lovers' embrace, and a tall pink and gilt marzipan candy castle that seemed to float upon clouds of spun pink sugar with marzipan sculpted likenesses of Kate, her dress spangled with sugar crystals, and Lord Herbert beside her, the two of them standing, arm in arm, upon the balcony of "the house where love dwelled," gazing down beyond the clouds to where black and white swans glided in graceful pairs upon a blue sugar moat.

He drove himself to vexation debating whether the eels should be jellied or stewed or served in a red wine or a cream sauce until our lady-mother quite lost her temper and snatched up a raw eel and slapped him across the face with it. His indecision over the cheeses was so maddening—he could talk of nothing else for days on end—that our lady-mother, at her wit's end, finally gathered up an armful of the white and yellow rounds that had been sent for him to sample and ran to the front door and sent them all rolling down the long, winding chestnut-lined avenue leading from the house to the main road. Poor Father ran after them, waving his arms in the air and crying frantically, "My cheese, my beautiful cheese!" But our lady-mother merely slammed the door, rolled her eyes, made a motion with her hands as though she were washing them, and went out riding with our Master of the Horse, Adrian Stokes, "who will not bore me to death by talking of cheese."

Undaunted, Father let it be known in the fish markets that he would pay well for a magnificent sturgeon, but that it must be "a veritable giant of a fish," so that every day fishermen came to the house vying to present the largest and handsomest specimen. Father actually went out amongst these rough, dirty, salty-tongued men, with their coarse hands, fishy fragrance, and weathered, nut brown skin, claiming it was a task of too vital importance to be entrusted to the steward or even the cook. We leaned from the windows and watched as Father personally measured and examined each fish himself with as much care as though he were buying a pedigreed stallion. He also expressed an interest in acquiring a porpoise to grace the banquet table, to be carried in on an ice-covered silver tray festooned with seaweed, oysters, crayfish, and crabs. The salad, he insisted, must be the largest ever seen in England and contain everything under the sun that might possibly be put into a salad, with sugared flowers, and all the vegetables that could be carved into whimsical shapes and figures. Of course, he had not forgotten about Kate's cake. "How could I?" he laughed when Kate asked. "My darling, don't you know I must have spent half my life thinking about cake? Why, if I had a penny for every time cake has crossed my mind I would be the richest man in England, mayhap even the whole world! So how could I possibly forget the most important cake of all—my beautiful Katey's wedding cake!"

Sure enough, the very next afternoon, he proudly marched a mincing little black-bearded Frenchman upstairs as Kate stood upon a stool before Mrs. Leslie, clad in only her shift, which, being of the most delicate cobweb lawn, left very little to the imagination. Father gently put Mrs. Leslie aside so that the worldly and blasé Frenchman might measure Kate's height, to thus ensure that the giant cinnamon spice cake—to be stuffed full of apples, walnuts, and raisins, both golden and black, and covered in gilded marzipan, Father promised, thus proving he had not forgotten—would tower over the "pretty little bride and her bridegroom too!" Kate gave a squeal of delight and flung her arms around the Frenchman and kissed his cheek, then fell to giggling because his moustache tickled.

To silence the outraged cries of Mrs. Leslie and Mrs. Ellen, who were both volubly insisting that this was not at all proper for the cook, a man—and a *Frenchman* at that!—to come in while the girls were all but naked in their shifts, Father extended his trusty gilt and pink and blue enameled comfit box, confident that it could make everything all right. It was newly filled with sugarplums, sweetmeats, candied violets, sugared almonds, cinnamon lozenges, crystallized ginger, marzipan, glacéed apricots, sugared orange and lemon slices, and anise wafers. In but a few moments all was pleasant as could be and the pastry chef was promising Kate the tallest, grandest cake ever seen at any wedding and regaling us with descriptions of the latest French fashions as we all laughed like lifelong friends and passed the comfit box amongst us.

Only Jane sat apart, crammed into the corner of the window seat with her bare toes tucked up under her and an old rat-gray shawl with moth-eaten fringe wrapped modestly over her shift. Through it all she never once looked up from her Greek Testament or uttered a word, not even when Father called out to her to come get some candy before it was all gone.

When he heard a tale of a genuine mermaid being exhibited at a nearby fair, Father, knowing that we three girls had loved mermaids from childhood—even Jane, though she was loathe to admit it lest it make her appear childish and frivolous in the eyes of Europe's most esteemed scholars—decided to hire the attraction away from the fair and have it shown at the wedding for all to marvel at. According to the painted placard outside the tent, the mermaid was supposed to be quite beautiful with long flowing hair like liquid gold, a tail that shimmered like dew-drenched emeralds, and a comb and necklace of red coral that she prized as remembrances of her ocean home. Father was so taken by the idea, that he procured the mermaid's services sight unseen. He said later that he didn't want to spoil the surprise for himself; he wanted to see it for the first time along with us.

But when the mermaid arrived at Suffolk House, our sumptuous brick and Portland stone London home, where we had moved the week before the wedding, it was such a ghastly shriveled brown thing that none of us could bear the sight of it. Kate, who dearly loved all animals, began to weep and pummel the chest of its keeper. "Oh you evil, evil man! The poor mermaid!" she wailed. "What did you do to it?" Whilst Jane simply arched her brows and said, "Ask rather what he did to the monkey and the fish that he cut in half and sewed together to make it." Whereupon Kate, realizing that *two* of God's creatures had been killed to create this monstrosity, slapped his face and ran sobbing from the room.

Above the waist, the sea maiden was quite dark-skinned and had the appearance of a shaven monkey, obviously a female one as its breasts sagged like a pair of empty leather purses, and it was wearing such a hideous grimace, revealing a fearsome set of fangs, beneath the coarse blond wig glued crookedly to its scalp, that it had obviously perished in the utmost agony. The lower portion was a scaly, dried, brown fishtail ineptly slathered with green paint and a few daubs of silver for good measure, and the coral necklace and comb were clearly pebbles that had been dipped in red paint and strung together with wire.

With a cry of disgust, our lady-mother flung it out the window, and the man from the fair scurried off in a high panic to reclaim his prize exhibit lest he have to find a more strenuous form of employment.

Crestfallen, Father stood before the fire, sweating in his new marigold velvet doublet, tugging nervously at his beard, and balancing first on one foot and then the other. At last, he sighed. "I had such hopes! A *genuine* mermaid, just think of it!" Then he turned to our lady-mother and said, "I . . . I'm s-sorry, Frances. But it seemed like such a brilliant idea at the time."

Our lady-mother folded her arms across her chest and glared hard at him. "Please, Hal, for all our sakes, tell me that you haven't any more of these *brilliant* ideas in store for us—I don't think I, or the girls, can stand it if you do."

Father opened and closed his mouth several times, nervously bit his bottom lip, and shuffled in place like a child sorely in need of the privy, then he hurriedly made his excuses and left, murmuring something about a pair of real unicorns garlanded in flowers for the girls to ride to the altar upon. I could not help but smile, but our lady-mother merely shook her head and rolled her eyes, while Jane tucked her feet up in the window seat, bit loudly into an apple, and bent her head back over her book.

2

That Whitsunday morning of May 25, 1553, I was up with the sun, already dressed in my new silver-shot plum damask and blue gray satin gown trimmed with seed pearls and soft gray rabbit fur, standing at the window, nervously twisting my amethyst and sapphire beads, and watching the dawn break like a great purple and orange egg, spilling its sunny yellow yolk out to seep over the sleeping city. As my sisters lay deep in their last sleep as maidens, silent tears coursed down my cheeks. Everything was changing when all I wanted was for it to stay the same. In but a few short hours, they would be wives off on their way to new lives, leaving me behind. Kate would be going not very far as it turned out; she wouldn't even be leaving London, just sailing down the Thames to Baynard's Castle, the Earl of Pembroke's ancestral seat, a stark medieval stone fortress, named for the Norman who had built it. And Jane and Guildford would be bundled off to the pastoral solitude of Sheen, a former Carthusian monastery in Surrey, where it was hoped that, in this bucolic setting, love, or at least friendship, would flower between them. I knew better than to expect an invitation to visit either of them anytime soon, and our lady-mother had already warned me not to pester and fish for one; both couples would surely want privacy and time alone together, and I would only be in the way; instead of a beloved sister, I would be the houseguest one forces a smile and endures while secretly wishing they would leave.

An hour later, wrapped in cloaks over their new embroidered lawn shifts, with their hair still up in curling rags hidden beneath their hoods, my yawning, sleepy-eyed sisters and an exhausted Mrs. Ellen, who had passed the entire night sitting beside Jane's bed to keep her from removing the hated curl rags, boarded a barge amidst a flurry of maids, including Kate's Henny and my Hetty, several seamstresses, supervised by Mrs. Leslie, and trunks filled with their wedding finery.

At Durham House, while the maids and sewing women flocked around my sisters, layering on the petticoats, lacing them breathlessly tight into their stays, and strapping on the padded bum rolls to lend an added fullness to their hips and a bell-like sway to their skirts, their hands fluttering with busy haste over their bodies from head to toe, making sure each lace was tied and each layer fell smooth, nipping and tucking, pinning and primping, snipping away stray threads, and making a quick new stitch where necessary, I sat alone by the window, my head resting against the cool, smooth glass, gazing down at the river. With my short stature I knew I would only be in the way if I tried to help, trampled underfoot and the scapegoat for nervous and frayed tempers. Thus, I alone saw Lord Herbert arriving with his handsome father, the Earl of Pembroke. But I kept silent. I didn't tell Kate. I knew that if I did she would shake off the maids and come rushing to the window, and I would always remember the look on her face as all her heavenly dreams came crashing down to earth.

The slight, sickly, whey-faced boy down below who stumbled and almost fell into the Thames while disembarking from the barge was no romantic hero. Indeed, his dashing, dark-haired father, so tall and slender in his black and silver brocade and velvet, with striking sleek silver wings at his ebony temples, was more likely to make a maiden's heart flutter. Poor Lord Herbert, even his hair seemed colorless! His clothes hung loose upon him, and even his hat seemed too large for his head, and the ostrich feather pinned to the sapphire blue velvet just seemed silly, not the graceful curling pure white plume on Lancelot's sparkling silver helm. No, this was not a strong, virile hero who had stepped out of a story to overwhelm his bride with bold embraces and kisses that burned like fire. This was another ailing animal to be added to Kate's menagerie, to be petted and pitied and nursed back to health. I could more readily picture Kate holding a cup of warm milk to his lips, stroking his hair, tucking him into bed, and telling him a story, more like a mother than a wife. I vowed then and there that I would close my eyes when the fatal moment came, when Kate approached her bridegroom at the altar; I just could not bear to see the disappointment upon her face.

"Look at me!" At Jane's despairing wail, I turned to see her shoving her way out from amidst the crush of maids and sewing women. *"Look at me!"* She flapped her hands futilely against the luxuriant richness of her gown as she stood, frowning, before the big silver looking glass even as Mrs. Leslie stepped forward to adjust the fall of green and yellow silk ribbons that floated down Jane's back from her crown of gilded rosemary and yellow gillyflowers. "I look as brazen as a bawd!" Jane cried, miserable and on the threshold of tears, as her hands twitched against the rich stuff of her skirts, itching to rip them away. She reached up and began to tug at the ruby necklace encircling her throat, insisting it was too tight. But our lady-mother slapped her hands away, hissing at her to stop lest she break it. How Jane *hated* that necklace! It was the one she called "Cousin Mary's bloody necklace" because the thin gold chain fit so snugly that the dark red rubies, shaped like tiny teardrops, created the illusion that her throat had been cut and blood was seeping from it, and the looser second and third chains, lined with the same rubies, made it appear as though drops of blood were dripping down to stain her breast. Since our Tudor cousins had, most strangely I thought, not been invited to the wedding, something which no one would explain to me, our lady-mother had sat Jane at her desk last night and made her pen a letter saying that though her dear cousin could not be with her on this most joyous day she would be wearing the necklace she had given her and thus would feel her dear presence hovering around her—"like a pair of loving arms," our lady-mother dictated—and Jane wrote obediently.

Seeing Jane's distress, I tried to suggest that the gold and jeweled gillyflower necklace that had been specially made would be far better on its own, that the bloodred seemed so jarring, like blood splashed upon the shimmering golden pallor of Jane's gown, but I was overruled. Our lady-mother insisted that Jane must wear the rubies so as not to offend our royal cousin, though I personally thought she would be far more offended by not having been invited. And besides, our lady-mother continued, with Kate standing beside her, glowing with the green fire of emeralds, Jane must have gems of a contrasting color but similar richness to adorn her.

"Stop it, Jane!" Kate, radiant as the sun itself in her cloth-of-gold and cream gown with her unbound hair blazing and bouncing down her back like ringlets of red gold fire, stuck out her lips in a pout and stamped her foot down hard in its dainty golden slipper, rattling her grass green emeralds, diamonds, and pearls. "Why must you try to spoil it? You're not the only one who matters! This isn't just *your* day. In case you've forgotten, there are two other brides, and I happen to be one of them, and while I cannot speak for Catherine Dudley, *I* want today to be happy, a *grand* and *glorious* day that will live forever in my memory so that when I'm an old lady I can tell my grandchildren about it, and I would like to spare them a description of my sister's glum and sour countenance sulking and brooding throughout the ceremony and feast. You look beautiful, as every maid has a right to on her wedding day, and I am sure the learned Protestants of Europe will understand and forgive you for forsaking those glum, dowdy weeds you favor for just *one* day, since it *is* your wedding day, and I'm sure God will as well; He is said to be most forgiving."

"Well said, Katherine." Our lady-mother nodded as she moved to straighten the crown of gilded rosemary and jeweled flowers that Kate's impetuous tirade had knocked awry and gently turned her around to untangle and smooth the vibrant rainbow of silken ribbons trailing down her back. "A tad peppery perhaps, but you show promising signs of practicality and reason. If Lord Herbert is ever given a diplomatic post, I trust you shall prove yourself a great credit to him, and not merely as an ornament he will be proud to display."

I wormed my way between my two sisters, standing glaring at each other, and reached out to take their hands.

"*Please,* don't quarrel," I pleaded, my voice trembling with the tears I was trying so hard not to shed. "This is the last day we shall all be together for what may be a very long time. We are sisters, despite our differences, and even if we cannot agree about things like dresses, we can at least agree to love each other and not let our differences divide us. *Please,* Jane, forget the dress, it doesn't *really* matter. It's just material to cover your body, and, for your own sake, as well as ours—we who love you and like not to see you sad and sulking—*please* smile and try to make the best of it. Like Father always says, 'If Life gives you lemons, slice them and sprinkle them with sugar; if the hand of Fate hurls almonds down on you, mash them and make marzipan.' And I *know* you can, Jane; *you're so clever!* And you are *so* beautiful. I wish you could see that, and that it is truly not a bad or sinful thing. How could it be when it was God Himself that gave you your beauty? And you do not have to choose. You can be beautiful *and* brilliant too! Verily I should think most men would account it even more of a marvel to see a beautiful woman display such a sharp intellect when most care only for primping and pretty clothes. And I'm sure, if you are kind and make friends with him, once Guildford sees how much your studies mean to you, he will not make you forsake them. They say he studies singing; so you could be at your books while he is at his lessons, you could both set aside time for your private studies, I'm sure of it!"

With a great rustling of stiffened petticoats and embroidered and shimmering skirts and sleeves, my sisters knelt down and put their arms around me and leaned their cheeks against mine, and I tasted their tears as well as my own.

"I'm sorry, Kate," Jane said softly, reaching around me to squeeze her hand. "I shall endeavor not to spoil your day. You are right, as is Mary. I have been selfish, and I am sorry."

"Thank you, Jane," Kate said in a tremulous, tearful little voice. "I'm sorry too. I should not have lost my temper. I know you are unhappy, and I am sorry for it, so very sorry; I wish there were some way, some magic words or a wand I could wave, that would make you as happy about your marriage as I am about mine."

"The heart in those words is magic to me," Jane answered, and I was nigh crushed between them as they embraced, but I was so happy they had made their peace that I didn't mind at all. "And I shall try," Jane promised, "as Mary with Father's deliciously sage words advises, to make sugared lemons and marzipan out of what Life has given me."

"With Guildford you already have the lemons and gilt for the marzipan, so all you really need is sugar and almonds." Kate giggled, and I opened my eyes and saw both my sisters smiling through their tears and laughing. And it felt good; I felt warmed by love, sunshine, and hope.

"Everything will be all right now," I whispered, but it was more a prayer rather than an assertion.

I took each of my sisters by the hand and led them to stand before the mirror. We smiled at each other. We knew what to do; the ritual was dear and familiar.

"The brilliant one!" Jane stepped forward and declared herself to the looking glass.

"The beautiful one!" Kate followed with a saucy smile and sashaying hips.

And then came I. "The beastly little one!" I piped.

And then our lady-mother announced that it was time for the brides to go downstairs. As we clung together, I felt my sisters' bodies, and the hearts within them, jolt and start at those world-changing words. Silently, they each pressed their lips against my cheeks, then stood and let the maids straighten the ribbons and cascading hair flowing down their backs and smooth down their skirts and sleeves one last time. Then, their hands still holding mine, trembling beneath the great, gracefully flowing fur-cuffed bells of their over-sleeves, we three sisters walked out to the top of the stairs. I stood and watched them descend, and then I turned and made my way higher upstairs to the musicians' gallery where I would stand and watch, "like a little angel from her cloud," Kate said. "Our angel," Jane added. And then they left me and went downstairs to meet their destiny, to become wives and leave maidenhood behind, just as they had to leave me.

Standing on my tiptoes, despite the protesting pains it caused to cry out in my back, hips, and knees, I folded my arms atop the rail and gazed down upon the scene transpiring in the Great Hall below. The musicians, costumed in silver, to make yet another of Kate's dreams come true, were playing a short distance from where I stood, and they smiled and nodded kindly to me. Being players, who had spent their lives roving, entertaining others to fill their purses, playing at both fairs and the private parties of the nobility, I was not the first dwarf they had seen, and they did not regard me with the same repulsion and superstitious dread as most did, and between songs one of them laid down his lute and brought me a small stool to stand upon, to take the strain off my toes and ease my aching joints.

The wedding passed in a gold and silver blur, through the shimmering wet veil of my tears and the blare of the music filling my ears, and then the feasting and dancing began and the musicians changed to a livelier tune. Though I could not see his face from my perch so high above, Father was, I could tell, as proud as a goose who had laid a golden egg as he presided over the long tables groaning beneath the weight of gilt platters heaped high with all kinds of dainties and delicacies he had chosen. There were towering pyramids of fruit and nuts, cheeses and sweetmeats, even little roast birds, and crayfish boiled to an angry red. There were so many, piled so high, that I feared they would collapse in an avalanche upon some unsuspecting guest who dared pluck a sugarplum from below. And in the center of it all an immense and awesome wonderland of a salad with every kind of salad greens, vegetables, roots, and sugared flowers that human imagination could possibly think of tossed and mixed into a great gilded basin shaped like a scallop shell, presided over by a large marzipan sculpture rising out of its midst, depicting a trio of mermaids made in the brides' likenesses, with carrots and turnips and all the vegetables that could be carved like fishes, sharks, whales, dolphins, and turtles swimming upon the leafy sea of salad greens. I could just imagine Father boasting that one way or another he was determined to have a mermaid for his daughters, and that though he had lost one he had gained three more and these even better as they were made of candy.

And of course there was the cake. At one point Father even swung a squealing, happy Kate up onto the table to stand beside it in her golden gown to show that, true to his word, it towered above her. Kate was so happy! She picked up her skirts to show her pretty ankles and dainty, twinkling golden slippers and pranced joyously around the cake as though it were her dancing partner, until she stopped, laughingly crying out that she was dizzy, and several gentlemen pressed close to catch her as, with a joyous whoop, she leapt into their outstretched arms. And, as though she were a little girl, they threw her high into the air and caught her several times before setting her on her feet again and relinquishing her to the timidly smiling boy who was now her husband. Kate plucked a sunny yellow dandelion from the salad and smilingly tucked it behind his ear and gave his cheek a hearty, smacking kiss before she grasped his hand and laughingly led him off to dance, while Father, groaning and salivating in an ecstasy of gluttonous delight, dug both his hands into the cake, tearing out two great handfuls, and brought them to his mouth. The expression upon his face as he chewed conveyed such bliss I was certain he was imagining that he had died and gone to heaven.

Seeing her with him, I gave a great sigh of relief, feeling the fear fall from my heart and sink away into nothing; what had been big as a boulder was now the tiniest, most miniscule piece of gravel. She didn't seem disappointed at all; she must have been looking at him through the eyes of love. I pressed my hand to my lips, and though she could not see me, blew a kiss to my lovely, loving Kate, wishing her all the happiness in the world.

I glanced over at Jane and Guildford, sitting at the banquet table, and wished I could see love lighting up their faces. There seemed to be an invisible wall about them setting them apart from the other guests; though they were surrounded by smiling, happy revelers, these two alone took no pleasure in the day, looking as though they wished they were any place than at this grand party meant to celebrate their nuptials.

Fastidiously nibbling on a slice of sugared lemon and occasionally sipping from a gilded goblet, Guildford Dudley looked bored and beautiful. But Jane just looked sad and very pale, her eyes, indeed her entire expression, dull and dead. From time to time Guildford would reach out and touch her hand, as though to assure himself that she was still alive. Each time Jane would flash him an annoyed grimace and pull her hand away.

"Jane, you promised!" I wanted to shout down at her.

Watching them sitting there together, so strikingly and discordantly apart from all the gaiety, I sighed and shook my head as my fingers fiddled with the cameo pinned to my plum damask bodice. It was a wedding favor, given to all the most prominent and influential guests. Specially carved by an Italian craftsman, it depicted Guildford Dudley's handsome profile, and was wreathed by golden gillyflowers creating a cunning little frame that could be worn as either a pendant or a brooch. I was so surprised that I had been given one, I thought myself of so little consequence, but Guildford himself had presented it to me when I arrived at Durham House. Still in his gold brocade dressing gown and slippers with his golden hair bound up tight in curling rags, he had waved aside the servants who rushed to help him and knelt down before me and pinned it to my bodice with his own lily-white hands, explaining that I more than anyone deserved to have some beauty in my life. The words were pompous and condescending, but I could tell by his smile and the look in his pale green eyes, and the very fact that he made the gesture when there were so many much more important people he could have given it to, that this was a genuine act of kindness. Guildford was really not as bad as Jane made him seem. As I spent more time with him, I began to think that there was more to Guildford Dudley than most people realized, that his flamboyant ostentation was part of a role he was playing, and the joke was truly on those who never bothered to look beneath the surface.

I watched with great interest as Father approached this dour couple. Smiling broadly, with a flourish, he presented each of them with a golden bowl heaped high with salad. I saw Guildford smile, his hand reaching out to touch Father's as he set the bowl before him. Jane sullenly shoved her salad away, and Father smilingly drew the shunned bowl to himself as he sat down between them. He waggled his golden fork at Jane, his scolding marred by the great smile that graced his face, before he stuffed his mouth full of salad and gave his full attention to her bridegroom, chewing and nodding assiduously at whatever Guildford was saying as a dandelion waggled up and down his chin, its stem caught in his beard. Jane folded her arms across her chest and glared hard at them, and harder still when Father, in a distinctly, and disturbingly, coquettish manner, leaned forward to feed Guildford some salad from his own fork, but neither of them appeared to feel the scorch of her censorious stare; they seemed lost in their own little world. Jane would later, most disparagingly, repeat some of their conversation to me.

His eyes on Guildford all the while, Father sipped from a golden goblet of "the splendid Rhenish" he had chosen and, laying a hand over Guildford's, asked how he found the wine.

Guildford smiled brightly and said, "Oh I just look to my right, and there it is every time! The servants keep filling my cup, so I keep drinking it. It must be very good wine; after all, why would anyone give me anything but the best?"

Beaming, Father leaned forward and looked past Guildford to address Jane. "Smile and be merry, Jane, you're the *luckiest* girl in the world! See what a clever, witty husband I have chosen for you?"

Jane just glowered. "I thought my lady-mother chose him for me."

"Well . . ." The smile on Father's face faltered, but only for a moment, and then he brightened. "But as her husband all her property is mine, and that includes her ideas, so, when you think about it that way, I did choose him."

To which Jane just rolled her eyes and snorted and wished she could disappear.

I was still watching them, marveling at Father's perplexing behavior, the way he kept feeding and reaching out to touch and caress Guildford so familiarly; such affection for a son-in-law seemed unwarranted and disturbing, indeed for even a naturally born son, or even a daughter, it would have been peculiar, there was a sensuality about it that made it appear so . . . *intimate*. I was thus preoccupied when Kate came bounding up the stairs, her gold and cream skirts hitched high so she wouldn't tear or trip over them. A footman followed her, carrying a big golden platter heaped high with a thoughtfully chosen selection of roasted meats, cheese, and sweets just for me. Kate, in the midst of the glorious whirl of her own wedding, had not forgotten me and had actually taken time to prepare a plate with all my favorites.

"Mary, I am *so* happy!" she cried, throwing her arms about me and hugging me tight. "May you be just as happy on your own wedding day! I wouldn't worry too much about Lord Wilton," she added, seeing my woeful, doubtful expression. "You've years to wait before you come of age, and someone better, whom our parents deem just as advantageous a match, may come along. Now that I am a married lady and shall be going to court, you may rest assured, I shall look out for someone better for you. I want my little sister to be happy! I shall pray every day that love will find you, Mary, so you can know this marvelous and immeasurable joy! You deserve it! And God and Life cannot be so cruel as to deny you this bliss because of a caprice of Mother Nature!"

The musicians could not take their eyes off my Kate. She was as radiant as the sun, so jubilant and vivacious, she made everyone smile. Kate laughed and thanked them heartily for their good wishes and the wonderful music, and when she spied one of them, the youngest, a tabor player, hungrily ogling my plate, she inquired if they had yet eaten. Ashamed at his lapse in manners and too shy to answer, the boy reddened and hung his head, so the sackbut player spoke for him, explaining that it was customary for them to take their share of the leavings after the banquet was finished and the guests had left the hall.

"But all the best will be gone by then!" Kate protested. "No, you simply *must* have something now, I insist!" Before any could stop her, she was flying down the stairs again, skirts hitched high with her long train bouncing behind her, and the footman rushing after, only to return a few minutes later with four more footmen, all of them bearing flagons of wine and high-piled, golden platters, to provide us with a little feast all our own.

"I wish I could stay and dance and enjoy it with you," she said regretfully, tarrying at the top of the stairs with a sad little smile, like one torn between two worlds, "but I must go back; they're waiting for me . . ."

"I know," I said, and squeezed her hand. "It's all right, Kate. We understand. Go and be happy."

"Mary . . ." She hesitated again. "I wish you would come downstairs. I don't like to think of you apart and lonely like this. Please come down . . ."

"I am not lonely. I am with my sisters on their wedding day; every time you think of me, I will be right there with you. And when you dance, through you, I am dancing. And this really is better," I assured her with a wave at the gallery. "I can see everything from up here; down there I would be lost in a swirl of skirts and see nothing but legs and asses. I would be bruised black and blue before the day is through from being jostled and bumped and trod on. Go on now"—I shooed her away—"your guests, and your husband, are waiting for you!"

With another hug and a kiss she was gone. I watched the sparkling train of her golden skirt skipping down the stairs after her, like a puppy's happily wagging tail.

The musicians took it in turns to play while others of their number ate. To my delight, several danced with me, and so gallant and kind were they that I felt sure they truly enjoyed it. I kicked my heels high with gay abandon and whooped with joy when they swung me high. All of them praised Kate, and I saw that my sister had captured a dozen more hearts that day. The young tabor player in particular would never forget her, or her kindness, and many years later when I chanced to meet him at a court celebration, I would discover, though he was much too shy to ever publicly declare it, that he had written the popular song "Mistress Sunshine" as a tribute to her, the beautiful young bride in her golden gown who had come like a dancing sunbeam up the stairs to the gallery bearing treats for the troupe of musicians who played for her on her wedding day.

Then, like a sudden rainstorm come to ruin a perfect day, everything seemed to go wrong. I rushed to the rail to look down as sudden screams and the noise of retching filled the air. Down below me in the Great Hall people were running and staggering every which way in a blind panic, falling to their knees, grasping their bellies, and being violently sick. There was the thunderous rumble of footsteps upon the stairs as they ran for whatever private rooms and privies they could find, or fled the Great Hall to relieve themselves in the pleasure gardens behind the house, and yet more rushed out into the streets or to the river and stumbled into their waiting barges, presumably to make their way home or to the nearest apothecary, though it seemed more than likely to me that the swaying current of the river would make them sicker before they reached their destination.

I saw Father, looking none too well himself, wading through the panicked crowd, carrying a green-tinged Guildford Dudley, who had apparently fainted, and lay back limp as a rag doll in Father's arms as he carried him tenderly upstairs. Guildford's mother, clucking like a frantic mother hen over her favorite golden chick, followed anxiously behind, then darted ahead to open the door to Guildford's bedchamber, herself green-faced and sweating profusely in her rust red satin gown, wringing her hands and crying for someone to fetch a doctor quickly.

High above in the musicians' gallery, we were safe and at no risk of being jostled, trampled, and crushed by the herd of frightened, confused, and puking humanity.

"The fish?" the flutist guessed, lowering his instrument.

"*Something* was off." The sackbut player shrugged, and all as one turned and looked warily at the table where the remains of our own little feast lay.

"It was the salad!" I piped up. "Everyone who is sick, I saw partake of the salad! Someone must have plucked some bad leaves, mistaking them for good and wholesome salad greens."

"Aye"—the hautboy player nodded—"I've seen this before. 'Tis what you'd expect from a city wedding; 'twould *never* happen in the country. People there know which greens won't gripe the belly and turn the bowels to stink water."

"Praise be!" they all chorused as we all heaved a great, grateful sigh that the sickness had passed us by, and the musicians struck up a lively air hoping to calm the ailing masses below us. Kate had not brought us any of the salad; the crowd around it had been so dense, and she was in such a hurry to bring us our treats. I had seen her tarry a moment uncertainly beside it, judging how long the wait would be, then, with a wave beckoning the footmen to follow her, rush on up the stairs to us.

Where was Kate now? Had she or Lord Herbert been stricken? Vainly my eyes sought to pick her out, but somehow I missed her in the crush of the crowd. I was tempted to risk being trampled and go in search of her, but the rebec player reached out his hands and gently stayed me, and, with a twinkle in his eyes, informed me that he had seen her and her bridegroom taking full advantage of the confusion to slip away, "and neither of them seemed even a wee bit sick to me, little mistress," he added with a wink. All the musicians laughed and nodded knowingly, many of them adding that the young Lord Herbert was a "most fortunate" and "a very lucky" man. The cittern player even went so far as to say he wished he could trade places with him for a night, but the lute player elbowed him sharply in the ribs and said he shouldn't speak so in the presence of the lady's sister, adding, " 'Tis not meet for such young ears."

Soon the Great Hall was all but empty. Only a few servants and Jane remained. My eldest sister sat calmly at the deserted banquet table. I saw her nonchalantly pluck up a peacock tongue, pop it in her mouth, and wash it down with a sip of malmsey wine before she meandered off in the direction of the Duke of Northumberland's library, showing not the least concern that her husband had been amongst those taken ill.

Since there was no longer anyone to play for, the musicians laid down their instruments, loosened the laces that held their silver-frilled collars tight, and gave their full attention to what was left of our feast. And I, knowing that both my sisters were well, was pleased to join them.

Some time later, a lady with her sleeves pinned and rolled up and an apron tied over her green and silver gown came softly up the stairs with a straw basket slung over her arm. She shyly inquired if we were well or, gesturing to her basket, if we had need of dosing. "I've celery tonic, mint and wormwood syrup, conserve of roses, quinces, ginger suckets, and sugared aniseeds, if you do; all good for calmin' a tempest ragin' in the belly." She was a petite, round-hipped, buxom little woman, who spoke with a broad country accent, but she was *very* pretty, with a wealth of golden hair that she had unloosed from its pins, blue green eyes like the finest emerald mated in true love with a turquoise, and a timid, tentative smile I longed to see cast aside its shyness and show its full glory.

She had such a kind face and a gentle way about her, with no hauteur at all; I liked her instantly. She didn't shy away from me in fear, avert her eyes, or look at me with pity or contempt or treat me any differently than she would any other little girl. In her eyes, I was normal, and I loved her for it, as strange as that may seem when I didn't even know her.

Of course, I knew who she was. I had overheard some of the other women laughing and making cruel sport of her while they were helping Jane and Kate to dress. The Dudley girls had spoken of her with blistering disdain and a scorching contempt, and had piled pity upon their brother, sighing again and again, "Poor Robert!" Her name was Amy Robsart, and she was Lord Robert Dudley's wife, the one he had married in hot lust at seventeen, but now, not quite three years later, no longer wanted, and loathed his youthful folly more than he had ever loved this sweet lady.

How sad, I thought, that her own husband, and the rest of his family, thought that she was too far beneath him to be welcome in their proud and illustrious company, when I, a mere child, could see that she was worth more than the lot of them put together. I wanted to tell her, "You deserve better," but I didn't dare risk such a presumption, though years later, when Amy lay dead, with a broken neck to match her broken heart, and her name was on everyone's lips, providing a banquet for the gossips and scandalmongers, I would always remember that moment and regret that I had not taken her hand and spoken up boldly. She truly did deserve better. Not only did her own husband fail her, but her own body did too—when she died under those most mysterious circumstances she had been suffering from cancer of the breast.

The rebec player gave the Lady Amy a randy leer. "Aye, mistress, our bellies are fine, but I'd take a dose from you any time." He smiled invitingly and made so bold as to ask, "May I trouble you for a quince from your basket, mistress?" which she gladly gave though it was clear he was not troubled by the bellyache.

Blushing a little, she started to turn away, but at the top of the stairs, she hesitated and added shyly that we were all most welcome to come down to the kitchen. "Now that all those taken sick have been settled, we've mincemeat tarts and gingerbread with hot cider to drink, and apples sprinkled with cinnamon and sugar roastin' in the fire, and 'tis a right lively company, sittin' 'round the hearth, singin' and spinnin' tales. And if you'd care to play for us, some country dances per'aps, if you know any, 'twould give us all much pleasure. And you can have all you wish of what's left of the feast, to eat now or to take away with you—'tis only the salad that's tainted. There's not a one ill who didn't eat of it, and it would be a right shame to see all the rest go to waste when there's so much of it an' not a thing wrong with it."

"Shall we, lads?" the sackbut player asked. "What say you, little mistress?" He smiled down at me. We were all in agreement that we should go, and the lute player gallantly gave me a ride on his shoulders—"I shall be your litter, my little queen," he teased—and soon we were down in the kitchen, where we were welcomed warmly as old friends and plied with all the gingerbread, cider, mincemeat tarts, and roasted apples we could eat. The Lady Amy took it in turns to partner each of the men with great gusto and grace in the vigorous and lively country dances, holding her skirts up high to show off her green stockings and her fast-moving feet flashing swiftly in their silver slippers. She never missed a step or stumbled at a high kick, and laughed as her partners spun her around dizzily and swung her high in the air, her hip-length hair flying out behind her like a banner of gold. For a time she seemed to forget her cares and I loved seeing her so high-spirited and light-hearted; many who never even knew her would say in years to come that she was a wan, wretched, and miserable woman, and though illness and heartbreak may have made her so, I can say with complete certainty that she wasn't naturally, nor always, that way. Whatever happened to her happened because of the deadly combination of Robert Dudley and cancer.

When she was not dancing, Lady Amy took me to sit on her lap, saying, if I would allow her the liberty and be so kind as to indulge her, she wanted to "pretend for a spell that you're my own little girl." I readily assented and together we listened intently to the storytellers, relishing each word, laughing, gasping, shuddering, and wiping away tears by turns, though as darkness fell, they turned more to tales of terror, ghosts, and beasties that made us shiver despite our nearness to the fire.

My parents and nurse, preoccupied with their own ails, had forgotten all about me, and I stayed up later than I ever had in my life. The first butter gold glow of dawn was already lighting the sky when the musicians took their leave, and the Lady Amy, marveling that she had been so remiss and not sent me to bed hours ago, scooped me up in her arms, balancing me against her broad hip, and carried me up to one of the guest rooms.

"But I don't want to go to sleep!" I protested as she stripped me down to my shift. And as the tears began to trickle down my face, she sat and stroked my hair and asked me why.

"Surely you are tired, poppet, I know I'm all done in. Look"—she lifted her foot—"I've danced a hole clean through my slipper!"

"Because when I lie quiet and still waiting for sleep I will not be able to help but think how much I shall miss my sisters," I said. "I've lost them both in the same day, and now they're both going away, to new homes, and I shall be all alone at Bradgate; Father and my lady-mother are so often away at court, and when they are home they are always hunting or hosting parties and have time for no one but their guests."

"Aye, I see"—the Lady Amy nodded—"and I know just what you mean about the thoughts that come to trouble one in the quiet stillness before sleep. What beastly little imps those thoughts are!" Then she brightened. "But I'm certain your sisters will be havin' you to visit soon. I'm sure they'll be vyin' for the pleasure of your company, and you'll find yourself feelin' you've no fixed home at all, you'll spend so much time on the road goin' from one to the other. While the young brides are settlin' into married life, if you get too lonely, you're welcome to come and bide a while with me at Stanfield Hall or Syderstone Manor; I still live with my parents as my husband has yet to settle on a proper establishment for us. He's so particular about these things, Robert is, and everything must be just so or not at all." She heaved a little sigh and shook her head, and I sensed sadness and frustration hovering in the air about her, but she quickly shook it off and smiled at me. "But you would be most welcome to visit anytime you like. I could take you out to see the sheep, we've three thousand of them, and the orchards; Syderstone has the best apples in England, I always say you've never tasted an apple if you've never sunk your teeth into a Syderstone apple. If you'd care to come durin' the harvest, we have the *grandest* party, with dancin' and music and a big bonfire and bobbin' for apples, and every one of the dishes laid on the table has apples in it in some form or fashion—from the meats to the sweets. Our cider is the *best* in the whole of England, and I challenge anyone to prove me wrong!"

"I would like that very much," I said, and thanked her for her kindness, secretly praying that my parents would allow me to go, and she sat beside me, softly singing a charming little song about a shepherd and his flock, until I drifted off to sleep, dreaming of fleecy white sheep, rosy red apples, and clanking cups brimming with golden cider.

Early the next morning, blinking and yawning in the watery yellow sun, my sisters and their husbands descended the stairs to board the barges that would take them away to begin married life. They were no longer little girls, but wives now, with their hair pinned up in nets of gold beneath their round velvet caps. It was such a sudden and startling transformation, as though they had crossed a threshold as little girls with free-flowing tresses and entered a new room as elegant young matrons with their hair primly pinned up. Now they must go away from me, from childhood and all that was dear and familiar, and learn how to please their husbands, order their households, command their servants like queens overseeing their own little realms, and endeavor to always be on pleasant terms with their in-laws.

Strangely, neither marriage had yet been consummated, the Duke of Northumberland and our parents having agreed on it for reasons I did not understand. Both couples were under strict orders and would be watched to make sure they obeyed, not to commit the ultimate intimacy until they received permission directly from Northumberland. Kate was twelve, almost thirteen, and she had been bleeding every month for almost a year, and thus was considered a woman, so her age was surely not the reason for this prohibition. Why it must be so with Jane and Guildford, at fifteen and sixteen, I could not fathom; many women were wedded and bedded and carrying their first child by the time they turned sixteen.

Kate looked radiantly happy, her face and eyes glowing, as she danced down the stairs in her gold-embroidered apricot velvet with peach and white plumes swaying gracefully atop her round velvet hat, and the magnificent set of fire opals she had chosen when Father brought the jeweler to her and said she might choose anything she wished from amongst his wares. When I saw her I almost wept—how I missed the sight of her coppery curls bouncing and bobbing as though with a life of their own. It seemed unnatural to see them pinned tight with diamond-tipped pins and confined inside the glittering prison of a golden net beneath her hat. As soon as she caught sight of her husband, waiting for her downstairs, she gave a cry of delight and ran to throw her arms around him.

But Jane moved as though her shoes were soled in lead, her gold-fringed and embroidered moss green velvet skirts dragging behind her like a dead weight. She looked as angry as the fierce and ornate fire-belching, ruby-eyed, emerald, sapphire, amethyst, and jade scaled golden dragon brooch her new mother-in-law had given her just before she came downstairs, kissing her once on each cheek before pinning it to Jane's hat, just below the puff of white ostrich plumes that made that hideous bejeweled dragon look as though clouds of steam were billowing from its pointed ears. Beneath her hat's round brim, Jane's face was pale as chalk, her freckles standing out stark as smallpox, and there were dark circles around her eyes, as though she hadn't slept at all.

Though his stomach had settled, and he had passed a peaceful night, Guildford, his face startlingly pale against the ornate gold-embroidered claret velvet of his traveling clothes, was still feeling weak and wobbly, and Father insisted on carrying him down the stairs and laying him gently in the barge and pressing into his hand a gilded pomander ball, scented with oranges and cloves, to mask the river's vile reek. He tarried quite a time, causing our lady-mother to tap her booted toe impatiently, as he tucked a fur rug around Guildford, caressed his golden hair, plumped his pillows, petted Fluff, nestled in the crook of Guildford's arm, and presented his "beautiful new son-in-law" with two comfit boxes—a silver one with icy green enamel filled with sugared aniseeds, mint lozenges, candied quinces, and crystallized ginger in case his stomach should trouble him again, and a gold one with sunny yellow enamel emblazoned with golden suns containing sugared lemon slices, "just because you like them, and because I like you, and these remind me of you, so I hope they will remind you of me and how much I . . . like you." Father blushed and rambled as our lady-mother sighed and rolled her eyes, saying aside to Guildford's mother that having such a husband was like having a little boy who never grew up.

"I'm so happy!" Guildford, suddenly all aglow, exclaimed, sitting up and hugging his knees and smiling. "I feel like singing!" He threw his arms wide, as if to embrace the sun above, and opened his mouth in readiness to let the first notes out.

"Oh no, Guildford, you *mustn't* do *that!*" his older brother John exclaimed, quickly throwing himself forward to clap a hand over Guildford's mouth. "All that puking last night will have left your throat frightfully raw."

"If you force it, you will only make it worse," his brother Ambrose cautioned severely.

"Quite right," his father, the all powerful John Dudley, Duke of Northumberland, agreed, so suave and smiling, gracious and benign that any who didn't know him and his reputation would never have guessed that here was the most ruthless and ambitious man in England, a man who would stop at nothing to get what he desired. "You might damage your voice," he continued. "Don't you agree, Maestro Cocozza, that Guildford should *not* sing?" He turned to Guildford's Italian music master, waiting to board another, rather crowded barge with Guildford's valet, hairdresser, the secretary who wrote all his letters and also read aloud to him, the French and Italian tutors Guildford considered vital to his singing aspirations, laundress, page boys, musicians, sewing women, the man who looked after his pets, the French pastry cook Father had given the young couple as a wedding present, and, just for Jane, the prim, black-clad Mrs. Ellen, who had with Jane's marriage risen from nurse to lady's maid.

With much flourishing of his hands and a spew of rapid Italian, the music master agreed, in the most emphatic terms, that Guildford should most definitely *not* sing.

I tugged Lady Amy's skirt to get her attention, and when she bent down I asked, "Does he not sing well?"

"Well . . ." Her smile faltered. "His talent doesn't quite match his enthusiasm. Which is a right shame since he loves singin' so, but, to put it as kindly as I can," she whispered, lowering her voice even more to make sure Guildford wouldn't hear, "when he hits the high notes he sounds just like a cat yowlin' in heat, he does, poor lad!"

"When he was fifteen, Guildford ran away from home and tried to join a theatrical company," the Duchess of Northumberland with a fond and indulgent smile, confided to our lady-mother, who was standing beside her, tapping her leather-booted toe and looking impatient and bored, "but the manager brought him straight home, and right back into my loving arms. He said that Guildford was not made for the stage. Even he could see how delicate and sensitive my darling is, just like a hothouse rose that would wilt and perish without his mother's love."

"I don't think that's quite what the man meant, Mother," Ambrose Dudley opined.

"Nonsense!" the Duchess cried. "What else could he mean?"

"Well, I took it to mean that Guildford can't sing to save his life much less to earn his bread and board," Amy's husband, Robert, the fifth surviving Dudley son, whispered back to her, and Ambrose and John nodded their heads in emphatic agreement.

"For shame!" the Duchess scolded her brood of black-haired boys. "I'm ashamed of you all! You should be *proud* of your brother's talent and accomplishments, not jealous!"

"Come now, Mother, you know we all love Gillyflower!" Robert retorted, using the family's pet name for their gilt-haired darling. " 'Twas just a jest! You wouldn't want Guildford to think too highly of himself and get a reputation for being conceited, would you?"

"My Gilded Lily conceited? *Never!*" the Duchess scoffed.

I found it rather touching that though they all, with the possible exception of the deluded Duchess, deplored Guildford's singing and strove vigilantly to keep him from embarrassing himself, none of them wanted to hurt his feelings by letting him know.

Guildford frowned uncertainly and reached up to stroke his throat. "Well, if you *really* think it unwise . . ." And since everyone was so quick to assure him that they did indeed think it "*most* unwise," he lay back against his pillows again. "Perhaps I should rest my throat for a few days. It does feel a trifle red . . ."

"I think that's a *wonderful* idea, dear!" his mother exclaimed, and all his brothers and sisters were quick to agree and praise him for his self-discipline and good sense.

"I shall have the apothecary prepare a soothing syrup and send it on to you," his sister, the recently married Lady Mary Sidney, promised.

"One that tastes good," Guildford stipulated. "If it doesn't taste good, I won't drink it!"

"I shall insist upon it," she promised.

"Threaten him with hanging," Guildford advised, "if it tastes the least bit vile or bitter, then he will be *sure* to make it *very* sweet."

"When he knows who it is for, I am sure he will make it just as sweet as you are!" Father breathed like a love-bedazzled maid.

"Of course he will." Guildford smiled and nodded confidently as he sank back against the velvet cushions, drawing the purring Fluff close against his chest and stroking his silky white fur. "If my beauty doesn't inspire him, fear of hanging certainly will."

"Oh what a wit you are!" Father breathed rapturously. "You have such a way with words!"

"They just spring up in my head like roses in full bloom, and I say them so that the world can enjoy them too." Guildford beamed. "It would be selfish to keep my thoughts entirely to myself."

"Beautiful *and* generous too!" Father sighed, and I could see that he was perilously close to swooning into the Thames. "I'm sure you sing as beautifully as a nightingale," Father said gallantly, "and I hope to hear you soon."

Then our lady-mother, who had had quite enough of this absurd spectacle, took command. "Hal, come stand over here beside me before you fall into the river! Now into the barge, Jane," she directed, pointing the way with her riding crop.

With a mutinous scowl and a marked ill-grace, Jane climbed into the barge and dropped down heavily beside Guildford and sat there with her back straight and her eyes staring forward. Even when Guildford reached out and playfully ran his fingers up and down her spine, she didn't relax or relent, only stiffened her spine even more.

As the oarsmen dipped their oars and began to row away, and we all waved and called out cheerful good-byes, Godspeeds, and good wishes, it gladdened my heart to see my stubborn sister relent and lean back against the cushions. Her hand went up to fuss with her hat. I suspected a pin was poking her and thought nothing more about it until she slowly, making a grand gesture of it, extended her arm straight out over the side of the barge and, following a lengthy pause, dropped the spray of white feathers, with the hideous dragon brooch her mother-in-law had just given her acting as an anchor, right into the dirty, reeking waters of the Thames.

"Oh, Jane!" I sighed, shaking my head as the Duchess of Northumberland gave an anguished cry of, "My brooch! My *beautiful* brooch! Look what that girl has done to my beautiful brooch!"

Then Kate, nestled up against Lord Herbert, with her head pillowed on his chest, and his arm close about her, beamed and waved at me as their barge glided past. At least one of my sisters was happy, I thought as behind me our newly extended family fell to brawling over the loss of the ugliest brooch I had ever seen. While I couldn't condone or applaud my sister's conduct, it truly was an unforgivable snub and most ungracious and ill-mannered, the brooch itself really was better off stuck in the muddy bottom of the Thames where it could offend no one's eyes except the fishes, as our lady-mother quite candidly informed the Duchess, who had begun to stagger and sway and clasp her head and call for her smelling salts. "I know I shall faint!" she cried several times while failing to actually do so. In the end, she had to be helped back into the house, supported between two of her sons, while her daughter ran ahead, calling for smelling salts and cold compresses, and her husband sent Robert riding fast to fetch the family physician and an apothecary.

When they had all gone back inside, and only Lady Amy and I remained, she smiled down at me and held out her hand and suggested we take a turn in the garden until all the ruffled feathers had been smoothed back down again. I nodded eagerly and gave her my hand. When my lady-mother called for me, I was sorry to leave Lady Amy behind with her husband and in-laws. After I turned back to wave at her, I saw the sadness on her face and impulsively ran back and gave her a hug as though a part of me knew that I would never see her again.

3

I was back at Suffolk House on what was to be my last night in London, helping Hetty pack my traveling chest, preparing to return to Bradgate on the morrow and dreading the long, lonely hours that lay ahead of me without my sisters. Regretfully, I folded away the lovely new gown I had worn to the wedding with sachets of crushed lavender nestled amidst its luxuriant folds and wondered when I would get to wear it again. I was heaving a doleful sigh and trying to resign myself to my fate when a letter came from Kate, bidding me come to Baynard's Castle. I was so surprised I had to read the letter through three times to make sure wishful thinking hadn't caused me to misread the words, and even then I couldn't quite believe it and handed it to Hetty for confirmation. Kate had scarcely been gone a week, and I had thought not to receive an invitation to visit either of my sisters for months and months. But, as Kate explained, since she and Lord Herbert were still forbidden to consummate their marriage, and she found it "wearisome, vexing, and dreary" being always chaperoned "like a pair of guilty prisoners" she craved my comforting presence, as both a sister and a friend, someone she could be free and easy with. "I cannot even touch my husband's hand," she lamented, "without people eyeing me like a hawk about to swoop down and pounce on a poor little mouse. They're afraid if they leave us alone for an instant I will ravish him."

I was so excited I could barely sleep and was bouncing on my toes, impatient as could be, to set off right after breakfast the next morning. I drove my poor nurse to such distraction that I set off for Baynard's Castle wearing a pair of mismatched gloves with my bodice only haphazardly laced in back because I could not stand still and dear old Hetty's eyes were not what they used to be. "Don't be cross with me," I said to her, "my cloak will hide it. I know you're excited too, to see Henny again." For her own dear sister was Kate's nurse, now, like Jane's Mrs. Ellen, raised up to serve as lady's maid. Everyone loved Henny; she was a plump, good-natured mother hen of a woman who doted on Kate and clucked over her constantly, and she was much sweeter than my sour, always complaining Hetty, who had misery in her bones, aching back, stiff fingers, tired old eyes, and just about everywhere else. Father had offered to provide Kate with a real French lady's maid, one skilled with perfumes, paints, and fashions, and nimble fingers for the styling and curling of hair, but Kate had wept and clung to her "dear old Henny" and refused to be parted from her, and Henny had wept too and wrapped her arms like a pair of protective wings about Kate and said, "I'll not have my chick painted like a French whore!" Then Father had offered around his comfit box filled with pink sugared almonds and nothing more was ever said about Henny leaving or a French maid.

At Baynard's Castle, I followed a footman up the grand stone staircase and walked in on a scene of utter chaos. Like two naughty children playing at house, Kate and Lord Herbert, whom Kate had christened "Berry" because "he blushes red as one and is just as sweet," received me in the large, spacious parlor that divided their bedchambers.

Dogs and cats, barking and meowing, hissing and growling, chased each other all around the room, clawed the furniture, or curled up in their baskets or napped or groomed themselves on the bearskin rug by the fire, and gilded cages crowded the windows in which a profusion of rainbow-plumed songbirds sang or chirped and flapped their wings against the bars, and a big blue and yellow parrot danced on his perch or hung upside down from a large ring suspended from the ceiling, while constantly demanding a cherry over and over again until I wished I had a whole basket of cherries to throw at him just to shut him up.

There were bowls of fruit, candies, and nuts, cups and flagons of wine, and platters of meat, cheese, and cake strewn over every possible surface, even balanced precariously upon the mantelpiece, and several garments and items of jewelry, vials of scent, combs, hairbrushes, and pins, bits of sewing, and the accoutrements of needlework, and several spoons and knives, all apparently laid down in scattered distraction and then forgotten.

In the midst of it all stood Kate, in a shimmering emerald satin gown that was more appropriate for a court ball than a quiet rainy day spent at home, her coppery curls, unleashed from their pins and held but loosely back from her face by a jade butterfly comb, cascading down her back as though she was bored with pretending to be a proper married lady and wanted to be a little girl again. She didn't see me enter nor hear the footman announce me, which was hardly surprising given the din created by her menagerie. She was preoccupied, plumping the pillows behind her husband's back as he reclined on a couch, looking pale and smiling weakly, in his quilted mulberry satin dressing gown and slippers. She perched on the edge of the couch beside him and a brown and white spaniel hopped up onto her lap as she sweetly coaxed the invalid to take a sip of milk punch. Two implacable, blank-faced servants in the Pembroke livery stood stationed at either end, eyeing the young couple vigilantly, ready to put a stop to any affectionate displays that threatened to grow too familiar, and Henny, a much more familiar and friendlier face, smiled at me from over her sewing. I was astonished to see that she was making a tiny yellow dress trimmed with sky blue silk ribbons—a *baby* garment! My jaw dropped, and I flashed a startled glance down at Kate's stomach as with a cry of delight she sprang up, dislodging the spaniel from her lap, and rushed to embrace me.

"Not for me, silly! How could it be when we're not allowed to . . ." She giggled. "For the monkeys! Look!" She pointed across the room to where the two little creatures were rudely snatching cakes off the table and gobbling them greedily as Berry on his couch eyed them nervously and shrank back against his pillows. "That's Rosamund." Kate pointed to the one dressed up like a little lady in a rose damask gown and hood. "And that's Percival." She indicated the other, clad in a handsome forest green velvet doublet replete with gold buttons and fringe and a round velvet cap with a jaunty plume just like a courtier in miniature. "Aren't they *adorable?* My new father, the Earl of Pembroke, gave them to me. He simply *adores* me! As does Berry"—she ran to hug and plant a smacking kiss on her husband's cheek—"they both spoil me so. I even have an ermine coverlet for my bed! Look what they gave me this morning at breakfast!"

She thrust out her hand to display an enormous emerald in an ornate gold setting. It was so ostentatiously large it made me wonder how Kate could even lift her hand. Lord Herbert favored me with a shy smile, wincing as Rosamund snatched the silver-tasseled nightcap from his head and Percival hopped up to "groom" his pale, lifeless hair until it stood up on end like stalks of wheat, then clambered down over Berry's body and took off his slippers and began slapping their leather soles together, gibbering with delight at the noise they made. Then the parrot flew from his perch and landed on top of Berry's head and resumed his imperiously squawked demands for a cherry.

Laughing, with puppies nipping at her trailing skirts, Kate ran to snatch up a blue glass bowl filled with cherries that was sitting alarmingly near the edge of the mantel, and began tossing them, one by one, to her parrot. "Isn't life marvelous? Truly, my dear Mary, it is delightful to be married! I never dreamed it would be this much fun!" Kate's aim went awry and one of the cherries hit Berry's nose.

With a cry of alarm, she thrust the bowl at me, never noticing that I fumbled and almost dropped it, and ran to him and began smothering him with kisses until one of their chaperones cleared his throat loudly then, finding himself ignored, stepped forward and took Kate's arm and gently pulled her away.

"Milady mustn't be so exuberant," he said, wagging a reproving finger at her. "She must show some restraint and not be so free with her affections; there are some who might misunderstand and think her a wanton."

But Kate just laughed and threw her arms around him. "Don't

scold me, Master Perkins, I can't help it; I'm just *so* happy! *So wonderfully, gloriously, blissfully happy!*" She began to spin around the room, and I marveled that with all the clutter and the bevy of boisterous animals crowding around her that she didn't trip and fall. "I wish all the world could be as happy as me! Oh, Mary!" She suddenly grabbed my hand and began tugging me across the room. "Come, I must show you Fussy's new trick! My little boy is *so* clever!"

She bent and caught up the little brown and white spaniel chewing on the trailing train of her skirt and rushed over to the table by the window where a handsome gilt and ivory set of virginals sat. She set the little dog down upon the table beside the instrument and lifted a big, sprawling, fat orange cat from the chair and sat down and began to play, her fingers gliding effortlessly over the keys as the little dog began to yowl in time to the music. "Who's a clever boy? Isn't he *wonderful?* So talented, so clever!" Kate enthused, then turned smiling to me. "Now if I can only teach the others . . .we'll have a whole choir! Just think, Mary, we might even be invited to court to entertain the King!"

I glanced over at Lord Herbert and saw that though this failed to fill him with delight, he nonetheless still forced himself to nod and smile out of indulgent affection for his bride.

Seeing the stunned expression frozen on my face, Henny took pity on me and offered to show me to my room, chidingly reminding Kate that I had only just arrived and as lady of the house she had neglected her first duty—to see to the comfort of her guests. But when Kate started to rise Henny stayed her with a motion of her hand. "Nay, love, Miss Mary and I are old friends. We'll manage just fine. You stay 'ere and care for your poor ailing 'usband." And, before Kate had a chance to protest, took me by the arm and hurried me toward the door just as Rosamund sat down before the virginals and, to Kate's delight, began banging out a series of loud, discordant notes upon the ivory keys that set Fussy yowling and made Kate beam like a proud mother and praise them both for being "so brilliantly clever!"

Just before I reached the door, I tripped and would have fallen had Henny not caught me. I glanced down to see what I had stumbled over. I blinked my eyes and shook my head and wondered if the din had driven away my wits. There appeared to be a large tortoise staring up at me. His shell, unless I was very much mistaken, was set with a fortune in precious gems.

"Aye, my lady, doubt not your eyes," Henny said as she took my hand again, explaining as we went, " 'is name is Trippy. Miss Kate chose it on account of everybody always trippin' over 'im. 'Tis another gift from the Earl of Pembroke; 'e dotes on so." She shook her head and sighed, and I had the feeling that this troubled her more than she dared say, as though she feared putting it into words might somehow make it worse.

When the door closed behind us, I took the opportunity to warily ask, though I dreaded the answer and prayed it would not be the one I expected, "Is it *always* like *this?*"

"Aye, Lord save us, Miss Mary, it is, from morn till night Miss Katey—for that she still is to me and always will be—is chattering away, singing, and bouncing off the walls; I 'ave to give 'er a strong dose o' valerian, lavender, and chamomile every night just to calm 'er down enough to sleep. Last thing I do every night before I lay me 'ead down, and first thing on rising, I pray that the Good Lord will see fit to move the Duke of Northumberland to send word that they may consummate their marriage, for if mother'ood doesn't settle our Kate down, Lord only knows what will, for I certainly don't!"

"Oh dear!" I sighed. I had so wanted to come to Baynard's Castle, to be with Kate, but now that I was there, I was half wishing the invitation had come from Jane instead; though she was moody and sulky, and I would soon be pining for the sunshine of Kate's presence, it would no doubt be quieter in the country in comparison to this combination menagerie and madhouse. Kate had always been bubbly and exuberant, but under our parents' roof, where our lady-mother ruled with a riding crop she was not afraid to use on our bare buttocks and backs if we misbehaved, there had always been an element of caution and restraint; now that had been cast off and, in the presence of two men ready and eager to spoil her and indulge her every whim, Kate had become a whirlwind of giddy wildness and nervous energy.

I heard the sound of breaking glass and winced as the dogs and birds raised their voices even louder. "Naughty Percival!" Kate cried. "Look at him, Berry! He has stolen the cherries and dropped and broken the bowl! Come here, you naughty monkey, and let me see that you have not cut yourself! Quick! Someone catch him! He's climbing the curtains! Down, Percival, down! You naughty, naughty monkey, I swear, one of these days I really will have to spank you! No, no, Rosamund, you *mustn't* play with the broken glass! Give that to me at once, you naughty girl! Quick! Somebody catch her!"

As the clamor behind the door grew even louder, with the parrot determined to outshout them all with his incessant demands for another cherry, I sighed and had to wonder if, when the time came for me to quit Baynard's Castle, I would leave my mind behind to join the clutter in Kate's parlor.

Over the next week, every day I bore witness to such scenes. The entire household seemed to revolve around Kate; pleasing her seemed to be the entire household's sole purpose in life. Her husband and father-in-law were like rivals to see who could spoil her most. On chilly mornings when Kate rose from her bed, her shift-clad body was instantly enveloped in a robe of purest white ermine. At every meal the table was laid with her favorite foods, and there was always a dessert as pretty as it was delicious to please her. The Earl of Pembroke was always giving her pets, songbirds in gilded cages, and new puppies and kittens, and he had given her all his late wife's jewels and was constantly buying her more. If Kate admired a sunset, the very next day a bolt of shimmering satin evoking its color would arrive in the arms of the dressmaker, ready to fashion whatever gown, cloak, or petticoat that would please Kate best, or a jeweler would come and open a velvet box to reveal a magnificent fire opal, ready to be set in a ring, pendant, or brooch, whichever Kate fancied most. If perchance, whilst strolling in the garden, she happened to enthuse about the beauty of the flowers blooming there, a jeweler would soon come bearing some beautiful bauble that captured them in an eternal sparkling bouquet of costly and precious gems. The dressmaker came to Baynard's Castle so often she might as well have set up shop there and hung her shingle from the upstairs parlor window.

Every day brought fresh delights for Kate. Packages arrived every day for her. And, more times than I could count, I saw the

Earl of Pembroke sit Kate upon his knee and hang a fortune in jewels about her throat, stroking and caressing her neck and adjusting the necklace and smoothing it down in front to ensure that it lay just right; other times I would watch him pin a brooch to her bodice, though I wished he wouldn't do that as it quite unnerved me the way his long, elegant fingers casually grazed my sister's small, pert breasts and seemed to linger there inordinately long. It just didn't seem right—she was his son's wife—but when I tried to timidly broach the subject with Kate she just laughed and shrugged it off. "Better that my in-laws adore than despise me, Mary. Now come," she would wheedle and cajole. "Smile and don't spoil it for me! Don't be sour and serious like Jane!" And Henny told me that the Earl of Pembroke always came into Kate's bedchamber every night, after she was already abed, to kiss her good night, standing proxy for his son as it was feared that Berry's "youth was insufficient to overpower and restrain his lust."

Kate took great delight in flirting outrageously with both father and son. Being older now, as I look back, I can better understand that she found the effect her feminine wiles had on these men heady and empowering, exhilarating; she was reveling in these new sensations, like a monarch drunk on power, only it was her beauty that intoxicated. But back then, when I was only eight, as I watched it all unfold before my youthful eyes, I felt only confusion and a deep, persistent fear that tightened like a noose around my throat and made it hard at times for me to breathe. But still my beautiful, vivacious sister flounced provocatively from the arms of one straight into the other. She was so free with her kisses and embraces, I prayed every night that God would grant her the will and good sense to better govern and restrain herself. She loved finding excuses to lift her skirts to show off her pretty ankles and sometimes, even more boldly, her knees, and give a glimpse of the plump and rosy flesh above her garters. Whenever Henny was helping her dress, primly tugging her bodice up high to show less bosom and cover the curves of her shoulders, Kate would stubbornly push and pull it back down. More than once, when she was down on her hands and knees playing with her pups, I noticed both father and son staring raptly at her bosom. But it did no good to voice my concerns to Kate. Every time I tried to talk to her about it, she would pout and implore me not to spoil it. "I'm just having fun!" she would insist. "Where is the harm in that?"

Sometimes, in the morning when she rose, Kate would summon her "darling Berry" to sit and keep her company while she made her toilette. He had given her a beautiful Venetian glass hand mirror; the handle was shaped like a mermaid, her tail and person beautifully jeweled and enameled, and her long golden hair, adorned with pearls and precious gems, flowed up, as though it were floating, spread out and billowing in the sea, to encircle and frame the costly glass. Kate had a shimmering seaweed green silk dressing gown, and she loved to let it slip from her shoulders as she sat at her dressing table and pool around her slender waist. There she would sit, like a mermaid sunning herself on a rock, brazenly bare breasted, leisurely brushing her hair, sighing and arching her back, and admiring her reflection in the glass while Berry gazed adoringly at her, discreetly drawing the folds of his own dressing gown tighter over his lap, as the cool morning air caused Kate's little coral pink nipples to stiffen. I noticed, to my dismay, which, by her worried face I could see Henny also shared, that when the Earl casually strolled in, Kate showed no concern and made no attempt to cover herself. The Earl of Pembroke would cross the room to stand behind her, and lay a hand on her bare shoulder as he gazed down long and admiringly, before at last bending to kiss her cheek and bid her good morning. Once he even brought a rope of pearls, a magnificent lustrous strand shimmering with hints of gold and green, and bent to drape it around her neck, saying as he did so, "Pearls for our pearl, but we must take care that this enchanting siren does not lure us to our deaths and doom." Though they seemed spoken only in playfulness then, given what came after, my memory always wants to tint them a more ominous shade. Such are the tricks of memory, which is why any writing their recollections many years later must take care.

Another time, I was there while Kate was lounging in her bath when Berry and his father came in, without knocking, each bearing a big straw basket filled with red and white rose petals—a coincidence or a subtle reminder of Kate's Tudor heritage?—which they upended over Kate's head. She sat up in the bath, bare breasted and bold, laughing, and stretched up her arms, urging them to bend down so that she might kiss them.

Though I know, even as my pen records these memories, these things sound so lewd, and my beautiful sister appears a heedless wanton, yet I cannot *bear* that any who read this might think of my sister in these lascivious terms. It is so hard to explain! But there was such an aura of innocence and blind trust about her as she did these things, my heart breaks all over again to recall it. Even though Kate clearly encouraged them, and most eagerly too, it is the men I blame most; in my eyes they were the despoilers of her innocence. Though she was growing into a beautiful, shapely woman, more so every day, her nakedness was like that of a baby—natural, sweet, and pure. But no matter how hard Henny and I tried, Kate simply could not understand how some might construe her behavior, how it could tar and feather her reputation forever and make people think her something she was not, and it might even lead some men to believe they could freely dally and trifle with her and treat her body like their own toy. Each time she would stare back at us, befuddled, with a quizzical frown crinkling her brow. To Kate it was all "good fun," and she simply could not comprehend how anyone could see it any other way; if they did, *they* were the ones who were lewd, not her, she insisted.

I didn't know how to say it without hurting her or seeming ungrateful and unkind, but, as much as I had wanted to come there, I now wanted to leave Baynard's Castle even more. I felt always a sick and queasy dread, like one standing beside a scaffold must feel, hoping, praying for a reprieve, while waiting to watch a loved one die. I felt such a great fear for Kate it tainted everything and sucked all pleasure out of life. My appetite deserted me, and many a time though I loved a certain dish and thought I wanted or even craved it, the moment it was set before me, fancy fled and queasiness took its place, and I could not bear to look at it let alone eat it. The very air seemed bad to me, and when I overheard the Earl of Pembroke telling his son that the young king was ailing, with "a cough and rheum following a mild attack of measles" and that his feet were swollen and he "ejects from his mouth matter sometimes colored a greenish yellow or sometimes the color of blood or even black," I didn't wonder at it. It seemed a very marvel to me that the whole of London wasn't ailing, infected with the same fear and malaise that beset me.

Another sleepless night when I desired a book from the library, I overheard the Earl entertaining a late night guest—the Duke of Northumberland. They were talking about Jane, and I heard Northumberland say: "She has imbibed the Reformed Religion with her milk and is married in England to a husband of wealth and probity, and the King holds her in the highest esteem for her learning and zealous piety. In time, she could be the thunderbolt and terror of the Papists." Even though they were praising my sister—Jane would have particularly liked that last bit—their words frightened me. They were plotting something, and I knew it, and I was so afraid they were going to do something that would hurt Jane more than a forced marriage to Guildford Dudley ever could.

Then, like the answer to my prayers, letters came flying like frantic doves from Surrey. Apparently its bucolic splendor had little effect on Jane. The newlyweds were scarcely settled in at Sheen before she fell ill. In a hasty hand, she dashed off frantic letters to "my sisters, the only ones I can trust," imagining herself being poisoned upon the orders of Northumberland. Though why her new father-in-law would want her dead I could not even imagine. Surely Guildford didn't find Jane so disagreeable that he must resort to murder in order to be rid of her? In a hysterical scrawl that sprawled across the tear-blurred pages, she told us how her skin was itching so abominably that she had to sit on her hands to keep herself from scratching it off, and even without the intervention of her nails, it was sloughing off on its own, peeling away in great flaky patches and strips that revealed a smooth, burning, tender redness beneath, and her hair was falling out, every time she ran her fingers through it, they emerged dripping with long chestnut strands, and she could keep no nourishment within her stomach, which ached inside and out, as though it contained a great, tight knot, both hot and tender, and whenever she tried to eat, one or the other end would soon disgorge it, leaving her even more sick and weak and sore. She said she spent hours, *agonizing* hours, squatting over a chamber pot with a basin balanced on her lap, never knowing from which end the sickness would erupt, and her belly and bottom ached so as a result she could hardly stand it; each expulsion brought fresh torment. *"I will die if I stay at Sheen!"* she insisted, underlining the words with such force that the pen bit through the page.

After a fortnight at Sheen, our parents and Jane's newly acquired in-laws finally gave in to her complaining and transferred the young couple to the handsome redbrick Thames-side manor of Chelsea, where Jane had spent such happy times with the Dowager Queen Catherine Parr. There it was hoped that nestled amongst the pink roses, lavender, strawberries, and peach and cherry trees Jane would recover her health and blossom like a rose, "all velvety, pink, and sweet, the better to tempt Guildford to pluck." Northumberland hoped the young couple "might become one soon," and by that time he wanted that young lady "restored to the full bloom of health and beauty."

But all Jane did was sit on a bench in the garden or park, staring morosely at the pink orange sunsets, sighing and lamenting the loss of Catherine Parr, and, I am sure, in the most secret depths of her heart, that handsome rogue, Tom Seymour, though in all the years since whenever I had dared remind her of that time, Jane's temper would erupt and she would stamp her foot and angrily rail that it was cruel of me to remind her of that girlish folly she had let befoul and besmirch her soul when all she wanted to do was forget her "wretched foolishness."

"Why can you not understand?" She would round on me, angry tears falling from her eyes. "It is a stain on my soul I can never wash clean no matter how hard I try!" Then with her hands pressed to her temples as though she wished to crush her skull to kill every memory of Thomas Seymour that still lurked there, she would dramatically flee the room.

I never could understand it; we all make fools of ourselves at one time or another in our lives, and each of us harbors memories that make us cringe, humiliating instances that cause our faces to flush red with the flame of shame or embarrassment, but why did my sister think it was such a crime to let a little love, however unworthy the recipient of it was, into her life? Why did my sister believe that feelings were a sign of weakness and failure? Why did she aspire to be like a pure and perfect white marble saint instead of a woman pulsing with life, love, and longings?

Even though I am her sister, I cannot say for certain, only that I sometimes think that Jane was afraid to be real and imperfect, and this inspired her futile and impossible quest for perfection; she spent her whole short life chasing a dragon she could never conquer and slay.

4

My mind was already pondering how I might best persuade our lady-mother to let me go and stay with Jane, to help nurse her back to health, when Kate bounded into my bedchamber one morning and shook me from my sleep as she shouted for Hetty to hurry and pack a trunk for me.

"Wake up, Mary!" she urged, shaking me insistently. "We're going to see Jane!"

Before I was even fully roused, she was skipping off, calling back over her shoulder that we would breakfast on strawberries and cream in the barge on our way to Chelsea.

I was still yawning and rubbing my eyes when Kate skipped ahead of me and, lifting her skirts high, exposing her limbs to the oarsmen's admiring eyes, entered the barge with a graceful, flying leap and plopped down against the velvet cushions. As the oarsmen began to row, I sat there still half asleep, trying to make sense of Kate's chattering and avoid choking on the cream-dipped strawberry she shoved suddenly into my mouth.

"I just *love* to breakfast on strawberries and cream!" Kate prattled as she nibbled daintily upon a cream-slathered berry. "Isn't this fun? We're going to the country, or as close as we can get to it without actually leaving London. We shall act as Cupid's sweet ambassadors and see what we can do to get Jane out of her sickbed and into her marriage bed. I don't have an arrow, but I am not without arms!" she said coyly, dipping her fingers down into her bodice and drawing out a small, ruby red glass vial, shaped rather like a heart, that she wore suspended from a black braided silk cord about her neck. "Courtesy of Madame Astarte!" she said cryptically.

"Whatever is that?" I asked. "And who on earth is Madame Astarte?"

But Kate would only giggle, shake her head, and say mysteriously, "All in good time, my dear Mary, all in good time. And see, I've something more!" She reached into her bodice again and drew out a letter and a folded square of age-yellowed paper. "The Duke of Northumberland has given me leave to be the bearer of good tidings—as soon as she is recovered, Jane and Guildford can become husband and wife in deed as well as in name! To celebrate"—she brandished the other paper—"I've a recipe for a special wine made from gillyflowers—Guildford's favorite!" More than that, no matter how much I pressed her, she would not say.

The barge had scarcely docked before Kate had leapt out and was running toward the house. I followed her as best I could, clumsily tottering on my short, stubby, slightly bowed legs, proudly shrugging off Hetty's helping hands and her offer to carry me. I had not grown an inch in three years, not since I was five, and had learned to accept—What good would it do to shake my fist up at God and rage against it?—that it was my lot to spend my life trapped in a child-sized body with a back and limbs that always ached like a bad toothache. From the grinding pain in my lower back and hips, I already knew this brief exertion would require the application of hot stones wrapped in flannel when I went to bed that night. I would never have the strong, shapely, and slender limbs that carried my sisters gracefully through life, beautiful, slim white legs, as pretty as porcelain, not thick stumps like mine, and marred by ugly, ropey, pain-pulsing, and bulging veins. I would grow old, as would my sisters and all that lives; I would wrinkle and wither and gray frost would douse the dark fire of my hair, but as I aged I would also go back in time and return to a toddler's clumsiness, and a day would eventually come when I would need a cane, or even a crutch or a pair of them, or if I had the means to afford it and spare myself this indignity, a pair of handsome footmen to carry me about in a gilt and damask chair.

I was standing on the threshold, blinking my eyes to accustom them to the cool dimness inside Chelsea, when I heard Jane's voice. "Kate? Is that you, Kate?" she called as she appeared upon the landing, staggering weakly and flailing blindly for the banister to support her.

What a sight she was! Even in her loose white nightgown I could tell she had lost flesh. Livid, puffy pink patches and flecks of flaky white skin marred her face and hands, even the bare toes peeping out from beneath her gown, and, I suspected, all the parts I could not see were similarly afflicted. We bolted up the stairs to meet her, and I saw that her nails were gnawed ragged and raw and the fuzzy braid that snaked crookedly over her shoulder when she bent to embrace me was not as thick as it had once been, and I could see pearly patches of scalp shining through in places.

"Oh, Jane!" I sobbed and hugged her tight.

But I could not give in to despair. Kate was already taking command. "Don't worry, Jane, we're here now, and we'll soon have you well. Mrs. Ellen!" she barked like a general at the black-clad figure hovering at the top of the stairs like a shadowy phantom. Kate was a married woman now, not a little girl to be cowed by years and authority, and she issued orders now as fearlessly as a queen, confident that she would be obeyed without question. "Bring me an apron, and one for Mary as well, and prepare a hot bath for your lady. And I want the water *steaming!* Henny, have my trunks brought up at once!" she ordered her own maid. "Come, Jane, come, Mary, we've much to do." And, taking each of us by the hand, she marched us upstairs as if she, and not Jane, were the lady of the manor.

Though she squirmed and squealed in our arms like a slippery wet piglet and cried for cold water, insisting that we were scalding her, Kate and I knelt beside the tub with aprons tied over our dresses and determinedly scrubbed every part of Jane's body with a pumice stone until all the old, dead skin had been sloughed off. Then we pulled her from the tub and massaged her all over with olive oil, even her scalp—Kate said it might help and keep more of her hair from falling out—until, at last, Jane stood before us all rosy and pink as a newborn, her tender new skin still smarting from our ministrations.

But Kate was not done yet. She bade Jane kneel with her head over the tub and rinsed the olive oil from her hair, then sat her on a stool and, after whisking the tears of regret from her eyes, took up the shears and with a sure and steady hand quickly cut Jane's hair just below her shoulders. "I've left it long enough to pin up," she said softly, gently running her fingers through the wet waves, "so when you appear in public with your hair pinned up under your hood with a veil in back, like a proper married lady, no one will ever know. And you'll see, it will soon grow back and be more beautiful than ever."

Jane nodded gloomily and murmured something about all being vanity and her head feeling "pleasingly light" as she reached for her shift, but Kate snatched it away. "No, let your skin breathe," she insisted, and, taking Jane by the hand, led her to the bed, which had been newly made, upon Kate's orders, with the silk sheets she had brought with us, and the old canopy and curtains had also been taken down and replaced with new cream and gold damask ones. Then, settling our ailing sister back against the pillows, she dosed her with the peppermint syrup she had brought to soothe Jane's stomach and instructed Mrs. Ellen to take *all* Jane's clothes away—"and I do mean *all,* Mrs. Ellen, not even a shift or even a stray stocking is to remain"—and have them laundered and *thoroughly* rinsed so that nothing remained that might irritate Jane's sensitive skin. She then proceeded to give instructions about Jane's diet, insisting that Jane was to have nothing but a weak chicken broth for a week, though as the week progressed, if Jane was better, she might increase its strength, and after another week she could add small portions of milk and bread before progressing to a little roast chicken, "unsalted and without seasoning," she said as firmly as though she were a graduate of the Royal College of Physicians. And she was to drink fennel tea every day and have a bit of crystallized ginger to suck on after meals and whenever her stomach felt likely to rebel.

While Jane recuperated, Guildford spent his mornings reclining, indolent as an emperor on a gold and silver brocade couch, resplendent in his favorite gold brocade dressing gown, tossing grapes to his yellow-crested white parrot, and his afternoons frolicking in the meadow, raising his voice to the glory of God and to serenade the sheep—he liked to pretend he was on the stage and they were his captive audience—and having daily lessons with Maestro Cocozza. Meanwhile, Kate—a much calmer, less frenzied, and more focused Kate without her husband and father-in-law around to flirt with and her menagerie to pull her attention in a dozen different directions—decided that we should busy ourselves with "Cupid's work" now that Jane was on the mend.

"We must do what all the scoldings, threats, commands, and beatings cannot and bring these two together, Mary! We must show our sister that it is possible to make the best of an arranged marriage and mayhap even find love and passion within it."

"How do you propose that we do that?" I asked. Jane's coldness and contempt, the rude and scathing remarks she repeatedly doled out, had hurt Guildford one too many times, and he now kept a wary distance from her. Whenever they were together I could tell he was most uneasy in her presence, and there was a nervous stiffness, a guardedness, about him, as he weighed and pondered his every word before speaking then glanced warily at her, as though steeling himself for the biting remark that would inevitably follow. For the life of me, I didn't know how we could ever make these two fall in love.

"To the stillroom, Mary!" Kate cried and, like a soldier charging into battle, she raced ahead, arm raised as though brandishing a sword, flourishing the paper covered with the faded, spidery handwriting of the mother-in-law she had never known detailing how to make gillyflower wine.

Unbeknownst to me, before we left Baynard's Castle, Kate had ordered the necessary ingredients and they were there in the stillroom waiting for us. While Kate stood before the long table, reading the recipe aloud to me, I poured, scooped, measured, mixed, and boiled as Kate dictated until the mixture of water, sugar, honey, yeast, syrup of betony, cloves, and gillyflowers—Kate had chosen yellow ones because they were Guildford's favorite—had cooled and was ready to be casked and left in the dark to ferment for a month.

When it was ready, we sampled our concoction, growing giggly and giddy as Kate confided her plan to me. We would, she said, set it in motion the next morning, after Guildford departed to sing in the meadow.

Curled up on the window seat, lost in the pages of her Greek Testament, Jane suddenly found herself being deprived of her book and divested of her clothes even as we dragged her down the corridor to Kate's room, leaving her dull brown gown lying on the floor like a mud puddle. I gaily flung her plain brown hood as far as I could before I slammed the door behind us.

We stripped our sister bare and plunged her into a tub of hot, rose-scented water and scrubbed her pink. Then, over her protests, after we had dried her, we tugged a loose, flowing gown of cream-colored lace and fine, pleated, unbleached linen over her head, ignoring her cries that without undergarments underneath it was most indecent.

"I won't wear this! I simply won't!" she wept and raged. "It is indecent, I tell you, *indecent,* no godly Christian woman would ever . . ."

But Kate only smiled and sang over her protests as she adjusted the silken ribbons and falls of lace on the bodice and sleeves, and I raised my voice to join hers as I circled Jane, carefully smoothing the long, trailing skirt, making sure the lace and pleats lay just right.

"You're so beautiful, Jane," I breathed. "This gown makes you look so womanly and soft, like a goddess of femininity."

When Jane broke free of us and ran for the door, I raced ahead of her, turned the key in the lock, and shoved it under the door to where Henny, our coconspirator, waited outside. I smiled sweetly at Jane's defeated face and took her hand and led her back to Kate, who sang of love and lads and lasses wooing and stealing kisses in pretty gardens as she combed her fingers through the wet, red brown waves of Jane's hair.

Jane broke away again, and while she pounded on the door, demanding to be let out, wincing and hopping around on one foot, cradling her toes, after she lost her temper and kicked it, Kate and I sat by the sunlit window while we waited for her hair to dry and busied ourselves with weaving daisy chains to adorn her neck, wrists, and waist, and an elaborate floral crown of scarlet poppies and golden wheat, with two grandiose upper tiers of pinks, marigolds, daisies, buttercups, bluebells, lavender, rosemary, dandelions, corn cockles, daffodils, peonies, periwinkles, forget-me-nots, pink sweet peas, lily of the valley, Canterbury bells, meadowsweet, yellow buttons of tansy, the feathery spikes of bright pinkish purple loosestrife, the blushing and freckled pink and white bugle blossoms of foxglove—"Like Jane will be when Guildford sees her thus!" Kate teased—the perky, purple pink pompoms of chives, and heart's ease pansies, the bold and vibrant popinjays of Mother Nature's bouquet.

"Now for Guildford!" Kate cried, proudly holding up the ornate wreath of golden wheat and yellow gillyflowers, scarlet poppies, snowdrops, sunny yellow St. John's wort, foamy white meadowsweet, marigolds, forget-me-nots, and heart's ease pansies her nimble fingers had just fashioned for our gilt-haired brother-in-law. "As every queen must have a king, and every king must have a crown!" How this game and these words would haunt us in later years! But we were young and innocent then of Northumberland's and our parents' schemes.

"Let me out, Henny, *I order you!*" Jane screamed, forgetting herself and kicking the door again.

"You heard what Lady Jane said, Henny!" Kate called in the prearranged signal. "You'd best let her out before she breaks the door or her toes!"

"Very well, Miss Jane," Henny said, and soon we heard the key turning in the lock.

As soon as the door swung open, Jane rushed out, right into the trap of Henny's and Hetty's open arms.

"Let go of me! Let me go!" she howled, thrashing, twisting, and squirming as Hetty's arms closed like a vise beneath her bosom and Henny caught her around the ankles and lifted her feet off the floor.

"To the meadow!" Kate trilled, carefully holding the beautiful floral crowns out before her as she skipped ahead of us and led the way downstairs, and I brought up the rear with the daisy chains draped over my outstretched arms.

As soon as we stepped outside, the musicians Kate had hired struck up a lively tune and began prancing alongside us, to escort the Lady Jane to where her bridegroom awaited her in the meadow. We had invited the servants to join our little party, and they had already carried out the casks of our gillyflower wine, and even as we approached, the girls from the kitchen were busily laying out a trestle table laden with a rich bounty of golden cakes, strawberries and cream, and meat and cheese pasties.

Every day it was Guildford's custom to go out into the meadow to dance and sing, letting his high notes soar free as birds as the sheep fled baaing before him. Most people shuddered and cringed when they heard him, but not Kate. Always kindhearted, she would shrug and say that the Bible did say, "Make a joyful noise unto the Lord, all the earth: make a loud noise, and rejoice, and sing praise." Guildford's efforts certainly seemed joyful and were undeniably loud. Nor could I bear to mock him, for in my heart I understood all too well his impossible, impractical dream; Guildford longed to be a great singer, just as I longed to be a woman normally and beautifully formed just like my sisters.

When Guildford heard our little party approaching, he paused midsong and stood there staring at us, a *very* pretty picture of golden-haired puzzlement.

"Don't let her go, not yet!" Kate cautioned Henny and Hetty as they set Jane on her feet. Instantly, they tightened their grip on her as the servants milled curiously around, watching us and whispering, wondering what was going on.

"Let go of me! Let go!" Jane squirmed and twisted in the vise of their strong arms. "You've dressed me like a dancing girl, a lewd, indecent dancing girl, at a pagan bacchanal, and I shall not be part of it, I tell you, I won't, I won't, I won't! I am a good Protestant maid! I am impervious to this lewdness. It shall not infect or touch me. The Lord shall protect me!"

"Calm down, Jane," Kate said as she carefully laid the floral crowns on the ground far enough away that Jane and her captors would not trample them. "You're carrying on as though this were a witches' sabbat, and we meant to roast babies on spits over a fire and make you sign your name in the Devil's black book. Look around you, feel the sunshine, smell the flowers, listen to the music, and see all the smiling faces that wish you well. All the evil and indecency you're imagining is all in *your* mind, not ours. There are no pagans, Papists, or witches hiding in the trees waiting to swoop down on you and force you into sin. Can't you see that God is in his heaven and smiling down on us on this *beautiful* day?" Kate paused to give Jane's cheek a pat as she walked past, nimbly evading a kick from our outraged sister, then seized my hand and rushed me over to the trestle table. "Quickly, Mary, before Jane breaks free!" She snatched up a cup and thrust it into my hand and then, with her back turned to Jane, stealthily withdrew the red glass vial from her bodice and spilled half its contents into the cup, then bade me take it *carefully* to the cask and fill it. "And *please,* Mary, do not spill even one precious drop!"

I did as she asked, then watched as Kate approached Jane and, with the strong-armed assistance of Henny and Hetty, forced her to drink and drain it to the dregs.

"Only a little longer, love, before it begins to work its magic," she said, stroking Jane's hair and kissing her cheek before she scooped up the crown she had made for Guildford and ran back to prepare a similar cup, with the last of the mysterious potion, then ran giggling across the meadow to where Guildford stood gaping quizzically at us.

"I am Love's humble handmaiden come to crown Your Majesty and present you with this loving cup from your queen, your loving bride," she announced playfully as she set the crown on his head, then offered him the cup, though to my eyes, Jane seemed none too loving as she snarled and twisted suddenly and kicked Hetty's shins quite viciously, causing my poor old nurse to cry out in pain.

Guildford's skeptically arched eyebrow conveyed that our thoughts were traveling along the same path, but he nonetheless graciously accepted, calling out, "Thank you, my queen!" as he raised the cup in a toast to her then downed its contents. "Very sweet," he pronounced as he passed the empty cup back to Kate.

"We used six pounds of sugar and almost as much honey," Kate proudly volunteered, and Guildford smiled and said indeed he did not doubt it.

Smiling, Kate skipped back to Jane, and together we decked her with daisy chains. It was easier now that she was standing still. Her eyes seemed larger and curiously vacant though she was staring straight at Guildford and a strange pink flush was slowly stealing over her, and I noted as I arranged a daisy chain around her neck that her bosom had begun to heave. When I glanced up and asked if she were all right, there was a strange, crooked little smile tugging at her lips, as though one side wanted to smile and the other was undecided whether to give in or continue to frown.

"Your crown, my queen!" Kate said as she set the ornate, towering floral coronet on Jane's head and I thrust a large bouquet into her hand. "Come, your king awaits!" Kate urged as she took Jane's hand and began tugging her toward Guildford. To my surprise, Jane didn't balk but nodded and began to follow, meek and docile as one of the sheep watching these curious goings-on from a distance. I, cheerfully playing the part of trainbearer, ran behind and caught up Jane's train and, with a wave of my arm, motioned for the musicians to join us. Surrounded by sprightly music, walking on a soft carpet of green grass studded with daisies, clover, and dandelions, with plump black and yellow honeybees buzzing around our ankles, we escorted our sister to her bridegroom.

There, on that glorious June day, in the lax formality of the meadow at Chelsea, far removed from the luxurious environs of Durham House where she had been married in a golden gown, Jane, with a guttural cry and a passionate lurch, flung her bouquet high in the air and lunged fiercely into the arms of Guildford Dudley and crushed her lips against his with bruising passion. He gripped her tightly and returned her kisses with equal fervor as we all cheered and the men tossed their caps and the women flung flowers in the air.

"Our work is done," Kate said as we exchanged a satisfied nod. We joined hands and skipped back to the wine cask to click our cups and drink a toast to the bride and groom and offer our heartiest thanks to Madame Astarte and her "passion potion."

While we sat on the grass, sipping our wine, Kate told me of her clandestine visit to the old gypsy witch in one of London's grimy back alleys. She described the ancient crone, dirty and stinking of garlic, stale, unwashed flesh, and sweat, who painted her old, wrinkled face with bold paint like a whore, ringing her mouthful of blackened stumps with the most vivid scarlet, and wore her dirty, matted gray hair in rainbow plaits of silk and satin ribbon tied with jingling bells, trailing down her back nigh to the floor; and clothed herself in glittery, mismatched rags of discarded and pilfered finery wherein teal damask with tarnished gilt threads mingled with rainbow scraps and tatters of dingy silks and satins, brocades, damasks, and velvets, to create a haphazard patchwork gown with a long, trailing train that followed Madame Astarte as though she were a great cat and it was her tail. Rows of clanking gold and silver bangles covered her wrists and ankles, and she let the nails on her bare feet grow into curving yellow talons that scraped the floor when she walked just like a cat with overlong claws. Madame Astarte had so many cats Kate claimed she couldn't take a step in any direction without tripping over or treading on them.

Suppressing her fear, Kate had boldly ventured into her lair, explained Jane's situation, and asked for whatever potion the old gypsy woman deemed most beneficial to remedy the situation. She crossed the witch's palm with silver and within minutes the red glass vial was in her hand, but ere she could depart the old crone was prying Kate's fingers wide and staring intently at her palm. With a sudden blankness in her eyes and a deadness in her voice, she monotonously chanted a dire prediction: "Your love is both a blessing and a curse to you and those you love. The greater your love, the greater your loss; the greater your passion, the greater your pain. You will die young and fair, starved for love, but his heart shall go on." Her words filled Kate with such fear that she turned and fled, gripping the precious potion tight over her heart and praying God forgive her for going against His teachings and trafficking with witches.

Once back in the safety of her bedchamber at Baynard's Castle, Kate flipped open her Bible and found the passage in Deuteronomy that was haunting her and read it with a thudding heart and a sudden sweat akin to that which comes with a raging fever.

There shall not be found among you any one that maketh his son or his daughter to pass through the fire, or that useth divination, or an observer of times, or an enchanter, or a witch, or a charmer, or a consulter with familiar spirits, or a wizard, or a necromancer. For all that do these things are an abomination unto the Lord: and because of these abominations the Lord thy God doth drive them out from before thee.

Shivering and burning all at the same time, salty tears and sweat running down her face, Kate fell on her knees and raised her clasped hands heavenward and begged God again and again to forgive her until she collapsed on the open Bible in a dead faint. When Henny found her and put her to bed and bathed her hot flesh with a cool, wet cloth Kate was still babbling deliriously. "*Please,* God, don't let it be true! Please, forgive me! *Please,* God, don't let it be true! I *had* to do it! I *had* to do it, for Jane!"

I never knew until she told me; Kate had kept her secret well. Henny had told me that my sister was ailing with the onset of her courses and to let her, and the household, rest in peace, so I had done as she suggested and enjoyed the quiet respite without insisting on seeing my sister. After all, it was only a trifling ail that afflicted most women every month, so I did not worry. Perhaps she only meant to be kind and didn't want to alarm me. Indeed the fever soon broke. But I wish I had known the truth, and that I had known beforehand what Kate intended to do. I would have gone with her and gladly shared her guilty burden of trafficking with that dirty, flea-bitten Circe. I would not have let that old hag hurt my beautiful Kate. I would have kicked her in the shin before she could mutter her evil prophecy, words that once heard could never be forgotten. Now I knew why I had a sense, though I could never put my finger on it and thought perhaps I was imagining it, that since her fever, Kate's gaiety seemed somewhat forced. But now, when I ventured this, Kate assured me that it was not true.

"I don't believe a word of it!" she declared, shaking back her curls and bravely thrusting her chin in the air. "I just hope the old witch's potion isn't as false as her prophecies! Love is the most beautiful, wonderful thing in the world; how could it ever, when it is true and given freely, hurt anyone?" She went on in a light, disdainful tone, ridiculing the witch's prophecy as she refilled her cup with our sweet, potent brew. "Here, have some more wine, Mary!" She snatched my cup and replenished it. "*False* love yes," she continued, "that is a sword that wounds, but *true* love, as *I* shall *always* love, no, *never!* It is only the absence of love and love denied and unrequited that hurts! *Me* to die starved of love?" She scoffed. "Whoever heard of such a foolish and ridiculous thing? It's absolute nonsense, I tell you! I cannot even imagine it! Speaking of starving, I'm hungry, let us have some cake!" Before I could say a word, she bounded up and jostled her way through the crowd congregated around the flower-decked trestle table.

Are you trying to convince me, or yourself? The question hovered unasked behind my closed lips as I watched my sister, laughing and exchanging pleasant banter with the common folk and servants as she piled a plate high with golden cake, ruby red strawberries, and big white clouds of cream for us.

I was sitting there half dozing, my belly contentedly full, my brain buzzing with gillyflower wine, and a silly smile plastered across my face, watching a yellow butterfly flit and dart from flower to flower, when Kate nudged my arm, knocking my cup from my hand and spilling what little was left of my wine.

"Look!" Kate cried, pointing as Guildford scooped Jane up in his arms and began staggering determinedly in a drunken zigzag toward the house as Jane clung to him and squealed with girlish delight and wantonly kicked her bare limbs in the air. "Now our sister will discover just how wonderful love can be! You will see," she asserted with a confident nod, pausing to take another very sweet sip of our golden gillyflower wine. "She shall thank me for this in the morning!"

But upon that point Kate was very much mistaken.

Late the next morning, Jane awakened with a fearsome headache, pounding like an anvil on a blacksmith's forge within her skull, stark naked and sore between her legs with Guildford sprawled blissfully beside her on his belly with one arm draped possessively across her breasts. She thrust him from her in disgust. Slowly, she sat up, cringing at the vile taste in her mouth and cradling her aching head. She swung her legs over the side of the bed, wincing at the pain, and startling at the blood crusted on her inner thighs, and staining the white sheet like a bouquet of rusty red blossoms. Her bare feet sank down and crushed the coronet of flowers Kate had made for her. Instantly it *all* came rushing back. Jane saw clearly that Kate was the culprit, the person responsible for her drunken despoiling. Snatching up the crumpled lawn and lace dress and struggling into it, Jane fled her floral-bedecked bridal bower, the room Kate had ordered arranged so beautifully while we were out in the meadow, with garlands of flowers draping the bedposts and petals scattered on the clean white sheets.

She was standing on the landing, seething, breast heaving, when she spied Kate and me poised to come up.

"You!" she hissed venomously, pointing a rage-trembling finger right at Kate. "*You* did this to me! You made a fool of me!" She struck her brow with the heel of her palm. "There was something in the wine, there must have been, and you put it there to make me forget myself! You made me give myself to that . . . that . . . *lack-witted popinjay!* I will *never* forgive you, Kate, *never,* as long as I live! From this day forward, you are my enemy, not my sister!" Then, in a frenzy of uncontrollable tears, she hitched up her skirts and ran, stumbling blindly, tripping and barking her shins on the stone stairs.

I saw Kate's heart break.

"Jane, wait, please!" Kate started up after her, but I, standing on a higher step so that I was of a nigh equal height with her, reached out and stayed her and shook my head, urging Kate to wait, to leave her be, and let her temper cool. But it was too late. All of a sudden we were engulfed in the voluminous, billowing folds of a pink gown and, freeing ourselves, looked up to find ourselves caught in a shower of falling finery. Jane was hurling Kate's clothes down at us and running back for more. I hugged Kate close as she clung to me and wept amidst the hail of dresses, hats, gloves, fans, jewelry, and shoes.

"Get out! Go! I don't want you here! I never want to see you again!" Jane screamed as she barked her shins and bloodied the creamy flow of her skirt trying to drag Kate's heavy oak traveling chest to the top of the stairs. Kate and I quickly jumped apart as Jane gave one last hard kick to the trunk and sent it barreling down the stairs, straight at where we had been standing. *"I hate you, Kate, I hate you!"* she screamed so fiercely the words seemed to rake and tear her throat raw, and I feared that when I looked up at her panting, red-faced figure glaring down at us with shoulders and breast heaving, I would see blood bubbling from her mouth. I could not fathom how she could unloose such a scream without doing internal damage.

Kate sank down onto her knees in a welter of rumpled finery and wept as I had never seen before.

"Come away," I said gently, tugging her hand, while Henny and Hetty silently appeared to gather everything up and pack it away inside the trunk that had landed on its side at the foot of the stairs.

I led my sister out to sit on the seawall, where we had passed many happy afternoons, eating cherries and vying to see who could pitch the pits farthest out into the river, contentedly swinging our feet, and watching the pink and yellow streaked orange sunsets. While we waited for Henny to collect the rest of Kate's things, I did my best to soothe her, promising that I would remain, and that when Jane's temper cooled I would do all that I could to convince her of the truth I knew—that Kate had acted out of the goodness of her heart, wanting only to see Jane find true happiness within her marriage.

"I was afraid her bitterness, contempt, and hate would destroy her," Kate wept in my arms. "She has a chance at love—I only wanted to make her see that! She can't be so cold as she pretends, so it *must* be fear, it *must!* I thought, if she could forget herself, just for a day, see what passion is truly like, she wouldn't be so afraid of it!"

"I know, I know." I patted Kate's back as the barge that would carry her away, back to Baynard's Castle and her wild, giddy, flirtatious whirlwind of a life, glided silently up to the water stairs.

While Henny and a footman saw to Kate's trunk, I walked my sister carefully down the smooth, worn stone water stairs, giving her every comfort and reassurance I could that "sisters quarrel but never stay angry for long" and that "all will soon be forgiven."

I stood and waved until she was out of sight, then I went back in to Jane with a prayer on my lips that the words I had just spoken were not just a comforting balm, that the wound truly would heal without leaving an ugly scar.

For more than a fortnight Jane kept to her chamber, maintaining a stony wall of silence, stubbornly refusing to see me or Guildford, who repeatedly banged on her door and demanded to know how she could refuse to fall in love with him. She admitted only Mrs. Ellen, but when she tried to remonstrate with her, assuring her that her sisters loved her dearly and had acted only with the best of intentions, and that Guildford was trying his best to be a good husband to her, Jane would turn her back and stop her ears, and in a loud, clear voice, that grew even louder every time poor Mrs. Ellen dared utter a word, recite Scripture, quoting, in maddening, monotonous repetition, the passage from the Book of Matthew about wolves in sheep's clothing.

I passed many a wakeful night worrying about how I could possibly make things right between my sisters. I could understand Jane's anger, how she felt betrayed, both by Kate and her own body, the volcano of emotions forcibly buried and concealed deep within that Madame Astarte's potion had caused to erupt in a passionate explosion that had left Jane no longer a virgin. But I knew that Kate, more than our parents, who had arranged the match, truly had Jane's best interests at heart. She could not bear to see the sister we both loved trapped in a loveless marriage, like a windowless cell so bleak and narrow one could scarcely take two steps in any direction, with barely an arrow slit in the wall to let the light in. She wanted to show Jane that she could have so much more.

Guildford, though vain and self-centered, and not the shining star of brilliance that Jane was, was not without kindness; he would, if Jane let him, be her friend and try to make the best of this marriage that neither of them had any choice about. But they had a choice within it, to be friends, kind, dear, loving friends, if they would, and, perhaps more, if they deigned to let Love enter and flood the sparse Spartan prison of Jane's soul. I wanted to tell Jane this.

Some days I stood at her door and talked myself hoarse, and on many of those sleepless nights I felt compelled to creep out and kneel there and pour out my heart, to try to make her understand that Kate had truly meant only good and not a bit of harm. But Jane kept her door locked and would not hear me, and through the muffling thickness of the heavy wooden door I heard her voice loudly reciting Scripture, sometimes in English, other times in Latin, Greek, or Hebrew, but I knew it was always the same verse: *Beware of false prophets, which come to you in sheep's clothing, but inwardly they are ravening wolves. Ye shall know them by their fruits. Do men gather grapes of thorns, or figs of thistles? Even so every good tree bringeth forth good fruit; but a corrupt tree bringeth forth evil fruit.*

A good tree cannot bring forth evil fruit, neither can a corrupt tree bring forth good fruit. Every tree that bringeth not forth good fruit is hewn down, and cast into the fire. Wherefore by their fruits ye shall know them.

One unusually hot July night, when I could no longer bear tossing sleeplessly in a tangle of sweat-sodden sheets, I rose from my bed to bind the sticky curtain of my hair in a tight braid, to give some respite to my neck, and to bathe myself with a cooling cloth. As I stood poised beside the basin, ready to dip the cloth, I heard voices below my open window. I recognized them at once—my father and Guildford. I heard every word they said, but to this day I wish I had not. I wish I, like Jane, had stopped my ears and taken refuge—even if it was a cowardly refuge—in the recitation of Scripture or just jumped back into bed and hugged a pillow tight over my head.

"Must you go?" Guildford asked in a sensual, sulky voice, and I could just picture his pretty lips pouting so seductively that he was just begging to be kissed. "The night is young and I'm *so* beautiful . . ."

Next came a groan, torn passionately from Father's throat and a rustle of clothing as though he were clutching another body close to his. "I can't fight it anymore! You taste as sweet as a sugared lemon!"

"Oh, Hal!" Guildford sighed.

"Don't call me Hal. My wife calls me Hal!" Father spoke the word *wife* so savagely, with such biting contempt it frightened me; it was as though he were stabbing my lady-mother with his words.

"Very well, I shall call you *Enrico,*" Guildford announced. "That is Italian for Henry; I asked Maestro Cocozza and he told me," he added boastfully as though making such an inquiry of his music master was some monumental accomplishment of which he should be very proud.

Another blissful sigh and the rustle of clothing, then Father said, "And I shall call you *Il mio amore,* my love, my sweet, *mio dolce . . .*"

The silence that followed told its own tale—they were kissing passionately. Then, with a breathless gasp of wonder, they broke apart.

"We shall be *so* happy together, when we are away from here, in Italy." Father sighed, dreaming their dream, their folie à deux, aloud. "My golden songbird that I keep in the gilded cage of my heart shall sing, his voice soaring like wings from the stage. You shall be showered with accolades, gold, jewels, and flowers thrown nightly at your feet by the adoring masses as you take your final bow, and I shall be right there in front every night, leading the applause, and every day I will bake the sweetest, most decadent, rich pastries . . ."

"Name your shop *Il Limone Zuccherato,* The Sugared Lemon, for me!" Guildford breathed, and another silence followed as I imagined their lips locked, their bodies crushed, close together, tart and sweet.

"But what shall we do for money?" Guildford asked. "When I sing, will the people throw enough money for us to live in the style to which we are accustomed?"

"Do not worry, my love, I shall supplement our earnings, from your singing and my pastry shop, at the gambling tables!" Father said, confident and reassuring.

Inwardly I groaned. Father was a *terrible* gambler. Some said he was the *worst* in London, and the higher the stakes, the better he liked it; his losses were astronomical, and we lived perpetually on the threshold of financial disaster. Dr. Haddon, our chaplain at Bradgate, had spoken to him *numerous* times, *pleading* with him, *begging* him, for the good of his soul and the sake of his family and to stave off ruin, to renounce this reckless and ruinous habit forever.

"What's one fortune?" Father said with what I could well imagine was a blasé shrug. "I can *always* win us another and another after we've run through that one, and then another! You shall stand beside me and be my good luck charm! With your beauty and my brains we make a *perfect* match!"

"Heavenly!" Guildford sighed and surrendered to Father's embrace one more time.

Quietly, even though the heat was stifling, I closed the casement and returned to my bed, with a sick, frightened feeling in the pit of my stomach. I didn't want to hear any more and wished with all my heart I could erase from my mind what I had already heard. It was too absurd; my father, the Duke of Suffolk, wanted to run away with his son-in-law to Italy, to live and love, in the most sinful way known to man, warmed by the sun, while one sang, on a stage he would most likely be hissed and booed from as he was pelted with rotten vegetables, and the other renounced his proud and noble heritage to run a sweetshop. It was mad, utterly mad!

No, Father, no! I sobbed into my pillow as I pounded it with my fists in pure frustration. *Guildford is meant for Jane! How can they ever become a loving couple if you come between them?*

The next morning there was no sign of Father, and when I discreetly inquired if perchance he had arrived during the night, I was met with blank and puzzled stares from the servants. Clearly his clandestine visit was intended for one person alone—Guildford.

❧ 5 ❧

On the ninth day of July, 1553, the country idyll, and with it Jane's self-imposed sulking isolation, came to an abrupt end when Lady Mary Sidney arrived, her barge gliding silently up to Chelsea like a black swan darkly silhouetted against a glowing orange sunset. She had come bearing orders from her father, the mighty Northumberland, to bring Jane and Guildford to Syon House "to receive that which has been ordered for you by the King." More than that she would not say, not even when my sister stamped her foot and demanded, imperiously as a queen, that she be told for what and why she was being summoned.

Guildford did not bother to ask questions. Excited as a child over the idea of an outing, he ran back inside to change his clothes. When he returned, elegantly garbed for travel, with Fluff purring in his arms, he paused to kiss his sister's cheek and called back casually to his valet to follow directly with his things, then settled himself comfortably in the barge, languorously against the velvet cushions, ready to be off. "This place begins to bore me," he declared, nonchalantly trailing his fingers through the water.

But, ever balky, endowed with a stubbornness that put every mule in Christendom to shame, Jane resisted, digging her heels in and claiming that she could not go, she was too ill to obey the

Duke's summons even if the King commanded it. She tugged, slapped, and fought against the determined hand Mary Sidney clasped around Jane's delicate wrist as she endeavored to pull her across the grass to the water stairs, urgently insisting that Jane *must* obey. "It is necessary for you to come with me, Jane; Father said you must come even if I must give orders to have you bound and carried into the barge, you *must* come *now!*"

With an anguished cry, Jane took refuge in unconsciousness and fell fainting to the ground. Before I could reach her, Mary Sidney had already summoned four of the bargemen, clad in the Dudleys' blue velvet livery with their proud emblem of a bear clutching a ragged staff emblazoned on their chests and sleeves. They easily lifted Jane up, a featherlight burden in her flowing gray silk gown, with her arms outstretched, and her legs straight, like Christ nailed to the cross, and gently carried her to the barge. They laid her on the cushions beside Guildford, who flicked some water onto her moon-pale face on which her freckles stood out like cinnamon stars, Guildford observed, adding languidly that if mathematics didn't bore him he would be tempted to attempt to count them. His sister did not dally; she clasped me beneath my armpits, despite my protests at this indignity, and nigh threw me into the barge, then climbed in herself and gave the order to "*Row!* Take us to Syon House!" as we crouched around Jane, rubbing her hands and fanning her, imploring her to open her eyes.

"Yes," Guildford drawled, "it is such a beautiful sunset; you really should look at it. Lying down as you are, you have the most splendid view; I almost envy you, but I don't want to take off my hat, it's so beautiful, or rumple my hair after all the hours I spent on these curls. But"—he heaved a martyr-worthy sigh—"methinks beautiful things—like me—are wasted on you; you just don't know how to appreciate the finer things in life—like me." With those words he snapped open the yellow enameled comfit box Father had given him and began nibbling daintily upon a sugared lemon.

I opened the collar of the white lawn partlet that modestly filled the low black-braid bordered square bodice of Jane's dove gray gown and pressed a damp handkerchief to her throat. She felt feverish to my touch, and I feared the nerve-induced illness that had lately plagued her was returning with a swift vengeance. Mary

Sidney quickly poured a goblet of spiced red wine, and as Jane moaned and her eyelids began to flutter, lifted her head and urged her to drink.

Jane sat up, sputtering wine and demanding that we turn around and take her back to Chelsea at once. *"I order you!"* she screamed, hurling the goblet of wine at the bargemen, and balling her hands into fists and futilely hammering them and her heels against the floor, but they, being Northumberland's men, ignored her, and Guildford petulantly ordered her, "Do sit still, Jane. You're rocking the boat and will bring on the *mal de mar*—that means seasickness," he added helpfully.

"I *know* it means seasickness. I speak perfect French, you nit-wit!" Jane spat back at him. "And it's not *mal de mar.* It's *mal de mer!*"

"Who cares?" Guildford shrugged, selecting another sugared lemon from his comfit box. "It's not the spelling that matters, only the meaning. And everything I say is very meaningful; isn't that so, Mary?" He turned to his sister for confirmation.

"Yes, dear, *very* insightful *and* meaningful," she promptly agreed, and our little voyage continued in bored, curious, and angry silence, making the two hours it really took seem like an eternity for all of us.

It was after nightfall when we arrived at the erstwhile convent of Syon that the Duke of Northumberland had converted into a country estate for himself as it was situated conveniently near London, so he need never stray too far from the throne and the puppet king whose strings he pulled. We passed through a long, torchlit corridor in which the gray stone walls were covered with ornate gold-fringed tapestries. The house seemed curiously silent, which had the unnerving effect of making our footsteps sound inordinately loud, and strangely deserted for a nobleman's house; there seemed to be no one, not one single servant, about to welcome or attend us. Just as Guildford was complaining that such laxity deserved the horsewhip, a door at the end of the corridor swung open and the Duke of Northumberland emerged, smiling broadly, to welcome Jane as though she were the only one there and the rest of us were invisible. Guildford was so astonished he couldn't even speak.

I watched my sister shy warily away from her father-in-law with fear and mistrust filling her eyes. But he ignored this and led her on, as we tentatively and uncertainly followed, through the door, into a room lit by hundreds of candles with a dais and gilded chair, clearly a makeshift throne, beneath a gold fringed scarlet canopy, at the far end. It was obviously a presence chamber intended for someone great and important to receive visitors or hear petitions.

As soon as Jane entered there was a great rustling as men and women, high born nobles all in fine array, and men who were clearly members of the King's Council in somber black robes and the heavy golden chains of office they were so proud to wear, broke apart and moved to stand in a double row, facing each other, clearing a path leading up to the throne. As Jane passed them, the ladies curtsied low and the men knelt, all of them murmuring soft and reverent words such as "sovereign lady," "Your Grace," "Majesty," "Your Highness," and "our gracious queen."

Jane gasped and leapt back and stumbled against Guildford's chest. From his arms, Fluff gave a loud hiss and, claws bared, slashed an indignant snowy paw at Jane's head, tearing the black veil hanging from her hood. "Now see what you've done!" Guildford petulantly wailed. "You've upset Fluff!" Whereupon he shoved her forward, as his father rushed to reclaim her hand and, walking backward, guided her, like a man pulling on the bridle of the most recalcitrant mule, to the throne even as Jane, meek and pale-faced, shaking with fear, repeating, *"No, no, no!"* dug in her heels and tried to wrench free, turn, and run away.

But Guildford wouldn't let her; he stayed right behind her and made sure she kept moving forward. "You cannot run away from this honor. It is your destiny, Jane," he said, patting her shoulder. "But don't worry, you have me, and I shall be glad to share it with you. We're young and beautiful and everyone will love us, once we do something about those plain, drab clothes of yours, of course; they're *so* dreary, no wonder you're so melancholy. And I *really* think you should have a henna rinse as soon as possible. Picture us standing side by side in the sun, you with your red hair and me with my golden. The people shall worship and adore us!"

I wanted to go to her, but Mary Sidney grabbed my shoulder and drew me back to join the others and gestured for me to follow her example and curtsy. Farther down the line, I saw Kate, standing between the Earl of Pembroke, in his long black robe and heavy gold chain, and frail, flaxen-haired Berry clad head to toe in the most delicate blue. Kate looked radiant in a beautiful gold-braided garnet satin gown with her hair glowing and free-flowing, dancing down her back like a cascade of crackling flames. Feeling my eyes upon her, she leaned forward and looked down the line, and when she saw me, her face brightened and she fluttered her fingers in a merry little wave before, at Berry's nudging, straightening her back and assuming a properly dignified pose.

"As head of the Council," Northumberland gravely intoned as he pulled the reluctant and tearful Jane along, "I do now declare the death of his most blessed and gracious Majesty, King Edward VI . . ."

Jane gasped loudly and staggered, and for a moment I feared she would faint. I noticed then that she was the only one who seemed surprised by this news; no one else reacted at all. Then our parents, smiling broader than I had ever before seen them, came from where they had been standing nearest the dais, to embrace and kiss Jane's cheeks. Beaming as he embraced her, Father declared that he was so proud of her, that she was the shining star of the House of Grey, and even though he had been disappointed at her birth that she was not a boy, she had with this newly attained glory atoned for that more than a thousand times over.

Northumberland cleared his throat loudly, and our parents resumed their places, and, oblivious to Jane's astonishment and distress, he continued his speech.

"We have cause to rejoice for the virtuous and praiseworthy life that His Majesty hath led, as also for his very good death. Let us take comfort by praising his prudence and goodness, and for the very great care he hath taken of his kingdom at the close of his life, having prayed God to defend it from the rule of his evil sisters.

"His Majesty hath weighed well an Act of Parliament wherein it was already resolved that whosoever should acknowledge the Lady Mary or the Lady Elizabeth and receive them as heirs of the Crown should be had for traitors, one of them having formerly been disobedient to His Majesty's father, King Henry VIII, and also to himself concerning the true religion. Wherefore in no manner did His Grace wish that they should be his heirs, he being in every way able to disinherit them."

As Jane shrank back from him in horror, still breathlessly murmuring, "No, No, No!" Northumberland, with a firm, unshakable grip, forced her up the steps of the dais, with a little help from Guildford, who gave a hard push to her rump. Poor Jane would have fallen face-first into the purple velvet cushions had Northumberland not deftly caught her beneath her arms and spun her around and sat her down properly.

"His Majesty hath named Your Grace as the heir to the Crown of England," he announced, moving to stand beside the throne and gesturing for Guildford to do the same, as he calmly clamped a hand on Jane's shoulder when she attempted to bolt up from her unwanted seat. "Your sisters shall succeed you if you should happen to die without issue . . ."

With these words, Kate suddenly became more important than she had ever been in her life, or ever imagined she would be, except to the man who loved her. Everyone turned to look at her, to appraise her, with calculating and conniving eyes, considering how she could best serve their interests. Until Jane birthed a child, or if she proved barren, or her babies died, Kate would be the heir to the throne. From now on, people would praise, admire, and flatter her more than ever before when it was only for her beauty, and they would look to her for favors and beg her to intercede with Jane or bring their petitions to her attention. Kate was now a young woman of *great* importance, after Jane, the highest ranking lady in the land, and I sincerely hoped Berry would be able to help her bear the weight that was about to descend upon her pretty shoulders.

"This declaration hath been approved by all the lords of the Council, most of the peers, and all the judges of the land," Northumberland continued. "There is nothing wanting but Your Grace's *grateful*"—he paused meaningfully as his eyes bored into Jane's and his fingers dug deeper into the tender flesh of her shoulder—"acceptance of the high estate which God Almighty, the sovereign and disposer of all crowns and scepters—never to be sufficiently thanked by you for so great a mercy—hath advanced you to. Therefore you should *cheerfully*"—his fingers bit harder—"take upon you the name, title, and estate of Queen of England, receiving at our hands the first fruits of our humble duty, now tendered to you upon our knees"—he paused long enough to kneel—"which shortly will be paid to you by the rest of the kingdom . . ."

With a gesture, he brought the whole room to their knees and every voice swore to be loyal to and defend "even unto death, our sovereign lady, Queen Jane."

With a wrenching cry, Jane levered herself up from the throne, staggered forward, then fell in a dead faint. Northumberland rose swiftly and stood staring down at her with a grimace of distaste, while Guildford, jostling Fluff from one arm to the other, bent to pull her skirt down into a more modest drape "as only the king and her female attendants should ever see the Queen's garters." The highborn lords and ladies made a great show of pretending not to notice. Only Kate and I attempted to break from their ranks and rush to assist her, but Pembroke and Berry held Kate back, adamantly shaking their heads, while Mary Sidney restrained me.

"Guildford, how well you are looking, you look good enough to eat!" Father exclaimed, breaking the awkward silence as Jane lay, defenseless and unconscious, upon the dais, with her hood knocked askew and her gray skirts trailing down the steps like dirty rainwater.

Guildford simpered and preened and, stepping down from the dais to stand before Father, did a little turn to show off his buff-colored doublet and matching hat, both trimmed with layers of white and gold lace, gilt and silk braid, and lustrous gold and white pearls. "Isn't it *delicious?* The color is called marzipan; my tailor says it is London's latest fancy. He says I should *never* wear anything that doesn't make people want to *devour* me!"

"More apt words have never been uttered since God created the earth!" Father agreed. "Mmmm . . . *marzipan!* A most delicious creation!" His eyes closed and his mouth fell open, and for a moment he seemed lost in a fantasy world before he recovered himself. "I *dream* of you in marzipan! A gilt marzipan sculpture come to life! How you tempt and tease and torment me!"

Guildford smiled. "I am constantly amazed by how well you understand me!"

There was a groan from the dais as Jane slowly sat up, rubbing the back of her head where it had struck the dais. "No, no," she said groggily, massaging the small of her back as she maneuvered herself around to sit upon the top step, hugging her knees and rocking back and forth, "the Crown is not my right and pleaseth me not! The Lady Mary is the rightful heir!"

"Nay." Northumberland shook his head as he reached down to jerk Jane to her feet, like a puppet master pulling the strings. "Your Grace does *great* wrong to yourself and your house!"

"Shut up, Jane, and do as the Duke says! You stupid girl, by the way you're behaving, anyone would think you were being forced into the tooth-drawer's chair instead of being honored with a throne!" our lady-mother exclaimed. "It is your duty to obey the last wish of your cousin, King Edward, entrusting you on his deathbed with safeguarding his kingdom so that the light of the Reformed Faith should not be snuffed out as it surely would if Papist Mary came to the throne! Do you want the Pope's good shepherdess leading us all back to the Catholic fold, bringing the Spanish Inquisition to our shores, and burning those who resist? Is that what you *really* want? To end the enlightenment and go back to the dark ages, the Catholic creed, selling of indulgences, and Latin litanies? Enough of that, Hal! Here! Wipe that drool off your face!" she snapped angrily, impatiently thrusting her handkerchief at Father, as she moved swiftly past him to take Guildford's arm, and, rather forcefully I noticed, urge him back up onto the dais "to stand beside your lady, until such time as we can have another throne made for you, Your Grace."

"A gold one set with emeralds to accentuate my golden hair and green eyes," Guildford regally dictated as he resumed his place on the dais, pausing to give Jane a shove that sent her flopping back onto the velvet-cushioned throne with her feet flying up in the air, then artfully draped his arm across its jeweled back and adopted an elegant pose.

Jane sat frowning and floundering on the plump purple cushions, then, wiggling to the edge and dropping to her knees, announced that she would pray to the Lord for guidance.

While all stood around glowering and glaring at her, rolling their eyes, and tapping their toes upon the stone floor in mute impatience, Jane raised her hands to heaven and implored the Lord above to give her a sign and tell her what she should do.

"You stupid girl!" our lady-mother, weary of waiting, lost her temper and shouted. "His silence *is* a sign! He is telling you that you should obey the will of your parents as the Scriptures say and accept the throne He has seen fit to vouchsafe you!"

For a moment Jane wavered, swaying on her knees, teetering on the verge of another faint, and then she gave in and nodded. Northumberland and Guildford each bent down and clamped a hand around an arm and lifted her back onto the throne, and Jane announced to the assembled company, "If what hath been given to me is lawfully mine, and it is my duty and right to succeed to the throne, may Thy Divine Majesty aid and grant me such spirit and grace that I may govern this realm to Thy glory and service."

"Well said, well said, God save Queen Jane!" Father led the company in a round of applause. "Now let us have sweet wine and sugar wafers! My daughter, the Queen, commands it!" He clapped his hands to summon the servants who instantly, as though they had been lurking just outside waiting for this moment, filed in with well laden platters, trays of golden goblets, and flagons of wine to fill them.

After partaking of these refreshments, the assembly broke up, Northumberland hastily enjoining Jane to get a good night's rest as she would make her formal entry into London on the morrow, via barge instead of the customary procession through the city streets, lest the populace, being partial to King Henry's daughters, show themselves quarrelsome and unruly. "The royal apartments at the Tower are being made ready for you as we speak," he added, "and from there, in a fortnight, you will go to Westminster Abbey for your coronation." Then he called for Mrs. Tylney, whom he had chosen to assist Mrs. Ellen as Jane's tirewoman, and Lady Throckmorton, whom he had appointed as Jane's chief lady-in-waiting, and asked them to escort "Queen Jane" upstairs and put her to bed.

Before the words had even left Northumberland's mouth, Kate grabbed my hand and determinedly barged ahead of Mary Sidney, who tried to hold us back, and elbowed Mrs. Tylney aside. "As the Queen's sisters we have precedence over all except the King," she sweetly explained, flashing a bright smile. Then, crooking a finger to summon Mrs. Ellen, who had arrived with Guildford's servants and had been standing awestruck at the back of the room through it all, we graciously allowed Mrs. Tylney and Lady Throckmorton, each holding a branched candelabrum aloft to penetrate the gray gloom of the former nunnery, to lead the way upstairs.

Alone in Jane's bedchamber, we undressed our sister, peeling off her gray gown and stripping her down to her sweat-stained shift. We guided her to sit upon the bed while I knelt and removed her shoes and stockings, and Kate divested her of her hood and unpinned her hair, dropping the pins into Mrs. Tylney's waiting hand. Through it all, Jane sat wide-eyed and trembling, murmuring over and over, "I should not have accepted it, it is not my right, it is not my right, I should not have accepted it . . ."

After Mrs. Tylney had answered a knock upon the door and conveyed a message from Guildford that he would sleep apart from his wife tonight as he owed it to their subjects to look his best upon the morrow, we dismissed her, along with Lady Throckmorton and Mrs. Ellen, sending her to inform Berry and the Earl of Pembroke that Kate would bide a while with her sisters and they should return to Baynard's Castle and not tarry for her sake.

We tucked our sister into bed and lay one each on either side of her, hugging her shivering body between ours. Though no words were uttered, I knew that in the face of the frightening enormity that Jane faced, like a knight alone against a great and fierce dragon, all had been forgiven. Jane squeezed Kate's hand and willingly laid her head upon her shoulder, and Kate smiled as tears rolled down her face and pillowed her cheek against Jane's hair, and I smiled too, thinking that it was like the sun showing its bright face through the rain and whatever happened we would weather this unexpected storm together—"the brilliant one," "the beautiful one," and "the beastly little one."

6

The next morning found us all baking beneath the blazing July sun, squinting and shading our eyes against the brightness as spreading wet blossoms of sweat bloomed beneath the arms of our sumptuous new clothes. Slowly, in a grand yet sedate procession, we boarded the big gilded barge that would convey us to the Tower of London, where Jane and Guildford were to await their coronation. Behind us, other nobles swarmed onto their own barges, to form a flotilla that would accompany us. Not a breeze was blowing, and all the colorful gold and silver embroidered and fringed banners hung slack, limp and lifeless, as the trumpets blared seemingly with the sole purpose of deafening us. Oh what a sight we were! Sumptuous and sweaty, beautiful but bedraggled! When I remember us now, I don't know whether to laugh or cry—we were both comical and magnificent.

Our lady-mother walked proudly behind Jane, like a golden galleon in full, majestic sail, hung with a fortune in diamonds and arrayed from head to toe in cloth-of-gold that the sun struck with blinding brilliance. Beside her, Father, in gold-embellished wine-colored velvet, reverently followed Guildford, holding up the hem of his long, ground-sweeping green-satin-lined white velvet cloak embroidered with golden crowns, yellow gillyflowers, and gold and silver lilies and roses.

Our lady-mother had insisted upon being the one to carry Jane's heavy green and white velvet train, profusely embroidered with red and white Tudor roses and golden crowns, while my poor sister tottered along, reeling like a drunkard, balanced precariously upon the four-inch cork platform soles of the chopines we had strapped to her green velvet slippers at Northumberland's insistence, to raise her diminutive form so that the people could see her better. She staggered and stretched out her hands before her like a blind woman trying to feel her way along as she boarded the barge and made her way to the purple velvet-carpeted dais where she was to stand, with Guildford, and their closest attendants, on display for the teeming multitudes thronging the muddy banks of the Thames. She took her place beside her husband, frowning deeply and tugging at "Cousin Mary's bloody necklace." Our lady-mother had herself fastened it around Jane's neck, ignoring her complaints that it was too tight and bit painfully into her neck, just as she ignored Jane's insistence that the green velvet headdress laden with jewels was too heavy and the pins stabbed her scalp like a multitude of tiny daggers. "One must suffer to be beautiful, Jane," our lady-mother answered, slapping down the little white hands that tried to pluck out the pins she had only just put in.

Beside Jane, Guildford stood smiling and waving with restrained elegance at the crowd. Each golden curl was arranged to gleaming perfection, and his beautiful body was clad in gooseberry green hose that looked as though they had been painted on and a white velvet doublet embroidered with golden gillyflowers. While behind him, beside Father, stood a radiant, smiling Kate, the heir apparent until Jane bore her first child, arm in arm with her husband and father-in-law, beautiful in spring green velvet and cloth-of-silver, the emeralds they had given her blazing green fire on her throat, breast, fingers, and ears, and in her hair, its color a bold, flaming reminder of her Tudor heritage.

I peeked out from behind our lady-mother and smiled and waved at Kate, who nodded back at me and called, "You look *beautiful,* Mary!"

At first it had seemed very likely that I would be left behind, our lady-mother insisting that I would be mistaken for a fool, a jester, that my very presence would make a mockery of this momentous occasion, but Jane, exerting her will as Queen, announced that I would walk behind our lady-mother, and have the honor of carrying Jane's black velvet bound prayer book—the one she was never without and most often wore hanging from a chain or cord about her waist—upon a white satin pillow. "You shall be the torchbearer of the *true* religion, the Reformed Faith, Mary!" Jane announced. And when our lady-mother continued her protests, Jane adamantly declared, "I shall not go without *both* my sisters!" Father set aside his comfit box, brushed away the sugar clinging to his chest, and said there was really no cause for concern since I would be dressed with such opulence no one could possibly mistake me for a fool unless they were one themselves.

So I walked proudly behind my sister, the scarlet-infused sable of my hair plaited with pearls beneath a deep green velvet hood edged with emeralds resting in nests of silver braid. I wore a gown of white satin embroidered with ornate flourishes of silver vines and leaves blooming with dainty flowers made of emeralds and pearls, and over it a loose, silver-braided green velvet surcoat flowing gracefully over my hunched and twisted spine. In my hands, like a sacred relic, I carried my sister's prayer book lying stark black against a white pillow. Originally four long silk tassels dangled from each corner, but Jane, despite the appalled gasps of those surrounding us, ripped them off one by one, saying, "God's truth needs no adornment!"

Behind me and Kate followed Northumberland, his wife, and their elegantly arrayed brood of sons and daughters, and the spouses of those already married. Only Amy, to my great dismay, was absent. When I dared pluck Robert Dudley's cloak and timidly asked her whereabouts, he glared down at me from his haughty height and said she was in the country where she belonged and could not embarrass him or anyone who mattered. Then he turned away from me, barely managing to conceal the disgust in his dark eyes, directed both at me and the absent Amy, whose very existence by then was enough to kindle her husband's anger. The Dudleys were trailed by the gentlemen of the Council in their long black velvet robes, white neck ruffs, and gold chains of office, the highborn lords and ladies who had been appointed to serve the royal family, and dozens of servants in the royal Tudor green and white livery and the Dudleys' blue velvet emblazoned with their proud emblem of a bear clutching a ragged staff.

As we set sail, I noticed that the people who thronged the riverbanks were very glum and silent. None of them waved or cheered. There were a couple of lackluster cries of "God save her!" as though they were praying for Jane's deliverance from a cruel fate, not celebrating her ascension to England's throne. The truth was they didn't know Jane; she was a stranger to them, unlike Princesses Mary and Elizabeth, whom they had watched grow up and come to love. They distrusted Jane; they saw her, and, given the circumstances, with good reason, as Northumberland's puppet, a tool to set his own son upon the throne.

"They don't seem very happy," Jane worriedly observed.

"Nonsense!" Guildford scoffed. "They are simply awestruck by my beauty—I mean our beauty"—he laid a hand on Jane's arm which she contemptuously jerked away—"and my majestic presence, which, with a little effort I am sure you will, my queen, acquire in time. King Edward was a poor, scrawny lad, a pale, puny weakling," he continued. "And, though accounted a most handsome man in his youth, his sire, Henry VIII, was a hideous, monstrous mountain of bloated, rotting flesh, and bald as an egg beneath his cap too. I've heard it said that three goodly sized men could fit inside one of his doublets. But *we*"—Guildford smiled—"are young and beautiful! Look!" He waved a hand out to encompass the mute and scowling masses. "Some of them are weeping from the sheer joy of beholding me—I mean us. Thank you, my good people, thank you, your tears are more eloquent testament of your adoration than your words could ever be!" he called out to them and blew them a single kiss.

"You idiot, you addle-pated ninny, they *hate* us!" Jane snapped. "You can't even see it; you're so besotted with your own beauty! You empty-headed nincompoop! I *hate* you!"

"My dear wife," Guildford said, favoring her with an indulgent smile. "I am not so empty-headed that it has escaped my notice that you have just admitted that you find me beautiful, even though you tried to hide it amidst a volley of insults. There is too much passion in your hate for me to be deceived and not see through it to what it really is—you love me and you know it. Everyone does; I'm very lovable! You shouldn't be ashamed, you know, I am your husband, so it is quite all right, even expected, for you to love and adore me like the sun that lights up your dreary little life. Besides, many find me beautiful, and how could so many people possibly be wrong? Now smile and wave at our people, Jane, smile and wave!" he coaxed, lifting her limp hand by the wrist and waggling it in the air. "That's it! You're doing splendidly! *Smile!* I said *smile,* not pout and puff out your cheeks like you have a toothache. And no glowering at me as though your eyes were daggers you want to bury deep in my heart, when we all know it's my fleshly dagger you want buried deep inside you instead. But you won't admit it, not even to yourself. You're frightened by your desires and fighting to deny them, but 'tis a losing battle, and your love, and lust, for me shall in time be the victor. It's inevitable—I'm irresistible! Now *smile* and wave! Watch me and try to be as wonderful as I am. Smile and wave! Smile and wave!"

"You're wonderfully *dreadful!* Pompous, conceited, vain, and I hate you!" Jane retorted, stamping her foot and nearly falling, grimacing as she twisted her ankle in her unaccustomed chopines.

"Wonderfully *desirable,* you mean, Jane," Guildford calmly corrected as he caught her arm to help steady her. "Look out there, my wife"—he swept a hand over the silent crowds thronging the riverbanks—"there stand our subjects, and every one of them wishes they could make love to me; I can tell by their smoldering eyes and silent, reverential awe. Not everyone who wants me makes so bold as to tell me so; some of them are shy, but I can *always* tell. When you're as beautiful as I am, you become accustomed to being the unattainable object of desire to so many people; why, I couldn't even begin to count them even if I wanted to try! How they envy you to have me in your bed! That is what each and every one of them is thinking, you've incited the envy of all London, you lucky girl!"

Jane just glowered at Guildford and tried to pull her hand away. But, despite his seemingly delicate beauty, he maintained a masterful grip upon her wrist, forcing her limp hand to flutter up and down, until the barge reached the Tower just as a deafening hundred-gun salute was fired to welcome them.

"I hate you!" Jane hissed when he finally released her wrist. "I'll hate you until I die!"

"Methinks the lady doth protest too much!" Guildford simpered to his brothers, who snickered and nodded.

"I'll hate, detest, deplore, and despise you until you die!" Jane stamped her cumbersome cork-soled feet and screeched like one of the cantankerous, old women who sold fish in the marketplace, heedless of our lady-mother's swiftly delivered pinch and hissed reminder that such undignified behavior did not become a queen.

"Then you'll cry when you realize how much you love and miss me," Guildford serenely surmised to the tune of his brothers' encouraging laughter.

"Hmp!" Jane snorted and, gathering up her full skirts and thrusting her nose disdainfully high in the air, started past him. Her indignant exit however was ruined when her chopines threw her off balance and she began to fall. But Guildford acted quickly; he caught and swept her up into his arms, and, as all those aboard the barge gave a hearty cheer, he carried her ashore and through the Tower gates.

After Northumberland stepped forward and most presumptuously accepted the keys to the Tower, which were always given to the new monarch upon their arrival, Sir John Bridges, the Lieutenant of the Tower, smiling back over his shoulder at Jane and Guildford from time to time, thinking them no doubt a pretty and playful pair of young lovers, began leading the way to the White Tower, where the royal apartments were. Kate giggled and snatched a basket of rose petals that had been intended to carpet the ground the new king and queen would walk upon from a startled page boy and rushed after them, flinging handfuls of red and white petals in the air so that they wafted down in a perfumed rain over Guildford and Jane.

"Do stop it, Kate!" Jane snapped over Guildford's shoulder. "You're wasting perfectly good rose petals that could be made into cough syrup!"

"To give to the poor no doubt, pardon me, my bride, the *Protes-*

tant poor," Guildford jibed. "*Not* the Papists for we *loathe* them and do not want to ease their coughs and sore throats, better that they should die and burn in Hell. Is that not an apt assessment of your way of thinking, my love?"

"It's no laughing matter! It is our Christian duty to feed the hungry, clothe the naked, and give drink to the thirsty! But unless they mend their ways and turn their back upon the Roman Church, they deserve to be damned and burn for all eternity!" Jane retorted heatedly, shaking her head hard to dislodge the shower of petals that had just landed there courtesy of Kate.

"You put covering nakedness before quenching thirst," Guildford observed. "How interesting! I'm rather surprised you didn't put it before appeasing hunger as well. After all, we don't want people falling on their food like naked savages, do we? No, far better that they should be clothed first before they even think of food and drink. Is that not so, my queen? You see, I am endeavoring to understand how you think. I do everything else so well, I should hate to think that I would fail to be a good husband."

"It is not a jest!" Jane cried, looking as though she was about to burst into tears.

Guildford heaved an exaggeratedly languid sigh. "Life is a joke, Jane. Better to laugh through it than to cry! Don't you think I know that everyone laughs at me? But what they don't know is that *I* laugh *first!*"

Just for a moment, as I waddled along, struggling to keep up and not let Jane's black velvet prayer book slide off the slick white satin cushion, I thought I saw the ghost of sadness in Guildford's eyes, but it flitted past so tantalizingly swift, I was never *really* sure, though in my heart I always felt certain that I had in that moment caught a glimpse of Guildford Dudley's soul. But whatever it was, he shrugged it off and laughed and Kate gave a joyous whoop and flung another handful of rose petals over their heads.

Once in the royal apartments, Guildford tossed Jane onto the bed and called for wine. "I'm rather parched," he added as Jane floundered amidst her full skirts and cumbersome train and kicked her feet in the clunky cork chopines and screamed for Kate and me to "get these things off!" We hastened to unbuckle the leather straps only to have Jane seize them from our hands and fling them across the room. She was aiming for Guildford but hit the big silver mirror he was standing in front of instead. Guildford calmly stepped aside, utterly unfazed, sipping his wine as the mirror shattered. "You shouldn't have done that; that's seven years bad luck," he remarked. "Now your eyes shall have to be the mirror I see myself in."

With a scream, Jane flung herself back on the bed, arms and legs wide, and began kicking her feet and pummeling the bed with her fists just like a child in the throes of a tantrum. Then, all of a sudden, she heaved herself up, her face flushed crimson and chalky pale all at the same time and covered with a pearly sheen of sweat. Nearly falling, tripping over her skirts as she went, she began tearing at her clothes, ripping laces and fastenings, desperate to get them off, slapping Kate's hands away and knocking me down when we tried to assist her. "I'm burning up!" she screamed. "These sweltering velvets are a foretaste of the flames of Hell, lit by the bonfire of our vanity! God save me! I can *feel* the flames already, burning inside me, devouring me!"

Without even trying to unfasten the clasp, she tore Cousin Mary's necklace from her throat, cutting the back and side of her neck, and letting the broken links of gold and deep red rubies fall like tears of blood onto the floor. Kate tried to go to her and press a cloth over the cuts, but Jane snarled like a mad dog and shoved her away. Once she had stripped herself down to her shift and torn off her garters and stockings, Jane raced across the room to the washstand where the heavy white porcelain pitcher and basin sat, lifted the pitcher high, and poured the water down over her upraised face, sighing with ecstatic relief as it drenched the front of her shift and dripped down onto her bare toes to puddle on the floor.

A lusty gleam came into Guildford's eye as he saw how the water had plastered the thin white lawn shift to her form and turned it nigh transparent. He thrust his wine cup into Kate's hand and said in a regal tone, "Be gone! The King would be alone with his Queen!"

Kate giggled and grabbed my hand and as we pulled the door closed behind us we couldn't resist peeping around and catching a last glimpse of Guildford struggling to lift our kicking, squirming sister into his arms, and carry her, fighting and protesting all the while, back to the bed.

"Kiss me the way you did in the meadow at Chelsea, Jane!" he urged as Jane snatched up a pillow and bashed him over the head, rumpling his beautifully arranged curls and sending white feathers wafting down over them like snow.

"Oh ho!" Guildford chuckled as he lunged to pin her down again. "I thought I'd married a dove, but I see I am saddled with a scorpion instead! But, nay, she shall *not* sting me; I shall saddle and tame her instead!"

As Jane continued to struggle and thrash beneath him, Guildford went on as though they were a loving couple having a delightful breakfast table conversation.

"Father thinks it's high time we produced an heir, and I agree." He nodded, darting swiftly across the great, gold, damask-covered bed when Jane managed to break free and grabbing her ankles and pulling her back to him. "A beautiful golden-haired boy," he continued as he nonchalantly flipped my sister over, flat on her back, just like a pancake, then clambered atop her, wrestling to get hold of her wrists. "Or girl. If it's a boy we shall name him Prince Gillyflower, and if it's a girl . . . Princess Gillyflower! It has a certain charm, don't you think? I think we should name all our children after flowers, so they will surround us like a beautiful bouquet. Wouldn't that make a fine portrait! The two of us sitting most regally clad upon our thrones with our children clustered about us dressed in clothes embroidered and adorned with the flower they are named for! Of course, all our children will be blond like me; how could they even contemplate being anything else?"

"You're a fool, a vain, contemptible, empty-headed fool, and I hate you, I hate you, *I hate you!*" Jane screamed and kept screaming until Guildford leaned down and stopped her with a kiss, and we hastily shut the door and slumped against it, hugging each other and giggling.

"No, Jane, you hate *yourself* because you desire me and feel betrayed by your own flesh and lust," were the last words we heard Guildford say, muffled by the thick, ornately carved wood, and then it was all moans, groans, and cries of delight, and Jane's "I hate you!"s were uttered with a breathless fervor that exposed them for the lie they were.

"She loves him." Kate smiled as she sat back against the door and hugged her knees. "She *really* loves him!"

The next few days passed in a constant flurry. Our lady-mother decreed that Jane must now dress to suit her royal station and called in a whole army of dressmakers, seamstresses, and embroidery women, and Kate and I were there to attend our sister as she thrashed and pouted her way through the fittings that followed.

I tried to placate her by choosing fabrics and designs of a more subtle opulence, but only the dark, stark, and plain would satisfy Jane, and these our lady-mother slapped away with the most emphatic disdain. Vainly I offered up silks and damasks in aquatic hues of blues and greens and jewel vibrant sapphire and emerald satins and velvets, but Jane thrust them away.

"People expect elegance and glamour from their queen," I endeavored to explain as I helped lace a glum-faced Jane into a high-collared midnight blue satin with a yoke, kirtle, and under-sleeves of the same blue stitched with shimmering jet flowers. "They will be so disappointed if you appear before them in plain black or gray. The people take pride in their queen's jewels and gowns, at seeing her look her best."

But Jane simply replied that they should look to their souls instead "and endeavor to purge and wean themselves of their pride and vanity." When I tried to coax her into a misty gray velvet with a low square bodice bordered with moonstones and pearls, Jane snatched the scissors from the nearest seamstress and snipped the jewels away, insisting that they be replaced with a border of plain black silk braid and that the neckline be filled in with a simple white lawn partlet devoid of embroidery.

But we persevered, bringing her gowns, kirtles, and sleeves in shades of cinnamon, mulberry, walnut, crimson, purple, ruddy embers, moss green, and a beautiful tawny rose brocade trimmed with pearls and rabbit fur.

In the end, Jane threw up her hands and cried, "Do as you will! I want neither the Crown nor the regal wardrobe that goes with it, but no one cares what I want! So do as you will; you will anyway, no matter what I say!" With that she stood stoic and still and flung her arms wide, as though she were bracing herself to be nailed to a cross, and shut her eyes, and let the seamstresses swarm around her.

While in the room across from Jane's, Guildford submitted to the tailors' ministrations with a kingly grace. I found that he welcomed my opinions when I, passing the open door, timidly said that gold embroidery would suit that cinnamon velvet far better than crimson. "You have an eye for fashion, little gargoyle," Guildford complimented me. "Henceforth I want you here for all my fittings. Get her a comfortable chair. One that will ease her back, not a stool, you oaf!" he barked at his poor valet. Thus I passed many pleasant hours comfortably ensconced amongst the beautiful fabrics and trimmings I loved so, while my brother-in-law, handsome as a sun god, stood unabashedly naked before me and let the tailors drape him with swathes of shimmering, jewel-colored satins, silks, brocades, and velvets, and even sat beside me, with our heads together, as we examined the various buckles, buttons, and brooches the jewelers brought.

Guildford was particularly excited about his coronation clothes, but simply could not set his mind on a single color, much to the despair of the tailors, who tore at their hair as they had already started, then stopped, six coronation suits already. "I shall be *perfect* in purple!" he would enthuse, then later that same afternoon declare, "I shall be *ravishing* in red!" or the next morning upon awaking decide, "I shall be *glorious* in green!" Then, while taking a turn in the Tower gardens, he would turn to me, nibbling uncertainly at his lower lip, and inquire, "Or should it be blue? I am *always* becoming in blue, and Mother says I am most piquant in pink. Just think how *striking* I would be in silver with my hair *blazing* like gold in the sun!"

But I just smiled and said, "If ever an occasion called for gold, this is the one." And Guildford nodded and smiled and finally made up his mind.

"What better occasion than one's coronation to deck oneself entirely in gold? I was *made* for gold!" he cried. Then he went on to fill the tailors' hearts with joy when he told them to go ahead and finish the other suits that languished in various states of completion—"for one can never have too many clothes, and I intend to be the best dressed king England has ever seen; if she is not careful I shall even outshine my own queen.

"I shall *dazzle* them," he went on. "When they see me, my subjects shall think they've died and gone to heaven and an angel stands before them! And upon the steps of Westminster Abbey, when Jane and I emerge, hand in hand, crowned, with robes of ermine flowing from our shoulders, I shall sing!"

"No!" Suddenly Guildford's brothers—Ambrose, John, and Robert—who had spent the day sitting at a nearby table playing cards, bolted up, sending chairs crashing and cards flying, as they shoved past the tailors. Their mother, who often observed the fittings, sitting on the window seat smiling over her embroidery and nodding approvingly at every word Guildford uttered, gently made her way to Guildford's side and laid her hand lovingly upon his shoulder.

"Darling," the Duchess said gently, "you don't *really* want to waste your voice on the common rabble—dirty, uncouth people who are incapable of appreciating the gift God has given you—do you?"

"It seems almost sacrilegious to me," John ventured.

"Yes"—Ambrose nodded vigorously—"and in your ermine robes—think how hot and heavy they shall be—you are apt to overtax yourself!"

"Yes," Robert added emphatically, "and what if you were to faint from the heat, excitement, and strain of it all? The people might think that their new king is a weakling. And you know the Spaniards and the French are *always* watching; their ambassadors shall be right there watching your every move and recording every word you speak so the story would soon spread abroad. And if they think you are weak, it could mean *war!*"

"You are right." Guildford nodded sagely. "How fortunate I am to have the benefit of my family's loving wisdom to guide me. Very well, I shall wait until the banquet, when I have been divested of my ermine robes, had my brow massaged with rosewater, and eased my throat with cooling wine, and then I shall sing for our noble and refined guests, who are certain to appreciate the precious gift I shall give them." Then, before his loving family could object further, he clapped his hands and called for the tailors to resume his fitting.

"My son is the most beautiful boy in the world," the Duchess of Northumberland said softly, admiringly, as she watched Guildford being draped in gold.

"Until he opens his mouth," Ambrose, standing behind her, added glumly as his brothers nodded.

Later that afternoon, when Jane was seated morosely on her throne in the presence chamber, the Crown was brought to her, by the Royal Treasurer, the Marquis of Winchester, to ensure that it fitted and, as our lady-mother said when she preempted the honor of placing it on her daughter's head, "to see if it suits."

Jane shrank from it, as though she feared it, even as the Marquis spoke comfortingly, assuring her that, "Your Grace may take it without fear."

"It is not my right!" Jane whimpered, but her protests fell on deaf ears as she slouched lower, cringing away from it, whining piteously as she suffered it to be set upon her head. She barely tolerated it a moment before she put it from her, letting it fall with a great clanking clatter onto the stone floor.

The Marquis of Winchester gave an appalled gasp, and our lady-mother gave Jane's arm a vicious pinch.

Guildford picked the crown up and held it at arm's length, eyeing it critically. "And where is *my* crown?" he demanded. "You haven't even come to measure my head yet!" He turned accusing, icy green eyes on Winchester.

"I—I—one shall have to be made, Your Grace," he stammered.

"No!" Jane cut him off savagely, snatching the crown roughly from Guildford's hands and thrusting it blindly at the Treasurer. "A crown *you* shall *not* have! *You* shall *not* be king! Your father thought to play kingmaker when they forced me to marry you, but he shall not succeed! I shall create you a duke, but *nothing more!*"

"I will be made king by you and by Act of Parliament!" Guildford insisted. "I shall settle for nothing less. It is an insult, and most demeaning, for you to be queen and I, your husband and consort, only a duke!"

"You will never be king! *Never!*" Jane shouted.

"Oh yes, I will!" Guildford countered. "If you don't make me king, I'll . . ."

Those lords and ladies standing nearest watched avidly with bated breaths and crowded as close as they dared, eager to see who would win this battle of wills.

"You'll what?" Jane demanded, folding her arms across her chest and glaring hard at Guildford.

"If you don't make me king, I'll"—Guildford gave a tantalizing pause before he rushed on, throwing the words down like a challenge to a duel—"I'll leave you forever and go home to my mother!"

Jane turned slowly, stretched out her arm, and pointed. "There is the door, you lily-livered, mollycoddled milksop, go on back to your mother; I'm surprised that you've even been weaned!" With these words she turned her back on Guildford and flounced sulkily back to slouch sullen-faced upon her unwanted throne. When Mrs. Ellen, so long accustomed to the role of governess, leaned over and whispered a gentle reminder about ladylike posture, Jane glared daggers at her.

"Yes, my love," Guildford said icily, "but you know it would be much simpler if you just called me Guildford, but I daresay a girl who reads Plato in Greek can't help showing off and striving to impress everyone with her vocabulary in any language even when there's no need!" Then he was striding out the door, the very picture of elegant indignation.

A few moments later, hearing a commotion outside, Jane bolted from her throne and hurled herself at the open window, leaning so far out I feared she would fall and ran to be ready to wrap my arms around her legs and act as her anchor if need be. Adopting the most imperious tone I had ever heard come from her, Jane called down to the guards, ordering them to stop Guildford from leaving the Tower. "Although I have no need of my husband in my bed at night," she said scathingly, in a loud, clear voice that would have made the most potent man wither, "by day his place is by my side!"

When Guildford reappeared, Jane ran up to him, and, for a moment I thought she was going to launch herself at him with arms swinging. But instead, she stopped, panting angrily before him, and, with her chin thrust high, announced, "Your father forced me to assume this throne that is not mine by right and shall be my downfall, but you shall not desert me like a rat fleeing a sinking ship; when we sink—and we will!—we shall go down *together!* If my life is forfeit because of your father, yours shall not be spared!"

"Oh!" Guildford sighed. "I am touched beyond words that you want us to be together until the day we die; is that not what you are saying, my lady-wife? Really, we *must* teach you to say these things in a sweeter and more romantic and affectionate way, a more feminine manner that does not instantly call to mind salty-tongued sailors. Even though *I* can see through these angry and insulting words to the truth that is in your heart, some might be deceived and take you seriously. We don't want the foreign ambassadors reporting back to their masters that the King and Queen of England hate each other and quarrel like a sailor and a fishwife!"

The assembled lords and ladies chuckled softly at Guildford's jest.

"Oooh!" Jane seethed, balling her fists and stamping her feet in frustration, before she stormed into her bedchamber and slammed the door. A moment later she opened the door again, stuck her head out, and screeched, *"I hate you!"* before slamming it again.

"Careful, Jane!" Guildford called after her. "People will think we're in love!"

But the argument didn't end there. That night after Guildford had slipped naked between the perfumed silk sheets and snatched away Jane's beloved volume of Plato's *Phaedo* and flung it across the room, his mother barged in, dark braids bouncing indignantly down her back, in her lavender damask dressing gown and lace-frilled cap. She was carrying a sumptuous gold-tasseled and embroidered emerald velvet dressing gown and a pair of gold-slashed green velvet slippers that she had kept for hours warming before the fire.

"Come, Guildford!" she said, holding the dressing gown out for him to slip his arms into, then kneeling to slide his feet into the slippers as though he were a little child. "I, your loving mother, cannot permit you to share the bed of such an ungrateful, undutiful wife who denies you the kingship that you deserve, and, as her husband, is your right!"

"Yes, Mother." Guildford nodded dutifully.

"You selfish girl," she continued to berate Jane as Kate, Mrs. Ellen, and I rushed out, in our night robes and caps with our hair hanging down in braids, from the adjoining room where Jane had asked us to stay the night. She had felt unwell after dinner and feared her fever was returning and wanted us near in the hope that our presence would deter a scene such as this one. "Don't you know that you owe your crown to us?" the Duchess demanded. "If it had not been for my husband, you would not be queen at all! We have given you the most precious jewel of our family—Guildford! How can you be so ungrateful? To deny him the Crown! Look at him! If any man deserves a crown, it's Guildford!"

"A bright, shiny gold one with emeralds to accentuate my eyes," Guildford interjected. "I want *everyone* to say King Guildford is the brightest coin in the realm! And I want my profile minted on all the coins too! Well, all the *gold* ones," he amended. "You can have the silver ones, Jane, since after all, you are queen."

"Is there no end to your vanity?" Jane glared hard at him, then turned back to the Duchess and said frostily, "The Crown is not a plaything for boys and girls. When I look at Guildford, I see a man behaving like a petulant child who has been denied a toy he covets."

The Duchess looked angry enough to strike Jane, but somehow she held back, and instead spun on her heel and marched out, calling, "Come, Guildford!"

"Yes, Mother!" Guildford called, then turned back to Jane. "I will not be a duke, I will be king! If you are queen, it only stands to reason that I am king!" Then he impulsively flung wide his dressing gown, exposing his body in full, naked glory one last time before Jane's wide-open, astonished eyes, to remind her what she would be missing. "Don't look to have me again," he said cattily, closing his robe and knotting the sash tight, "unless I am crowned king. Only then will this jewel again be yours!" With a toss of his golden curls, and his perfect nose haughty high in the air, he followed his mother out the door and down the torch-lit corridor to the bedchamber she had ordered prepared for him.

Fluttering her hand over her heart, Kate sank down onto the foot of Jane's bed. "Oh my!" She shook her head again as if to clear it of the vision of Guildford's nakedness. "Jane, if I weren't already married . . . if I didn't love Berry so much . . . Oh, Jane! I would swap husbands with you in a heartbeat! Guildford is so very . . ."

"Vain, arrogant, childish, petulant, absurd, vapid, conceited, insufferable, ignorant, and empty-headed!" Jane unleashed a furious rush of words. "He's the worst kind of fool—the kind who thinks he isn't one! I hate him! If it were up to me, I would say, 'Take him!' but you're my sister, Kate, and I love you, and I wouldn't wish Guildford Dudley on my worst enemy! A knife in the eye is almost preferable to spending even one hour with him!"

"Well . . . yes"—Kate nodded slowly—"but he's *so* good-looking! Everyone has faults, Jane; can't you find it in your heart to be a little more tolerant and forgiving and try to regard his flaws as charming little foibles? After all, he's *so* good-looking!"

"No!" Jane said adamantly, lying back down and pounding her pillow hard. "I wanted my sisters here to comfort me, not to lecture me! Everyone is against me! No one cares about me and what I want and how I feel," she cried, and promptly burst into tears, and both Kate and I had to rush to comfort her while Mrs. Ellen went to prepare a soothing draught that would ease her into a quiet sleep.

For the rest of their marriage, Jane and Guildford would sleep apart no matter how hard Kate and I tried to bring them back together. Their hot pride consigned them each to a cold and lonely bed.

The days rolled slowly past, and I watched my sister's eyes grow dark shadowed and purple brown, mottled bruises blossom on her bare arms where she kept pinching herself in a vain attempt to wake herself up from the nightmare her life had become.

In her bedchamber, clad only in her shift—now the plainest garment she was allowed to wear—Jane would stand and stare at the many ornate clocks that the courtiers had, most curiously, given her as gifts. There were clocks of gold, clocks of silver, many beautifully enameled, and yet more clocks made of ebony, ivory, exquisitely painted porcelain, jade, carved stone, honey-hued oak, and gleaming, dark, varnished cherry. They sat on every suitable surface, covering every table and lined up in neat rows upon the mantels of the great stone fireplaces that warmed Jane's rooms. Her fingers would reach out and move the gilded hands around the ivory faces.

"If I were superstitious, I would take the gift of so many clocks as an omen that, for me, time is running out," she said, although she was only fifteen.

The illness that had beset her in the early days of her marriage had returned; her skin had begun to peel and itch again and her hair to fall from her scalp; she burned with a persistent fever, and her stomach ached both outside and within as though a great, taut knot were lodged there and rejected all nourishment, and her bowels became once again watery and impulsive. She took to her bed, growing weaker as she refused to eat, insisting that it was all the work of Northumberland, he was having her food laced with a slow-acting poison and the only way she could save her life was to continue to deny Guildford the Crown, for the moment she relented and consented her life would be over, stolen by a killing dose.

Though neither of us liked Northumberland, or doubted he would have any qualms about poisoning anyone who stood in his way, Kate and I were certain this was not true. This belief was born only of Jane's fear, and we tried to allay her suspicions by acting as her food tasters. But even though neither of us ever showed the slightest sign of sickness, still her fears would not perish. And the more Jane refused to eat, the sicker, and weaker, she became, turning away even from her beloved books, and only lifting her head to sign, without bothering to read, the papers the men from the Council laid before her. It was only when Kate began to bring her food prepared, under her strict supervision, from the kitchen at Baynard's Castle that Jane began to rally. Within a few days, she was able to leave her bed and sit at the head of the Council table again.

She began to make an effort, saying if she must be queen, then she would be one who made a *real* difference. She banged her fists and slapped her palms down on the Council table and spoke heatedly about using her power to break the yoke of Rome, to smash idolatry, the veneration of the Virgin Mary, and the whole panoply of Papist saints, of freeing the people from the shackles of popish rituals and Catholic ceremonies that dazzled the eyes and duped the soul, and with their insistence on Latin that only the educated could understand, deafened the majority to the *true* word of God. She vowed to let God's light shine clear, pure, bright, and true, not doused and diffused through the rosy stained glass of Catholicism, and to make a brave new world where people didn't pander to superstitions and worship the baker's bread, plaster saints, and jeweled crucifixes, or try to buy their way into heaven by purchasing indulgences. She said her reign must be for the greater good, that God, in His infinite wisdom, must have chosen her to be England's and the Reformed Faith's champion, as our cousin Mary, if she became queen, would most surely deliver England as a bridal gift to Spain and bring the Inquisition to these shores, and this might even lead to the very name of England being obliterated.

She also spoke about giving her royal patronage, monies, and aid to various charities in London to benefit poor widows and orphans and the deserving poor—by which she meant the Protestant poor or those willing to forsake Rome and embrace the Reformed Faith—and of sponsoring schools to nurture and encourage a love of learning in both boys and girls, and of doing something to remedy the debased currency that made English coins a joke throughout Europe where it was derisively referred to as "fairy money" as the coins themselves weren't worth the values stamped on them. Jane said and planned so much. But no one was really listening, except Guildford, who chimed in, "And don't forget clothing the naked, that's really important, oh and feeding the hungry, and giving drink to the thirsty of course, but, by all means, cover the naked first, Jane!"

The men on the Council let Jane talk but took their orders from Northumberland. The truth was, they only supported Jane's queenship out of cowardice and fear, because Northumberland had threatened and intimidated them, and they feared what he might do to them and their families if they opposed him. All of them, along with most of the nobility, had profited well by embracing the Reformed Religion. The spoils and plunder of the religious houses had made them all very rich. They had acquired wealth, lands, and the former monasteries and abbeys that stood on them, which they had either demolished to build anew or converted into lavish homes for themselves, and all the gold and silver plate that formerly adorned the altars now filled their cupboards, and precious jewels that had decorated shrines and reliquaries now adorned their persons. Thus they now lived in fear of the ascension of Mary, the punishments, reprisals, and loss that would surely follow as she endeavored to restore the religion she considered the only true one. Surely this included returning all properties she regarded as stolen, and the monks and nuns who had been beggared by the dissolution would be rich once more, while England's nobles would be considerably poorer, and once again the tithes would flow into the Pope's coffers, and the greedy cardinals would descend like a flock of avaricious red birds upon England again.

Inside the Tower, rumors reached us that the people were rallying around our cousin Mary, "the one true queen." Already she had amassed an army thirty thousand strong. Whenever I looked out the window, I saw the frantic preparations to mount a defense against her. The Tower teemed with armed men, and carts rolled in and out piled high with weaponry, ammunition, and other supplies to feed and equip an army. But Jane didn't know any of this; she had taken to her bed again, simmering with fever and trying to escape a life she didn't want into the sweet oblivion of sleep.

As soon as Jane was proclaimed Queen, Northumberland had sent his son Robert out, riding proud and arrogant, confident that he could never be defeated, at the head of an army of five hundred men to capture Princess Mary, but she eluded him. So it was imperative that someone else, someone more experienced, go, and bring her back to the Tower, a captive in chains. Northumberland wanted to send Father and had persuaded the Council that this was the wisest course. Northumberland knew that he was the glue holding this fragile reign together, and without him to threaten, domineer, and intimidate the Council their instinct for self-preservation would assert itself and they would flee to throw themselves on the mercy of Mary, even if they must forfeit their church spoils to save their lives.

Northumberland sent word, asking that Jane rise and receive the Council as they had business of the utmost importance to discuss with her; business that could not wait even one more day.

Mrs. Ellen and Mrs. Tylney tenderly raised her from her sickbed and covered her nightshift with a robe of ermine-bordered crimson velvet. They led her to sit in a gilded chair and bathed her face and hands with rosewater, while Kate brushed her hair. I brought a golden circlet for her head, but Jane mutely pushed it away. At a nod from Mrs. Ellen, I ran to let in the Council, but at the door I suddenly looked back. What a woebegone little figure she was! Sitting there, her bare toes barely brushing the floor, pale-faced and wretched, her eyes deep-sunken and dark-circled yet bloodshot and rimmed in red from weeping. Impulsively, I ran back and fetched a footstool and knelt to set her little white feet upon it. Only then did I open the door.

They strode in and, after kneeling to show their respect, stood around my sister's chair like a flock of blackbirds, solemn-faced in their long black robes. All except Guildford, who was the last to arrive, sauntering in, a vision in gold-decked rose satin with Fluff purring in his arms. After bowing curtly to Jane and dutifully kissing her limp, fever-damp hand, he went to sit on the window seat and amuse himself by dangling a string for Fluff to bat his paws at, appearing utterly indifferent to what the Council had to say.

When Northumberland told Jane that Father must leave, to lead her army and fight for her throne, Jane fell to weeping, insisting that "no, *we*"—for the first and only time I heard her invoke the royal *we*—"have need of him here! He must tarry here in our company!"

She sat there hunched in her chair, looking *so* small in that voluminous red robe, shuddering and sobbing, I thought assuredly those black-robed men were moved by pity. Father forced his way through their black-robed ranks and gathered Jane in his arms, holding her tight, as her shuddering gradually subsided, and her sobs turned to hiccups, assuring her that he would not go, that he would never leave her.

He drew his trusty comfit box from his doublet and gave Jane a piece of candied ginger to suck, and then he turned to address the Council. "Gentlemen," he announced, "I shall tarry here as my daughter desires and my Queen commands!"

They huddled together, voices rising high then dropping low, and thus it was decided that Northumberland should be the one to go. But it was not pity that moved them, it was just another one of those games that powerful men play, a canny maneuver to get Northumberland out of the way, to break his hold and set them free. No one cared what became of Jane.

Finally they bowed and, in solemn silence, filed out, with only Northumberland lingering long enough to glower at Jane and say, "You will regret this." But Jane, slumped weakly in her chair, seemed not to hear. And then he too was gone.

Father tenderly gathered Jane in his arms and lifted her from her chair. She laid her head gratefully upon his shoulder, and, still sucking on the thumb-sized nugget of crystallized ginger, he carried her back to bed. He laid her down and sat beside her, stroking her hair and telling her a story about a plain little oatcake who sat weeping at the roadside because all the other pastries were prettier than she was, crowned or filled with fruits and nuts, sprinkled with cinnamon, drizzled with honey or rich dollops of cream. Then along came a gingerbread minstrel with black currant eyes and a red currant smile, gaily adorned in red, gold, and green marzipan motley, skipping and prancing down the road, playing his flute and singing his song as he went his happy-go-lucky way. Seeing the oatcake damsel's distress, he knelt before her and gently asked, "Why do you weep?" When she sobbed out her wretched plight, he promised that she would be the most beautiful of them all. He took cream and dyed it pink with berry juice and slathered it upon her and decorated her with sliced strawberries, pale green gooseberries, and black currants. Then all the other pastries crowded around and proclaimed the little oatcake plain no more. She was so fair, in fact, that nothing would satisfy them but that she must become their queen.

"And the oatcake was so grateful to the gingerbread minstrel that she married him that very hour, with a mincemeat pie presiding as their minister and a pair of fruit suckets as witnesses, and made him her king. In a grand ceremony attended by all the pastries, comfits, custards, cakes, pies, wafers, and sweetmeats, the fat and wobbly red jelly archbishop replaced the gingerbread minstrel's motley marzipan fool's cap with a crown of gilded marzipan and gave him a cinnamon stick scepter and a sugarplum orb to hold, and he took his place proudly beside his queen as everyone cheered and threw curls of candied orange peel and raisins in the air. And they all lived happily ever after in their pink, spun sugar palace and had a dozen spice cake babies."

"Thank you, Father," Jane said sleepily as her eyes fluttered shut, and he bent to stroke back her hair and press a kiss onto her fevered brow. And then—Oh, Father!—he went and spoiled this tender moment by turning to Guildford, who had come to stand leaning against one of the gilded bedposts and listen to the story, hanging enthralled on every word.

"That is the *most beautiful* story I have *ever* heard!" he sighed, pressing a hand over his heart. "It makes me want . . . it makes me wish . . ."

"Yes?" Father asked eagerly as though his entire future hung upon Guildford's answer.

"It makes me wish that I had a piece of gingerbread right now!" Guildford exclaimed.

"Then let us away to the kitchen and see if we can find some," Father said, and gallantly gave his arm to Guildford. Like two naughty children, they hurried away together, with Father confiding to Guildford that he had made the cream that iced the oatcake pink in honor of the beautiful rose satin doublet Guildford was wearing, leaving Jane to slumber obliviously as her time as England's queen was fast running out.

After Northumberland rode out, regal as a king himself, at the head of his army, with his handsome dark-haired sons—Ambrose, John, and Robert—all of them in feathered helms and gleaming new silver breastplates, it all started to fall apart.

First the Treasurer absconded with all the gold, rushing to lay it at the feet of the woman he considered the rightful queen, and then the other councilors followed. They gathered in their black robes and gold chains around the Great Cross in Cheapside and filled their caps with coins and flung them high into the air. As the people scrambled for this bounty, the Council proclaimed Mary Tudor "the one true queen" and cried, "God save her!" Then they were off, racing as fast as their horses could carry them, to kneel before Mary and declare their loyalty unto death, insisting that they had only followed Northumberland and acknowledged the usurper Jane out of fear for their lives and the well-being of their families.

From her stronghold, the thick-walled, impregnable castle of

Framlingham, where Mother Nature provided a feminine touch to relieve the starkly martial atmosphere with golden irises blooming in vast profusion around the moat, Mary Tudor sat regal and straight-backed in her purple velvet, surrounded by tapestries depicting the life of Christ, and announced that she would give £1,000 worth of land to any man who captured Northumberland. Thus was the doom of the most unpopular man in England sealed; it was only a matter of time, and everyone knew it, even the man himself. On the march to capture Mary, Northumberland looked back and realized all was lost. He no longer had enough men to mount an attack; they had been slipping behind the hedgerows and scurrying into the deep gullies, making their way back home to their families or else deserting to Mary. He had no choice but to turn back. He dismissed his men and said, "Go where thou wilt," and walked boldly into the Cambridge marketplace. He filled his cap with all the gold coins he and his sons had upon them and flung the contents high in the air, as they all cried out, "God save Mary, the one true queen!"

The Dudley men were soon arrested and led back to London in chains as the people hissed and reviled them, shouting, "Death to the traitors!" They pelted them with horse turds scooped from the street, rotten eggs, and cabbages; some even brought their chamber pots to hurl the contents at the detested Dudleys, who walked tall and proud through this rain of filth as though they were being showered with gold and silver.

On the days when Jane, through sheer will, dragged herself from her bed, she sat listlessly, wan and feverish, upon her unwanted throne, decked in her undesired finery, tensely awaiting the end, watching the number of her attendants steadily dwindle. And Guildford, to whom she had contemptuously thrown the dukedom of Clarence, like a bone to a dog, kept to his own rooms, dining in state with his ducal coronet perched upon his golden head while his musicians played, having fittings with his tailors, and filling the Tower with an ungodly screeching as Maestro Cocozza diligently plucked out the scales on the ivory keys of the virginals.

Then it was all over. It lasted just nine days; people would later speak of it in awe as "the nine days' wonder." I remember so well that tense, hot day, July 19, 1553, when Jane, in gold-embroidered, spice-orange velvet, sat tensely upon her throne beneath the crimson canopy of estate, which seemed to weep golden tears, as all the bells in London rang, and an ecstatic nation, delirious with joy, danced in the streets, flung their hats high in the air, and cried, "Long live our good Queen Mary, long may she reign!"

Wine flowed freely in the conduits, strangers embraced strangers, and nine months later many babes would be born, and the female ones christened *Mary* in honor of the woman whose ascension they had been celebrating during the conception. Suddenly the great, carven double doors slammed open and Father rushed in, golden spurs jangling noisily on his high leather boots, a big, sticky bun clutched in each hand, and his mouth rimmed and auburn beard crusted thick with cinnamon and sugar like hoarfrost. At first we could not understand what he was saying and stared at him blankly, trying to puzzle out the mumbled jumble of pastry-muffled words. He quickly gobbled down one of the buns to free one hand and swallowed hard, wiping his mouth with his tawny velvet sleeve. He strode across the room to Jane. Ever one for a dramatic gesture, Father leapt up and ripped the canopy of estate down from over Jane's head. "You must put off your regal robes, my daughter, and content yourself with a private life," he said with a crestfallen sigh before turning to the remaining bun for consolation.

"I much more willingly put them off than I ever put them on," Jane answered. "Out of obedience to you and my lady-mother, I have grievously sinned. I most willingly relinquish the Crown."

But Father wasn't listening. He crammed the last bit of bun into his mouth and pulled a jet-beaded rosary from his pocket, and out he ran, waving it wildly in the air for all to see, ignoring Jane's plaintive question, uttered with a sense of great relief as she slumped back gratefully against the velvet cushions of her unwanted throne: "Father, may I go home now?"

But it was too late, Father was already gone, and I doubted he had even heard. I caught a glimpse of him from the window, dancing a joyful jig on Tower Green, waving his rosary in the air, and shouting, "God save Mary, the one *true* queen, long may she live and reign! Ho there, you, old woman by the gate! I'll have two more of those buns; I think they must be the best in London!"

When Guildford wandered in and was told what had just happened, he just shrugged. "Here today, gone tomorrow." He sighed.

"Now where is Maestro Cocozza? Now that the Devil is done tempting me with the lure of a golden crown, it's time for my music lesson. I must work even harder now. Since I am a duke's son, I have always had to work *very* hard, to prove myself, as no one takes me seriously, so this is *really* a blessing in disguise. Just think how much harder it would be if I were King; then they would only applaud out of politeness and to flatter me. I could croak like a frog or yowl like a cat in heat and they would still throw roses at my feet and tell me how wonderful I am. But I don't want that—I want them to *really mean it!* I want people to hear my voice and *weep!* Because it's so beautiful," he added as an afterthought, lest there be any misunderstanding.

While Guildford's voice was soaring zealously over the scales, displaying a great zest to conquer, Kate skipped in. She was wearing a new gown of "ashes and embers," which she twirled prettily to display. A pert, little, round, feathered hat of dark gray velvet trimmed with orange roses crowned her cascade of coppery curls, long ropes of black pearls swung and clacked about her neck all the way down to her waist, and her favorite fire opals flashed against her throat, breast, and fingers. She was carrying the most adorable little dog, a tawny bundle of fluff with eyes like black buttons and a turned-up tail that it fluttered like the most graceful plume. Kate had even tied an orange satin bow around his neck.

Jane was by then lying listlessly on her bed, stripped down to her shift, with a cold cloth draped over her brow, trying to ease her pounding head and cool the persistently simmering fever that stubbornly refused to leave her, but she raised her head long enough to chide Kate for being so pretentious. "Embers and ashes indeed!" she scoffed. "Why not just call it dark gray and orange since that's obviously what it is?"

But Kate just smiled, set down her little dog, and went to take Jane's hand.

"Are you all right?" she asked.

"I am glad to put off this regal burden as I never desired it," Jane answered. "Truly, by accepting it I showed a great want of prudence. But what's done is done," she said stoically. "We can never go back, only forward, and I must wait and face whatever punishment is decreed for me."

"Cousin Mary will understand that none of this was your doing," I tried to reassure her, telling her what I indeed believed as we had never known anything but kindness from our royal cousin. "You must write to her and tell her all that happened, that you never desired this and knew nothing of it beforehand, that you were forced to accept the Crown. Put the blame where it belongs, on Northumberland, and I am sure she will pardon you."

"Of course she will! It doesn't even bear brooding about!" Kate declared, hopping up and crossing the room to examine the glittering heaps of finery, some yet unfinished, others just waiting to be stored away with sachets of lavender in the great gilded and carved wardrobe chests.

Across the room, Kate and I exchanged glances. Each knew what the other was thinking. We smiled, and Kate darted back to grasp Jane's hand as I scrambled down from the bed and took the other one.

"Just one last time!" Kate said as we pulled Jane from the bed and led her to stand in the center of the room.

We acted as her handmaidens and bathed her naked body with rosewater before lowering a fresh lawn shift edged in gold embroidery over her head. While I knelt to roll gold-embroidered white stockings up Jane's limbs, tie her white satin garters below her knees, and ease her feet into a pair of new golden slippers, Kate laced her stays and fastened a padded bum roll around her narrow hips to lend a feminine fullness there and give her skirts a beautiful bell-like sway. Then came the petticoats, new, white, and crisp. And then . . . it was time for the dress! A pale, walnut-colored silk figured with grandiose gold arabesques, whirling and swirling everywhere, to beguile and bedazzle the eye, over a rich, diamond-latticed petticoat of gold upon gold. The full gold and white striped sleeves were slashed with cloth-of-gold and garnished with loops of pearls and gold and diamond clasps, with frills of golden lace at the wrists. It was the dress that would have been her coronation gown.

Kate pinned a gold and pearl filigree brooch to the low, square bodice. I handed Kate a necklace of golden dewberries interspersed with pearls, and she fastened it around Jane's neck, then, dipping into the jewel coffer herself, Kate chose a long, v-shaped gold necklace set with diamonds and beautiful deep green agates, each one carved with a star, that ended with a great tassel of Venice gold that hung almost to Jane's waist. Around her waist, I fastened a girdle of gold filigree and pearls with a beautiful ornament of gold and dangling pearls attached to the end, but Jane unclasped this and asked that I bring her black velvet-bound prayer book from the table beside her bed and attach it there instead, which I did. Then Jane obediently slipped her arms through a sleeveless robe of ermine-bordered gold brocade that Kate held up for her.

I brought a stool for Jane to sit upon, then Kate, whose nimble fingers had always been clever with coiffures, brushed Jane's still shedding hair, which still hung only a little ways past her shoulders, and braided it with gold ribbons and ropes of pearls, and rolled it up into a becoming little bun speared with diamond-tipped pins and crowned her with a delicate circlet of gold filigree and pearls.

When Jane was ready, the three of us went to stand before the big, silver looking glass that had been brought in to replace the one Jane had broken her first day in the Tower.

There we stood, Jane in her golden royal regalia, Kate in her fashionable embers and ashes gown and feathered hat, and me in my deep green damask blooming with teal roses.

"Go on," Kate prompted, giving Jane an encouraging nod.

Jane hesitated only a moment before she stepped up to the mirror and declared herself, "The brilliant one!"

Kate followed, with a sunny smile and a pert sashay of her hips. "The beautiful one!"

Then I stepped forward. "The beastly little one!"

We clung together and laughed until we wept. But Kate would not let us give in to sorrow.

"Come, Mary!" She rushed around to gather up the hem of Jane's heavy golden robe, and I hurried to help. Jane, casting her habitual solemnity aside, to be once again—just one last time!—a little girl playacting, pretending to be queen, raised her chin high and swept grandly out into the presence chamber and took her place upon the throne for what we all knew would be the last time.

Kate and I arranged the folds of her robe gracefully around her feet and sat on the top step of the dais, each of us reaching up to take one of Jane's hands, as we waited for the inevitable.

As the wild jubilation continued outside the windows, with a party on every street in London, joy spilling from every door and window, we sat and waited. Guildford peeped in for a moment then disappeared. We shared a glance, disdaining him for being a coward, for deserting us. But we misjudged him. A little while later he reappeared in his splendid gold coronation suit with a servant walking behind him, carrying a gilded chair. At a nod from Guildford, the man placed it on the dais next to Jane's throne and Guildford sat down. Kate smilingly relinquished Jane's hand, and Guildford took it, and this time Jane did not pull away.

Thus Sir John Bridges and the guards found us, sitting as though we were posing for our portrait. Very gently, he informed Jane and Guildford that they must vacate the royal apartments and come with him now.

Hand in hand, Jane and Guildford descended the dais, as grand as a king and queen about to lead the opening dance at a court ball, and as she swept past us both, Kate and I reached out to smooth and straighten the folds of her gold and ermine train. As they faced their guards, Guildford turned to Jane and leaned down and gently kissed her lips.

"I am sorry," he said, "for depriving you of the pleasure and consolation of my body these last days."

"That's quite all right," Jane answered, then added as a soft, hesitant afterthought, "I forgive you."

"Of course you do." Guildford nodded understandingly and smiled, still holding her hand, massaging the back of it with his thumb. "I'm much too beautiful for anyone to stay angry at for long."

Then the guards led them away. At the last moment, Jane shrugged off her royal robe. " 'Tis a great, cumbersome thing, and I shall not be needing it where I am going," she explained as she bunched it up as best she could and tossed it to Kate. In the open doorway, she paused and turned back and implored us to "please tell Mrs. Ellen to bring my books."

Then she was gone.

Mercifully, a dungeon was not our sister's destination. Speaking soft and gentle, to try to allay her fears, and gesturing for the guards to fall behind as they crossed the Tower Green, Sir John escorted her to the pleasant home of the equally pleasant gentleman gaoler,

Master Partridge, and his wife, which adjoined his own fine timbered residence, and possessed an excellent view so she "could sit by the window for hours and watch all the doings and comings and goings" at the Tower. She might even, if she liked, walk out to enjoy the gardens and fresh air or to feed the Tower ravens.

"A pack of greedy voracious pets they are, my lady," Sir John said fondly as one of the big, black birds lighted in his path and gave a great squawk before taking wing again. "You are to be treated well, my lady," he assured her, "and have naught to fear from any of us." He paused and added meaningfully, "We know 'twas all none of your doing, and though some would adjudge you a traitor, you are an innocent one and have every hope of receiving the Queen's pardon in due course; it's sure to come when things have settled some."

The Partridges were a well-named couple, plump, amiable, and smiling. Introducing themselves as "Nate and Nelly," they greeted Jane warmly as though she were their much-loved niece. Mrs. Partridge had even baked some apple tarts to welcome Jane and told her that she was "bound and determined to put some meat on your poor bones." Mrs. Ellen and Mrs. Tylney were already there. It turned out that there was no need for us to convey Jane's message; they had anticipated her desire and were already busily unpacking the plain garb that Jane preferred, putting her beloved books on the shelves, and arranging her desk before the window, so she would have the best light for writing. Nelly Partridge herself had already made up the bed fresh with fat, goose down pillows and a bright quilt "to help chase out any gloom from the room."

Poor Guildford was not so fortunate; he was taken to the Beauchamp Tower, albeit to a commodious and comfortable cell that he was to share with his brothers, and the Dudleys' wealth afforded them many luxuries denied to common prisoners. Guildford was even allowed to have Fluff and all his fine clothes with him, and many delicacies and fine wines for their table. They even had apples to feed to the porcupines in the Tower menagerie, to which the brothers had taken a fancy.

There was no more we could do at the Tower, so we hired a barge to take us back to Baynard's Castle. Kate kissed me and said,

"All will be well," and even let me hold her little dog, whose name she said was Cinnamon.

But all would *not* be well, and even more unpleasant news awaited us at Baynard's Castle. A maid met us at the door and said we must go straight in to the earl's study. The Earl of Pembroke had, with the rest of the Council, thrown a cap of gold in the air and declared himself all for Mary, and he would not suffer his only son to be bound in "pernicious wedlock with the daughter and sister of traitors." Kate's marriage—fortuitously yet unconsummated—must be annulled right away. Her things had already been packed and sent on to Suffolk House, and all her animals too, and she was to be turned out, to go to the devil or wherever pleased her; it was a matter of complete indifference to her formerly fond and indulgent father-in-law, who now stood there staring at her as though she were a loathsome, leprous thing he could not bear the sight of.

With a heartrending cry that brought tears to my eyes, Kate fell on her knees and clung to him, sobbing out her love for Berry and begging that he let her stay. Spying her husband, watching covertly from behind a velvet curtain, Kate reached out an entreating hand to him, but he hadn't the courage to defy his father and, with tears in his eyes, and mouthing the words "I'm sorry!" Berry turned away.

"Kate"—I pulled at her and pleaded—"do not so humble and demean yourself before this man; neither he nor his cowardly, milksop son are worth it!"

But Kate would not hear or heed me, and her tears fell on the Earl of Pembroke's shoes like rain as she groveled shamelessly, forgetting all pride and thinking only of love.

In desperation, she lunged up and grabbed Berry's arm, forcing him to stand with her before his father.

"You cannot annul our marriage," she said boldly, lying blatantly. "It has been consummated. We defied Northumberland's edict, and I may be with child." She laid a hand on her belly. "Surely you would not want to risk your grandson being born a bastard? Berry is frail and sickly, and you have no other son, or daughter either, so unless he gets a son, your line will die with you!"

Oh, Kate! My jaw dropped and I shook my head as I stood there, dumbfounded. I could not believe what she was doing. What did she hope to gain by this deception? Time to drag it out and be hurt all the more? A slow torture instead of a swift end? She could not hope to have the chance to get Berry alone and make the lie true. If he decided to be patient and wait to see if Kate bled, Pembroke would be sure to have them watched even more vigilantly than ever before. *Stop, Kate, stop!* I wanted to shake her and shout. *You are fighting a losing battle that you cannot win! Recollect your pride and leave this sorry wretch and his sniveling boy with your head held high! You deserve better and you can find it!*

The Earl of Pembroke took a step forward and stared straight into the stormy ocean of Kate's blue gray eyes, still glimmering wet with the tears of her heart.

To her credit, Kate proved herself to have a better card face than our father ever did. He scrutinized her hard, but Kate held her ground, her face inscrutable, and in the end he could not say whether she was bluffing. She had succeeded in planting the seed of uncertainty . . . for what little it was worth.

"Is this true?" He turned to Berry.

"I—I—" the young man hung his head and stammered, his blushing face proving the aptness of his nickname. "I—do not know! *Please,* Father, do not ask me anymore; I cannot bear it!" Then he burst into tears, covered his face with his hands, and ran out, weeping volubly, from fear or heartbreak or both I could not rightly say.

"Very well"—Pembroke nodded—"we shall see." He summoned a servant and bade him take Kate upstairs, to her former bedchamber, now stripped bare of her belongings, and station men outside her door to ensure that she made no attempt to leave and no one entered without his permission.

I stepped forward then, clutching Kate's hand, determined not to let go. "Where Kate goes I go!"

Pembroke snorted and shrugged. "What care I, little grotesque? You are of no importance, an ugly, worthless thing that can neither help nor hinder." He gestured impatiently for us both to leave his study and mount the stairs to the room that would be our prison until he set us free, whenever that would be.

Did an hour pass or two or even three? I could not say. We could have looked at the clock, of course, but somehow this didn't occur to us. Kate and I lay silently on her bed, with her little dog between us, staring at the ceiling and holding hands, tensely awaiting we knew not what. Did he mean to keep us here until her monthly bleeding proved the lie? Or had he something more sinister in mind?

Finally the door swung open and Pembroke came in accompanied by the most bizarre creature I had ever seen. I sat up and blinked and rubbed my eyes, but I was not dreaming. Standing at the foot of the bed staring at us with gold-lidded evil eyes was a filthy hag arrayed in even filthier finery, made of hundreds of colorful and glittery scraps of rich materials haphazardly stitched and patched together to form a jagged, ragged rainbow motley. Her face was painted like a harlot's, bold scarlet outlining a mouth filled with blackened stumps. She wore her dingy, dirty, graying hair trailing down her back in a gay messy tangle of little braids plaited with silken ribbons every color of the rainbow, gold and silver tassels, and even tiny bells. Golden hoops drooped from her ears, and stacks of clanking gold bangles adorned her wrists and ankles. The nails on her bare feet were long and yellow with sharp tips like daggers—did she file them to create those sharp points? I marveled that walking unshod on the earth or stone floors hadn't blunted or broken them. Even before Pembroke introduced her as Kate's "old friend, Madame Astarte" I knew who she was; I recognized her from Kate's description. But how did *he* know? Both Kate and I started and exchanged puzzled looks. Had he had Kate followed?

But there wasn't time to ponder it. From amidst the filthy folds of her skirt of many colors, Madame Astarte drew a bottle that looked to be filled with black bile.

With a swift movement, she grasped Kate's head, forcing it back, and put the bottle to her lips. "Open or I'll break those pretty pearly teeth!" she threatened.

With a shriek, I launched myself across the bed at that wicked Circe, clawing and biting with all my might.

"Run, Kate, run!" I cried, but Pembroke barked an order to the men outside the door to stop her as he pulled me off the witch and threw me contemptuously into the corner. I heard Kate scream my name, and she started to run to me, but Pembroke caught her, and she kicked and flailed as he bore her back to the bed and held her as he shouted for Madame Astarte to do her business fast.

My head had struck the wall, and for a moment or minutes, I sat there dazed and stunned watching through a starry dazzle as, with sharp scarlet-painted nails digging into Kate's chin, drawing pinpricks of blood, Madame Astarte forced my sister to drain the evil bottle to the dregs.

"Drink this, my pretty," she cackled as Kate thrashed and kicked, helpless against the two of them. "It will void your womb if there is anything in it. If not, I pity you the more for the cramps it will make claw and grip you from within until you wish you are dead."

And then it was over. They were gone. The door was shut, locked from without, and we were alone again. Kate ran to me and knelt beside me, clasping my face, urgently imploring me to speak to her. I groaned and sat up straight, assuring her I was fine, even as I noted the fierce ache in my spine where my hunched back had struck the wall.

"Can you stand?" Kate asked, helping me to slowly rise, but then she gave a great gasp and doubled over, clutching her stomach. "Hurry, the chamber pot, Mary!" she cried as the pain brought her to her knees.

The agony my Kate endured! She was not with child, and there was little within her bowels to expel, and once it was all gone the cramps continued, sharp as knives, making her gasp and cry out, and all I could do was hold her, bathe her face, and be there for her. I sang and told her stories, trying to help her mind rise above the pain that gripped her tight like an iron-gloved hand squeezing inside her, determined to wring her dry. I wanted to undress her to make her more comfortable, but she slapped my hands away, even as the beautiful embers and ashes gown grew heavy and soaked with sweat, wrinkled and twisted by the agonized jerking and writhing of her limbs. No, she said, she wanted nothing to delay our departure, she wanted to be ready the very instant we were able to go.

The sun set, and the stars came out to twinkle then faded away. With the first light of dawn, Kate took a deep breath, sat up, cried out, and doubled over again. I scrambled across the bed and tried to make her lie down again, but Kate shoved my hand away. Slowly she straightened her spine and, taking a deep breath again, tried to stand. She failed and fell down beside the bed, yet she would not stop; determinedly she dragged herself across the floor and hammered on the door.

She was kneeling there, hunched and shivering, when Pembroke appeared. She said not a word, but her eyes bored into his, burning with hatred. The silence was answer enough to suit him, and he stepped aside, gesturing that we were free to go. I ran to help Kate as, using the doorjamb, she pulled herself up. I let her lean on me, to give her what support I could, praying that my frail, crooked body did not buckle beneath her weight. I was terrified that she would fall down the stairs, hindered by the heavy, damp, bedraggled skirts and petticoats that tangled about her limbs. I wanted to turn back, swallow my pride and implore Pembroke to be kind and carry her down, or summon a servant to assist her, but Kate hissed at me through her pain-clenched teeth, *"Don't you dare!"*

Gripping tight the banister, she made her way slowly down and stumbled out the front door, which led out to the street; better that than risk the damp, slick stone of the water stairs. I left her sitting on the front steps, gasping, hugging her knees, gritting her teeth against the pain, and rocking back and forth, while I ran to hire a coach to take us to our parents' London house. The coachman was kind, and seeing Kate's distress, he came down from his box and carried her and set her gently inside his battered old coach that stank of urine and sour wine. But Kate was so grateful for his kindness that when we reached Suffolk House and he had carried her inside, where Henny waited to cluck over her, she pulled the wedding ring from her finger and laid it in his coarse, leathery palm with a fervent *"Thank you!"* Of course a coin would have sufficed, but such an extravagant gesture was typical of Kate. "My shining golden moment of proud defeat!" she said with a bitter, biting flippancy as she took one last look at the gold ring before she fell fainting at our feet.

Shortly afterward we received a document attesting to the fact that Kate's marriage had been formally dissolved. The same would soon happen to me, and I would find myself shunned and set aside, for not even Lord Wilton, the great war hero who had survived the Battle of Pinkie Cleugh, was brave enough to marry a traitor's daughter. Our betrothal, never publicly announced, was swiftly dissolved, and many never even knew of it until it was all over. They would shake their heads and sigh, and some would even presume to pat my shoulder and condole with me over my lost opportunity. But the truth was I didn't care; there was no love lost for me to lament over. I had never been one to wear my heart on my sleeve as ripe pluckings for any handsome gallant, much less a hideously disfigured braggart old enough to be my father living on his laurels and gory glory. I would sooner not marry at all than have a man who patted me on the head like a faithful spaniel when I fetched his slippers and plumped the pillows behind his back as he sat by the fire, growing ever more cantankerous and whiny, and endlessly reliving his old campaigns until I wanted to scream and seize one of his swords off the wall and run him through myself.

"Though we never met, we are well rid of each other," I said, and everyone commended me for putting on a brave face to cover my supposed disappointment.

☙ 7 ☙

Our lady-mother would not allow us to be tainted by Jane's disgrace. "When a fox is caught in a trap sometimes it chews off its own leg to save its life," she said savagely as she shouted to Father, complaining of boredom in his bedchamber across the hall, to stay in bed. "*Feign* fearing for your life, Hal, if you haven't the wit to do it in truth! And enjoy that soft, comfortable bed while you can, for tomorrow you may be in the Tower if I cannot persuade the Queen to clemency!" She added this as she elbowed Henny aside and gave Kate's corset laces a vicious yank that made my sister, standing there clinging to the bedpost as though for dear life, wince and cry out, while I, in my new blue black velvet, sat and watched in silence, nervously fingering the sapphire and diamond crucifix our lady-mother had herself fastened about my neck while Hetty braided my hair with ropes of pearls.

But though I sat mute and pliant, inside my heart was *raging.* It was all so unfair! We were going to court to plead for our family's fortune and Father's life, but when I asked our lady-mother what about Jane, she sternly rebuked me and cautioned me not to mention my sister's name or refer to her at all even with the most subtle hint before our cousin, the Queen. It wasn't right! Jane was to be sacrificed, when she had done naught but obey our parents and her father-in-law. She had never wanted the Crown; she had been all along the pawn of ambitious, greedy, power hungry men, all of whom had turned tail and run to our royal cousin and saved themselves, and now Jane was a prisoner with no one to speak on her behalf. It wasn't fair! She amongst them all, even our beloved father, was the one most deserving of mercy!

"Pinch your cheeks to give them color!" our lady-mother hissed in Kate's ear as she gave the laces another sharp tug that I feared would snap Kate in half then knotted them tight. "Remember to smile, albeit demurely; you must subdue your sparkle," she counseled, though somehow, looking at Kate's pale and sickly face, I didn't think that would be a problem. "Anything more risks appearing unsuitably brazen given your current circumstances."

My sister teetered and seemed on the verge of fainting as she clung even tighter to the gilded bedpost. Yet she whispered softly, obediently, "Yes, my lady-mother." My poor Kate, all the fight and spirit seemed to have been wrung out of her by that vile black potion; she was so quiet now, so listless and pale, so caught up in her own woes that I feared she too had forgotten about Jane.

But our lady-mother didn't care how weak and wobbly Kate was, that she was loathe to go to court and appear before the all-appraising eyes as a divorced and disgraced woman, and even perchance see her former husband and father-in-law basking in the Queen's favor while we knelt before her as rosary-clutching, crucifix-wearing penitents.

"Too pale! You're whiter than a bedsheet, my girl; that will *never* do!" Our lady-mother sighed and stormed out to fetch her own rouge pot, pausing to shout again at Father, who was now whining petulantly for sugared almonds, while Kate, now arrayed in gold-flowered brocade the color of dried blood, sank down onto the foot of the bed and let Henny fasten a diamond crucifix about her throat and brush her beautiful hair, adorning it with diamond and pearl flowered combs, but otherwise leaving it unbound like a virgin's—our lady-mother's way of advertising the fact that Kate was again available and still a good and, most important of all, an *unsullied* catch—not just barely used and like a virgin but a virgin indeed.

"Remember who you are!" our lady-mother said fiercely as she

gripped Kate's chin hard and began to paint her lips and cheeks. "Queen Mary is seven years past thirty. Her womb has been the bane of her existence, bringing her great pain every month since she first began to bleed—'strangulation of the womb' the doctors call it—and even if she should overcome her old maid's timidity and marry, until she bears a son, *you* are heiress to the throne! She cannot abide Elizabeth! So stop moping and hold your head up high, and I *promise* you, a day *will* come, when that weak, sniveling boy will *beg* you to take *him* back, and you can gaze at him with *withering* scorn and say, *Nay!* You shall have better, my love, far better than the Earl of Pembroke's puny son! The boy's character is as weak as his knees, and the same is probably true of his cock too! You married a jelly, but trust me, my Kate, you are well rid of him! *I know*—I married a jelly too, that ninny lying across the hall braying like an ass for sugared almonds when his very life is at stake, but *I* made it work for me. Take that lesson to heart, Kate, though the Lord and Law teach us that the husband rules and it is the wife's duty to obey his every wish and whim, I as your mother tell you that you, as a wife, *must always* find a way to gain the upper hand; you will be lost and miserable if you don't! Now smile!" she commanded and held up the mermaid hand mirror.

"Look at yourself! Such beauty should never even know what sorrow means! Your beauty is your fortune, my love; you can make men bleed and beg for you and use them as you will and never lift a finger even if they think that *you* are *their* pretty plaything; learn from this misfortune, my daughter, and use your power well while you can; beauty does not last forever, and one day you'll wake up and discover that without your beauty you are *nothing!*"

"Yes, my lady-mother." Kate nodded, staring straight ahead, her eyes blind and unseeing, and I was certain she had not heard a word. Thankfully, our lady-mother, already primping before the looking glass in her garish salmon velvet spangled with gold beads and diamonds, and trimmed with red fox fur, wasn't paying attention; she was preoccupied with stuffing a stray strand of Tudor red hair back into the golden net, fluffing the orange, pink, and white plumes on her velvet hat, and slathering yet more rouge on her cheeks, so Kate's docile answer was enough to content her.

I don't know how we did it. I don't know how we found the

strength to walk into the presence chamber, a parade of penitents in finery instead of sackcloth and ashes, with censorious eyes glaring at us from all sides, and kneel humbly before our royal cousin. Kate faltered and almost fainted when we passed the Earl of Pembroke, who stared straight ahead and through her like glass, and watery-eyed Berry, whose doughy belly made him look like a blueberry in his blue velvet doublet, but at least he had the decency to blush and hang his head in shame. But I held Kate's hand tight, letting her feel the bite of my nails, willing her to feel my own strength flowing into her and stay on her feet. She squeezed back and gave me a grateful little smile, and we continued our slow, torturous progress, following our lady-mother up to the gilded throne upon the crimson-carpeted dais where our royal cousin sat gowned in regal purple beneath the gold-fringed canopy of estate, squinting her shortsighted eyes at us.

It all passed in a blur that, when we discussed it later, neither Kate nor I could recall clearly except in a few sharp fragments like shards of glass picked up from the muddy river silt. I remember kneeling several paces behind our lady-mother and staring entranced at her gold-spurred bloodred Spanish leather boots as she knelt laboriously, with creaking, protesting stays that made those standing nearest snigger, before our royal cousin. Kate recalled our lady-mother's sausage-fat pink fingers twisting and tugging at the numerous chains of diamonds and ropes of pearls that encircled her thick, florid neck, pointedly caressing the most prominent jewel of all—a great diamond crucifix as large as a man's hand, while her other hand clutched the pink coral rosary at her waist. She *swore* we had seen the error of our ways and embraced the *true* faith and pleaded for Father's life, claiming that Northumberland had secretly administered a slow-acting poison, to influence Father's behavior and put him in fear of his life; compelling him to bend his will to his own if he hoped to attain the antidote and live. And our poor father yet languished, our lady-mother said, an ailing and befuddled invalid uncertain of his life, with a priest's comforting presence keeping vigil at his bedside, aiding in his prayers, which he uttered fervently every waking moment, imploring God to spare him and that Her Majesty Queen Mary find it in her heart to be merciful to her loyal and loving kinsman who, though he had never wavered in his love for her, had been led most grievously astray by the Devil's henchman Northumberland.

"My husband, as Your Majesty well knows," our lady-mother said apologetically, "is a weak and foolish man, and, alas, he fell into the power of Satan's emissary—the evil Northumberland. I tried, with a wife's gentle persuasions to dissuade him, but alas"—she sighed—"it is a wife's duty to obey her husband and be guided by him, not to counsel him or try to usurp his power."

I choked on my laughter and had to quickly feign a sneeze when she turned and glared furiously at me.

I remember our proud lady-mother, sweating and red-faced, crawling laboriously on her fat knees up the stairs of the dais to kiss the hem of Cousin Mary's purple velvet gown and then receive her embrace and a kiss on each cheek. Then Kate and I were there, in our cousin's arms, feeling her soft velvet sleeves enfolding us like a pair of purple wings, and the hot yet dry caress of her lips brushing our cheeks and the overpowering odor of her musky perfume mingling with her sweat on that hot July day.

"We are family," the new queen magnanimously declared, "and all is forgiven!" Though all, I would later discover, didn't include Jane; she had been conveniently forgotten, like dust a lazy servant had swept under the grand Turkey carpet.

I gazed up into our royal cousin's pale, pinched, and lined face, half blinded by the rainbow of jewels bordering the purple velvet hood that crowned her faded hair as the sun poured in through the high arched windows and struck them, and prayed God that she could read my mind as I gripped her hands and silently beseeched her to be kind and merciful to Jane.

But Cousin Mary merely smiled and bent down to pat my cheek as she whispered, "You need not be in awe of me now that I am queen, little cousin; you are still as dear to me as ever." Then Kate was in her arms, as Cousin Mary crooned over her and caressed her face—"so pale, my pretty Kate!"—and condoled with her over the loss of her husband and, taking the pearl rosary that hung from Kate's waist and wrapping it comfortingly around her pale, bloodless fingers, promised that God would provide a balm for her wounds if she asked Him to. "*Pray,* Cousin Kate, *pray,* and in God's love you will find a *greater* consolation than in the arms of Pembroke's lad."

Kate nodded blankly and answered softly with a dazed, "Yes, Your Majesty." She looked ready to fall over in a faint, and I quickly moved to help guide her down the dais as we retreated, backward, curtsying thrice as royal etiquette demanded.

Cousin Mary said more, but neither Kate nor I remembered. We felt as if we were watching it all from under water and the babbling current muffled our ears; it all seemed so foreign and far away as though it were happening to someone else and the scene was being played out in a foreign language that neither of us could comprehend. And then it was all over, and we were home again, back at Suffolk House, and our lady-mother was calling in the dressmakers again, to outfit Kate and me for court, where we were to go and live and serve our gracious queen as ladies of the bedchamber, and at the same time sternly shaking a finger at Father, who had padded in in his velvet slippers with his comfit box in hand and his valet in tow bearing a gilded tray groaning with fruit and cream-filled pastries and pretty marzipan cakes. He sat pale and shivering by the fire in a cinnamon and white, swirled, brocade dressing gown, listing to our lady-mother insisting that he must, when questioned, say that he did not remember, that he had been ill, and in fear—*deadly* fear—for his life, and that he must lay *all* the blame upon Northumberland and say that he had given him poison that had made him follow docile as a dog wherever he led, even unto the folly of committing high treason.

"Yes, dear." Father nodded distractedly as he nibbled on a piece of marzipan.

"But what about Jane?" I asked.

"Shut up, Mary!" our lady-mother hissed as she swung around and dealt me such a slap that I, sitting on the foot of Kate's bed, fell backward, my legs actually flying up over my head, in a somersault that would have been comic had it all not been so very tragic.

Seeing our woebegone, tear-streaked faces, Father came and sat down between us. He gave us each a sugar roll and put his arms around us.

"There, there"—he patted our shoulders—"it's not so bad;

think of all the wonderful pastries and sweetmeats you shall have to eat at court! Cakes filled with berries in wine and slathered with rich cream, honeyed pear tarts in flaky golden crusts, marzipan cakes with gilded frosting—mmmm . . . *edible gold!*—bitter oranges and tart lemons made sweet with shimmering coatings of sugar crystals, tangy candied figs and apricots, candied cherries bright and fine as rubies, red jewels to delight the tongue, sugarplums, almonds hidden inside shells of colored sugar, mincemeat pies, moist golden cakes sodden with cinnamon syrup, and the subtleties—just think of the subtleties, my dears!"

As our lady-mother rolled her eyes, he mused rapturously about these wonderful works of edible art, wrought from spun sugar and marzipan, in marvelous, miraculous, and magnificent designs, confectionary art and architecture, made especially for the Queen's table, by confectioners who deserved to stand shoulder to shoulder with the world's most brilliant architects. "I've never understood it! Why are the greatest architects remembered but the best pastry cooks forgotten? Where are their memorials? I'll tell you—melted like sugar in the rain! Oh the fickleness of humanity! It makes me want to weep!" he cried and reached into his comfit box and shoved another handful of sugared almonds into his mouth.

Kate and I just sat there, staring down at the sugar rolls growing sticky in the heat of our hands. It just wasn't fair! We were to be ladies-in-waiting, to live in luxury at court, with dancing, feasting, and beautiful clothes, and a generous allowance for each of us of £80 per annum, while our sister was to languish in prison with the shadow of the ax hanging over her. Just as Nero fiddled while Rome burned, our lady-mother was draping our shoulders with pale orange satin to see which of us it suited best and debating whether the gold braid or vermilion silk fringe made the best trim, and Father was railing against the unjustly forgotten pastry cooks of bygone centuries. There seemed to be no justice left in the world!

8

To appease the fears and keep—or win—the good regard of her nobles, Queen Mary decreed that they should keep their church spoils and plunder, that while the religion would in time be restored, the properties and goods would remain where they were, in private hands. But there were other things that made the men squirm uneasily in their seats around the council table—Queen Mary seemed to trust Senor Renard, the Spanish ambassador, more than she did any Englishman. She deferred to him at every turn. And though it was true these men, most of whom had betrayed and sacrificed my sister to save themselves, did not merit great trust, they were all Englishmen born and bred who would put their own proud little nation before the interests of any foreign country and fight for it unto the death.

It all seemed such a fraud to me! My family and many of the men who now sat on the Queen's Council had, until a scant few weeks ago, been Protestants, ardent devotees of the Reformed Religion, yet now we all decked ourselves with rosaries and crucifixes, listened to the priests' Latin litanies, and marveled at the miraculous moment when the bread and wine became the body and blood of our savior Jesus Christ, and never missed a Mass.

"We are all turncoats and hypocrites," I said to Kate one day as we were dressing in the room we shared at Greenwich Palace, donning the russet and black velvet livery we wore during our daily attendance upon the Queen, saving our finery for evenings, holy days, Sundays, special celebrations, banquets, balls, and feasts.

Kate vehemently agreed, adding, albeit softly lest the walls have ears, that she herself believed that Princess Elizabeth had it right and that there was but one Jesus Christ and all the rest was naught but dispute and debate over trifles.

As I finished lacing the back of her gown, Kate turned and in all seriousness said to me, "I believe in the Lord Jesus Christ and try to honor and live by his teachings, I read my Bible, follow the Ten Commandments, and say my prayers; why is that not enough, Mary? Why must we be either Catholic or Protestant? Why must lives be ruined and sacrificed for either faith?"

"Heaven only knows." I sighed as I stepped up onto the trunk at the foot of our bed and grasped the bedpost so Kate could return the favor and lace mine. "For I certainly don't!"

Meanwhile, in Master Partridge's house, Jane waited, through the sweltering heat and summer storms. *Wait*—that was really *all* she could do. She had already written and justified herself as best she could to the Queen.

Day after day she passed sitting tensely by the window, quietly observing the gate to see who came in and out, warily watching the Tower Green, gazing at the Beauchamp Tower, where Guildford and his brothers were kept, and the chapel. All the while the fever burned slow and steadily within her, making the August heat even harder to bear. Mercifully it never rose alarmingly high, never enough to drive her out of her senses into the arms of delirium, or to require more than cooling compresses, but it never departed either.

From her window, Jane watched our royal cousin ride through the Tower gates in triumphal procession, amidst heralds and trumpets and splendidly arrayed nobility, mounted on a white palfrey caparisoned in gold embroidered white velvet nigh down to the horse's hooves, with Cousin Mary herself in grand purple array embroidered with a blinding blaze of gold and a jeweled coronet casting rainbows over her faded hair and haggard face.

Before we hastened to take up her train, Kate and I waved and blew a swift kiss to Jane, just to let her know that we had not forgotten her.

And Jane was there at her window, to observe in stern and disapproving silence the Catholic requiem Mass Queen Mary ordered in memoriam of the late King Edward. Though, in fairness to our royal cousin, I must say this was more for her than for him, for she had already given Edward the stark Protestant funeral service at Westminster Abbey that he would have wanted. Kate and I, as well as our lady-mother, walked, veiled and black clad, each of us with a large silver crucifix on our breast and a black onyx rosary in our hands, behind the new queen, amidst priests in embroidered and brocaded robes and miters and swinging censers that engulfed us in perfumed blue clouds of incense that made us cough and feel light-headed.

And Jane was there at her window to watch Northumberland embrace the Catholic faith in a desperate ploy to preserve his life. Whenever she saw him being escorted under guard to hear Mass in the Tower's chapel, she pounded the glass and loudly denounced him as "a hypocrite," "an evil fraud," "a base and false man," "a white-livered milksop," and "the devil's imp." She accused him of "trading the beautiful temple of God for Satan's stinking, filthy kennel" and shouted, "Whoso denieth Him before men, he will not know Him in His Father's kingdom!" But if he heard her, Northumberland gave no sign, studiously bowing his head over his book of hours as a pearl rosary swung from his hand, the dangling silver crucifix catching the last rays of the dying sun. Sometimes his sons followed after—Ambrose, John, and Robert—a penitent trio of bowed, dark heads, but strangely never Guildford. Later I heard that when he was coaxed to convert, to try to save himself, Guildford—vain, foppish, frivolous Guildford—replied that since his wife valued the Reformed Faith so highly he didn't think "it should be cast off lightly like one suit of clothes for another."

On the twenty-third day of August, Jane was there at her window to witness the poignant farewell between Northumberland and his sons, outside the chapel where he had just heard Mass for the last time. Stoically, he bade each boy a fond farewell, until he came to Guildford. It was then that Northumberland's famous composure deserted him. He pressed his golden boy to his breast again and again and wept and kissed him, before Sir John Bridges gently parted them and led Northumberland away to die upon the scaffold, where he once again renounced the Reformed Religion and implored the Queen to be merciful to his children, and remember that they had only obeyed their father as all good and obedient children were reared to do.

But there was reason to take heart; the night before her coronation, when I knelt to remove Cousin Mary's gold-embroidered, rose velvet slippers, while Kate brushed and braided her long, lank hair in readiness for bed, hoping to coax the faded, dingy, orange and gray strands into holding a wave on her day of triumph, Cousin Mary dismissed her other ladies. She bade us to sit beside her and, with her arms draped affectionately about us, confided that she could not bear to have a pall of sorrow cast over the morrow, she wanted it to be a happy day for all, so we must banish our fears and know that Jane had naught to fear from her.

"An innocent girl should not suffer for the crimes and greed of others, and my conscience, and my heart, will not allow me to condemn unjustly. I know it may seem an unjust punishment, but your sister is safer where she is at present. She is housed in comfort and treated with great kindness. As soon as I am married and have borne a son, then, when no man can dare raise a banner in your sister's name, to try to claim for her a crown I know she does not want, then it will be safe—for her and for me—to set her free. For now, I am protecting her by preventing any man from using her as his pawn; when I restore Jane to liberty I want her to be *truly free,* to know that no one can ever do that to her again. She is a young woman, not a weapon, and youth and beauty are fleeting, *I know,* and I want her to be able to enjoy them before they slip away."

Jane was there, as we knew she would be, watching from her window, upon that sultry September morning when the long, splendid coronation procession assembled in the courtyard, led by Queen Mary seated resplendently in a golden litter in sumptuous ermine-bordered, gold-embroidered sapphire velvet and a dazzling coronet of jeweled flowers like a spring garden sprouting from the lost and faded glory of her hair.

For that occasion, I made two red silk petticoats trimmed with golden lace, for Kate and me to wear beneath our new crimson and ermine gowns. Upon each I embroidered three golden butterflies, working a concealed initial into the wings of each—*J, K, M.* When we emerged from the royal apartments, to take our places in the procession, we boldly went to stand before Master Partridge's house, so that Jane could see us. We lifted our skirts to show our petticoats, the three golden butterflies, and we held up three fingers then pointed up to Jane, then back at ourselves, to show that we had not forgotten her, that we were still together, sisters three, and nothing could divide us.

"The brilliant one," Jane mouthed.

Then it was Kate's turn—"The beautiful one."

Then mine—"The beastly little one."

Jane watched us climb into a gilded chariot where a discreet crimson-carpeted step had been supplied to put me at an equal height with Kate. It was with glad and excited hearts that we waved gaily back at Jane as the trumpets sounded and the long, winding procession headed out the Tower gates to progress slowly through the city to Westminster Abbey. We blew kisses back to her, hoping to convey to her that soon, *very soon,* all would be well, we had the Queen's word upon it, and she would soon be free, to live quietly with her beloved books and Guildford and perhaps—how Kate and I hoped!—learn to embrace the joys of being young, beautiful, and to taste and savor the fruits of love. We still believed that love was possible between Jane and Guildford; if Jane would only stop fighting desire as though it were a demon sent to tempt and torment her.

But we didn't know then that Senor Renard was holding Prince Philip, the dazzling golden Spanish bridegroom, out, tantalizing, before Queen Mary, dangling the man whose portrait our royal cousin had fallen in love with like a carrot before a donkey's nose, trying to compel her to condemn Jane, making it so that Mary must choose between Jane's life and the love she had always longed for. But in those days our cousin was still clinging strong to clemency, wringing her hands, and crying, "I *cannot* find it in my heart to put my unfortunate kinswoman to death." Vainly she tried to assure Ambassador Renard that "every requisite precaution will be taken before I set the Lady Jane at liberty." But by these assurances he would not be placated, and Mary's dream of marriage with her gold-bearded Spanish prince seemed to drift further and further away, until, I think, she too began to see that Jane stood between her and the most incredible, fierce desire she had ever known.

Jane was still a prisoner the blustery October day when she turned sixteen. We were afraid she would think that we had forgotten her, so we wanted to do something special to let her know that even though our bodies were apart we, her loving and devoted sisters, were always there with her in spirit. Through Mrs. Ellen, we sent her a rich plum cake and a beautiful but, by court standards, plain, new gown of the more modest cut Jane favored. It was made of velvet of that most delicate hue of blue known as milk-and-water with its modest square-cut bodice edged with luminous moonstones. Mrs. Ellen ignored Jane's protests and dressed her in it and brushed and crowned the red-kissed brown waves of her hair with a delicate pearl chaplet. With the connivance of Mr. and Mrs. Partridge and Sir John Bridges, we arranged that Jane be encouraged to walk in the walled garden after supper and enjoy the breeze off the river.

How Kate and I relished imagining the scene that followed! Kate pleaded a headache and to be excused from her duties that night, and I was allowed to stay with her, and we lay side by side on our bed, imagining Guildford Dudley clad head to toe in shining white stealing up behind Jane and gently cupping his hand over her mouth so she would not scream. With his own body, he would press her against the side of Master Partridge's house, letting her feel his desire, and there, in the shadows of the weeping willow tree, sheltered by the lilac bush, lift her skirts and make sweet love to her. Even when the rain began to fall and the lightning flashed across the darkened sky, Kate and I imagined them clinging all the closer, feeling the full scorching heat of their passion in the chill of the autumn rain.

But Jane always knew how to spoil a good dream. The next day Mrs. Ellen told us that, after their passion had been spent and Jane had pushed Guildford into a mud puddle, she rushed into the Partridges' kitchen, soaked to the skin, breathless, and bedraggled, and frantically sought lemon juice and vinegar. She had made a great mess, which she did not tarry to clean up, attempting to pour both into a wine bottle, then bolted up the stairs to her bedchamber, ripped off her sodden clothes, and flung herself naked upon the bed. She spread her legs wide, and, with a rage-fueled brutality akin to rape, shoved the long, slender neck of the bottle inside her cunny, thrusting her hips high as she poured its tart, stinging contents inside her.

When Mrs. Ellen tried to intervene, fearing that Jane would do herself an injury, Jane snarled like a mad dog and slapped her hands away, shouting, "Leave me be!" and Mrs. Ellen quietly withdrew to sit upon a stool in the corner. Later, when Jane lay curled upon her side and wept because the mixture stung and burned her inside, and she ached from the bruising force of the bottle she had thrust into her secret center, she rejected all Mrs. Ellen's attempts to comfort her and ordered her to get out.

"Leave me be! Leave me be!" she sobbed to the rhythm of Mrs. Ellen's softly retreating footsteps.

When I heard about it later, I sighed and shook my head and felt the salty prick of tears stab my eyes. There was a battle betwixt angels and demons raging inside my sister, so heated, confused, crowded, and clouded by smoke and writhing, warring bodies, sometimes it was impossible to tell good from bad, friend from foe, or who would triumph in the end. I loved my sister, but I despaired of ever understanding her. Why must she fight against herself and push away any who would love and comfort her? Why did she relish the role of victim and stage her life for sacrifice? Why did she reject pleasure and choose pain time and again?

These questions I can ask, but never answer, and I wonder sometimes if Jane even could. Perhaps the truths were too deeply buried to ever be unearthed. Some things are not meant for the plain light of day and prefer to dwell in darkness; some things are better left hidden no matter how much curiosity needles us.

9

On a bitterly cold November morning, Kate and I huddled together in our furs and stood amongst a great crowd on a busy London street to watch Jane and Guildford walk to the Guildhall in London, where they were to stand trial. We tried not to be afraid. Everyone said it was just a formality. Proper form must be observed, and since Jane had technically committed treason, albeit most unwillingly and under duress, she must still be condemned, but everyone knew the Queen intended to assert her royal prerogative and issue a pardon.

Though the people stood and stared, and did naught to shatter the peace of that bitingly cold morning, a number of halberdiers in uniforms as bright as blood splashed on the snow surrounded the prisoners, each man walking with the gleaming head of his new-polished ax turned out to show that the accused had not yet been condemned. We tried to catch Jane's eye, but she kept her head bent over the black velvet prayer book she held open before her, her lips moving silently over the words I hoped would give her enough comfort to see her through the coming ordeal. She wore stark, unadorned, black velvet, with an equally plain hood with a black silk veil fluttering in back. Mrs. Ellen and Mrs. Tylney, also clad in austere black, followed a few steps behind. Mrs. Ellen held a black velvet cloak lined and collared with fur over her arm, and when she saw Jane shiver, she unfolded it and started to step forward.

But Guildford, walking beside Jane, a vision in black velvet slashed with white satin and festooned with pearls, with a gay bouquet of pinks, violets, and his favorite yellow gillyflowers cut from silk to brighten the winter gloom pinned festively to his feathered hat, fell back a step and took it from her. He moved behind Jane and most tenderly draped it around her thin, trembling shoulders. But Jane never even looked up, much less glanced back, and I sincerely doubt she uttered even one word of thanks. Guildford, with a sorrowful expression, let his hands fall from where they had lingered on her shoulders and fell back in step beside her.

Kate and I clung together and waited, our eyes never once leaving the doors of the Guildhall. I don't think even a half hour passed before they opened again and the procession emerged to make the return journey to the Tower. Although we knew what to expect, it was still like a hard slap that left us reeling. This time the ax heads were turned to point toward Jane and Guildford, and the silent masses fell back with pitying and horrified gasps, some even daring to softly mutter "God save you!" to the condemned. Kate clutched my hand hard. "It's just for form's sake, it's just for form's sake," she kept repeating, as though by sheer repetition she could convince herself, and me.

Why should it not be true? After all, we had no reason to doubt our royal cousin. Though, in truth, I would have felt much better if, during the times we had spent with her, Jane had responded with a loving sweetness and sincere gratitude instead of rudeness and hostility. Every time I looked back and remembered Jane's behavior at Beaulieu that Christmas I felt sick to my very soul. I could still hear Jane taking Mary's lady-in-waiting to task for curtsying to the Host, quipping about the baker making Christ, and noisily breaking wind while Cousin Mary regaled us with stories of the saints' lives. Deep down a part of me feared, though Cousin Mary would deny it and try to bury it beneath layers of politeness, that Jane had indeed turned our kinswoman into a secret enemy. If it came down to a choice between a sulky girl who turned her back on priests and farted when told how the pious and worthy virgin

Saint Lucy had plucked out her own eyes when her pagan betrothed admired them and cried, "Here, take them! Now leave me to God!" and a golden Spanish prince, handsome, lusty, and devout, we all knew who our royal cousin would choose. I had seen the way her eyes devoured his portrait; it was the same way Father looked at plates of marzipan and Guildford Dudley, and our lady-mother regarded Adrian Stokes, the same hungry intensity, subtle and slow-burning, biding its time, trying to be patient while waiting to burst into passionate flame.

Our royal cousin was fortunate, as only a queen can be, that she could always justify her choice by claiming Jane was a liability, a life that had to be sacrificed for the greater good, and that her marriage to Philip was an act of duty, not of passion, to ensure the succession. But no one would be deceived. They would only see a lust-mad old maid hankering to lift her petticoats for a golden-haired lad eleven years her junior, and they would all laugh and gossip and whisper and mock, but none of them would rush to be Jane's champion either; the nobles at court cared only for themselves, and Jane's so-called friends, all the bookish scholars safely away in Protestant-friendly Switzerland and the Low Countries, were not knights in shining armor ready to ride out and rescue the lady-fair. And Jane was, in the end, worth more to them as a martyr—a young and beautiful martyr.

But Jane seemed oblivious to it all and displayed no concern; not even the faintest flicker of emotion flitted across her pale face. She never once lifted her head from her prayer book, and Guildford, walking beside her, stared blindly straight ahead, moving like one in a trance. Then, all of a sudden it seemed to strike him, like a blow coming out of the dark, and he staggered and stood still a moment, then fell back to walk several steps behind Jane and hung his head to try to hide the tears now pouring down his face. I remember the teardrop pearls trimming his beautiful, black velvet hat fell forward, and it looked like even his hat was weeping too for beautiful, doomed Guildford Dudley, and the white plume that crowned it quaking, like a shaking fist, out of sheer fury at the unfairness of it all.

A lady in a rabbit fur cloak standing near us shook her head and sighed at the woebegone sight passing mute and dazed before us—

"How can they be so unkind to someone so beautiful?"—speaking words that Guildford himself might have uttered when the verdict was read. Both my sister and her unwanted husband had been condemned "to be burned or beheaded at the Queen's pleasure."

Kate knelt down, despite the snow that soaked through her skirts and chilled her knees, and hugged me so tight I thought she would squeeze all the breath out of me. We clung together, two sad little girls, fourteen and nine, swathed in rabbit fur, but ice-cold inside, and wept, feeling the hot tears turn to ice upon our wind-chapped cheeks.

In the days and weeks that followed, Jane could not rest; lit from within by the fire of fever, tormented by long, slow-dragging days and so many sleepless nights, she would nervously walk the floor, pacing back and forth, wall to wall, constantly reciting, as if to instill herself with courage: "Be constant, be constant: fear not any pain, Christ hath redeemed thee, and Heaven is thy gain." She had begun to fear that God was testing her with this imprisonment and was terrified that she would fail. No longer could she find forgetfulness and solace in her beloved books; she was too consumed with worry about what would become of her.

While we danced and reveled through the Twelve Days of Christmas and the New Year, Jane sat by the fire and stared at Mr. Partridge's Yule log, wondering if "to be burned or beheaded at the Queen's pleasure" would be her fate in the new year of 1554.

When she walked out into the biting winter air, Jane stubbornly refused to look up at the wall walk of the Beauchamp Tower, where Guildford was allowed to take his daily exercise. He would stand there and watch the river traffic, no doubt remembering the days when he had glided in grand style along the Thames reclining on the velvet cushions of his family's barge. He would stand and stare at London Bridge, where the heads of traitors were impaled on metal spikes and picked down to pearly bone by the ravenous ravens before their bare skulls were hurled into the river to make room for more. No doubt he wondered if his and Jane's heads would soon join them. Sometimes he watched Jane, gazing down at her, as though willing her to look up and wave at him. But she never did.

I always wished she had. One smile, one wave would have meant so much. Though they were kept in separate quarters, they were together, as prisoners condemned to die, yet they were alone because Jane willed it.

The New Year brought disaster instead of the peace I knew Queen Mary craved. The country was as unquiet, fearful, and restless as Jane's own feverish, fear-racked mind. People feared the coming of Philip. They were afraid he would bring the Spanish Inquisition with him as a bridal gift and that we would all lose ourselves under the red cloak of Spain. The Queen was so besotted with the prince of her dreams, giddy as a girl, she would sing and hum snatches of songs throughout the day and sit for hours gazing lovingly at his portrait. Time and again she would declare, "I shall love him *perfectly* and *never* give him cause to be jealous!" never knowing how cruelly others mocked her for it, laughing behind her back, and how so many guffaws quickly became coughs as she passed. The idea that our aging, spinster queen could ever give a man as handsome as Prince Philip, and eleven years younger than herself, cause to be jealous, was utterly absurd. To Prince Philip, this was a marriage of state, yet in her heart our royal cousin had transformed it into one of smoldering passion. And when she heard rumors—as those cruel-minded mockers made certain she did—of his exotic and alluring mistresses and baseborn children, she made herself sick weeping, and only the Spanish ambassador's assurances that this was naught but false and malicious gossip could make her dry her eyes and smile again.

Senor Renard was urgently endeavoring to persuade her that Jane must die. He was also fanning the flames of Mary's fear and suspicion of her own half sister, Elizabeth. "Elizabeth is greatly to be feared," he cautioned, "for she has a power of enchantment; she has inherited her mother Anne Boleyn's sorcery"—knowing full well that just the mention of Anne Boleyn's name was enough to rekindle all our royal cousin's most deeply embedded grievances, reminding her that she had been the loved and adored princess until the woman she always called "The Great Whore" came along and ousted both Mary and her venerable mother, the pious and devout Catherine of Aragon, from Henry VIII's fickle affections.

Trouble was brewing, and you could sense it, even smell it, in the air. Thus it came as no surprise that in the county of Kent, a fine-figured, auburn-bearded man called Thomas Wyatt the Younger, the son of the poet who had at one time rivaled Henry VIII for the love of Anne Boleyn, began to raise an army, inciting others to join him. He intended that they should march on London, hoping with this show of might and force to dissuade Queen Mary from marrying Prince Philip. Wyatt would always afterward insist his sole aim had been to show Her Majesty that her people loved her but feared the threat of foreign domination that came hand in glove with the marriage. But some whispered that there was more to it—a secret scheme to wrest Mary from the throne and replace her with Princess Elizabeth, or Jane.

Then misfortune came to darken our doorstep once again. Our lady-mother was in London with the Queen, basking and reveling in her favor, flaunting her new jewels and gaudy velvets, gambling and making merry, and riding out with the royal hunt or alone with Master Stokes for a brisk, vigorous canter every chance she got, thus she failed to be properly vigilant where Father was concerned. If ever a man needed an alert and watchful wife it was Father. Left to his own devices in the country with his horses and hounds and recipe books filled with sweet things he was always pestering the cook to make, he was in a most vulnerable state when the charismatic Wyatt came calling. Father fell under the man's wicked spell and foolishly, nay *idiotically,* agreed to join him provided that, if Queen Mary failed to see reason, Jane would be restored to the throne as England's queen.

But the people loved Queen Mary more than they hated Spanish Philip. She made a rousing speech at the Guildhall that made the Londoners fall in love with her all over again. And when Wyatt came, the people closed their doors and hid from him. He was, in the end—though there were a few tense moments when we feared all would be lost—soundly defeated and taken in chains to the Tower.

After it was all over, rotting corpses hung from gibbets on every street corner, and dangled from the trees and London Bridge, which had more heads displayed on it than anyone could ever remember seeing before. London was an ugly, stinking place we longed to run away from, but we could not forsake our sister. Sometimes it seemed as though ugly, leering corpses had risen from their graves to take over the city and frighten the wits out of the living. Whenever we went out, traveling between whichever royal palace the court was in residence at and Suffolk House, where our lady-mother presided grandly over bountiful banquets and the gambling tables, Kate and I clutched pomander balls stuffed with oranges and cloves to our noses, but it did little good; there was just no escaping the stench of death.

Father never even made it to London. Five miles outside of Coventry, his men deserted him. He fled alone, in hasty panic, lamenting that our lady-mother was not there to do his thinking for him. He made his way to Astley Park, one of his Suffolk estates. There, hunted like prey himself, pursued by packs of barking hounds, he panicked, and, as he ran across the Great Park, through the sticky, slurping mud that sucked off his boots and dense curtains of relentlessly pounding rain, cast off all his clothes and, running in a zigzag motion, flung them far and wide. He hurled himself to the ground and rolled in the mud, thoroughly coating himself, "like a roast in spicy batter" he would say after, hoping to erase his scent and fool the dogs. Then he ran, clutching his beloved comfit box against his pounding heart, pausing only to try to paste some fallen leaves around his loins with mud for modesty's sake. As his pursuers gained on him, he sought a hiding place and endeavored to cram his great, dough-soft body inside a hollow tree, in which he became hopelessly, and most uncomfortably, and indecently, stuck. "It seemed like such a good idea at the time," he would afterward say when attempting to justify his outlandish behavior. As the hounds brayed, held back by their keeper, and the soldiers stood about laughing, woodsmen were summoned with saws and axes to carefully extricate our cold and miserable father from the tree's embrace. He emerged pale as a ghost, a broken and defeated man who realized he had been a fool to try to make a deal with the Devil, like the greedy man in that old story his tutor used to tell him as a lad who had sold his soul for a sack of gold only to discover upon opening it that it contained only chestnuts. Father was doomed. His mud-caked body covered once again with his cast-off clothes, he was led in chains back to London.

Jane, who had heard the confusion and panic in the city, the distant din and chaos of Wyatt's rebellion, but not known the cause of it as neither Master Partridge nor Sir John Bridges had the heart to tell her, sat at her window and watched Father's sad arrival. She turned to Master Partridge and demanded to know the reason for his arrest. At his honestly given answer, she sank down on her knees, hugging herself and weeping silently, all hope gone, knowing that our royal cousin would not dare let her live now. Mary could no longer afford to be merciful. The only freedom Jane would ever have would come when the headsman's ax set her soul free.

That same day, our royal cousin signed the death warrants for Jane, Guildford, and Father. Afterward she closeted herself alone, weeping, in her private chapel, with a miniature of Jane in one hand and one of Prince Philip in the other. She emerged hours later, puffy-faced and swollen-eyed, with a plan to send her own chaplain, the kindly Dr. Feckenham, to try to convert Jane. What a feather that would be for the cap of Catholicism—to convert one of their most fervent and fanatical opponents! And, with Mary soon to be married, and, God willing, a mother, and Jane no longer a heretic, but a good Catholic, it would soon be safe to release her into a life of quiet seclusion. Dr. Feckenham was well chosen; he was not a sour-faced, grim, and pedantic priest, but a smiling, jovial man, the very soul of kindness, and, having been imprisoned for his faith during King Edward's reign, he could sympathize and well understand Jane's predicament.

But Jane was ever wont to turn her back and stick up her nose at Cousin Mary's kindness.

"I am ready to receive death patiently and in whatever manner pleaseth the Queen," she icily informed Dr. Feckenham.

Yet the scholar in her could not resist his challenge, one last opportunity to show off her much touted brilliance, and dispute with him on various theological points upon which their faiths diverged. To the tune of the hammers wielded by the workmen building her scaffold on Tower Green, they debated the number and nature of the sacraments and the miracle of the Mass, the mystical moment when the bread and wine became the body and blood of Jesus Christ. But Jane would not be moved, not even to save her life; to her, her soul was more important, and she would rather die for what she saw as the truth than live a lie.

"Well, my lady, I see we shall never agree," Feckenham most dolefully concluded.

"Not unless God turn your heart," Jane woefully answered, for in Feckenham she had seen that not all Catholic priests were the devils she imagined them. Here was a man, a kind, fatherly man, whose faith was as sincere, devout, and strong as her own, and even though he had failed to sway and change her, he would not abandon her, but would, as a friend, if she would allow it, stand by her to the very end. And for this great kindness, with tears in her eyes, Jane thanked him.

When Feckenham bade her farewell, leaving her to prepare to face death upon the morrow, she laid her hand upon his sleeve and spoke, regretfully, of Guildford. "He is innocent and only obeyed his father in all things as all children are brought up to do."

Then she turned her back on him and went and knelt beside her bed to pray.

Jane would never know the sacrifice Kate made to try to save her. Afterward, we would both try to forget, to pretend it never happened. When the Earl of Pembroke, her former father-in-law, cut off Wyatt's advance, Queen Mary rewarded him with a diamond ring from her own finger. He knelt at her feet and, with tears shimmering on his proud, patrician face, slipped it onto his smallest finger, the only one it would fit, and vowed he would wear and cherish it until the day he died.

Afterward, I saw the Spanish ambassador draw him aside. Little and unnoticed, I heard their urgently exchanged words—the Spaniard's evil serpent's tongue urging Pembroke to persuade Queen Mary, who was wont to let kinship and sentimentality sway her, that Jane *must* die, she could not be allowed to live, it was too dangerous.

I made the mistake of telling Kate. That night, when the clocks struck midnight, Kate, her hair rippling down her back like a curtain of flame and clad in her sheerest lawn shift edged with Spanish blackwork embroidery, silently covered herself in a cloak of black velvet, drew up the hood to hide her face in shadows, and went to him. I begged her not to go, but without a word, she gently but firmly pushed me away. She gave herself, she surrendered her virginity, that most precious gift a woman can give but once, to a man who had already hurt and wronged her, to try to save our sister's life. He was the most powerful and influential man at court, the richest earl in England; only his word stood a chance of outweighing the Spanish ambassador's, and if he spoke up for Jane his words might be enough to tip the balance in her favor, to our royal cousin's natural tendency toward clemency. Pembroke promised, but he exacted a price—Kate must give herself to him; only then would he speak for Jane.

But Pembroke lied, as I knew he would, and showed himself once again to be a cruel and evil man. He never spoke one word espousing mercy for Jane. Instead, he joined the others, his voice amongst the loudest, calling for her death. He used and soiled my sister, then parroted the Spanish ambassador—Jane was a traitor and must die as traitors do. The head that presumed to wear a stolen crown must be taken, Pembroke said, and called it justice.

When Kate came back to me at cock's crow, sorely used and tearstained, her shift torn and bloody, moving as though each step hurt her, I wordlessly opened my arms and let my shoulder soak up the tears that followed.

"When he held, kissed, and caressed me, and when he . . . loved me," her voice wavered uncertainly, and she nibbled her lower lip as she looked up at me with her tear-bright eyes, "though I know 'loved' is not the right word for it, he excited and repulsed me as no other man ever has. I detested and desired, loved and hated him, all at the same time. The feelings were all a jumbled red-hot mass in my mind, and whenever I tried to sort them out and make sense of it all I got burned, so I stopped trying, like a drowning person who stops fighting and just lies back and starts floating, drifting along wherever the current carries them. I wanted to stay, yet I wanted to go, to draw him close and hold him near, yet to bite and kick, scratch like a hellcat and fight my way free of him, and of me, because I didn't like myself when I lay with him. But at the same time I was me, and I knew I couldn't escape myself; I am what I am, and there's no good fighting it. All I could do was kiss, caress, and cling. I was wholly in his power, because I wanted to be even though I didn't; I was myself, yet not myself. Oh, Mary, for the first time, I think I understand what it was like for Jane with Guildford! And he hurt me, Pembroke hurt me, I knew he would, I didn't want him to, and yet I did, and I knew it must the first time, it is like that for every maid, yet I welcomed it, I invited it, and he hurt me. Oh, Mary, it was both agony and bliss!" Her voice broke in anguish, and she fell to weeping in my arms again, clinging to me as though only I could save her.

What did you expect? You played with fire and got burned, a little voice inside my head said. But my mouth never moved except to kiss the bright curls as I held Kate close and willed the pain to leave her, to soak into me, along with her tears. I could bear it. There were many things I could have said to my sister, but I hadn't the heart to actually say them; all I could do was hold her, and hold her again when she realized Pembroke's treachery and duplicity. Jane was doomed, and he had helped decree it, just as he had helped thrust an unwanted crown upon her. People are always apt to forget that which they do not wish to remember. They always see themselves in the light that flatters and favors them most and try to ensure that others do also. That is why I have never trusted memoirs, not even those writ by saints.

10

Though we loathed to go abroad that chilly morning of February 12, we *had* to, it was a mission of mercy our hearts could never say no to. Though we had begged, pleaded, wept, and humbled ourselves as we never had before, our royal cousin refused to allow us one last hour with Jane; even when we fell sobbing on our knees before her and pleaded for time enough for just one kiss, one embrace, to say good-bye, the answer remained the same—*no!* Cousin Mary turned her crimson velvet back on our tears and said when we were older we would understand, that she did this for our own sake, to spare us even greater pain. When Kate persisted, she held up her hand and said, "I will hear no more. Leave me now," and dismissed us. But she later sent a message saying that we might, if we wished, go and give what comfort we could to Guildford. He was in a state of terrible agitation because Jane had refused to see him when Cousin Mary offered to let husband and wife spend their last night on earth together. So Kate and I put on our furs and set out for the Tower.

Guildford spent his final morning in a flood of tears, bewailing his misfortune, and that Jane would not be with him on his last walk. "We should have taken it together," he sobbed into Kate's lap, while I knelt and stroked his back, as we both tried our best to comfort him in the absence of our—I must say it!—*selfish* sister.

Jane had sent word through Sir John Bridges that "if our meeting could have been a means of consolation to our souls I would have been happy to see Guildford, but as our meeting would only increase our misery and pain, it is better to put it off for the time being, as we will meet shortly elsewhere, and live bound by indissoluble ties."

We tried in vain to make him see the message of hope hidden in Jane's words, but Guildford only shook his head and wept all the more, wretched and inconsolable, in our arms, afraid to die alone, with no one to hold his hand and take that final walk with him.

"I don't want to die!" he sobbed. Desperately, he implored us to find a blond beggar to die in his stead and then go away with him to Italy where he could do what he had always wanted to do—*sing!*

But it was just a frantic fantasy, one last grasp at a dream that all of us knew could never be.

Though not bound to us by blood, Guildford was the only brother we ever had—all the sons our lady-mother ever bore died before they had scarcely drawn breath—so we did what we could for him. We calmed and bathed him with chamomile and lavender, and then we dressed him. Though some might have objected to two maidens handling a young man so intimately, Guildford was like a little frightened child beneath our hands, and it was all entirely innocent; his nakedness stirred nothing save sorrow that one so young and fair was about to die at only seventeen.

Kate chose for him an elegant, black velvet doublet slashed with cinnamon satin and black silk hose and gently made sure the lace-trimmed collar of his white lawn shirt was laid open wide, to leave his pale neck bare and vulnerable for the ax. As he sat, docile as a child in his chair, sipping his chamomile tea, Kate, her nimble fingers always so clever with coiffures, arranged the gilded curls of Guildford Dudley for the very last time, and as I watched, I plucked at the dyed russet plume on his black velvet cap to give it a jaunty curl before I gave it to him.

"Thank you, Mary." Trying so hard to be brave, Guildford smiled at me. "It is very cold outside and my head is very beautiful;

it would be frightful if I caught cold in it," he said, and set it on his head at a rakish tilt, and I caught the self-mocking twinkle in his gooseberry green eyes for one last time.

When it was time for us to go and Sir John Bridges was at the door, Guildford suddenly cried, "Wait!" He gathered up Fluff from where he lay curled and sleeping on the bed, held him close to his heart for a long moment, and kissed and caressed the sleek, silky white head, then came and laid him gently in Kate's arms. "Please take care of him for me. He likes a bowl of cream every morning for his breakfast," he added, his voice breaking, just like our hearts.

With tears in her eyes, Kate promised that Fluff would be spoiled, "like a king among cats," and we embraced Guildford one last time, and then we parted before the tears could drown us all.

We wept all the way back to Greenwich Palace, where we must hasten into our russet and black liveries to attend the Queen, and when we climbed out of the hired barge, we left the cushions sodden with our tears.

In our room, Kate gave Fluff a saucer of milk, kneeling down on the floor beside him, stroking, petting, kissing, and making much of him while he regally lapped it up. We helped each other change into our liveries, then we walked the floor, back and forth, tensely waiting, watching the clock, knowing that, all too soon, our sister's soul would depart this earth. A maidservant came, sent as an act of kindness from the Queen, and brought us a late breakfast since she knew we had not had any and did not want to see us faint and lightheaded when we came to her. But neither of us wanted it, though we hadn't the heart to refuse and send it back to the kitchen lest our royal cousin think us ungrateful and disdainful of the gesture.

The kitchen wench was just departing when Kate suddenly ran across the room and jerked her back inside. "I want your clothes!" she said. I watched in astonishment as my sister, who had always had a maid or me to help her, wrenched off her gown, not caring what she tore, until she was down to her shift and stays. She left her petticoats pooled on the floor and ordered the trembling and astonished girl, "Strip!" Fearing that Kate had lost her mind and might do her some injury, the girl nervously complied.

As she struggled into the girl's plain buff-hued homespun gown, Kate kicked her torn and discarded livery at her and ordered her to put it on, as she could not walk the palace corridors without decent cover, and fetch something for me to wear. "*Anything!* A sack will do, if that's all you can find. *Hurry!*" she cried when the girl dithered and wept about my size and said she did not know what to do. *"Run, damn you!"* Kate stamped her foot to speed her on her way, then turned and quickly shucked off my gown. As it rose over my head, I heard tearing and popping and knew our liveries would require much labor before we could wear them again, if we even could.

Kate was gathering up the wild riot of her flaming curls with such haste it was as though they burned her hands and thrusting them inside the maid's linen cap when the girl returned clutching a rough-woven sack that, by the dusting it left on the floor and my skin, must have contained flour. Kate ran to her sewing basket and quickly cut a hole in the bottom for my head and two on the sides for me to stick my arms through, then thrust it over my head and helped me wiggle into it. Then, seizing up the maid's apron and knotting it around her waist and stumbling into her oversized wooden clogs, she grabbed my hand and rushed me out the door, even as I one-handedly struggled to remove the jewel-tipped pins from my hair and unloose the ropes of pearls plaited into it. These I left lying on the floor like a child's discarded toys.

We flew down the water stairs, heedless of the slickness that put our necks and bones in peril, and, for the second time that morning, spilled into a barge. Kate flung a handful of coins at the bargeman and bade him row to the Tower as though his very life depended on it.

"Kate, what are you thinking?" I cried. "This is madness! We are due to attend the Queen; she will surely punish us!"

"I don't care!" Kate said defiantly, and turned and shouted for the bargeman to row faster. "We *must* be there for Jane, Mary. We *cannot* let her die alone!"

Hearing Kate say it gave me all the courage I needed.

"For Jane." I nodded and reached out to hold Kate's hand.

We almost didn't make it. We were too late for Guildford; he had already been dead almost an hour. His head and body, wrapped in a bloodstained sheet, had already been carted back from Tower Hill. We would hear later that Guildford had, at the last moment, found his courage, and as he knelt before the block, he declared that he would die "doing what I love best, and, this time, no one shall stop me! Lord." He turned his gooseberry green eyes heavenward. "Here is my voice; I shall send it soaring high to heaven to meet Your angels as they come to carry my soul home to You!" He flung wide his arms, closed his eyes, and threw back his head, and unleashed a loud and joyful voice that pathetically endeavored to climb all the way to heaven. Wincing, as the crowd cried, "Lord, have mercy on our ears!" the startled executioner snatched up his ax and lopped Guildford's glorious golden head off in a single stroke.

We would later learn that Jane had stood by her window and watched his lonely last walk to Tower Hill. Guildford stared straight ahead and never paused or even once looked up as he passed beneath her window. She was still there afterward to witness the return of his bloodied corpse in the cart, catching a glimpse of golden curls peeking from the folds of the winding sheet. Then the tears Guildford had once predicted came, and Jane sobbed out again and again "Guildford! Guildford!" and fell weeping into Mrs. Ellen's arms, muffling her sobs against that good lady's black velvet shoulder. "The ante-repast is not so bitter that you have tasted, and that I shall soon taste, as to make my flesh tremble," she said in a tearful rush and then, raising her head, swallowing back her tears, continued. "But that is *nothing,* Guildford, to the feast you and I shall this day partake of together in Paradise." Then she went and knelt down beside her bed and prayed that God help her find the courage to bravely endure her final hour. "Lord, Thou God and Father of my life, hear this poor and desolate woman, and arm me, I beseech Thee, with Thy armor that I may stand fast, gird me with verity and the breastplate of righteousness."

"Hurry, Mary, hurry! Jane needs us! We have to be there for her! We cannot let her die alone! We cannot!" With a strength I feared would wrench my arm from its socket, Kate pulled and dragged me through the crowd, heedless of the legs I banged into and the toes I trampled. She determinedly shoved and elbowed her way through, as the drums beat and the Tower chapel's bells tolled, taking me with her, all the way up to the very front, close enough to reach out and touch the scaffold.

Wearing the same black velvet gown and hood she had worn to her trial, with her head bent over her precious prayer book, our sister was already mounting the thirteen steps of the black-draped scaffold.

As she stepped onto the straw-covered planks, Jane hesitated a moment, taking a step back, toward the reassuring black-robed presence of Dr. Feckenham, while Mrs. Ellen and Mrs. Tylney, nigh blinded by their tears, hovered anxiously behind, waiting to divest her of her cloak and headdress and make sure the pins holding up her hair were secure so it would not fall down and impede the ax and thus prolong Jane's agony.

Jane handed her prayer book to Sir John Bridges, to whom she had promised it as a remembrance, and in a timid, tremulous little voice courageously, and correctly, asserted, "If my faults deserve punishment, my youth at least and my imprudence were worthy of excuse. God and posterity will show me more favor."

Then she let her ladies do what they must, shying fearfully away from the tall, muscular-armed, black-hooded executioner as he knelt and gently asked her forgiveness. Forcing herself to be brave, Jane gave it and laid the traditional coin in his palm. As he motioned her toward the block, Jane, like a teary-eyed little girl craving reassurance, asked, "You will not take it off until I lay me down?" He answered most kindly, "No, my lady."

Her eyes rising to watch the ravens circling overhead, her voice faltering, cracking, and halting, rising high then dropping low, Jane addressed her last words to the crowd.

"Good people, I am come hither to die, and by a law I am condemned to the same. The fact, indeed, against the Queen's Highness was unlawful and the consenting thereto by me, but touching the procurement and desire thereof by me or on my behalf, I do wash my hands thereof in innocence, before God and the face of you, good Christian people, this day." She paused and wrung her hands as though she were indeed washing them. "I pray you all, good Christian people, to bear me witness that I die a true Christian woman, and that I look to be saved by none other means, but only by the mercy of God, in the merits of the blood of His only son, Jesus Christ. I confess when I did know the word of God, I neglected the same, loved myself and the world, and therefore this plague or punishment is happily and worthily happened unto me for my sins. Yet I thank God of His goodness that He hath given me a time and respite to repent. And now, good Christian people, while I am alive, I pray you to assist me with your prayers."

When I looked around me, as many bowed their heads and dropped to their knees on the snow-crusted earth, I saw there was nary a dry eye in sight.

Upon the scaffold, Jane turned and looked uncertainly to Dr. Feckenham. "Should I say the Miserere psalm?" she asked. At his nod, she knelt, still facing the crowd, and after a moment he did too, and their two voices, hers softly speaking English, and his sonorous Latin, blended together in the recitation of the "Miserere mei, Deus" as his hand reached out to hold hers.

Have mercy upon me, O God, according to thy loving kindness: according unto the multitude of thy tender mercies blot out my transgressions.

Wash me thoroughly from mine iniquity, and cleanse me from my sin.

For I acknowledge my transgressions: and my sin is ever before me.

Against thee, thee only, have I sinned, and done this evil in thy sight: that thou mightest be justified when thou speakest, and be clear when thou judgest.

Behold, I was shapen in iniquity; and in sin did my mother conceive me.

Behold, thou desirest truth in the inward parts: and in the hidden part thou shalt make me to know wisdom.

Purge me with hyssop, and I shall be clean: wash me, and I shall be whiter than snow.

Make me to hear joy and gladness; that the bones which thou hast broken may rejoice.

Hide thy face from my sins, and blot out all mine iniquities.

Create in me a clean heart, O God; and renew a right spirit within me.

Cast me not away from thy presence; and take not thy holy spirit from me.

Restore unto me the joy of thy salvation; and uphold me with thy free spirit.

Then will I teach transgressors thy ways; and sinners shall be converted unto thee.

Deliver me from blood guiltiness, O God, thou God of my salvation; and my tongue shall sing aloud of thy righteousness.

O Lord, open thou my lips; and my mouth shall shew forth thy praise.

For thou desirest not sacrifice; else would I give it: thou delightest not in burnt offerings.

The sacrifices of God are a broken spirit: a broken and a contrite heart, O God, thou wilt not despise.

Do good in thy good pleasure unto Zion: build thou the walls of Jerusalem.

Then shalt thou be pleased with the sacrifices of righteousness, with burnt offering and with whole burnt offering: then shall they offer bullocks upon thine altar.

Then she stood and, in a rare display of kindness, turned back to help the old man rise. Impulsively, she bent and kissed his cheek and whispered, "I pray to God that He abundantly reward you for your kindness to me."

Turning hurriedly away, as though she feared she must move fast lest her courage falter and cowardice well up to take its fragile place, she faced the block and fell to her knees in the straw. She motioned urgently for Mrs. Ellen to quickly bring forth the blindfold and bind her eyes to blot out the world she was about to leave. Just before her eyes were covered, she gazed once more, fearfully, at the headsman and implored, "I pray you dispatch me quickly!" To which he nodded. "Aye, my lady."

But Jane had misjudged the distance between herself and the block, and when, blindfolded, she moved to lay her head down, she found only empty air. This nigh chased her courage away. Her hands rose, frantically groping before her. *"Where is it? Where is it?"* she sobbed plaintively.

It was such a sad and pitiful sight. Everyone felt sorry for her. But no one dared move. And then history records that "one of the standers-by took pity," but I can tell you that it was my brave Kate, unrecognized in her serving woman's disguise, with the fire of her hair doused and hidden by a borrowed linen cap, who broke from the crowd and clattered up the wooden steps in her clunky, cumbersome clogs. She laid a comforting hand on Jane's shoulder, letting it linger there one long and loving moment. Those watching never knew they were witnessing two sisters saying farewell. Then, moving swiftly, Kate gently guided Jane's hands and helped her lay her head down on the hard, scarred wooden block that had seen so many deaths.

"We love you, Jane," Kate afterward told me she had whispered.

Jane had whispered back, "Don't cry for me, Kate; by losing this mortal life, I gain an immortal one!"

Swallowing down her tears, Kate clattered back down again, and while her back was yet turned, Jane cried bravely, "Lord, into Thy hands I commend my spirit!" and the ax fell with a great thud, cutting through Jane's skin and bones to bury its blade in the wood.

I was watching Kate's face, not the scaffold, when the ax fell. She shut her eyes, but the tears seeped out. She breathed deeply, shakily exhaled, and whispered, "Fare thee well, my dear Jane!" Then she squared her shoulders, opened her eyes, took my hand, and began swiftly pulling me back through the crowd, away from the scaffold. "Don't look back, don't look back," she kept saying until the words lost all meaning.

I didn't. So neither of us saw, though we heard, when the executioner held our sister's head aloft by her hair and spoke the traditional words, "So perish all the Queen's enemies! Behold the head of a traitor!" Behind us we heard the crowd marveling that so vast a quantity of blood had come out of one little girl.

Jane was gone, but she would live on, and posterity would indeed favor her. Almost overnight it seemed poems, ballads, and pictures celebrating her courage and faith, her youth and beauty, were sprouting up like weeds, recited and sold on every street corner. She had captured the public's imagination and become a tragic heroine. Had she been a toothless, gray-haired hag of fifty, instead of sixteen and beautiful, it might all have been a different story, but there's something about that scene that fascinates and titillates, that excites and ignites, stirs the blood and kindles lust—the blindfolded beauty kneeling there, neck and shoulders bare and white as snow, as a sacrifice to the spinster queen's lust for a golden Spanish prince, and the fountain of blood gushing out of that frail, slender neck to stain the pure white snow, like the red blossoms of a maiden's blood on the sheets of her bridal bed. That is how the world, and posterity, will remember my sister.

Mrs. Ellen, who had faithfully remained to tend Jane's corpse, came to the palace that night and brought us each a long, wavy lock she had cut from Jane's head before she tenderly wrapped our sister's poor, broken body in a sheet and laid her, beside Guildford, in the musty, dusty crypt of St. Peter ad Vincula, the Tower's sad and bloody chapel, where Anne Boleyn and other condemned traitors lay entombed. Later I would have Kate sit, hang her head low, with her hair falling like red gold rain around her face, and snip from the nape of her neck a long strand. She would do the same for me. I would braid and weave them together, forming a pair of roses, one for each of us to keep and cherish, comprised of three shades of hair cut from the heads of three sisters—"the brilliant one," "the beautiful one," and "the beastly little one"—skeins of ruddy chestnut, fiery, blazing copper, and ebony harboring a secret scarlet, together forever, bound and united, divided not even by Death's cruel scythe.

Mrs. Ellen also brought us Jane's treasured Greek Testament. After she had gone, we found, written inside the cover, upon the blank pages, a letter addressed to Kate. I was a little hurt. Was there nothing for me? I flipped to the back, hoping to find a message for me on the last blank pages, but there was nothing.

"Maybe there's something here for both of us?" Kate suggested as I gave the book back to her and we sat, side by side, on the fireside settle and she read it aloud.

> *I have here sent you, good sister Katherine, a book the which, although it be not outwardly trimmed with gold, yet inwardly it is worth more than precious stones. It is the book, dear sister, of the law of the Lord. It is His Testament and Last Will, which he bequeathed unto us wretches, which shall lead you to the path of eternal joy. And if you, with a good mind, read it, and with an earnest desire follow it, it shall bring you to an immortal and everlasting life.*
>
> *It shall teach you to live and learn you to die. It will win you more than you should have gained by the possession of your woeful father's lands. Within these covers are such riches as neither the covetous shall withdraw from you, neither the thief steal, nor the moth corrupt.*
>
> *Trust not the tenderness of your age shall lengthen your days, for as soon, if God will, goes the young as the old. Wherefore labor always to learn to die. Defy the world, deny the Devil, and despise the flesh, and delight yourself only in the Lord. Be penitent for your sins and yet despair not. Be strong in faith and yet pre-*

sume not and desire with Saint Paul to be dissolved and to be with Christ, with whom even in death there is life.

Rejoice in Christ as I trust I do and seeing that you have the name of a Christian, as near as you can follow in the steps of your master, Christ, and take up your cross. Lay your sins on His back and always embrace Him. And touching my death, rejoice as I do, good sister, that I shall be delivered of this corruption, and put on incorruption, for I am assured that I shall for losing of a mortal life win an immortal life.

Pray God grant you and send you of His grace to live in His fear and then to die in the true Christian faith from which in God's name I exhort you that you never swerve neither for hope of life nor for fear of death. If you will deny His truth to lengthen your life, God will deny you and yet shorten your days. And if you will cleave to Him, He will prolong your days to your comfort and His glory to which glory God bring me now and you hereafter when it shall please Him to call you.

Farewell good sister, put your only trust in God who alone can help you. Amen.

Your loving sister,

Jane

Kate flung the book to the floor and threw herself into my arms.

We clung together and wept, both of us surprised to discover that we had any tears left.

"I would rather my brains rattled around in my head like seeds in a gourd than live a scholar and die a martyr!" Kate cried. "I want to *live,* Mary, to *love* and *be loved!* I must embrace the flesh; I *cannot* despise it, no more than I could ever follow in Jane's footsteps!"

As I retrieved the book, I noticed the ribbon tucked inside that Jane had used to mark her place. It was a broad glossy bloodred satin ribbon. I drew it out and beheld the words *For my sister Mary* embroidered across the top, and beneath it, also in neatly stitched gilt letters that seemed to shimmer and dance in the firelight, these five verses:

Death will give pain to the body for its sins, but the soul will be justified before God.

There is a time to be born and a time to die; and the day of our death is better than the day of our birth.

Live to die, that by death you may gain eternal life.

If my faults deserve punishment, my youth at least and my imprudence were worthy of excuse. God and posterity will show me greater favor.

Peace I leave with you, my peace I give unto you: not as the world giveth, give I unto you. Let not your heart be troubled, neither let it be afraid.

She had not forgotten me after all. Every time I read a book and needed to mark my place, Jane would be right there with me.

Then, long before we were done weeping, while our eyes and faces were yet red and tear-swollen, it was Father's turn to lay his head upon the block and die. We could not be there for him. Though our royal cousin, to our surprise, never said a word about our disobedience the day Jane died, the night before Father's execution we were summoned to sleep upon a pallet at the foot of her bed, as two of her ladies-in-waiting always did, and she kept us close all the morrow, reading aloud to her and embroidering until the deed was done. But afterward we were allowed to go into his cell and claim his personal possessions.

Upon his desk, amidst drawings of cakes, candies, pies, pyramids of fruit, and great, fantastical marzipan and spun sugar subtleties with copious notes below mouthwateringly describing them all, we found a crumpled, tear-stained letter. It was from Jane, written the last night of her life.

Father,

Although it hath pleased God to hasten my death by you, by whom my life should rather have been lengthened; yet I can so patiently take it, as I yield God more hearty thanks for shortening my woeful days, than if all the world had been given into my possession, with life lengthened at my own will. Albeit I am well assured of your impatient dolours, redoubled manifold ways, both in bewailing your own woe, and especially, as I am informed, my unfortunate state. Yet, my dear father, if I may without offense rejoice in my own mishaps, herein I may account myself blessed, that washing my hands with the innocency of my fact, my guiltless blood may cry out before the Lord, "Mercy, to the innocent!"

And yet, though I must needs acknowledge, that being constrained, and, as you know well enough, continually assayed; yet, in taking the Crown upon me, I seemed to consent, and therein grievously offended the Queen and her laws; yet do I assuredly trust, that this my offense toward God is so much the less, in that being in so royal estate as I was, my enforced honor never blended with mine innocent heart.

Thus, good father, I have opened unto you the state in which I presently stand, my death at hand, although to you it may seem woeful, yet to me there is nothing more welcome than from this vale of misery to aspire to that heavenly throne of all joy and pleasure, with Christ our Savior, in whose steadfast faith (if it be lawful for the daughter so to write to the father) the Lord that hitherto hath strengthened you, so continue to keep you, that at last we may meet in Heaven with the Father, Son, and Holy Ghost. Amen. I am,

Your Obedient Daughter Until Death,
Jane

I thought it was rather harsh—even if it was true. And Father was such a sensitive man, a great overgrown boy really, no wonder it had made him weep. Yea, it was true that he should not have sought the Crown again on Jane's behalf, in a rebellion she knew nothing about, and would have wanted no part in if she had, and by doing so he had sealed her doom and his own. Yet seeing her letter, stained with Father's tears, made me cry. *Oh, Jane, how could you?* Father must have felt she was pouring salt into his wounds!

Yet, perhaps her thoughts had traveled the same lines. Perhaps Jane had regretted her harshness. After she sent him this letter, Father asked his gaoler to take her the pretty prayer book bound in gilt-embellished yellow leather Guildford had inscribed and given him, before the tragic power play that had turned our world upside down, and ask his daughter to please write some words of comfort inside it and send it back to him with all speed.

As Kate and I stood peering down at the book as it lay open in my hands, I could not help but wonder what Jane had thought when she opened it and read Guildford's own elegantly writ inscription.

> *Your loving and obedient son wisheth unto Your Grace long life in this world, with as much joy and comfort as I wish myself, and in the world to come, joy everlasting.*
>
> *Your most humble son to his death,*
>
> *Guildford Dudley*

But did it *really* matter anymore what Guildford and Father had been to each other, and who was to blame, and for what? The time for cattiness, cruel reminders, blame, and malice had passed. Like the obedient daughter she had been brought up to be, Jane dipped her quill and wrote beneath her husband's words:

> *The Lord comfort Your Grace and that in His word wherein all creatures only are to be comforted. And though it hath pleased God to take two of your children, yet think not, I most humbly beseech Your Grace, that you have lost them. But trust that we, by*

leaving this mortal life, have won an immortal life. And I, as for my part, as I have honored Your Grace in this life, will pray for you in another life.

Your Grace's humble daughter,
Jane Dudley

Was the *Dudley,* I wondered, her subtle way of reminding him that, despite what mad, foolish folly they might have shared, whether carnal or innocent infatuation, Guildford was really hers?

"Poor Father." I turned to see Kate standing beside the bed cradling his dear old blue and rose comfit box against her breast. Tenderly, she lifted the lid.

"Look, Mary!" She held it out for me to see. "He left it for us."

Kate sat down and patted the bed beside her. I joined her there, the two of us gazing down at the pretty auburn-haired marzipan mermaid that was all that remained inside it.

Gently, Kate lifted it out and let the bare-breasted sea siren lie upon her palm as reverently as though it were a consecrated wafer.

"Shall we?" she asked tentatively.

"For Father." I nodded.

Kate hesitated for a moment, and then she quickly lifted the mermaid and snapped her in half at the waist.

I took the green scaled tail from her and quickly popped it in my mouth, while Kate did the same with the remaining half.

Then I put my arm around her waist, and she did the same, and we leaned against each other. "Poor Father!" we sighed and savored his memory along with the last piece of candy he would ever give to us.

11

Father's foolish head was stuck on London Bridge as a warning to other would-be traitors, but bits of his beard still billowed in the breeze, and the ravens had yet to pick it clean when we received a most curious summons from our lady-mother bidding us to put on something pastel and pretty, "to bring a burst of spring to these dreary winter days," and come at once to Suffolk House for a "celebration of sweet delight."

"Whatever can it mean?" Kate wondered as I stood at the foot of our bed in my gold apple–patterned spring green brocade and laced her into a gown of pale rose damask figured with delicate silver roses. "How can it be a 'sweet celebration' so soon after Father and Jane are gone?"

"I cannot even imagine," I sighed. "Life will never be the same without them. I am so afraid nothing will ever be sweet again, Kate."

"Don't say that, Mary," Kate pleaded. "We have to be brave; life is for the living, so we *must* find things to look forward to, things worth going on for. Sweet times *must* come again! But, now . . . it is *too* soon."

When we arrived at Suffolk House, we were ushered into the downstairs parlor where, in a blaze of what must have been a hundred candles, our lady-mother, thinking perhaps that the candlelight would be kind and flatter her, stood before the great marble fireplace. Her hair, now an alarming cherry red—she had obviously been overzealous in applying the henna—was flowing down her back, girlishly unbound, though she was galloping hard and fast toward forty. Upon it sat a lavish crown of gilded rosemary, lavender, meadowsweet, red and white roses to remind all of her Tudor heritage, deep purple violets, marigolds, and the white star-shaped blossoms known as love-in-a-mist. She was holding a large golden goblet and wearing a loose, flowing gown of creamy white damask beneath which her uncorseted body jiggled like five frightened piglets squirming and writhing in a vain attempt to free themselves from the sack they had been sewn into. When she took a step toward us, I heard the jingle of spurs, and glanced down to glimpse the sharp-pointed toes of black leather riding boots peeking from beneath her gown.

"Come, my daughters"—she held out a hand to us—"and embrace your stepfather!" With a sweeping gesture, she indicated the bashful, blushing figure of our Master of the Horse, Adrian Stokes, who seemed to be trying to hide himself in the shadows as though he were afraid to face us. "Here, my love"—she pulled at his scarlet satin sleeve—"come and drink a loving cup with me!" She pressed the goblet into his hand.

"Pinch me, Mary!" Kate whispered, clutching hard at my hand. "Wake me *now;* I *must* be dreaming!"

"Methinks I am having the same nightmare," I whispered back as we stood and stared at the blushing, bashful black-haired boy standing sheepishly beside our lady-mother in his garishly bright, scarlet satin doublet adorned with golden bugles all down the front and along the sleeves.

To his credit, Master Stokes seemed overcome with a burning hot shame and found it exceedingly hard to meet our gaze. Instead, he stared at the floor, studying his gold-slashed, scarlet shoes as though he could not quite believe that these were truly his feet.

"Well?" our lady-mother demanded, hands on hips. "What are you waiting for? Come, now, don't be shy—embrace him!"

"I would sooner hurl myself into the Thames!" Kate cried. "Mother, *how could you?* He's only *twenty!*"

Without daring to meet Kate's eyes, Master Stokes mumbled that he would be twenty-one on Tuesday.

"Yes, my love, and we shall have a party, a very grand party!" Our lady-mother smiled indulgently as she patted his arm and smacked a kiss onto his cheek and her hand stole mischievously behind to give a greedy and unsuspected squeeze to his buttocks that made Master Stokes nearly start out of his skin.

"Mother!" Kate cried, shaking her head incredulously. "Father has not even been dead two weeks! *Could you not have waited?"* She turned away, her hand rising to try to hide her tears. "You didn't even wear widow's weeds for him!"

"Come, Kate." I caught hold of my sister's hand. "You're wasting your words and your breath! She's not even sorry Father is dead; she *can't* be . . . to do *this!"* I waved a disgusted hand at Master Stokes. "He's young enough to be her son!"

"I—I—" Master Stokes began to stammer, looking first at our lady-mother as though, still accustomed to a role of servitude, he was awaiting her permission to speak. "Perhaps we did marry in haste. I—I—I always liked my lord of Suffolk and was greatly saddened by his death. When I first came to Bradgate, as a lad to work in the stables, he always had a smile and a treat from his comfit box for me. Truly, I mean no disrespect to his memory! If you like, we could drink a toast to him and light some candles 'neath his portrait."

"Sit down and shut up!" Our lady-mother shoved Master Stokes toward a chair and aimed a kick at the same buttocks she had just been squeezing. "I didn't marry you for your conversation!" Then she swung around, her gown billowing out like a great white sail behind her, and grabbed Kate's wrist, twisting it roughly. *"You stupid girl!"* she hissed. "I thought you had more sense! I didn't have time to mourn, and your father is as dead as he'll ever be, so what's the difference when by my actions I could still save *something?* Or did you want to see it all lost because of your foolish father—Bradgate and Suffolk House and what lands and monies we have left, that he didn't gamble away? I had to save something, and by marrying beneath me, and forsaking my rank as Duchess of Suffolk, to show the Queen this family has no more royal pretensions,

I have accomplished that! I did what I had to do, and you two ungrateful little girls should fall on your knees and thank me for it! Think you I liked giving up my title to become plain Mistress Stokes, even if it did land me a lusty young lad in my bed? Aye, I've saved the homes and money, but I've sacrificed my title, and now wherever I go people will snicker behind my back, because I've married a boy young enough to be my son, as Mary so rightly says! But I have two daughters and their futures to think of!"

"And *yourself!*" Kate shouted.

"Yes, myself!" our lady-mother acquiesced. "I've done my duty all my life, and now I *deserve* a husband who will make me happy! I've more than earned it! Forget about your worthless father, that spineless lout with a brain as soft and doughy as his body! I am the daughter of a queen, and the niece of a king, and I deserved far better than Hal Grey!"

She paused to draw breath and fan her flushed face, then, with a defiant toss of her head, went to sit on the gilded arm of Master Stokes's chair, ignoring its ominous groan, and arranged herself as though she were posing for a portrait of a doting wife. She stroked his hair and bent to nibble on his ear, while he blushed and glanced away as her hand dipped down to rove inside his shirt and playfully tweak a nipple, hard enough to make him squirm, wince, and squeal.

"Jane and Guildford too," she continued as she snatched the golden cup from Master Stokes's hand and drank greedily from it. "They're all dead and nothing can bring them back! Though I do regret poor Guildford; the *dear* boy wanted me to run away to Italy with him to manage his singing career. He paid me a great compliment when he said that even though I am a woman I was still the most formidable person he had ever known, and he felt confident that none of the theater managers would ever *dare* to cheat or shortchange him if I were there minding such matters. He was right, of course. Poor Guildford!" She sighed. "God rest him!"

She daintily selected a sugarplum from the golden tray beside Master Stokes's chair and popped it into her mouth, washing it down with a great gulp of wine. I watched disgustedly as a red rivulet dripped from the corner of her rouged mouth and trickled slowly down to stain the bodice of her white gown. It made me think of blood, and I had to close my eyes as my belly churned sickly inside.

"Come on, Mary!" Kate, swatting the tears from her eyes with her sleeve, seized my hand and dragged me toward the door. "We can't stay here!"

"I . . . I think it's going to rain!" Master Stokes called after us.

"Then don't go outside and stare up at the sky with your mouth open else you might drown!" Kate shouted back at him as she slammed the door and pulled me out into the London night, forgetting our fur cloaks in her haste.

"You should be happy for me!" Our lady-mother thrust her head out the parlor window and shouted after us as the rain began to lightly fall. "Your father is as dead now as he will be in a year, and instead of hiding it and living secretly in sin, I am legally wedded and well and rightfully enjoying the black-haired boy God has sent me as a reward to console me and share my bed! By heaven, I *deserve* him! At least I had the decency, the honesty, not to pretend!"

"Oh go boil your head, Mother!" Kate shouted back at her and kept on walking, pulling me along after her, as the first bolt of lightning stabbed the darkened sky, and the boom of thunder drowned out our lady-mother's angry reply.

"Kate!" I tugged at her hand. "Surely we should get a coach or a barge? It's dark, and it's not safe for us to be abroad, alone, defenseless, and dressed as we are. The city is full of danger, and we are walking straight into it!"

But Kate wasn't listening. Even as I tugged one sleeve and the wind fiercely grabbed the other, Kate kept walking, fast and furious, and didn't stop until we stood staring up at London Bridge. The rain-slickened gray stone shone silver in the lightning's bright white flash, and the traitors' heads, in various states of decay, leered ghoulishly from the metal pikes their pitch-dipped necks were impaled upon. An eyeball dangled from the socket of one of the freshest, while others looked leathery and weather-beaten, their flesh stripped away to reveal the bones beneath.

Kate drew me to stand in a nearby doorway, and huddling back in a corner, her arms wrapped around herself for warmth, she slumped down. "Now we wait."

"Wait for what?" I asked, yet in my heart I already knew the answer. Kate was waiting for a later hour, for the traffic on the streets and bridge to disperse, for all to be in their beds so none would be abroad to witness the bold act she intended.

Kate's eyes were fixed on the bridge, staring at the heads—or one particular head—and she didn't bother to answer me. I knew it would be futile to tell her she could not have it, not without the Queen's consent. The heads were left on London Bridge until all the flesh was gone, then the bare skulls were tossed into the Thames to make room for more. It was part of the punishment—that they could never lie in their graves whole. Only if the Queen granted consent could their families take them down for decent burial. Jane and Guildford had fortunately been spared this fate, but not Father. I knew our lady-mother would not be asking for his head; all she wanted to do was forget, and to make the Queen forget too, and she would beat us if she knew we had dared revive memories she wanted to sink, like Father's clean-picked, wind-buffed, and rain-polished skull, to the muddy bottom of the Thames.

But she had underestimated Kate. Kate wouldn't have it. She would save him, and damn the Queen's permission and our lady-mother, she would do it, daring all for love, just like she always did. *All for love*—that was my sister Kate; that is the epitaph that should adorn her grave, for there are no truer words to describe her than that motto she lived by all her life.

I must have fallen into a doze. I started awake as a flash of palest pink and silver flew past me. Kate was up and running; before I could reach out a hand to try and stop her, she was gone, running toward London Bridge as the rain lashed her, and the wind tugged and howled at her as though it were outraged by her audacity and determined to do what I couldn't—stop her.

Every time my heart beat I felt as though it would burst out of my chest and that I would look down and see it protruding, pulsing and dripping blood onto the golden apples that figured my beautiful green gown. I was too afraid to even pray as I watched Kate climb tenaciously to the top, fighting the wind all the way, and make her way along the bridge until she reached the grotesque cluster of weather-ravaged, raven-picked, and rotting heads. I wondered if wherever he was Father could see his rash and daring daughter, leaning far out over the rail, being pelted by silver needles of rain as she reached for the spike his head was impaled upon. Poor Father! His dull, dead eyes stared out blindly into the storm, the scarce tufts that were all that was left of his luxuriant auburn beard billowing, as the wind buffeted him like a parody of our lady-mother boxing his ears.

But she could not reach it, strain and strive as she might.

"Kate!" I ran out into the rain. "You'll *never* reach him! *Please,* come down before you fall!"

Kate straightened, wind-whipped and breast wildly heaving, and stared down defiantly at me. *"Never say never to me!"*

She hitched up her skirts and swung her leg out, straddling the rain-slickened rail, and shimmied along, as agile as one of her pet monkeys, even as the wind ripped the hood from her head and snatched away the silver net and pearl-tipped pins, unleashing a riot of waist-length copper ringlets to ride the wind like writhing red gold snakes, turning my sister into a beautiful Medusa lit by the blinding white flash of lightning. Was the boom of the thunder the great God Zeus laughing at this bold wench even as he desired her? Was the wind His way of trying to pull her into His embrace? Or would she slip and fall into the Thames, a beautiful sacrifice for His brother-god Neptune? *Oh, Kate, Kate, come down, Kate!* my heart cried as tears rolled down my face. *Cease this folly! Forget the head! Father is dead, and you cannot save him now! No one can! The head is just a head, and not worth risking your life for!*

Grasping the rail with one hand, Kate leaned far out and reached for Father's head. She started to slip, and I nearly died, sweating and burning despite the cold rain. She righted herself and sat for a long time, watching as her little pink shoe plummeted into the black water below. It sank without a sound, and any splash it made was swallowed up by the lusty, gusty wind. In the blinding flash of lightning that followed, I saw the determination in her face, and I knew she would never stop until she had his head or fell to a watery grave.

She tried to push her hair back, but it came right back, slapping her in the face, plastering itself over her eyes, nose, and mouth like a tangle of orangey red seaweed. Undaunted, Kate reached down and fumbled beneath her skirts and tore off a pink silk garter, leaving her white stocking to fall and droop around her ankle. Squeezing her knees tight around the rail, she gathered her hair back, like a horse's tail, and tied it tightly with the garter. Then she was ready to try again. I wanted to turn away. I couldn't bear to look, and yet I *had* to. She really was fearless, my bold, brave Kate! I could not have done it!

She really should have been dressed all in black to appear less conspicuous, or even better as a boy for ease of movement, but Kate had not planned this, or if she had, she never told me. Yet, despite the danger and encumbrance her clothes presented, the artist in me would not have altered a single stitch or shade. She was a *glorious, terrifying* sight to behold, there in the pouring rain, wind-whipped skirts of soft rose and silver and white petticoats flapping like the wings of terrified birds fighting to ride the wild, raging wind, to stay aloft and not be beaten down, illuminated by the silver-white, diamond-bright flash of lightning against the midnight sky. I wish I had been blessed with the talent to paint her, so the world could see her just like that instead of the insipid, pale, lifeless, black-and-white-gowned likenesses that are all that is left to show the world Lady Katherine Grey.

Then she had him, cradled safe against her breast. It was all over except for her descent, and surely God would not let her slip; if she was going to fail, if she was going to fall, surely it would not be now.

Carefully, most carefully, she shimmied back down. Wordlessly, she gave me Father's head to hold while she struggled to raise her heavy, waterlogged skirts and wiggle out of one of her petticoats.

Poor Father! I caressed his leathery, wind-burned cheeks. Most of his beard was gone, taken by the ravens or other birds to build their nests. I liked to think someday I might look up, at the nests in the trees in the parks and gardens of the Queen's palaces, and see auburn skeins from Father's beard woven into their nests.

Silently, Kate held her petticoat out to me, like a cradle, to lay Father's head in, but first I kissed his brow, and Kate did the same before she tenderly swaddled him in the sodden white linen.

I stood for a long moment and eyed my soaked and shivering

sister with breathless wonder. I still couldn't believe that she had done it. The wind had yanked and stolen away the garter that bound her hair, like a lovesick swain playfully snatching a ribbon from his sweetheart's hair to wear as a love token upon his hat or sleeve. She was minus one slipper, and I feared the frosty slush that covered the ground would be smitten by her fair toes or pretty little foot and take a token too. Her gown hung limp, hugging every curve, clinging to her limbs, so that she had to fight its waterlogged embrace for every step. The lightning flashed a vivid silvery white, and I saw frozen raindrops clinging to her hair like little diamonds. Her teeth were chattering, and there was a wild gleam in her eyes, a blue gray storm themselves, that spoke both of triumph and disbelief. She looked half drowned, a sorry, sodden sight, yet to my eyes she had *never* been more beautiful.

"Come on, Mary!" Clutching Father's head to her with one arm, she held out her hand to me and I took it.

Then off we went to the Church of St. Botolph's-Without-Aldgate, where I still visit Father every Sunday. Once there we gave Father into the care of the minister. He still keeps Father safe, locked inside the cupboard in his study, in a glass casket filled with sawdust that is regularly replenished—Father's leathery flesh soaks some vital nutrient from the wood shavings that keeps him tanned, as though he still rode to the hounds every day. Dr. Reynolds always receives me kindly, and together we share a cup of wine and drink a toast to Father, whom he remembers warmly as a feckless man he occasionally counseled against his gambling, but always generous and kind.

As the church bells tolled midnight, Kate took my hand again and we disappeared into the dark and rainy night to sneak back into Greenwich Palace, now that Suffolk House, still celebrating a wedding that to my mind made a mockery of the sacrament of holy matrimony, seemed even less of a home to us than it ever had before. Our lady-mother I realized now was the bedrock, the firm and solid foundation our family was built upon, but Father—fun, silly, wild, reckless Father with all his schemes and dreams and his ever-present comfit box—had been the heart of it.

❧ 12 ❧

Perhaps our royal cousin truly believed Kate's health had been broken by the series of cruel blows that had befallen our family—the loss of Jane and Guildford, followed fast by Father, and now our lady-mother's ludicrous and humiliating marriage to our former Master of the Horse—or maybe she just felt sorry for us. Not a word was ever spoken about the disappearance of Father's head from London Bridge. She kissed us each upon the cheek and gave us each an opal rosary and leave to retire from court. "Go home and grow strong; replenish your strength," she said as she bade us farewell.

Kate and I returned to Bradgate alone, with only a few servants to attend us. Our lady-mother remained in London, cavorting shamelessly, and most lustily according to the servants' gossip, with her new husband. "In exchange for sacrificing my rank, God has given me a most diverting boy to amuse and console me!" she said in defiance of the ridicule and laughter, thumbing her nose at those who marveled that she had married so far beneath her.

We reined our horses in at the foot of the long, winding drive lined with chestnut trees. We sat slumped wearily in our saddles and stared up at the house as the March winds tugged at our dust-caked riding habits and the feathers on our hats. It seemed a whole lifetime had passed since we had last been here. When we rode away to London, to see Jane and Kate married, I didn't realize I would be so long away from the only place I had ever thought of as home. The great rosy-bricked rectangle that had started life as a hunting lodge sixty years ago stood in the center of a sprawling, green deer park, flanked by silver streams and verdant forests so dense it was said one could wander twelve miles or more without ever glimpsing the sun, and beyond them, the slate hills towered in the distance. His pride swollen with the honor of having married a king's niece, Father had added two tall red-brick turrets with stained glass windows depicting hunting scenes to make the house look less like a big brick box. He had tried to fund their construction with his endeavors at the gambling tables but had garnered only greater debts. From the pointed red-tiled roof of each fluttered our family's proud banner of green, yellow, black, and white silk, and our parents were always vigilant for the least sign that the sun was beginning to fade them and had them replaced regularly; for this they kept a sewing woman in residence who did nothing but make new banners.

Without Jane and Father, Bradgate wouldn't be the same; it would be an empty shell of a house with its heart torn out. I would miss Jane's sullen seriousness, coming upon her curled in a window seat with a book in her lap and an apple in her hand, and Father, always with his comfit box, bringing us treats from London and coaxing the cook to "bake more goodies" so that the house always smelled of sugar, cinnamon, and marzipan, a plethora of spices and all the sweet fruits of summer.

There were some woodsmen working nearby, trimming the trees, and they paused and respectfully knelt and doffed their caps to us, silently offering their condolences upon our two great losses. The man nearest us had left his ax—a new one by the look of it—leaning against the tree he was attending and the sun struck its blade. Rather than shield her eyes, Kate stared straight into the blinding yellow glare. Before I could stop her, she sprang from the saddle and ran and seized the ax and began chopping madly. Clumsily, she staggered backward, tottering under its unwieldy, unaccustomed weight. But she persevered and swung the ax, again and again, all the while weeping wildly, sobbing for Jane and Father, crying hysterically that Jane and Father had lost their heads so the trees at Bradgate must too in remembrance of them.

"Take up your axes and 'head them! 'Head them like they did Jane and Father!" she commanded the woodsmen. So frighteningly persuasive was the crazed wildness in her eyes, that they quickly took up their axes and obeyed.

I stood silently by and didn't dare interfere until Kate dropped the ax and fell to her knees, panting and weeping, with bloodied blisters marring the beautiful white hands she held out to me, as though I could somehow heal the hurt. I gestured quickly for the woodsman to reclaim his ax and coaxed my sister back into the saddle and onward to the house. As we rode on, the air was filled with the sound of vigorous chopping, the whack of blades driven hard into wood and the grunts of strong, sweaty men pulling them free and swinging again, and again, until by day's end, when they went home with aching shoulders and backs and blistered hands, every one of the chestnuts that lined the approach to Bradgate stood a bare, ugly trunk, their leafy green heads lying toppled on the grass beside them to be cut into firewood and carted away on the morrow.

But by then Kate was already abed, having cried herself to sleep before the last lush green head fell, while I stood at the window and watched the destruction with tears in my eyes. *So wasteful!* I thought as I silently wept for Father, Jane, and Guildford, their lost and wasted lives, Kate's lost dream of love, so cruelly snatched away, and the destruction of the beautiful chestnut trees we three sisters had sat and played in the shade of, climbed, and gathered blossoms and nuts from. They had always been there all our lives, already grown tall and glorious by the time Jane was born. Bradgate didn't seem the same without them either, and I shuddered to think of our lady-mother's wrath when she beheld the stark, ugly, naked trunks, crudely chopped at various heights, when she at last returned to Bradgate. *At least we shall be well warned and ready to face her,* I thought, *for we shall surely hear her screaming from the road.* I shuddered again and hugged myself as I pictured her red, angry face and her arm wildly swinging her riding crop, hearing the smarting swish as it slashed the air until it found flesh to strike. In my mind I already felt its sting, splitting flesh and welling blood. I would take the blame; Kate had suffered enough, and I could and would spare her this.

Behind me, on the bed, Kate stirred, sobbing in her sleep, but did not waken.

"I wish there were something I could do to make our world right again, to turn back the clock and bring them all back, but I cannot. I have no magic. I am only a little girl!" I whispered feebly. But my sister, twisting in her sorrow-racked slumber, did not hear me.

At least she was still alive. I went and stood by the bed and clasped my hands and prayed, "*Please,* don't ever leave me, Kate!"

Kate burbled a few more little whimpers—they were growing mercifully fewer and fainter—and rolled over in bed, and I let myself imagine that they were an answer, reassuring me that she would never leave me alone, that she would be right there with me, in body as well as in spirit, until the day I died.

Dwarves with twisted bodies like mine rarely made old bones. Our bodies grew more contorted with age, which could squeeze and crush and damage our inner organs, our lungs were notoriously weak, and we were plagued by pains in our joints, like the grinding agony in my lower back and hips that sometimes left me prostrate, lying completely flat for days. All these ails only grew worse with age.

It was only cruel mischance that Jane, the firstborn, had also been the first to die at only sixteen. So surely Kate—sunny, vibrant, healthy Kate—who longed for life, not a glorious death and martyrdom, would be the last of us to die.

I gazed at my sister, her beautiful copper ringlets strewn across the pillows like a blazing, red gold banner shimmering in the sun, and pictured her many years from now as a gray-haired old grandmother dying peacefully in her bed with all her children and grandchildren clustered lovingly around her to see her tenderly into God's embrace. "That is the way it *should* be. God, *please* let it be so!" I fell on my aching little knees and prayed with all my heart and all the fervor of a frightened little girl who had just lost her eldest sister and father. *"Please! Please!"* I prayed until the words became an incoherent murmur and I fell into an exhausted slumber myself and lay upon the floor curled like a puppy beside Kate's bed.

13

After we returned to court, we made a pact to put the past behind us, to only look forward, and never again look back. We would welcome and embrace the future wholeheartedly since we could do nothing to change the past. We had to let it go lest it drag our hearts down to sink like stones in the river to be mired in the mud forever. We had to break free of the anchors that weighed our hearts down and swim for shore where life, and maybe even love, waited, and not drown. We couldn't wear mourning for Jane and Father, and in order to survive and thrive at court, we had to cast the black velvet from our hearts as well, and Kate had to learn to love and wear red again without thinking of blood. After one last lingering look and one late night of tears and bittersweet memories, we packed our treasured mementos of those we had loved and lost away in boxes and hid them beneath our bed.

After that, time seemed to speed up, like we were racing through life, and we seemed to dance, fast and furious, through the years; they flew by so swift, like falcons flying after sparrows, intent upon the kill, and we too had to kill every moment lest it leave us free to do what we had promised never to do—to pause and ponder and look back upon the past.

But for my Kate, though she smiled, danced, and made merry,

life at court was in truth sheer torment, and she cried into her pillow every night. She just could not *bear* having to see Berry every day, to brush his hand by happenstance in the course of a dance, or in obedience to the carefully laid choreography in a masque, to find herself sitting near him at a joust or picnic and see the attentions he paid to the other ladies, or to have their eyes meet across the banquet table and then to see him turn away and engage another in conversation. She had me make a beautiful soft orange and strawberry pink gown for her, the shades carefully chosen so they blended beautifully, but not so pallid and meek that the eye would pass them by. When she put it on, she would sashay past or linger near Lord Herbert in this beautiful dress that had been designed to cry out *Notice me! Notice me!* bouncing on her toes, with an eager expression like a dog begging for a bone, copper curls shimmering in the light of the candles or the sun as she twirled them idly around her fingers or tossed them over her shoulders.

But it was all in vain. Berry simply turned away and asked another lady to dance or walk in the garden with him, and Kate would be plunged back into despair, crying into her pillow every night and pushing her plate away so that the flesh fell from her bones and our lady-mother would feel the need to grasp her chin tight, bruising the milk-pale skin with the brutal pressure of her meaty thumb and fingertips, and remind her, "Without your beauty, you are *nothing!*"

I used to pray every night that Kate's heart would heal and she would see that it was not *really* Berry the boy she was in love with, but Love, the *idea* of loving and being loved. Kate, unlike many men and women of our class who married for convenience, practicality, and to obey parental dictates, took the pretty and sentimental words of the marriage service seriously, and when she spoke them, her heart was in every syllable. *Let her find a new love,* I implored the Lord, *one who is truly worthy of her and will never forsake, hurt, or disappoint her, one who will be faithful and love her unto death like the great loves the minstrels sing of.*

Cousin Mary, to her credit, always treated us well, as though she were, in some small way, trying to atone for taking Jane from us.

One day she drew me to sit beside her as she sat gazing with the most desperate yearning at Titian's portrait of Prince Philip.

"I know you will understand, little cousin, being what you are," she said delicately. "Though I am not malformed like you, I too always thought the great loves the minstrels sang of would be denied me, that Love would always shun and pass me by. So you *must* understand, now that I have found him, I *cannot* . . . I *dare not* . . . let him go. I am not so much a fool as to think I could do better, and Love, who has deigned to look at me for once, may never do so again if I snub the great and precious gift he has given me."

In truth, I *did* understand, yet I could not forgive the taking of Jane's life. A part of me, in my child's anger and anguish, cursed Cousin Mary and hoped that she would find only misery with her Philip. But afterward, I fell on my knees and begged God to forgive me, for evil thoughts rashly uttered in anger, lest the misfortune I had wished upon another rebound upon me and the only sister I had left. Jane was gone, and whether Cousin Mary found joy or sorrow with her Spanish prince, it would not bring her back.

When Kate brushed the Queen's hair on her wedding day, Cousin Mary, with tears in her eyes, took Kate's hand. "You are young and beautiful. You've already had one chance, and you will have another. You will not be alone forever; women as beautiful as you never are. But this is my *last* chance. Philip is my last hope, and I *must* have him—for the True Faith, for England, so I may give birth to a son, a Catholic prince, to rule after I am gone, and for me," she admitted at last, lowering her eyes as though half-shamed by this admission. "I ask you to please understand." She drew Kate to stand beside her, before the big, silver looking glass. "Look"—she lifted the heavy mass of Kate's hair, like a nest of writhing copper snakes—"see how bright your hair is. See all the gold twining like true lovers embracing with the red. Now look at mine." She lifted a lifeless hank of her own dingy and lackluster yellowy orange gray hair. "They used to call me Princess Marigold, but all my gold has been spent in loneliness and sorrow."

That was the closest Cousin Mary ever came to apologizing for what had happened to Jane. The truth is lust triumphed over cousinly love. Jane died to make an old maid's dreams of love come true, but she died in vain. Some would say I should find consolation, a sort of bitter victory, in that. But I don't. My sister died at only sixteen, the reasons don't really matter; none of them are good enough to justify it or heal the wound in my heart. In the end, all that really matters is that she died, not how it affected the grand scheme of things; I can't, and never could, think of the world as a giant chessboard and the people I love as pawns upon it, won and lost in the game of life.

But our lady-mother was overjoyed by the favor our royal cousin showed us. She crowed and preened and strutted in private, vowing that Kate would be England's next queen. She went on, maddeningly repetitious, her face glowing as she gloated about how she had known Queen Mary from girlhood and knew her womb to be "rotten fruit," "too moist for any seed to take root," and "unfertile ground unlikely to sustain a life" even if Prince Philip succeeded in planting one there. Gleefully she related how scores of physicians had been summoned to treat Mary for "strangulation of the womb," to bleed her from the sole of her foot to try and ease the painful retention of blood that caused her womb to swell and ache, and bring forth her monthly flow to relieve her. "Such women are poor breeders," our lady-mother said. "If they whelp at all, their babes are sickly and soon die, so we've *nothing* to fear from the rotten fruit of Mary's womb! A day *will* come when I will see my daughter crowned queen! *This* time, *all* shall be done *right!*"

Once, as a pointed snub to Princess Elizabeth, who balked at attending Mass and often made excuses, claiming to be unwell, even feigning to faint outside the royal chapel or loudly complaining of a bellyache, Queen Mary strode past her half sister to take Kate by the hand and bade her walk beside her, *before* Elizabeth, while loudly praising my sister as a "good Catholic maid." When our lady-mother heard she was delirious with joy. She celebrated by drinking and dancing all night with Master Stokes then dragging him off to bed at cock's crow to service her until she fell into an exhausted sleep around noon.

Through it all, Kate kept silent, never daring to tell our lady-mother that she did not want to be queen and prayed every day that God would bless our royal cousin with a child of her own and thus spare her. Indeed, what good would it have done if she had spoken up? It would have only led to more angry words and blows. "I shall wait and hope this cup shall pass me by," Kate told me in the privacy of our room, "and that I shall not be made to drink from it, for I've no desire to; I find it a vile and bitter brew, more poisonous than pleasurable, and sometimes it even kills. I would rather be queen of my husband's heart, to rule our household, with our children, pets, and servants as my loyal and loving subjects, than be empress of all the world." But our lady-mother would only have laughed and called Kate a fool and boxed her ears while deploring her daughter's lack of ambition.

While Kate had all the praise and glory, I found that I was subjected to less mockery after the courtiers saw how greatly our royal cousin favored us. It was wonderful beyond words to be spared the jibes and insults, even though it meant I was more or less ignored. No one thought I would ever be queen like Kate, so there was no need to try to curry favor and make a fuss over me. So I kept silent and watched. Many young men flirted with Kate, and young women sought her friendship. We had gone, almost overnight, from being reviled as turncoats to being revered as royal princesses, at court, though not by the people in the streets. Some even detested us as Elizabeth's rivals, though we never saw ourselves as such.

But people see what they want to see and are often blind to the truth. They feared we would usurp the succession as our sister had. Elizabeth did not love or even like us and was more to be feared than Mary. Elizabeth would be swift to punish any who *dared* come between her and her one true love—England. She would never forgive or be merciful and passive. No, Kate and I agreed; better to die outright than be regarded as Elizabeth's enemy.

So many people longed for Elizabeth, including the lascivious golden-bearded Philip who was now the Queen's husband—palace gossip said he had peepholes drilled in the wall so he could watch Elizabeth undress and bathe. And to most of the common people, Elizabeth was England and their last link with their beloved Henry VIII. Loving Philip had cost Cousin Mary most of her people's love, and many thought she cared more for Spain than she ever did for England. The people's love affair with the last *true* Tudor princess, the vibrant, flame-haired Elizabeth, only grew more passionate as England erupted in a blaze of persecution that sought to burn out every trace of the Reformed Religion. People went to the stake praying with their dying breath for Elizabeth's ascension, for her to come to the throne and deliver England from this evil.

It was an exciting and frightening time to be alive. In gowns of silver tinsel and Our Lady's blue satin, with crowns of silvered rosemary and blue ribbons on our unbound hair, we were there when Mary finally married her prince, and Kate was amongst the maids chosen to dance with Prince Philip at the wedding feast. She laughed and told me afterward that when he lowered her after the high lift in the volta, his tongue had flickered out like a snake's to lick and delve inside her ear and his hand had cupped her breast and compared its size and sweetness to the oranges in the garden of his father's palace.

We were there, in close and daily attendance, the two tragic times our royal cousin's womb bore phantom fruit. We knelt and prayed with her in her private chapel and took it in turns with the other ladies to read her prayers, psalms, and saints' lives, and sat for hours sewing and embroidering baby clothes. How Cousin Mary praised the rows of pretty roses I embroidered around the hems of those little white gowns! She would trust no one but me with this delicate task, declaring, "Our little cousin Mary's roses are the prettiest!" Soon many ladies of the court were vying to have me embroider roses on the hems of their petticoats, to peek out whenever they lifted their skirts. For us girls who wore the Queen's russet and black livery by day, to emphasize the grandeur of the royal garb, for our wary cousin feared any who might outshine her, it was a fun and harmless way for us to add a little color and uniqueness to our bland attire. Eventually I was stitching not just roses but all manner of flowers, in both becoming and unusual combinations—like pinks mated with marigolds; periwinkles coupled with yellow primroses; country daisies and the petite yellow buttons of tansy; chamomile blossoms and scarlet poppies nestled amongst golden wheat; bluebells and buttercups; festive red-berried and thorny-leaved holly alongside mistletoe with a profusion of white berries to tempt a lover's kiss; deadly poisonous but pretty purple monk's hood and jaunty yellow Turk's cap; purple-pink thistles amidst spires of lavender; purple-kissed blue forget-me-nots and pure white lily of the valley; or those great sweet-scented snowballs of heavenly white blossoms known as guelder roses that bloomed in May but bore poisonous red berries in autumn, and in my embroidery I could show both incarnations side by side.

Some ladies even craved garden vegetables, healing herbs, bountiful branches laden with dangling fruit, or beds of ripe berries encircling their hems. Even in the evening, when they might wear their own splendid attire, they still wanted to wear the floral bordered petticoats I made for them, often in colors brightly contrasting their gowns. At any moment as the ladies danced past, one might catch a beguiling glimpse of vibrant yellow daffodils beneath a purple velvet gown, bright pink peonies peeping out from underneath a brazen scarlet skirt, blueberries bursting ripe with flavor beneath a luscious pear silk, or even globe artichokes spreading their leaves beneath sunset orange satin. One might even catch a quick glimpse of the vibrant pink of the apothecary's rose hiding beneath a matron's modest mouse gray velvet, or spy the pink-speckled white bugles of foxglove, or even a row of flamboyant heart's ease pansies blooming beneath a widow's black weeds.

For the more daring and coquettish ladies, the ones who liked to lift their skirts especially high during the dance, I embroidered flights of beautiful rainbow-winged butterflies or fat black and yellow bees fluttering up their stockings from ankle to knee. Even Cousin Elizabeth, then still at court under the Queen's wary, watchful eye, had me do a sumptuous silver and gold border of roses dotted with pearls on a cream taffeta petticoat to wear with the new silver and gold brocade gown Prince Philip had given her, ostensibly to satisfy his wife's complaint that Elizabeth dressed too plainly, seeing it as a secret message encoded in her clothes to show the Protestants that she was with them and only paid lip service to the Catholic creed. But it was all great fun, and for the first and only time in my life, I knew what it was like to be popular and sought after. It felt good to be important, even if it was for such a frivolous, flighty thing.

As each of the Queen's phantom pregnancies progressed, we were there to cater to her cravings for great bowls brimming full of mixed peppers, orange slices, olives, and goat cheese, and afterward to pat her hands, hold her head when she bent retching over the basin, and nurse and comfort her through the agonizing attacks of heartburn that inevitably followed these repasts.

As her suspicion, jealousy, and hatred of Elizabeth increased, we obediently sat and listened to her zealously recounting the lurid tale about how Elizabeth's mother, "the great whore Anne Boleyn," used to have the lowborn lute player Mark Smeaton concealed inside a cupboard in her bedchamber, to come out and pleasure her whenever she lay down naked and opened her arms and legs and called for "something sweet." She would pace back and forth, tear at her thin hair with her clawlike hands, and rant and rage about Elizabeth, insisting that she did not deserve the people's love, and was a bastard with not a drop of Tudor blood in her, though one only had to look at Elizabeth to know this was a mad delusion; none of the children King Henry sired ever resembled him more. But it sorely rankled our royal cousin to know that Elizabeth held the people's heart in the palm of her hand and had youth and patience on her side. She was shrewd enough to know that her chance would come; she had only to wait for it and the crown would be handed to her on a purple velvet cushion. There was no need for her to embroil herself in the dangerous schemes her sister imagined; Elizabeth was no fool. But every time a new conspiracy was uncovered or whispered of, Queen Mary was convinced Elizabeth was at the heart of it, and no one could persuade her otherwise.

Then, all of a sudden, Time tired of this frantic pace, dug in its heels, and slowed to the gait of a lazy, old snail. I remember *exactly* when it happened—the morning I awoke to my first monthly blood. I was thirteen then and fearing that I would never bleed; both my sisters had shed their first woman's blood early in their twelfth year; for them it had been like a belated New Year's gift. I remember Kate's courses started for the first time on St. Valentine's Day, and she saw heart shapes in the red stains on her sheets and declared it a sign that she would be lucky in love, but Jane thought it was all a confounded nuisance and went on to preach a ponderous sermon about Eve in the Garden of Eden.

How excited I was when I awoke and found the rusty red roses of womanhood blooming on my sheets. I bolted from my bed and rushed to the looking glass, hoping to see some change, praying as

I ran that God had worked a miracle, and I would find that overnight "the beastly little one" had been transformed, like a butterfly emerging from its cocoon, into a beautiful, shapely, and slender young lady just like Kate. Yet one glance told me that during the night, when I had passed obliviously in my slumber from child to woman, neither Father Time nor Mother Nature had left a gift for me to mark the occasion. I was still no taller than a child of five, a crouch-backed little gargoyle, and I knew that no corset, no matter how rigorously laced, would ever sculpt my stocky, tree-trunk torso into an exquisite hourglass like Kate's. And if I were to ever dare tread a public measure, the movements of my short, thick, vein-rippled, bowed little legs, fortunately hidden by my skirts, would occasion mockery, giggles, and glee instead of compliments on my nonexistent grace. When I raised my night shift with my still stubby fingers and walked back and forth before the icy cruel, silvered glass, I saw that I still had the same waddle-wobble walk. *Nothing* had changed, and I knew it never would; I would be stuck inside this ugly, ungainly, squat little goblin's body until the day I died and God set my soul free.

"Mayhap in Heaven I shall be a raving beauty," I sighed and said to the sad, ugly face staring back at me from the looking glass. Then the tears came. So suddenly they took me by surprise. I wept as though great stones of sorrow had been suddenly set down upon my shoulders and chest, threatening to crush me with this painful grief. I wanted my sister; I wanted Kate. But we no longer shared a room; that privilege had been taken from me and given to another, and I was left to sleep alone. No one wanted to share a bed with "Lady Mary Gargoyle." I wanted to run howling down the corridor and pound on her door in my bloodstained shift and throw myself into Kate's arms, but womanly dignity and pride won out over a child's rage against unfairness. I would keep my blood a secret, for in truth, what did it matter that I was now a woman? There would never be a husband, a man, to love me. My body might as well be dry and barren, yet my heart, I knew, would always weep tears of blood for the carnal comforts and fleshly pleasures that would ever be denied me because of what I was. Unfortunately there were no nobly born dwarf lads at court who could be mated with me, only the lowborn tumblers and fools in jingle bells and motley who came to entertain, and to them I was of too high an estate to ever be trifled with. Instead of desire in their eyes, I saw scorn and envy; unlike them, I did not have to make silly faces and cut capers to put food on my table; I was a duke's daughter with royal blood in my veins, born to live and die in comfort and ease. If Fate ever decreed that I should hold a scepter it would not be tipped with jingle bells to be waggled at a laughing crowd while I rolled my eyes and stuck my tongue out.

The young Lady Jane Seymour, the late Lord Protector's daughter named in honor of his sister, "the third time's the charm queen" who had died giving Henry VIII the son he desired above all things, was now Kate's best friend and bedmate. This Lady Jane was assuredly one of the most delicate, gentle-hearted creatures God ever created, so sweet that indeed it hurt my heart to hate her. She had made a point of befriending Kate in the dark days just after Jane's death, when most of the court hypocritically shunned her as the sister of a traitor and a turncoat who had renounced the Reformed Faith to save her life and family fortune when many of them had done *exactly* the same thing, and a divorcee at only fourteen whose much-envied beauty and the flirtatious wiles she had boldly exhibited in the company of her former husband and father-in-law made her virtue suspect. But pale, ethereal Lady Jane in her gowns of her favorite heavenly blue reminiscent of the Holy Virgin's robes had no patience for such things. Perhaps it was because she knew she was not long for this world? Her lungs were weak; fever often brightened her cheeks and pallid, blue-violet eyes, making them glow with a watery luminosity that only made her more beautiful, especially since she had not had the misfortune to inherit the Seymours' prominent and beaky nose that usually marred their women's otherwise fine features. Her hair was the fairest I had ever seen, a shimmering silvery blond that always made me think of angel wings, but she often bemoaned was too limp to hold even a vestige of a curl. No matter how long her maid labored twining it around the hot irons, it would fall flat, hanging straight to her waist, slick as silk, defying all pins, before the irons even had a chance to cool or for Lady Jane to make her way downstairs to whatever celebration she was preparing to attend in the Great Hall.

I didn't lose my sister all at once. The change happened gradually. Though I didn't begrudge her a friend, I could not help but resent anyone who came between us. My sister was in truth my only friend and I had great need of her. But the five years that separated us, though they had always seemed so inconsequential before, and I had always been old for my years, now seemed of a sudden so very great. I wanted to stop it, and the polite, bland smiles that Kate now favored me with as though I were a stranger, or a mere acquaintance at most, instead of the sister who knew and loved her best. But I couldn't. When I tried to talk to her about it, she dismissed it as nonsense, jealousy, or just my imagination.

In truth maybe there were elements of all three tossed into the brew of emotion bubbling inside of me. I only know that whenever she was with Jane Seymour I felt as though a pane of thick glass divided us and I was always on the outside looking in, futilely trying to get her attention, trying to gain back the time Kate no longer had for me. It only made things worse when Lady Jane, with kindness in her forget-me-not eyes, would smile shyly and hold out her hand and invite me to join them, for I knew that if I did that pane of glass her gesture had banished would soon come back again, and I would feel an outsider, an intruder, an eavesdropper spying on them. So I schooled myself to proudly decline, turn my back, and thrust my nose up high, and walk away from that outstretched hand.

Even if my cold rebuffs hurt that gentle lady, I had to protect myself since no one else would. I knew that being with them, seeing the happiness they shared, would hurt me because I could never be a part of it. Knowing that it had once been mine made the pain even worse.

At court all the maidens who served Her Majesty slept two to a bed; it was deemed a special privilege or a sign of great disfavor for any to have a room all to herself. But this Lady Jane was often troubled by coughs and fevers, so few relished sleeping in the same bed with her lest they catch some vile contagion or her coughing and feverish tossing deprive them of a restful sleep. At first, Kate would only occasionally creep down the corridor in her shift and bare feet to pass a night giggling and gossiping with her friend, but then a day came when, with the Queen's permission, she packed her things and moved them to Lady Jane's room. Every night thereafter I would lie awake, wishing and hoping that Kate would come creeping down the corridor to spend a night with me, but she never did. I would picture the two of them, braided and frilled night-capped heads together, gossiping and giggling long into the night, just like Kate and I used to do, and weep into my pillow and wonder if God would ever see fit to send me someone to ease my loneliness. Kate said God had given her Lady Jane as a replacement for our own Jane, the sister He had taken home to Him, but who, if any, I wondered, would He give me to take Kate's place?

But at least Kate was getting better. Her heart was healing, or so I thought. I remember seeing her one night, with a handsome dark-haired boy in gold-piped crimson velvet. I watched with a glad heart as he maneuvered her into a corner to steal a kiss after she had danced, the most beautiful damsel of all, in a masque, draped in a gold lace mantle over a green and purple gown embroidered with golden pearl-dotted vines and festooned with bunches of purple and green wax grapes, and beneath it, I noted with pleasure, the petticoat I had embroidered for her with bouquets of scarlet roses bound with golden bows and clusters of grapes. He caressed her bright hair, as he pressed forward, and so dazzled and smitten was he by her radiant beauty and charm as they bantered softly and smiled into each other's eyes that he absently plucked grapes from the clusters in her hair and had already eaten three before Kate laughingly inquired if he was aware that they were made of wax. Kate let him steal another kiss, and he caressed the side of her neck with hands that looked so soft and tender they made me *long* to be in her shoes.

When his hand traveled down to gently cup her breast, Kate let it linger there for a moment while she savored his kiss before she laughed and danced away from him and ran to grab the hand of one of the court graybeards and, his potbelly jiggling, pulled him out to join the other dancers in a lively gavotte. I watched with a sad and happy heart, knowing that it would be Lady Jane Seymour, not I, who would laugh about it in bed with her that night. How I missed her and those sweet, sisterly confidences whispered against our pillows while all around us the palace slept.

I stood in the shadows and waited for her. As she and Jane Seymour walked past, heads together, giggling, on the way to their room, I boldly reached out and caught her skirt. Kate paused and stared down at me, and I saw the flash of impatience, and annoyance, in her eyes. When I did not speak and glanced meaningfully past her at Lady Jane, unable to keep the reproachful glare from my eyes, she demurely lowered her head and murmured that she was rather tired and would await Kate upstairs.

"Well, what is it, Mary?" Kate turned back to me, arms folded across her breasts.

Still I persisted. I *had* to know. "Do you love him?" I asked hopefully.

"Who?" Kate asked irritably, as though she had no idea what I was talking about.

"The dark-haired boy in crimson. I saw you kiss him, and you let him touch your breast. He's very handsome, Kate, and he has kind eyes."

With a flippant, world-weary laugh and a toss of her flame-bright curls, Kate said, "It was *only* a kiss, Mary! It meant *nothing!* I was just having fun; isn't that what I'm here to do? Love is a snare." She said this suddenly, with a brittle vengeance filled with unshed tears that threatened to seep through the cracks. "I made the mistake of getting caught in it. But don't let it get you, Mary. Don't you make the same mistake! If you do, you'll *never* be free! It bites deep, holds tight, tears you when you try to pull free, and even if you do get away, it always leaves you marked with a scar so that you can never forget it, no matter how much you dance and laugh and let pretty boys kiss and fondle you."

She laughed again, as though she were trying to pretend it was all a jest, and twirled away from me, dancing down the corridor with an obviously feigned gaiety, on her way to join Jane Seymour.

"I don't believe you!" I called after her. "Your words are a shield; you're just trying to protect your heart because you don't want to be hurt again!"

Kate froze, then whirled around and stormed back to challenge me. "What do you think that *you* know about love?" she demanded.

"More than you think," I answered boldly. "Those who have never had it, who have had to learn to live without it, knowing it is something they can never realistically hope to have, but still nonetheless yearn and dream of it, know its worth far better than those who have had it given to them free and gratis all their lives, and will go on to love and love again, just as you will! Losing Berry isn't the end, Kate. You *will* find love again, or it will find you, I haven't a doubt of it!"

Breasts heaving, Kate stood and stared at me as though I were her enemy, and, for a moment, I feared I had gone *too* far, that she hated me, there was such anger in her eyes. But then, abruptly, she gave a great sigh, briefly shut her eyes, then turned and walked away.

"I'm tired. Good night, Mary." She tossed the words back coolly over her shoulder along with the hot blaze of her curls, but I thought I detected a quiver of tears hovering just beneath the words. As her steps quickened as she neared the stairs, I knew that this would be another night when she cried herself to sleep. Only it would be Jane Seymour, and not I, who would be there to hold and comfort her.

The next afternoon Queen Mary sent for me. She had sensed my unhappiness, I think, after Kate deserted me. When I entered her quiet, darkened chamber, where all the curtains were drawn tight against the sun that so cruelly hurt her poor, tear-swollen eyes, she was alone, bereft and grieving for her golden Spanish prince who had sailed away, never to return, leaving her alone with another phantom baby filling her belly with false hope. She sat on the floor, trailing black veils like a widow and straggling, dirty, matted hair that was now entirely gray but for a few pale yellowy orange streaks. *It shall have to be cut off,* I thought with a pang of alarm, knowing how sensitive Cousin Mary was about her hair, *for not even Kate will have the patience to comb the tangles out.*

She squinted hard at me, then her lips spread in a wide smile, showing swollen gums and the ugly black and yellow stumps of her few remaining teeth. She held up two dolls—a pair of little ladies arrayed in exquisite gowns she had made. There was a small chest nearby overflowing with more. Tiny gowns, kirtles, cloaks, petticoats, slippers, and headdresses spilled out onto the floor, and her sewing basket beside it, surrounded by scraps of gorgeous fabric and skeins of gilt thread, her silver sewing scissors, and a pincushion speared with pearl-tipped pins and shaped like a pomegranate that was a precious relic of her mother. She handed me one of the dolls, a little raven-haired lady in lemon velvet crisscrossed with gold piping and pearls, and bade me sit beside her whilst she cradled a honey-haired damsel in tawny rose brocade.

I was thirteen and fancied myself too old for dolls, so I felt a trifle foolish, and embarrassed for her as well as for myself, but I didn't dare disobey nor could I bear to disappoint someone who had been so kind to me, one I knew to be in such pain, mayhap even dying if the whispers gliding like serpents through the palace corridors were true.

The hours dragged slowly past as we dressed and undressed the dolls and enacted little dramas with them. Suddenly she turned and rummaged in the chest and brought out two more dolls—a replica of herself in her sumptuous black velvet wedding gown, so densely embroidered with gold you could barely see the black beneath, and a male doll, golden-haired, with a little golden dagger of a beard decorating his chin, clad in gold-embellished white velvet and a bloodred cloak embroidered with pearls and golden thistles. She started to give him to me, but then, with a horrified gasp, as though she could not believe what she had almost done, snatched him back and hugged him possessively against her breast and glared at me with crazed eyes that *dared* me to try and take him from her. I didn't know what to do. Thankfully the moment passed, and she realized that I was no threat. With tears rolling down her face, she thrust the doll fashioned in her own likeness at me. Then, though she was crying so hard she could scarcely see, we reenacted the couple's nuptials until Queen Mary collapsed weeping on the floor and her two most devoted ladies-in-waiting, Jane Dormer and Susan Clarencieux, emerged silently from the shadows to help her back to bed.

"Go away, little gargoyle," Susan said over her shoulder as they led their weeping mistress away. "This is no place for you."

As I closed the door behind me, I heard Cousin Mary's sobs grow into keening wails as she cried for her Philip.

Soon she was dead. We were bathing her corpse and dressing her for the last time in the blue velvet and ermine gown she had worn on her coronation day, carefully pinning it to conceal how loose it hung upon her emaciated frame. Kate's clever fingers worked wonders with the dirty, matted hair, snaring it in a golden net beneath a coronet of spring flowers formed of precious gems.

As we worked silently over her corpse, outside the bells tolled and the people sang and danced in the streets, and wept with joy, to welcome the young woman they called "Our Elizabeth." She was the phoenix that had risen from the ashes of all the Protestants "Bloody Mary" had burned to cinders along with her popularity, throwing her people's love onto the pyre and eradicating all memory of the once-beloved "Merciful Mary" and the even more dimly remembered "Princess Marigold." Now her death was cause for jubilation, a national holiday that would be celebrated for many years to come.

As Kate rubbed rouge onto the gaunt cheeks that were like yellow wax in the candlelight, our eyes met over that poor, pathetic body and we silently wondered, now that Elizabeth was queen, what would become of us. Elizabeth, unlike Mary, had never favored or befriended us, but neither had she been cruel, only coolly indifferent; to Elizabeth we were just there, like pieces of furniture. I hadn't told Kate, but I had already set to work embroidering a petticoat with red and white Tudor roses and the crowned golden initials *ER,* "Elizabeth Regina," as a gift for her, to show that we had no royal pretensions, we weren't pretenders to the throne, and we wanted only peace, not to be embroiled in conspiracies and schemes. I prayed Elizabeth would read correctly the message embroidered in those royal roses of red and white petals that symbolized the union of the houses of York and Lancaster. Our very survival might depend on it.

14

With the advent of Elizabeth, Lady Jane Seymour's health began a sharp decline; her bad days now far outnumbered her good. The Queen didn't like having a fever-bright consumptive with a hacking cough too near about her and often gave her leave to retire from court to her family's country estate, Hanworth, in Middlesex. She sent Kate with her as "a remedy against loneliness for a young girl so accustomed to the crowded life at court."

To our immense relief, Queen Mary's demise had not substantially altered our position, except we, like most of the court, were Protestants again. We rode once more in golden chariots clad in ermine-banded crimson as part of an even more splendid coronation procession, and wore again our red silk petticoats with the golden butterflies in remembrance of our lost sister. We also retained our privileged posts as ladies-of-the-bedchamber.

But Elizabeth, though graciously cool and largely indifferent to me, was always very wary of Kate. Though Kate would have gladly gone on her knees and sworn that she didn't want to be queen, she wanted only to be happy, as a wife and mother, that a loving, happy household was the only kingdom she coveted, it wasn't enough. Elizabeth knew that as long as she remained the unmarried "Virgin Queen," which she seemed bound and determined to do despite the confusion and consternation it caused, Kate would be regarded as the heir presumptive; thus many would flock around and flatter her and even devise plots to bring her to the throne sooner rather than later.

There were many in the world who thought Elizabeth's claim to the throne tenuous at best. Those who refused to acknowledge the marriage of Henry VIII and Anne Boleyn said Elizabeth was a bastard born of an illicit and illegal union, and thus the Crown should go to someone more worthy and of unblemished pedigree, someone like my sister Kate, and her resemblance to the "Tudor Rose," Mary Tudor, "The French Queen," was often favorably cited. There were even whispers of a Spanish plot to abduct Kate and marry her by force to Philip's imbecilic son Don Carlos, a youth who took fiendish delight in torturing animals and servants. But Kate wanted no part of any of it, and certainly none of Don Carlos and his manias and madness. If anyone dared try to speak to her about her "royal destiny," she would stop her ears and flee their presence as fast as she could.

That was why, I thought, it pleased her so much to escape the court, to travel by a slow horse-drawn litter to Hanworth with her invalid friend. It was the *only* way Kate could know *true* peace, away from the maelstrom of plotting that was Elizabeth's court. "Deliver me from this viper's nest of intrigue!" she would always cry as she bolted down the steps into the courtyard and leapt, unassisted, into the litter, impatient to be off and away from it all, looking forward, never back, not even to wave at me.

But there was more to these visits to Hanworth than I ever knew until much later. That was where she met Ned again. Edward Seymour the younger, the handsome Earl of Hertford, who had once, briefly, been our sister Jane's suitor.

As though Fate had decreed it, Kate told me when she finally bared her soul and confessed all, nigh two years after that fateful day, she had been wearing a robin's egg blue gown—the very same color she had worn that long ago morning when they had first met on the stairs at Bradgate—when Ned Seymour, the sun making a golden blaze to burn out the brown of his hair, descended the sunken stone steps into the garden where Kate was busily gathering a pretty bouquet to brighten his sister's sickroom.

Gallantly, Ned insisted that he must help her. As he bent to pluck the blossoms, his hazel eyes gazing deeply into Kate's stormy blue gray ones, he let his fingers brush against hers as he handed them to her. He showed himself exceedingly well versed in the lore and secret language of flowers and recited what each blossom stood symbol for.

"Purple iris for a message," he began. "Like the one hidden in this bouquet. Scarlet poppies because everyone deserves one fantastic, extravagant folly in their life, like a foolish or impossible love"—he smiled knowingly at Kate—"even if the memory makes us cringe forever afterward."

His words conjured memories of Berry and made Kate blush. To give her a quiet, private moment to compose herself, Ned knelt over a patch of purple blue blossoms.

"Jacob's ladder," he announced. "To bid thee, fair maiden, come down to me like an angel from heaven and bless me with your love and favor."

Then he was down again, enthusiastically reaching for more.

"Goldenrod"—he twirled the feathery spire of golden flowers around by its stem before giving it to her—"for encouragement, for I would have that from you, just as I would give it. Snowdrops for consolation, that we might find comfort together, and be a balm to each other for the many sorrows and disappointments that have dotted our lives like a field of these dainty white flowers."

Both paused to ponder the many painful losses that had scarred their families and the day they knew would inevitably come when they would both lose a beloved sister and friend—the Lady Jane Seymour.

But Ned was quick to shrug off his sorrow.

"Daffodils!" With an excited grin he bent to gather some of the jaunty yellow flowers that could always coax a smile out of any who beheld them. "To herald a new beginning, and—dare I hope?—a new love." He paused and stared deep and hopefully into Kate's eyes before breaking away to snatch up some sunny yellow flowers. "Here! I know you like yellow, so we must have celandine—for the joys yet to come, for all that we have to look forward to!"

Like a man possessed, again and again Ned swooped down to

gather more flowers, thrusting them into Kate's hands then darting back for more. "Like a seagull diving for fish," Kate would later laugh when she recalled this scene for me.

"Lilacs for the first stirrings of love; lily of the valley to welcome the return of happiness; larkspur so that your heart may be as light and gay as the lark's song; crocuses for joy and gladness; red roses for passionate love, white for purity, and pink for your perfect grace—your movements are as beautiful as your face." He paused to take a breath and just to look at her, long and deep, like a parched and thirsty man who had just stumbled out of the desert drinking his fill from a welcome oasis. Kate would say afterward it felt like a whole lifetime passed in that moment, before he resumed gathering flowers again.

"Honesty for honesty, of course, that most precious gift which lovers should *always* give to one another; periwinkles for tender memories to cherish, like the day I met a little girl in a robin's egg blue dress fraught with worry over her beloved cat. Pinks for love pure and true; ranunculus for one so radiant and charming it would be a grievous sin not to tell her so. And here"—he brandished a posy of fragrant little pink flowers—"sweet peas for the most delicate, delectable pleasures. Look at them, blushing, bright pink, like the lips both above and below, visible and modestly hidden beneath your petticoats, that I *long* so much to kiss."

Then, as though fearing he had said too much, and that Kate might slap his face, he rushed on, snatching up more flowers.

Yet he could not stop. He had dared be bold and still Kate lingered.

"Honeysuckle for lovers entwined in passionate embraces who dream of each other whenever they are apart both by night and by day; vetch because I would cling to thee; gentian because you are so *very* dear to me; Canterbury bells for constancy." He added a generous spray of the swaying purple blue bells to Kate's already overflowing bouquet.

"Pink gillyflowers to remind us to always remember a love that should never be forgotten, yellow for fidelity and devotion, and white to tell you how sweet and lovely you are. And sweet-scented white stock, because you will *always* be beautiful to me even when your hair is white as snow and wrinkles web and crinkle your face. You will always be as beautiful to me just as you are now." His fingers caressed Kate's as he added these to her bouquet.

Then he was gathering a feathery and ticklish spray of leafy greenery.

"Ferns for sincerity," he explained. "To stand surety for the truth in every word I speak to you. Feverfew for warmth like the yellow sun at the heart of their white petals; wallflowers, red gold like your hair"—he dared twirl a curl around his finger—"for faithfulness in adversity. And lungwort because you *are* my life, like the air my lungs breathe; you, and hope of you, of someday calling you mine, keeps me alive. And these flamboyant beauties—heart's ease pansies—to remind you, *my* flamboyant beauty"—he gazed possessively at Kate—"to think of me, always and fondly. Peppermint for warm feelings because that is how I would have you think of me; rosemary for remembrance and a love that never forgets or dies; and forget-me-nots because I can *never* forget you and hope you never will me. Lastly, this pink cabbage rose"—he thrust it boldly into the center of the by-then enormous bouquet—"as a confession of my love in case you have any doubt."

I remember every word and blossom. I would later weave them all into an intricate beribboned border, the most elaborate I had ever embroidered, around a petticoat for Kate.

Kate threw back her head and laughed. Had her hands not been brimming over with so many flowers it took both her hands to hold them, she would have applauded in sheer delight. She thought it all gallant flattery and was awed by the smooth and silky delivery, as polished as an actor in a play; he had never once faltered over the flowers or their meanings.

"These flowers were intended for your sister," she observed. "Should I *really* carry her such a bold and ardent bouquet? Truly, sir, it seems overly . . . *passionate* for an invalid."

"Nay"—Ned shook his head, his eyes never once leaving Kate's face—"they are all for you and none other, Mistress Kate. For Jane we shall have to pick another, with purple coneflowers for strength and health, and flowering hawthorn to express our deeply cherished hope that she will soon recover; she will like that. But the message in *this* bouquet is, as you say, too overwhelming for an invalid, though I daresay if she knew, it would gladden her heart immeasurably to know I had picked it for you, just as she picked you, the most beautiful rose in all of England, for me. She planned this, you know. She conspired with Fate, who first put you in my path many years ago when I was sent to woo your sister, and now my sister, by bringing you here, has done the same. Call it what you will, my Kate—for you *are my* Kate—God, Fate, or Jane, we were meant to be together."

"When I looked from my window"—he pointed up to it—"and saw you here in a gown bluer than the sky, the same robin's egg blue as I remembered, with your hair shining in the sun, bright as a robin's red breast, in the midst of this garden, like a beautiful little blue egg in a nest, I knew I must put on my blue and red doublet too"—he touched his chest—"and come down to you, so that we two might be one as we were meant to be." Then, offering her his arm, he asked, "Now shall we add some ivy to finish this bouquet, for steadfastness, an attachment that ends only with life itself?"

That was the moment Kate decided that Berry was rotten and felt love for Ned Seymour ripen, full and beautiful, in her heart. Like Eve plucking the apple, then and there she gave her heart to him. I wasn't there to stop her, though 'tis folly to think I could have. Kate was ever one to follow her heart wherever it led, oblivious to any danger, pain, or obstacles that might lie in her path; even if it brought disaster crashing down onto her own pretty head, she would race blindly ahead, her eyes always on the pretty prize, never glancing at the ground and the ruts and rocks that might trip her up, following Love as though it were a pretty golden butterfly she must hold within her reverently clasped hands. "All for love," that was ever my Kate. It was her blessing, and her curse.

I saw so little of my sister over the next two years we were all but strangers. I rarely saw her except when she wanted some pretty embroidery for her petticoats or a new gown. Though I noticed, whenever I passed her in the palace corridors or glimpsed her at some celebration, there was a new lightness in her step, she seemed to always be smiling, and I often caught snatches of a song on her lips. Though her best friend was dying slowly, her bloom fading fast, Kate was dancing through the days just as she did the nights, until the schemers wore her nerves down to a shadow, and she and Jane Seymour must retreat back to Hanworth again.

Even our lady-mother's sudden death did not dampen Kate's newfound joy. We had been distant and cordial since her remarriage, but, like dutiful daughters, we donned mourning black and went to Suffolk House to wash and dress her body in preparation for the grand funeral Elizabeth had generously arranged to honor our lady-mother as she was the daughter of a queen. She was to be laid to rest amidst pomp and splendor and illustrious ancestors in Westminster Abbey, conveniently forgetting the fact that she had lost her title when she married so far beneath her. Kate and I shared the role of chief mourner. Though it should have been Kate's alone as the eldest, she insisted. As we led the ponderously slow procession, with black-clad maids behind us helping to bear the burden of our heavy black velvet trains, we stared straight ahead and tried to ignore the tittering in the pews about how our lady-mother had perished. In bed with Master Stokes, just as November 20 became the 21, she died with her boots on and smiling, seized by a sudden stroke.

"She went like that," our boyish young stepfather had informed us, snapping his fingers to illustrate the swiftness. "I do not think she felt any pain though—she was greatly smiling and just afore that had given me every indication that she was well pleased." Indeed, the embalmers, mindful of the deceased's dignity, had used bands of linen and small weights to give our lady-mother's dead face a more appropriate expression for when she lay in state, for which Kate and I were most grateful.

Nor a year later, when the court reeled with scandal and my own heart grieved the loss of one I scarcely knew but remembered fondly, was Kate's glowing happiness the least bit diminished. The Lady Amy, Robert Dudley's wife, who was rumored to be ailing with a cancer of the breast, had been discovered dead, with her neck broken, at the foot of a staircase, yet the hood remained straight upon her head, and her skirts were not disarrayed as one might expect after such a fall. Many cried *"Murder!"* and pointed at Lord Robert, and the Queen's reputation was also besmirched by the scandal. Gossip raged that they were lovers, and that Lord

Robert, grown weary of waiting for God to take his unwanted wife home to Him, and fearing that Elizabeth might succumb to one of her many foreign suitors, had taken matters into his own hands and had Amy killed, thinking her demise would clear the way for their marriage and another coronation at Westminster Abbey from whence he would emerge crowned King Robert I of England.

But Elizabeth knew better—Robert Dudley wasn't worth a kingdom. Even when Lord Robert was sent away to await the inquest's verdict and the court was ordered to don mourning for Lady Dudley, Kate still smiled and sparkled and showed the world how beautiful she looked in black.

Eventually a day came, after Robert Dudley had been welcomed back at court, after the inquest had adjudged Amy's death an accident, and we were allowed to doff our mourning and don colors again, when Kate came dancing into my room. Spinning in her long maroon velvet cloak, with pink roses blooming in her cheeks, and her eyes bright as stars, a blue ostrich plume billowing gracefully on her hat, to match the border of blue roses I had embroidered on the petticoat peeking from beneath the hem of the elegant apricot satin gown embroidered with maroon roses and vines I had made for her, she came to rest, kneeling beside my chair. I was hard at work on the petticoat she had begged of me, the one I would come to know only after it was finished as "Ned's bouquet." She put her arms around me and kissed my cheek, and I giggled and pulled away as the feather on her hat tickled me.

"It's your own fault, you know," she laughed. "You chose the feather and fashioned the hat, and most becoming it is too," she added as she turned to admire herself in the looking glass. Then she told me that she *must* have a nightcap, "the most *beautiful* nightcap *ever* made, and I want *you* to make it for me, Mary," embroidered all over with deep purple violets and trimmed with silver-veined lace, with a purple satin bow to tie "just so" beneath her chin. "I *must* have it and *soon,*" she insisted.

"All right," I sighed indulgently. "You shall have it." I gazed hard at my sister, then shook my head and sighed again. "If I didn't know better, I would think you were in love."

"Just in love with life, Mary," Kate said with a merry trill of laughter. "Just in love with life!" It wasn't exactly a lie. I just didn't know it then. But, to Kate, Ned Seymour was her life.

Before I could ask any more questions, she was gone; with a another quick kiss, and a song on her lips, she danced out my door again, glad-hearted, featherlight, and diamond bright.

I just smiled and shrugged it off, chuckled, and shook my head at Kate's latest caprice. It made my heart glad to see her so happy and light of step, always smiling, with pink roses blooming in her cheeks again. Mayhap it was stupid or naïve of me, but I *never* thought it had aught to do with any man. Kate didn't seem to favor any particular gentleman; she danced and flirted with many, and sometimes even let them kiss her—in quiet corners, forest glades during hunting parties, velvet-curtained alcoves, and moonlit gardens. Twice or thrice, that I knew of, she even let their fingers delve inside her bodice or rove daringly beneath her petticoats. Best of all, she had forgotten all about Berry; she could now pass him by without a glance. She was done moping and weeping for what she had lost and could never have again, and I hoped she now realized that he was never worth it. But I *never* saw her single Ned Seymour out or show any sign that he was special; she treated him with the politeness due the brother of her best friend and nothing more. I don't even recall that I ever even saw them dance together or heard her mention his name. I saw them nod and smile in passing and exchange polite greetings and comments on the weather and Jane Seymour's health, but that was all.

So I shrugged and went on with my sewing, foolishly surmising that flowered nightcaps were set to become the latest fancy, and soon other ladies would come knocking at my door with little velvet purses filled with coins or pretty trinkets and other gifts, prattling of ribbons, laces, and the flowers they favored. God help me, I never thought it was anything more! I should have laid down my sewing and gone out and boldly confronted Kate, grabbed her arm, stared her down, and gotten to the heart of the matter, but I, to my everlasting regret, didn't. I sat and sewed and did nothing.

15

On a blustery December morning, two years after Elizabeth had come to the throne, when Kate was twenty and I was sixteen, the Queen would hunt anyway despite the cold, cold weather. Elizabeth defiantly declared the air "bracing" and that she was not afraid of its bite. I heard that Kate was ailing and had sent Henny to beg that she might forgo the pleasure of the hunt and remain abed. Since I was never a good choice to follow the hunt, being too likely to get in the way and be trampled, Elizabeth readily gave me leave to stay behind and tend my sister. "Lady Jane Seymour is ill too," she tartly commented as I snipped a stray thread from the hem of her evergreen velvet riding habit, "though it would be more remarkable if she were well."

As soon as I could, I made my curtsy to the Queen, thanking her again, and rushed to the room Kate and Jane Seymour shared, expecting to find them both coughing and feverish.

I burst in without knocking. A startled cry greeted me, and I whirled around to see Kate standing before the looking glass as Lady Jane finished lacing her into the gown of butter yellow satin bordered with rich golden braid and embroidered all over with hundreds of dainty royal purple violets with gold-veined green leaves, that I had only put the final stitches in the week before at

Kate's anxious urging. I had thought to have more time with it; after all such a gown was better suited to springtime, so surely in the deep of winter there was no need to hurry, but Kate had wept and stormed, stamped her feet, and pleaded with me to make haste, insisting that she must have it and soon. But when I asked her why, she shrugged it off as merely "a fancy to be clothed in spring when outside the world is all snow and ice." She had come to my room to check its progress every day, sometimes twice or even thrice. Only when the last stitch had been put in did this fearful, frantic impatience fall from her like a dead rose petal.

"What are you doing here?" Kate rounded on me angrily.

"I—I heard that you were ill," I stammered.

"Well, I'm not, but don't you *dare* tell anyone! My cloak—quickly!" Her rude snappishness, so unlike Kate, told me that she was very nervous about something.

But Lady Jane seemed to understand, and as she draped the heavy, fur-trimmed, forest green velvet cloak around Kate she paused to give her shoulder a comforting pat.

"Kate . . ." I took a step forward and put out a hand to her, but she brushed me aside.

"*Go away, Mary!* I haven't time for you now!"

I thought I caught a flash of purple and white as Kate snatched up her green velvet reticule and stuffed something inside. Then she was gone, out the door as though her life depended on it, leaving Lady Jane to flash me an apologetic smile as she quickly threw on a cloak of blue velvet edged with gray rabbit fur and hurried out after her, even though the rapid pace brought on a violent coughing fit.

I know I shouldn't have, but I followed them. Even though it was very difficult, as they chose to brave the busy London streets instead of taking a barge, and I was much jostled and even knocked down twice, I refused to stop. Soon I found myself standing in Cannon Row, watching as my sister and her friend hurried up the steps of Hertford House, Ned Seymour's fine redbrick London residence. As though he had been watching for them, Ned Seymour himself, in a brown velvet doublet richly worked with gold, opened the door and let them in. He came out onto the stoop and glanced swiftly left and right before he followed them inside and shut the door. *How curious,* I thought, *to see a nobleman open his own front door.* The Seymours were wealthy and had many servants. Why had Kate and Jane come out unchaperoned when both had ladies' maids who might have accompanied them? Kate had always put great trust in Henny, who had been with her since birth, and was robust and strong-armed enough to make any man who might have dared accost the girls think twice. Something strange was happening, and I was determined to know what.

Boldly, I squared my shoulders and strode toward the door, only to nearly be knocked down by Lady Jane Seymour as she ran out in a swirl of blue velvet and gray fur. She caught me before I fell, and her face paled even more if that were possible, and the spots of red in her cheeks glowed even brighter. But she didn't try to stop me.

"It's not right to keep it from you. You're her sister, and you should be there," she murmured as she took her hand from my shoulder and hurried away, down the street, intent on some seemingly urgent errand.

I squared my shoulders and walked straight into Ned Seymour's house, unhindered and unannounced, and followed their voices into the oak-paneled parlor. Kate's green velvet cloak lay draped over the fireside settle, and they stood embracing before the hearth's bright warmth. They broke apart, gasping guiltily, at the sight of me. Ned murmured something about seeing to the refreshments and hurried out, leaving Kate alone to face me.

"What are you doing, Kate?" I asked wearily, for I was suddenly very tired of deceptions, secrets, and games. I wanted only to have the truth full plain even if it killed me.

"We're to be married, and you can't stop us!" Kate said hotly with a defiant toss of her curls, which I noticed now were crowned with a wreath of gilded rosemary, purple velvet violets, periwinkles, heart's ease pansies, and yellow gillyflowers: a bridal coronet, all fashioned from silk and velvet, to bring warm, bright, and beautiful spring into cold, wet, white, and gray winter.

Married! I staggered back, as though the word were a dread disease I would avoid. Only if Kate had told me she had the plague, I would *never* have drawn back. I would have stepped forward and done anything and everything I could to save her. *Oh no, no, no, no!* All of a sudden I felt faint and reached up to clasp my head, to make sure it didn't float away, it felt so dizzy, sick, and light. Now I understood. They were marrying in secret because it was the only way; Elizabeth would *never* give her consent to Kate, with her royal Tudor blood, marrying Ned Seymour, scion of a powerful family with Plantagenet blood, albeit a dilute strain, coursing through his veins. It was too dangerous and potent a combination to allow Elizabeth to sit easy on her throne, and heaven knew she already had cause to be vigilant and wary. As much as she was loved by her people, she was hated by many who had the power to finance a rebellion or pay an assassin.

And if Kate should conceive a son . . .

If Kate gave birth to a boy, all who opposed the petticoat rule of Elizabeth would know *exactly* where to turn; they would think an infant male was better than any full-grown woman, even one as shrewd and savvy as Elizabeth. Some might even be tempted to usurp the throne in that child's name, even if Kate wanted no part of it. She and her son would become, like Jane, innocent pawns in the game powerful men played, men who would not scruple to take Elizabeth's life, just so a Tudor crested instead of cloven betwixt the thighs, and untainted by talk of illegitimacy and debate about the validity of his parents' marriage, could sit upon England's throne.

"Kate, this is *madness!* Think what you are doing! You are defying the Queen! You know you cannot marry without her permission—neither of us can! Elizabeth is *not* Mary; she doesn't love us! Elizabeth's a tigress, fighting for her life and throne, kill or be killed, and she will *not* hesitate to kill you if she has to! She'll *always* put herself and England first because, to herself and most of her subjects, she *is* England!"

"Stop it!" Kate put her hands up to block her ears. "You're only trying to scare me, but I won't let you! *I won't!* It will not come to that; I won't let it!"

I crossed the room and took her hand, which I saw now wore a pale blue diamond, pointed at one end, like a great glimmering tear. "Kate," I sighed, "I am not your enemy; do not treat me as such! Talk to me, as your sister, and your friend, as you used to. Confide in me!"

With a great, heaving sigh, Kate sank down onto the settle and hung her head. I came and stood before her, taking both her hands in mine.

"Kate, look at me," I pleaded.

"I'm sorry I didn't tell you, Mary. My heart has been troubling me sorely, but I did what I did only to protect you. If you didn't know . . . no one could blame or hurt you." She pulled one hand away from mine and caressed her yellow and purple skirt. "You made my wedding gown, even though you did not know that was what it was, with your love for me in every stitch, as in every garment you have ever made for me. It's *so* beautiful! So how could I even think of shutting you out? On the happiest day of my life too!" She raised her head and gave me the full glory of her smile. "I love him, Mary! I have to follow my heart, even if it leads me into danger. We will keep our nuptials secret . . . for now, but later . . . someday . . . when the time is right, I will go on my knees before the Queen and confess all and do whatever I must to assure her I harbor no royal ambitions, I make no claim, now or ever, for myself or any children I may, God willing, bear. I will sign or say whatever I must to renounce it all, permanently, and Ned and I will go away, to live quietly in the country. All I want—for myself and for my family—is love and to be happy."

It was a beautiful dream, but I couldn't quite believe it could ever come true. I hated myself for doubting, but I couldn't help it; to do otherwise would be willful blindness and self-deception. I hung my head, so that she would not see my tears.

"I don't want to lose another sister, Kate. I don't want to see you die a traitor's death or rot your life away in prison. No man is worth such a sacrifice."

She reached down and cupped my face between her soft hands and smiled at me. "That will *never* happen, Mary; God wouldn't let it. What I do, I do for love—all for love. All will be well in time; you will see. You're just scared and imagining the worst. But our union was meant to be, all signs point to it, and God *will* bless us. *I know!* And, even if it did—but it won't!—you're *wrong,* Mary! Ned is different from other men; he *is* worth *any* sacrifice Love demands of me. Sometimes the greatest loves come hand in hand with suffering and sorrow. If you would have music to dance to, you have to pay the players; 'tis only just and fair." She shrugged and smiled brightly, as though this were a trivial matter like doling out coins to a troupe of musicians instead of *treason*.

I wished with all my heart that I could believe and share her auspicious euphoria, but I couldn't keep the fear from clutching my heart like a hand of ice. It made me shiver and not even Kate's warm smile could melt the fear away; I was afraid it would never leave me.

I took a step forward and reached up and gripped my sister's shoulders and stared deep into her bright, joyful eyes that were blind and heedless to all danger. "Kate, for God's sake, listen to me and see reason. If you do this fool thing, if you marry Ned Seymour you are committing treason—high treason! You can be burned or beheaded at the Queen's pleasure or sent to rot in a prison cell!"

But Kate just smiled at me. "Don't worry, Mary; everything's going to be all right! But . . . just in case . . . you were *never* here, and if you say you were, I shall deny it and say you are lying to try to protect your sister's honor."

That she would say such a thing told me clouds of concern lurked behind that sunny smile. Kate wanted to believe everything would be all right, to think she could will into being the bright future she wanted so much, but doubt and worry would dog her steps like trainbearers she could never shake off or leave far behind her.

With a smile and a carefree laugh, she was up and dancing across the room as Ned came back in, smiling broadly over a great silver tray laden with heaping platters of sliced meats, a sampling of cheeses, fresh baked bread, festive piles of dried and candied fruits and nuts, sliced apples draped with melted cheese, glass bowls filled with sweet, syrupy berries stewed in wine, creamy custard, a compote of honeyed pears and another of peaches, candied violets arranged upon a pretty yellow plate to match Kate's wedding dress, and at the heart of it all, a pretty pink cake made with raspberries crowned with candied pink cabbage roses. "A sweet repast for my sweet," he said as he set it down on a table where goblets and bottles of wine were already arranged. Kate gave a delighted squeal and clasped her hands as she admired the cake, lamenting that Father was not here to enjoy it with us, he would have been so pleased.

"He always loved raspberries and said pink was a heaven-sent color for confections!"

"I am glad you are here, my soon to be sister Mary." Ned smiled as he knelt down to face me. It was very kind of him to do so; many enjoyed the lofty feeling of superiority they experienced when they towered high above and looked down on me. He had a very pleasant face, and a smile so charming and disarming, and there appeared to be genuine warmth in his hazel eyes. I had to stop myself from impulsively reaching out and brushing back the wing of sun-lightened brown hair that fell over his brow.

Looking at him, this great, smiling overgrown boy of twenty, I could almost believe he loved my sister as much as she loved him. But there was always *something,* I can't put it into words; I only know that it was *always* there, niggling at the back of my mind, never letting me truly trust Ned Seymour. Possibly my soul was too sullied from all the ambitious machinations I had witnessed almost from the cradle, power plays, coups, conspiracies, and court intrigues; perhaps it made me overly conscious of the royal lines that would be united with their marriage and what this could mean for their, and their children's, futures. Kate was, after all, the unacknowledged heir presumptive, and thus a splendid catch for any ambitious young man, and one with Plantagenet blood in his veins could make much of that if he were so inclined, and might even consider such a wife worth feigning love for. After all, many had pretended passion for far less. How many men since time began had declared their love just to woo a maiden into bed? Maybe it was because this "great love" had blossomed so suddenly? To my suspicious mind it just seemed too choreographed, too much like a romantic stage play; those sweet dreams we want to believe but know rarely do come true. Or perhaps it was just that I was too cynical to believe in love at first sight? Or maybe Kate was right—I was scared and imagining the worst. I just don't know.

"I know it broke Kate's heart to think you wouldn't be here. And now you are here, and it all ends happily!" Ned's face brightened with a broad smile. Oh my, he was *very* comely! "It was meant to be," he declared, making so bold as to kiss my cheek, before he rose and went back to Kate. He led her to sit upon the settle and stood beside her, smiling down at her, as she gazed up at him, holding her hand, until the moment we heard the front door open again.

Her face terribly flushed and her shoulders shaking with a hacking cough, that by the looks of the handkerchief she tried to conceal, squashed tight in her fist, had brought up blood, and by its violence had shaken her fair hair from its pins, Lady Jane came in, tugging with all her fragile might at the hand of a big, black-gowned man with a long, tangled, greasy, and unkempt red beard.

"This way, Father, this way!" she cried between coughs, pulling hard at his hand and urging him toward Kate and Ned as he was apparently incapable of walking straight and finding the bridal couple himself. As he weaved his way across the floor, his unsteady gait aping the undulations of a slithering snake, he brought with him the fumes of the tavern, along with those of his own unwashed body, and his bleary, bloodshot eyes roamed the room as though the bride and groom might be hiding on the ceiling or concealed in a corner. As he stood, belching and swaying, before the bridal couple, I discreetly moved away; as I was shorter than the others, and thus nearer his nether regions, the stink of urine was unmistakable and undesirably near my nose.

Many burps and hiccups and fumbled words marred the marriage service he tried to read from the *Book of Common Prayer* he held upside down in hands like a pair of great pink bear paws, their backs thickly covered with coarse red hair. But Kate and Ned never seemed to notice, their eyes rapt and adoring, never leaving each other. They smiled, clasped hands, and spoke their vows staring into each other's eyes. Kate, I know, spoke straight from her heart.

Then it was over. They were man and wife and kissing and clinging passionately. A puzzle ring of five interlocking gold bands had joined the sky blue diamond on Kate's left hand.

Not daring to wear it openly at court, when she removed it to put it on a long golden chain so that she might wear it always hidden safely in the warm crevice between her breasts, Kate let me read the verse engraved on the five bands:

As circles five, by art compact, show but one ring in sight,
So trust unites faithful minds, with knot of secret might,

Whose force to break but greedy Death, no one possess power
As time and sequels well shall prove, my ring can say no more.

With joyous good humor, and more than a little relief, we all laughed as we bade the wine-sodden priest good-bye. He tottered out, pocketing the purse of gold Lady Jane gave him, and taking two bottles of wine from the table, one red and the other white, and raising them by turns to his mouth, suckling greedily as an infant from one and then the other as he made his way out onto the London streets, miraculously without walking into the wall or falling down the front steps. No one ever thought to ask his name. If he ever gave it, not a one of us recalled it. There was no paper; though I was a novice to such matters, I would learn later that there should have been a paper that we all signed—bride, groom, priest, and two witnesses. But no one thought of that. Kate had been married before, so she should have known, but she was just too happy to think. The priest, who should have known this business better than any, as Ned and Kate were not the first couple he had ever married, was too drunk to realize the omission. It was not, at first glance, all that serious; after all, a couple's agreement that they were wed was considered legally binding. It would only become a crucial issue in this case because of who the bride and groom were and their nearness to the throne.

Kate and Ned exchanged mischievous glances, nodded to one another, and whooped with joy as she flung her floral crown in the air and he did the same with his feathered cap. Then, seizing her hand, he bounded toward the stairs, calling back over his shoulder to his sister and me, "Eat, drink, and be merry, for my bride and I shall be!"

"A moment, my love!" Kate laughed and spun away from him. She embraced first Jane Seymour. "We really are sisters now!" Then, after pausing to retrieve her reticule from the settle and pull out the nightcap she had stuffed inside, she knelt before me and held it out, like a sacred offering, to me. "Will you put it on me, please?" she asked.

Tenderly, I brushed back the wealth of red gold curls and set the violet-embroidered white linen cap upon her head, tweaked the lacy frills, and drew the long purple satin ribbons around and beneath her chin to carefully tie a beautiful bow.

"There now." I nodded, smiling through my tears, which, Kate couldn't know, sprang from fear rather than joy. "Off you go!"

"Thank you, Mary!" She hugged me tight and kissed my cheek, then she was off, dancing across the room. At the foot of the stairs, she gaily announced, "I'll never be Queen of England, and that's fine with me. I don't want to be, not even in my dreams. All I want to be is queen of my husband's heart and our home. But every girl should feel like a queen on her wedding day, and I want to go to our marriage bed for the first time happy as a queen on her coronation day. That's why I asked you to embroider regal purple violets on my nightcap—for today this is my crown!"

As she twirled around and darted up the stairs, without a backward glance, her eyes upon the future, not the past, I saw embroidered beneath her skirts the intricate floral border of the bouquet Ned had picked for her. She was also, I noted, wearing purple woolen stockings, dyed to match the violets I had embroidered on her nightcap.

Lady Jane and I remained in the parlor, the silence broken only by her coughing and my footsteps as I paced restlessly back and forth. The refreshments sat on the table untouched. We knew better than to talk; we would only fall to quarreling. Jane thought she had done a wonderful thing by bringing her brother and best friend together. She was like one looking through a stained glass rose seeing only love and romance, but I saw the shadow of the ax hovering above the neck of my sole remaining sister. I saw danger and treason. Beside that, to me at least, this great love they supposedly shared mattered very little. It wasn't worth Kate's life.

Two hours later they were bounding back down the stairs, ludicrously unkempt, neither of them being accustomed to dressing themselves without assistance. In spite of ourselves, Lady Jane and I laughed and rushed to help them set right the many clumsily, missed, or wrongly fastened buttons, hooks, and laces, for we must all hasten back to court, before our absence was noted; for so many of us to be gone at the same time would never be dismissed as mere coincidence. We didn't dare take chances.

"But what of our banquet?" Kate asked. "It seems a shame to

waste it, especially that beautiful cake! Father would weep in Heaven if he knew!"

"We shall take it with us and have our wedding feast in the barge," Ned declared. He then carefully picked up the tray and asked Kate, "Will you bring the wine, my love?"

"A movable feast! What a splendid idea!" Kate smiled as she snatched the bottles up.

"I'll bring the cups," I volunteered, and carefully gathered the four golden goblets as best I could against my chest and hoped I would not drop them. But Lady Jane, to my immense relief, insisted on taking half my burden and relieving me of two. So it was settled, and we all followed Ned out to the water stairs where he whistled and hailed a barge to convey us back to the palace. We laughed and feasted all the way, gladly sharing our bounty with the bargemen, who were unaccustomed to such luxuries. Just before we passed under London Bridge, where Father's head had been displayed, we each raised a piece of the beautiful pink raspberry cake up high, as though we were lifting our goblets in a toast, "to Henry Grey, Duke of Suffolk, God rest his soul!" Kate laughed and whisked the tears from her eyes and fed Ned a bite of cake, and he did the same, then they fell into each other's arms, kissing hungrily, long and deep, tasting sweet raspberries and cream upon the other's mouth.

We arrived just in time to race into the Great Hall and take our seats around the banquet table, though our bellies were already well stuffed; it would not do to miss dinner. No one suspected anything. As far as the Queen and court knew, Kate had recovered from the headache that had kept her abed, Lady Jane's cough was neither better nor worse, I had spent the day sewing and tending them, and Ned had been absent on business for his family.

As Kate, Ned, and Lady Jane exchanged smiles and triumphant glances, like children who had crept into the kitchen and stolen a tray of cherry tarts, reveling in the knowledge that they had gotten away with it, I knew it was only a matter of time before we were found out.

After dinner, when the dancing began, and for the first time Ned led Kate out to dance, I knew it was the beginning of the end; their love was too bold and blatant to be missed. That night, when

Kate turned me out of my own room in my shift and bare feet, shoving me out without even a shawl to cover myself, to "go and sleep with Jane," so that her "Sweet Ned" might come and couple with her in my bed, I started counting the days, knowing that each one that passed, though I might sigh with relief at its end, carried us ever closer to the inevitable discovery. Kate and Ned would give themselves away—of that there was no doubt.

16

They were reckless. It was as though they *wanted* to get caught. Ned would tweak her coppery curls, steal a swift kiss, and call her "Countess Carrots." To which Kate, by wedded right the Countess of Hertford, would feign offense, lift up her nose, and haughtily declaim that her hair was red gold, or copper-hued, if you prefer, but certainly *not* orange like a common carrot. Sometimes he would pull her into a quiet corner and lift her skirts. As the court traveled from palace to palace, as each one required cleansing of the filth and stench, they made a game of coupling in every one of them, in any convenient nook and cranny, empty room, privy, alcove, quiet corridor, or garden bower, anywhere they could, and as often as they could. I grew weary of being turned out of my own room at night to sleep with the cough- and fever-racked Jane Seymour so they could roll about merrily in my bed. They were like little children playing, and when I tried to scold them, they hung their heads in mock-shame, glancing slyly aside at each other and stifling their sputtering giggles, as they nodded and mockingly answered, *"Yes, Mother Mary,"* then went out and did exactly as they pleased.

Unbelievably, they cast all caution to the wind. Even I, a virgin of sixteen, knew that Ned should have withdrawn without spending his seed, and there were teas Kate could have drunk as a safeguard against conception, and even sheaths known as "Venus Gloves" sold discreetly beneath the counter in glove shops that I had heard the gentlemen of the court whisper about. I had even heard women confide in each other about their own techniques, speaking of wax pessaries and wads of cloth or little sponges soaked in lemon juice or vinegar they inserted before the carnal act.

But Kate acted as though she knew better. Whenever I tried to talk to her, she would toss her hair and thrust her nose into the air, and say that I should not talk about such matters; it was "immodest and unseemly for a girl of my youth, as yet unmarried, to know of such things and presume to speak of them." But secretly wed in a court with a thousand eyes and an ear at every wall and door was neither the time nor the place for them to chance a child. What were they thinking? Simply put, they were not and I could not, then or now, understand why.

Sir William Cecil, Her Majesty's shrewd secretary of state, must have suspected something. He arranged to have Ned, "the fine and upstanding young Earl of Hertford," accompany his worrisome, dissolute nineteen-year-old son Thomas on a tour of France and Italy. Cecil hoped a good dose of culture and a dash of diplomatic service might calm young Thomas's wild streak and, if not quite curb, at least refine his taste in wine, women, and where he spent his money and time. It was an honor Ned didn't dare refuse, and in truth, I could tell by the look in his eyes, that unmistakable ambitious gleam I had seen so many times lighting up our lady-mother's eyes, that he didn't want to. He was, after all, an up-and-coming young man from a prestigious family that had been tarnished by both his father's and his uncle's executions, and he was eager to restore, and enhance, if he could, the luster. "Such opportunities come but once in a lifetime," he said to Kate, trying to hold and kiss her as she raged and cried.

They quarreled about his going one day, then kissed and made up in the royal orchard the next, with Ned hoisting Kate's skirts as showers of apple or cherry blossoms rained down upon them. They quarreled again, perhaps only for the sake of the sweet reconciliation in the orchard that would follow on the morrow. Angry words, tears, slamming doors, furious footsteps retreating fast, then kisses, cries, sighs, and whispers in a shower of perfumed petals, for a whole month that was the pattern. Ned said he would go, then he would say nay, for Kate's sake he would stay; then Kate would say no, she was being selfish and he must go, 'twas a grand opportunity he must not squander for her sake, they were young and had their whole lives ahead of them; then Ned would agree and say he would go, then Kate would weep and rage, and they would inevitably end back in the orchard again, in the throes of tears and torrid passion.

During one of those afternoons of love in the orchard Ned hung around her neck a golden chain from which a deep blue sapphire dripped like a great tear, emblematic in both shape and hue of his great sorrow in leaving her, he said. Yet more kisses, caresses, tears, quarrels, reconciliations, protestations, accusations, denials, avowals, and acceptance followed, day after day. The whole thing sorely vexed and wearied me, and many times I was tempted to shout at them to "decide and have done with it!"

One day I caught Kate crouched in a corner, greedily sucking limes, her face, neck, and fingers coated slick with the tart juice, and the drained flesh of at least a dozen discarded fruits and their torn and shredded peelings scattered on the floor around her. I knew she was in trouble, even as she denied it, shrugging it off as just a sudden craving, the way Father would sometimes wake in the night with a sudden insatiable urge for a quince and pomegranate pie. She fled from me, feigning lightheartedness and laughter, even as I shouted after her what we both knew, that she had never liked limes before. "You hate limes and you know it! You know what this means!" But Kate laughed and ignored me.

When she came to my room to try on the new gown I had been making, an elegant lemon damask with a quilted pearl-latticed petticoat of russet satin and matching under-sleeves, she complained that I had been stingy with the material and made it too small, that the waist pinched and needed to be let out and the bodice was too tight.

"That's because you're breeding! 'Tis no wonder," I said, "the way you and Ned have been going at it without precaution or care. You make rabbits look like models of decorum!"

Still Kate denied it, first accusing me of coveting the material to make something for myself and cutting it too small to try to save enough for me. "If you wanted it so much, Mary, you shouldn't have offered it to me!" Then, just as quickly, contradictorily, laughing, bending to hug me and kiss my cheek, craving my pardon, cajoling me to forgive her as her nerves were sorely jangled by the thought of parting from her "Sweet Ned." She stood, tossing her bright curls, and flippantly declaring that she was simply "growing fat and happy nourished by my Sweet Ned's love!" But I was not deceived. For the life of me, I could not tell why Kate was being willfully blind to such an obvious truth. I could see it and others would too in time.

I implored her to accompany me to London, to secretly consult a midwife, but she refused. She kept insisting that she was not pregnant and that she would not stoop to the "indignity of an examination to prove it."

"It's *my* body, Mary, and if I was with child, I think I would know it! Surely *I,* a *twice-married woman* of twenty, know more about these matters than you—a *virgin of sixteen*—do!"

Lady Jane Seymour was too busy dying to intervene. I was tempted to go and try to talk to her, in the hope that she could accomplish what I could not, but I hadn't the heart to trouble a soul I knew to be in the act of departing. On her deathbed, she clasped both Kate and Ned by the hand and told them to "be kind to each other and never forget how much you love each other." They each solemnly bowed their heads, kissed her fever-hot hands, and promised faithfully so the young woman who had brought them together and engineered their marriage could die in peace, believing that she had in her brief life, like a guardian angel or a good fairy, done the two people she loved most a great service and ensured their lifelong happiness.

So Ned sailed away with Thomas Cecil in May, still grieving for his sister, leaving Kate alone, carrying a child she still denied, to fend for herself at the Virgin Queen's court, while he enjoyed a lush, lusty spring in luxurious, lascivious Paris and spent a wild, sultry summer in sunbaked Italy. Everywhere the two of them went they drank to excess, lost vast sums at the gambling tables, hunted, danced, and whored, and spent money as if it were water. I heard

Master Secretary Cecil complain that he had known men to live an entire year abroad on what the two of them spent in a single month.

Before he left, Ned did at least one sensible thing; he gave Kate a deed in which he acknowledged her as his wife and bequeathed her lands with an income of £1,000 per annum, thus providing her with some financial security, and even more importantly, legally binding, written proof that they were married. If only Kate hadn't promptly misplaced it! Then none could have said they were merely pretending after the fact, to try to save her honor and prevent their children from being branded bastards. The date on that deed, drawn up and signed *before* Ned's departure, would have proved it was a truth, not a lie that came after Kate was found to be with child. Poor Kate, thinking only of love, not money, never realized the *true* import of that document, how it might have made *all* the difference in the world.

In a fit of tears and foot-stamping pique, Kate stopped letting me make her dresses, saying she could not abide my comments about her widening waist and "milk-swollen teats" and sought the services of another dressmaker instead, crying out before she slammed the door that she would not let me so much as sew up a hem for her if her life depended on it. But soon she was back, crying in my arms, now that Jane Seymour was gone, and there was no one else she could turn to. She had heard that Ned had sent baubles—some pretty enameled bracelets—to some other ladies of the court, but nothing for her. Though Ned would later claim that he had sent the bracelets to Kat Ashley, the Queen's childhood governess and now the Mother of the Maids, charged with overseeing the welfare of all the unmarried girls who lived and served at court. He had done this, Ned said, so that Her Majesty might have first choice, then Mistress Ashley was to bring the rest to Kate and, after she had made her selection, let her, his "well-beloved wife," distribute them amongst the other ladies, but "the old gray Kat was now in her dotage and had obviously muddled it."

It was a neat excuse, tidy and pat, *almost* believable, especially knowing dear old Kat and how befuddled her mind was growing. But I didn't believe it. Though she refused to admit it, Kate clearly had her doubts. And where were all the letters he had promised? He had vowed to write every day so it would be as though she were right there experiencing all the wonders of foreign travel right alongside him. Thomas Cecil, young, drunken rakehell that he was, obviously found time to write; the badly spelled wine-blotched letters he sent back to his rowdy companions at court were filled with amusing anecdotes of Ned dragging the drunken lad out of a fancy Parisian brothel after he had made a complete ass of himself by delivering an off-key serenade and proposal on bended knee to a probably poxy doxy, and tales of bawdy, balmy nights spent cavorting and frolicking nude with beautiful, buxom Italian peasant girls in olive groves by moonlight.

One letter passed with great amusement around the court detailed a night when Thomas and Ned and their female companions had all spontaneously stripped off their clothes and leapt naked into a wooden vat to stomp the grapes with their bare feet, dancing upon them as the musicians played, then fell to making love, changing partners, then changing partners again. When they emerged from the vat, they were stained purple all over and had to take many baths and even resort to pumice stones and vinegar scrubs before they were clean enough to be presentable. Everyone at court had a good laugh over it, except Master Secretary Cecil and Kate, who each in their own way found these reports most distressing, only Kate must bear her pain in private.

Again I held my sister as she wept then tried in vain to convince herself that it didn't mean anything, Ned was a young man, after all, and young men were apt to do this sort of thing. She pointed the finger of blame at Thomas Cecil; he was clearly a bad influence and her "Poor Ned" had found it impossible to curtail him. Thomas might even have discovered the truth about their marriage and used this knowledge to blackmail Ned into doing as he willed. "My poor darling!" Kate cried, horrified by the thought of this cruel coercion, imagining her "Sweet Ned" making love to another woman in a vat of grapes to keep their secret safe.

Privately, I was convinced she was grasping at straws, but I didn't have the heart to tell her so. I knew Thomas Cecil; he had once traded his best horse to a peddler lurking outside a tavern for a jar of cream guaranteed to make his cock "as big and hard as a battering ram," and another time, while visiting a London fair, he had given his fine Spanish leather boots in exchange for a recipe to turn his father's dairy cows' milk to wine. He had actually interrupted a Council meeting by running in barefoot brandishing the recipe, bursting with excitement to tell his father how he had just made his fortune. The idea of such a man blackmailing anyone into doing his bidding was absurd beyond words.

Soon there came a day when Kate could deny the truth no longer. She fainted while following the hunt. Only the quick intervention of the Queen's Master of the Horse, and some said lover, Robert Dudley, kept Kate from being trampled by the horses' hooves. She was carried in a sweaty swoon by litter back to the palace while the Queen, who could "not abide these weak and frail, fainting females," went on with the hunt.

I had stayed behind to do some sewing and I heard about Kate's fall from a pair of gossipy maids who had come in with fresh sheets to make up the Queen's bed.

I found Kate in her room, her crimson velvet riding habit and feathered hat cast aside, crouching, half kneeling, half lying on the floor, in her shift and red stockings, holding her belly and retching into the chamber pot. I ran to gather back her hair and found it soaking wet and reeking of sweat, and her skin was burning, oily and a-shimmer with it. I said not a word and stood patiently by until she was finished, then I gently helped her up. When she stood, I reached out and boldly laid my palm upon her belly. I felt life stir within it. Kate lowered her eyes to look at me, and I raised mine to meet hers. There was no use denying it anymore.

"Don't say it," Kate pleaded, soft and tremulously. "*Please,* Mary, don't say, 'I told you so.' "

"Come here." I opened my arms to her, and with a great sob, she dropped to her knees and came to me.

"Mary, what shall I do? I am so frightened! Ned hasn't answered my letters, though I dare not tell him. What am I to do? The Queen will think me wanton, when she finds out . . ."

"Then we shall have to ensure that she does *not* find out," I said decisively. "We will have to withdraw from court when your time is near, and the child shall have to be farmed out with a wet nurse; none must know it is yours. Later, we can discreetly arrange its adoption by a respectable couple, nice people," I assured Kate, seeing her stricken expression, "who truly want a baby."

"No!" Kate cried, leaping away from me as though I had suddenly grown horns and a forked tail. "*No! No! No!* I will not give up my baby!"

"Would you rather give up your head?" I asked plainly.

"Oh!" Kate sighed, sitting on the floor, leaning back upon her palms. "What a mess I have made of it all!"

I agreed but chose not to rub salt in her wounds by saying so. Instead, I held out my hand, to help her rise, and said simply, "Come, we needn't think of these things right now. There is much to be done, and we must get started. We must conceal the truth as long as we can."

I brought out Kate's darkest dresses and set to work letting out the seams. I made Kate stand still and took her measurements, this time with neither of us commenting on the changes in her figure. I worked in silence. When I brought out the increasingly fashionable farthingale, I silently thanked God and the Spanish for this birdcagelike undergarment, belling out around Kate's hips and limbs; it would help us hide the truth even longer. I would buy canvas and cane, or whalebone, if it could be had, and create a new one in which the stiff circular bands, which gradually widened as they descended to the hem, grew subtly wider earlier in their descent. That coupled with the dark colors she would be wearing, and lacing her stays tight as I dared, would make Kate's waist seem smaller above her fuller skirts. And—another stroke of luck—the Queen, being very vain of her beautiful, long-fingered white hands, greatly favored fans, great, graceful spreads of ostrich plumes, black or white, or dyed delicate or vivid hues. I instructed Kate to make a habit of holding her fan open, down low, near about her waist.

As a special gift, I bought a length of beautiful coal black velvet, lined it with charcoal gray satin, and made Kate a long, full, flowing, sleeveless surcoat to which I then added a narrow edging of white miniver. I stitched a row of beautiful braided silk charcoal gray frogs down the front so that she might wear it open or closed as she pleased. She would later don it for the miniature Lavinia Teerlinc would paint of the young mother holding one son and expecting another that would later become one of my greatest treasures. As a peace offering, to put the past months of stormy scenes and secrecy behind us, I embroidered a new petticoat for her with a border of pomegranates, both whole and halved, replete with pearl seeds, and bunches of pretty purple violets tied with yellow ribbons to recall the colors of her wedding gown. When Kate saw it she hugged me and wept, she was so very grateful and pleased, and promised never to ever keep anything from me again.

We had to be careful and clever and watch every step. Any slip could send us skidding straight into the arms of disaster. There were a few close calls. One night, Kate, unthinkingly, sat down at a banquet and greedily devoured an entire gilded platter heaped high with gingered carrots. She was about to raise the empty platter to her lips and lick it clean, so ravenous was she for the gingery glaze, when I caught her. Another night she danced with a young gallant she had once allowed some intimate familiarity with her person. When he sought a repetition and groped her breasts he drew back, startled, insisting that they had grown larger. I feared all was lost for us. But Kate feigned indignation. She pouted and said he had either remembered wrong or confused her with another lady, and if that were the case, she could not have meant that much to him after all. With a playful slap of her fan to his arm, coupled with a carefree smile, she danced away.

'Twas then I decided that Kate must give up dancing. Even though she complained and cried, I was adamant. I knew that it would not be easy, for Kate loved dancing, and she was so lively, graceful, and light of step that she was one of the court's favorite dancing partners, and always a favorite with the Master of the Revels for prime roles in the masques. But the more vigorous dances might hurt her child or even bring on her labor prematurely—I had heard of such things happening—and in the intimacy of the dance her partner's hands might discover her precious secret. At last, I agreed to compromise and let Kate continue to dance the more sedate, slower measures, devoid of lifts and leaps, where couples walked instead of skipped and pranced, and naught but their hands touched, lest her total abstinence from the dance be remarked. But when it came to the more lively measures, I held firm, and Kate began to suffer a series of misfortunes—badly sprained ankles, toothaches, sudden headaches, a sole come off her shoe, and I had even been known to surreptitiously bump someone from behind so that their wine or a plate of food spilled on Kate's gown so that she must quit the Great Hall and go change.

As though things were not complicated enough, just when we thought that part of our lives was well behind us, the duplicitous Earl of Pembroke and his whey-faced son came back, sniffing like hounds around Kate's petticoats, bearing gifts, and voicing hopes of a reconciliation, a remarriage, now that Kate was no longer in disgrace, and many thought, if the Queen died without issue, she would become England's next queen. All sly Pembroke wanted was the Crown for Berry, but, to our shared dismay, we might have to make use of this pair of weasels after all.

Though Kate waited "with an anxious heart" for Ned's return, her letters to him went unanswered. With tales of his frolics with French ladies and dalliances with buxom Italian peasant girls reaching our ears, and no word to allay Kate's fears, how could we not wonder if he had forgotten her? What if Ned, knowing full well that they could not reveal their marriage without braving the Queen's wrath, had decided it was not worth the trouble and just to pretend it had never happened at all? With Lady Jane dead, the deed lost, and the priest, Father Never-Known-Name, long gone, there was no one but me who could say it had happened at all. But as Kate's sister, and naturally loyal to her, and knowing my sister shamed and facing ruin, how much validity would my words truly carry? Ned might very well choose to save himself, but Kate, though she was not the first, and would not be the last, young woman at court to find herself with her belly full but a husband lacking, would be ruined. She would be forced to leave court and any hopes of another marriage would be dashed forever; she would be branded a light skirt, all her flirtatious ways recalled, and no respectable man would ever have her.

No, it could not be, I decided. Ned must look to himself, as I was certain he would anyway, but I must act fast to save my sister from certain ruin, even if it meant she must reunite with those who had hurt her so badly before. She could, if she would, use them to her own ends now.

Naturally Kate balked, not wanting to forsake her "Sweet Ned," or commit what she knew to be bigamy and adultery in her heart, but I was always more practical and pragmatic, and held firm to the only course I could see likely to have a fortuitous outcome.

"They hurt you once, now they can save you, so use them the way they used you!" I said. "What choice do you *really* have? You know better than to trust Elizabeth to be merciful! You are younger and fairer, and many men smile upon and favor you, and your legitimacy is undisputed; our parents were well and truly married long before you were born. If you are found out, you are handing Elizabeth the perfect excuse to get rid of you. Here are your options, Kate: At best, she, and all the world, will see you as a wanton with a full belly and no golden band on her hand and banish you to live out your life in the country. At worst, if she discovers you are indeed married, without royal consent, and to Ned Seymour, thus uniting your Tudor blood with his Plantagenet, you are both—you my sister and your 'Sweet Ned'—facing the Tower or even death—to be burned or beheaded at the Queen's pleasure. Or"—I paused pointedly—"you can do as I suggest, seduce Berry, let him have his way with you, and discover you are with child and quickly, confess to the Queen and secure her permission, marry him again, and we will find a midwife who harkens to the voice of gold rather than her conscience to assist us and arrange an 'accident' to fool Berry and his father into thinking that your labor has come on prematurely. Men are notoriously and blissfully ignorant of women's matters, and would rather not know the details. You can wrap Berry around your little finger and banish any doubts he might have if he has wit enough to have any, which I very much doubt."

Kate grasped her head and paced before me. "I don't know, Mary. I . . . you must give me time, I must think . . ."

I rushed and stood straight before her, boldly blocking her path, and when she tried to turn away from me, I grabbed her skirt and made her stay and look at me. "You haven't time, Kate! If you are going to do this, you must do it *now;* before you are showing too much for even a fool like Berry to be deceived. Any woman of experience, even one who has grown up accustomed to seeing her mother or older sisters and cousins breeding, could see the secret you carry if she saw you unclothed, but Berry, you *can* fool! A weak constitution and a timid, fastidious nature have kept him from being as active in carnal pursuits as most young men his age, and he has no mother or sisters, so I'm willing to wager that he will find you only pleasingly plump. You're older now than when he knew you, you were only fourteen when you parted, so 'tis natural your body would have grown fuller and rounder. So what will it be, Kate—Elizabeth's fury leading to exile and ruination; trust that Ned will do the honorable thing and come back like a knight in shining armor on a white horse and rescue you just so you can brave the Queen's wrath together and rot in prison or die for your treasonous presumption; or marry Berry again and, as Father used to say, make marzipan out of the almonds that are given you? *It's now or never, Kate! Make your choice!*"

"Marzipan," Kate whispered through tremulous lips. "I shall endeavor to make marzipan out of the almonds." She nodded, and breathed deep and shakily. "Will you help me, Mary? Tell me what to do?" In that moment all traces of the worldly and sophisticated woman of twenty vanished. My sister stood before me, shaking and weeping, as scared and helpless as a little girl.

"You *know* I will," I answered.

I bade Kate lie down and rest with a cold compress over her tear-swollen eyes while I set the scene. I sent Hetty, heedless of her grumbling, for candles, at least a dozen, all white and sweet scented, I stipulated. Their soft golden glow would be flattering and deceptive and work for us, like a faithful friend, to help hide Kate's condition and the fact that she had been weeping. I gave orders for the fire to be lit, with apple logs to give a pleasing scent, and for the copper tub to be brought and filled with water just as hot as Kate could stand. Then I drew Kate to my desk and had her pen a note, which I dictated as I arranged and lit the candles, bidding Berry come to her "now, my beloved, for I cannot bear to spend even one more hour without you." While Kate's devoted Henny, with a bewildered expression, but knowing better than to presume to ask questions, went to deliver it, I found Berry's miniature at the bottom of Kate's jewelry coffer and laid it on the table beside her bed, as though she had been gazing upon it often and thinking of him. Then I helped Kate undress, gathered her curls up loosely so they would easily fall down, got her into the tub, and tossed in handfuls of dried red rose petals, lavender, and chamomile.

"You know what to do—charm him, be playful as a kitten, my Kate!" I kissed her cheek and withdrew into the small adjoining room where Kate's maid usually stayed as Berry's footsteps stopped outside the door.

I cringed back against the wall and wished the walls weren't thin as parchment. Like a flirty little girl I heard Kate's breathy coquette's voice calling, "Come in, Berry, darling! I haven't seen you in such a *long* time; I've missed you so!"

Always soft-spoken, all I could hear was a low murmur whenever Berry spoke.

I heard the water slosh, and in my mind's eye I pictured Kate sitting up. "Will you wash my back? My front too? And my . . ." A delighted little giggle, then Kate was urging, "Take off your doublet, Berry dearest, and your shirt too. I don't want you to ruin such beautiful velvet by getting it wet because of me."

Soon she had coaxed Berry out of the rest of his clothes and was exclaiming, wide-eyed, I could well imagine, in feigned alarm. "Oh, Berry, it's *so* big! I'm frightened! Hold me!"

She must have hurled herself into his arms. There was a creak as they fell as one onto the bed, followed by more giggling. Then the expected sounds that accompany coitus, for in truth, I cannot be sentimental and call what happened between Kate and Berry on that bed "lovemaking."

After Berry left, I went to her.

She looked at me with tear-bright eyes. "I didn't lie, Mary," she said with a tremulous little smile. "When I told him they were tears of love. They are—for Ned, not Berry! That old, childish love has long grown cold and dead." She lay flat on her back and rubbed her belly. "I did this only for the sake of my child. He, or she, shouldn't suffer because I loved, and trusted, Ned Seymour. I must learn now to be self*less* instead of self*ish*; my child must now come first, and better that he—for I *do* believe I carry a boy, I don't know why, but I do—should grow up to be the Earl of Pembroke than Kate Grey's bastard."

Kate continued to entice Berry, admitting him to her bed several times, but to our frustration, he seemed content to draw out and just enjoy the dalliance.

"It's time, Kate," I finally said, after I had dressed her in the subtly altered farthingale and laced her as tight as I dared, and she stood before me gowned in black and evergreen velvet holding a fan of dyed emerald ostrich plumes before her waist. "Lie down upon the bed. When Berry comes to escort you to the Great Hall, I will let him in, and we shall pretend you fainted, and you must weep and tell him you suspect you are with child. We dare not tarry any longer. He *must* propose *tonight!*"

But Berry didn't come; instead, a servant in the Pembroke livery came bearing a letter.

"Here, Mary." Kate thrust it at me. "You read it. Berry's hand is atrocious and my head really does ache."

Mayhap Berry was cleverer than we thought, or his wily, treacherous father was doing his thinking for him. Did someone talk or start a rumor? Did Ned himself, during a drunken carouse, let the truth spill out and leak back to London? I only knew, all hope of Berry remedying the hurt he had once caused Kate, by saving her now, was gone.

"To cover your own whoredom, you went about to abuse me," he wrote. *"Having hitherto led a virtuous life, I will not now begin with loss of honor to spend the rest of my life with a whore that almost every man talks of. You claim promise of me, madame, when I was young, and since, confirmed as you say at lawful years, but you know I was lawfully divorced from you a good while ago. And if through the enticement of your whoredom and the practice and device of those you hold so dear, you sought to entrap me with some poisoned bait under the color of sugared friendship, yet (I thank God) I am so clear that I am not to be further touched than with a few tokens that were, by cunning slight, got out of me, to cover your abomination. I require you to send me, madame, all letters from me that reside in your possession as well as my portrait, or else . . . to be plain with you, I will make your whoredom known to all the world as it is now, thank God, known to me, and spied by many scores more."*

Though I loathed to give in to him, I knew it was safer to return some now meaningless tokens than risk Berry acting upon his threats. I gathered up Berry's letters—Kate had saved every one he had ever written her, tied in bunches with cherry red ribbons—along with his diamond-framed miniature, and went to his room.

When the servant let me in, I, without a word, tossed them with great contempt onto Berry's lap.

"Your sister is nothing but a whore!" he called after me, but I ignored him. "You vile, god-forsaken goblin, do you hear me?"

"No, my lord"—I paused at the door to answer—"like many dwarves, deafness plagues me; I am stone-deaf in my left ear and not inclined to listen to you out of my right." It was a lie of course, but I didn't care. I smiled to myself at his confusion and closed the door before he could think of a suitable answer.

In July, Kate was in her seventh month, and it was high time we were making plans. Since we could not see her safely wed to Berry, and it was too late to try to dupe some other young man, and by the way many were now looking at her, some tales must have spread.

As our wretched luck would have it, when we were on the verge of asking leave to withdraw to Bradgate, with myself this time feigning illness to draw attention away from the fuller figured Kate, the smallpox came, striking down the Queen when she went for a walk, with her hair still wet from her bath, and caught a late-summer chill. Though it meant Elizabeth was too busy fighting for her life to fix a keen eye on Kate, it also meant that we must stay, as Elizabeth now had great need of all her ladies. I begged Kate not to go too near, for fear that she might catch it, or it might harm the child inside her. I took upon as many of her duties as I dared. I was already ugly, with a body and face that would never lure and tempt a lover; so what mattered it if I emerged from this ordeal with my face scarred, ravaged, and raddled by the pox? All I cared about was keeping Kate and her child safe.

Burning with a fever so hot it hurt our hands to touch her, lapsing often into unconsciousness, with her entire face and body, even the inside of her mouth, covered with red pustules, many gave Elizabeth up for lost and began looking to the future. For many, that meant Kate. My poor, frightened sister hid in her room, cowering in fear of the Crown, and wept every time there were footsteps in the corridor or a knock upon her door, fearing they had come to force it upon her just like they had done to Jane.

Many of the ladies resented Kate's absence, scoffing at my claims that she was ill, with a fever and aching head, making snide remarks as we followed the German physician's orders and gently rolled Elizabeth's fever-flamed body into a many layered cocoon of red flannel and laid her on the floor before a blazing fire to "sweat the disease out." Nay, they said of Kate, she was ill only with her own vanity, selfishly trying to save her pretty face, while they sweated and risked the pox. Lady Mary Sidney, Robert Dudley's sister, was the most devoted of all the Queen's attendants and hardly left her side until she was out of danger. Poor Lady Mary suffered the full horror of the disease. Once amongst the fairest ladies of the court, she was left as foul a woman as the smallpox could make her and would never again appear in public without a velvet mask or a thick veil.

But Elizabeth survived. "Death possessed me in every joint," she would say. Soon the pustules dried and the scabs fell away, leaving her marble-white skin relatively unscathed. But to her dismay, her famous Tudor red hair did not fare as well. The fever's fire must have singed and weakened the roots, and it began to fall out in hanks and handfuls, and every time we brushed her hair or she raked her fingers through it more would come out.

While the Queen still rested abed, nigh bald beneath her gold-embroidered nightcap, fitful, bored, and irascible by soft candlelight—Dr. Burcot, the German physician, had ordered this as her eyes were not yet strong enough to brave bright light—waiting for the wigmakers to work their magic and restore what she had lost, Kate made the mistake of wearing a gown of deep purple satin. The glossy fabric shimmered in the candlelight, and as she bent to set down Her Majesty's breakfast tray, Elizabeth's envious eyes lighted upon the rich, rippling cascade of red-gold hair falling over her shoulders. She knew all too well that many had looked to Kate when her own life was at stake.

Like a cannonball, Elizabeth shot from her bed and hurled herself at Kate, screaming at her to "take that presumptuous rag off!" and tearing at it with her nails. "You think yourself fit to wear the royal purple, do you?" Elizabeth's anger spared nothing. She raked Kate's pale skin raw, leaving behind long red scratches welling with blood. Even when the purple gown and the grape-and-rose-festooned petticoat beneath were ripped to shreds, her fury didn't abate. As Kate stepped back, inching gradually to the door where she might summon help, and brought up her hands, trying to shield her face, the screaming royal harpy's talons caught and tore the laces that held up Kate's farthingale. Down it fell, around Kate's feet. She tripped over it and fell sprawling at Elizabeth's feet. Though her stays were laced as tightly as we dared, her belly showed big and round as the moon beneath. She was in her eighth month—we *almost* made it.

The rain of blows stopped as Elizabeth stood, wild-eyed and staring, and then she was bellowing for the guards. *"Take this slut to the Tower!"*

They marched my sister through the palace, refusing her even a cloak to decently cover herself. Her things, they said, would be sent later. They paraded her shame before the court, her bulging belly covered only by her white lawn shift and leather stays, scratched and bleeding from the Queen's crazed assault, with her lip burst, her nose dripping blood, and her left eye swollen nigh shut.

Forsaking all dignity, I hitched up my skirts and ran after her, heedless of the titters my waddle-wobble and bowed limbs provoked. Kate saw me and dug in her heels. "I must speak to my sister," she said. "I must tell her what things to send me." When they took hold of her arms, to compel her to keep walking, she spun around and laid a hand meaningfully upon her belly. "The child could come at any moment, and there are certain things I *must* have."

They nodded and withdrew just a little ways, but it was enough.

Kate knelt and enfolded me in her arms, both of us knowing that this might be our last embrace. As she kissed my cheek, she whispered quickly into my ear. "You know *nothing* of my marriage, Mary, *you were never there!* Let me do this for you; let me save you, as you tried to save me. Hold your tongue as you love me; do not cause me greater pain by letting me see you, my sister, punished for what I did."

Moments later, she was gone, whisked away to the Tower, and God alone knew if she would ever come out or perish within its grim, bloody walls as Jane did.

17

At Traitor's Gate, when she slipped and fell on the slimy, wet stone steps and banged her belly, Kate feared she had lost everything. She sat, tears streaming down her battered face, cradling her stomach, crooning to her unborn child, and praying that everything would be all right, that no cramps would seize her or blood rush from her womb vacating it of life. She felt her child move and thanked God. When he came to help and gently raise her, she smiled up at Sir John Bridges, the kindly old lieutenant of the Tower, who still harbored in his heart fond memories of Jane.

She was housed in comfort, albeit of a shabby sort, with cast-off furnishings left over from our sister's nine-day reign. There were three old stools covered in faded green damask, some musty, moth-eaten tapestries, and a pair of mismatched chairs, one upholstered in plum purple velvet that our sister used to sit in, the other in tarnished gold brocade that had been Guildford's favorite fireside chair. *"It makes me feel like they are here with me,"* Kate would write to me, from the desk that used to be Jane's.

She was subjected to intense interrogation; day after relentless day they tried to break her, but they could not shake her. Through it all, Kate stoutly maintained that she was a wife, not a wanton, but when asked to prove it, of course she could not do it. She insisted that the only witness to her marriage, the Lady Jane Seymour, was dead. When asked what of me, surely she would have wanted her sister, her only close relation, who served at court with her, and thus was conveniently close at hand, to be there on this most joyous of days, Kate said nay, she had kept her nuptials secret even from me, because I was the only sister she had left and she loved me. She wanted to ensure that only she and Ned, who knew full well what they did, should suffer the consequences. When queried about the priest, Kate could only recall he had been big and red-bearded. If she had ever been told his name, which she doubted, she had forgotten it. They asked her to produce any documentation to prove her marriage valid, even a letter in which Ned addressed her as his wife, but she could not do it; they had been discreet in their correspondence, and Ned had proved, despite his promises, to be a poor letter writer. As for the deed, Kate had no choice but to admit that she had lost it.

Ned Seymour had been summoned home, and when his ship docked at Dover he was taken straight to the Tower for questioning. But his interrogators fared no better with him than they had with Kate. "Both sing the same song," they reported.

The lengthy investigation concluded with a verdict that theirs had been a "pretend marriage." The child Kate was carrying was declared illegitimate, and Ned was fined the walloping sum of £15,000 "for seducing a virgin of the blood royal." Both would remain in prison at the Queen's pleasure; they must simply wait for her wrath to cool however long it took, even if it be days or whole decades.

When on the twenty-fourth day of September 1561, at half past noon, Kate's body bucked on the molten red waves of pain and her son, Edward Seymour, the Viscount Beauchamp, emerged into the world, my joy was sadly subdued. I had been hoping for a girl. That petite phallus between her infant son's thighs made him a dangerous rival for Elizabeth's throne, poised to become the pawn of factions, the centerpiece of conspiracies; his sex made him more of a threat than Kate herself had ever been. Ned, Kate, and their baby boy formed a potent and powerful trinity, as pretty as a picture to look upon; one could almost imagine them painted as king, queen, and prince. As such, they were a threat Elizabeth took seriously and would have been a fool not to. Even if the three of them harbored no regal ambitions of their own, no matter what they said, what they signed, even if Kate publicly renounced all claim to the throne for herself and her heirs, it didn't matter, it was what others might do in their names. One could be a pawn and unwilling; Jane had taught me that. As much as I loved my sister and loathed to think of her a prisoner, in truth I could not blame Elizabeth; it would have been the most dangerous folly to throw wide the prison doors and set them free.

But Kate wasn't thinking about that. How she delighted in her son! She regarded all he did with breathless wonder, marveling at each little movement, smile, and gurgle. She called him her "little sunbeam," "the light of my world," who lit up her "gray and dreary life." Motherhood wrought a wondrous change in Kate—how I wished I could have actually seen her!—passionate, capricious Aphrodite, light as the sea foam she had been born from, had become bountiful, nourishing Demeter, devoted to her child with a depth of feeling that made any carnal love seem callow in comparison.

She sent me letters telling me how she would sit by her window, nursing her son, and watch the pink dawn spread across the city and dream she had a gown of that color, and that she could *"go to that chamber where my sweet love lies sleeping and kiss him awake." "I languish for want of him,"* she wrote. She must have said as much to her gaolers, for one of them took pity and presumed to play the role of Cupid. Each night he would lead Ned to her door, let him in, and lock the lovers in together for the night, returning at dawn to retrieve him. Kate was in ecstasy over "the sad and splendid solitude of these nights of love" during which they felt as though time had stopped and they were the only two people left alive in the world.

In another of her letters, Kate described how the heavy oak headboard, carved most fittingly with cherubs and floral garlands, of her bed battered the wall when they were at their pleasures, causing bits of stone to chip away and shower down upon them. "Proof of our passion!" Kate would say as she gathered them up into a little red velvet bag, which she would keep as a souvenir of their nights together. *"I pity the poor queen,"* she wrote of Elizabeth, *"alone in her big bed every night, unable to marry the man she loves, and never to feel a babe suckling at her breast."*

Of course they weren't thinking about precautions. They were busy living only for the moment, grasping greedily at what time they had together, and Kate soon found herself with child again. She was overjoyed. Kate loved being pregnant; she thought carrying and giving birth to a child was the most worthwhile and rewarding experience a woman could ever know. But Elizabeth was *furious;* she vowed that Kate and Ned would never meet again. And the gaolers who had helped them soon found out for themselves what it was like to be prisoners in the Tower.

Kate's second son, Thomas, was born on the cold morning of February 10, 1563. By then, Kate, having observed two birthdays in prison, was sunk deep in a dark despair that not even her "little sunbeam" could lighten. It wasn't right, she said. Her sons should be in a proper nursery, with games, toys, and pets, and nursemaids to look after them, and they should have other children to play with and be free to frolic in the fresh air and sunshine, and there was their education to think of, and when they were a little older they should have ponies to ride. "Will we ever be free to walk in the sun, to walk out and gather wildflowers?" she wondered.

Indeed, freedom, of a sort, would soon come. Elizabeth decided that she could keep them in the Tower no longer. But she would not bring them to trial either. I overheard her telling Cecil that the English people ever loved an underdog; her own mother, Anne Boleyn, had been hated and reviled, until she stood trial. She had emerged from that ordeal transformed into a tragic heroine. The English people would be apt to fall in love with Kate—a beautiful young mother in love with her husband, guilty only of having royal blood in her veins and marrying without the Queen's permission. Better to consign them to a quiet country oblivion than to risk the public rising as their besotted champions.

She timed their departure well, during an outbreak of plague in London, when her subjects were more concerned with their own survival than the succession and scandal.

Until the very last moment, Kate thought her children would be going with her. Then a pair of white-capped and aproned nursemaids came out into the courtyard. Kate brightened at the sight of them, thinking they had come to join her little household. Without me or her loyal Henny she had realized just how much she missed female companionship. But no, the women showed themselves stern and unsmiling as each took one of the little boys and carried them to another litter. Kate barely had a chance to kiss them goodbye. They wept and reached out for her over the nurses' hard and unyielding shoulders, and Kate had to be restrained from going after them. She would have fought those women with everything she had, but the kindly Sir John Bridges held her and let her weep in his arms, and bade her "take comfort, madame, they are going to be with their grandmother and your husband, their father; they shall not be reared up amongst strangers." Only that, and the hope that they might someday be reunited, kept Kate from falling apart. *"We just have to wait for the Queen's anger to cool, and then we shall all be together again,"* she wrote me hopefully, and I knew Kate well enough to know that by trying to convince me, she was also trying to convince herself.

Denied a proper farewell, not even a parting kiss or even a handclasp, Ned and Kate, kept apart and watched with all vigilance per the Queen's decree lest Kate conceive again, stared longingly at each other across the courtyard, which suddenly seemed as wide as an ocean, Kate would later confide. One of the guards, moved by the gold Ned slipped him, or even genuine pity perhaps, brought Kate a bouquet of red and white gillyflowers, bound with red and white silk ribbons, with a note from Ned.

> *My sweet and lovely Kate,*
> *My heart breaks that I cannot be with you. I will never forget you.*
> *Yours until the day I die,*
> *Ned*

Kate buried her face in the flowers and wept, watering them with her tears. Then each climbed into a leather-curtained litter and took to the road, going their separate ways. Each was thoughtfully provided with a pomander ball filled with herbs to protect them from the virulence. Sitting up all night, burning the candles till the sun came up, so that it would be ready in time, I made my sister a petticoat embroidered around the hem with beautiful tussie-mussies, nosegays of sweet herbs believed to keep away the plague. I dearly hoped that my loving stitches would keep her safe. As long as she wore the garments I made for her, I hoped she would remember that she would be clothed in love.

Elizabeth chose to be kind in her own way, though it was very cruel to Kate. She could have sent the boys to board with strangers, but she gave them into the custody of their formidable grandmother, the Duchess of Somerset, and sent them to Hanworth, in Middlesex, where Ned would also be going to live, under house arrest, in his boyhood home, forbidden to cross its boundaries or have any communication with the outside world except by letter.

She might have done the same for Kate and sent her to Bradgate, but she did not. Elizabeth could never forgive Kate for her beauty or her impetuous nature that always let passion have free rein, for being a free spirit while Elizabeth was earthbound in chains of duty also forged by painful and bitter experience; Kate trusted blindly and followed her heart, but Elizabeth never could. So instead of going to a home familiar and dear, where she might see kith and kin every day, as Ned would their sons and his mother, Kate was sent deep into the English countryside, to Gosfield Hall in Essex, home of the aged and gallant knight Sir John Wentworth and his lovely silver-haired wife, Lady Anne. This elderly couple, both in their seventh decade of life, were given to plainly understand that Her Majesty "meant no more by this liberty than to remove the Lady Katherine Grey from the danger of the plague," and that she was a prisoner, to be kept strictly isolated, and forbidden to have "any conference with the Earl of Hertford or any person being of his household either." I could only hope and pray that these new gaolers would be kind to Kate and learn to love her. For I knew my Kate could never live without love. I could not be with her, except by letter, and she had lost her "Sweet Ned" and her little boys, so God must, in His infinite kindness and tender mercy, give her some other love; to deny her would be a death sentence.

18

Redbrick and turreted, just like Bradgate, only larger, with wide glass windows that invited the sunlight in, surrounded by pretty pleasure gardens and fishponds stocked with golden carp and bordered with yellow irises, Gosfield Hall was heaven on earth compared to the hellish, horrible prisons Elizabeth could have sent her to, and I hoped Kate realized and was grateful for it. I was, but I could not even thank Her Majesty.

After Kate was sent from court, the first time I saw Elizabeth, in a pearl-embroidered ivory gown and one of her magnificent new red wigs festooned with pearls and white ostrich plumes, I trembled as I sank down into the requisite curtsy as she passed. She paused before me and reached down to cup my chin, lifting it so I would look at her.

"Do not think to plead for your sister, little gargoyle, for I will not hear you."

"Yes, Your Majesty, I understand." I nodded, gulping down my fear.

Elizabeth's shrewd dark eyes bored into me like nails.

"Yes . . . I believe you do." She nodded. She walked on, only to stop again and look back. "I have been a prisoner too, and I do not forget what it is like to be young and trapped behind thick walls and iron locks, to wonder if each day will bring death, and if you will ever be free to walk in the sun. I have a long memory, Lady Mary."

Elizabeth would always put England first, and though it was of necessity hardened and often hidden lest others see it as a sign of vulnerability, she still possessed a heart. I truly think, after the hot temper and wounded vanity that had fueled her vicious attack on Kate had cooled, the only anger that remained was at Kate for being such a fool, for marrying Ned Seymour heedless of the consequences.

It is easy to say that Elizabeth, being Queen, with the power to condemn or pardon as she pleased, ruined Kate's life, but that is not entirely true. Kate was a woman grown, not a child, and she knew the danger and the consequences, and she did it anyway. She willfully chose to make love in the arms of danger. By doing so, she left Elizabeth little choice. Elizabeth did what she *had* to do, but not without some care and comfort for Kate, though many angered and outraged by her fate forgot that. A queen who rules alone in her own right has to be ruthless if she wants to survive and hold her throne. It could have been *much* worse; she could have left Kate to rot and die in a damp, rat-infested cell, sleeping on lice-ridden straw, with water and moldy bread her daily meal, or killed her outright, but Elizabeth did neither, and I always remembered that, even when others forgot.

The Wentworths—thank You, God, for answering my prayers!—*adored* Kate and doted upon her like a daughter. They did their best to make her comfortable, giving her a beautiful and spacious suite in the west wing overlooking the gardens. They tried, heaven knows they tried, to help her find peace and some measure of happiness in her new life.

When Kate arrived at Gosfield Hall she was already mired deep in black depression. She rejected her finery, shunning the bright colors she adored, and wore only black, like one in mourning. Ned's miniature, worn on a black silk cord about her neck, the great tear-shaped sapphire on its long golden chain, which Kate would often sit and listlessly finger, calling it the "emblem of all my sorrows," and the rings he had given her—the sky blue diamond and the golden puzzle of her wedding ring—were her only adornments. *"I know every line of his dear, handsome face,"* she wrote me. *"I wear his miniature always over my heart and feel like it goes deeper, as though the lines were etched deep into my heart instead of Lavinia Teerlinc's featherlight brushstrokes barely caressing the canvas."*

At first, she slept a great deal. Sometimes she even took sleeping draughts, preferring the oblivion of sleep to wakefulness without Ned and her boys. *"Sometimes I wish I could sleep the rest of my life away,"* she wrote me. *"Morpheus is very kind to me; he does not send me dreams to torment me, instead he gives me sweet oblivion, a refuge, a haven, where I can escape from the pain and rest in peace."* Time no longer meant anything to Kate, only that each dawn heralded a new day without those she loved most, and dusk meant another night alone in bed without her "sweet bedfellow" beside her.

Whenever she was not wearing it, she kept Ned's picture on the table beside her bed alongside the miniature Lavinia Teerlinc had painted of the young mother, proudly displaying her baby son. Though it made her feel vain to pass so many hours staring at her own likeness, this was the only picture Kate had of her firstborn, and she often bewailed the fact that there had not been time to have a picture painted of little Thomas. When her own imploring letters received no answer, she begged me to write to the Duchess of Somerset and ask her to have a picture painted of Thomas, but I was also ignored.

When she was not sleeping or weeping, Kate spent hours bent over her desk, writing endless letters to Ned, pouring out her love, reminding him of the passion they had shared, always signing herself "your constant, loving Kate." Even though they were too young to read them, she wrote often to her "sweet boys," just so they would know how much their mother loved and thought of them every waking hour. It was the only way she could still be a part of their lives, to make sure they didn't forget her, but she didn't know that they would never be delivered, that she was just wasting time, paper and ink, and breaking her heart; her boys would never read her letters; their grandmother burned them.

She addressed countless missives to the Queen, begging her forgiveness, *"for my most disobedient and rash matching of myself with-*

out Your Highness's consent," and to Sir William Cecil, imploring him to intercede on her behalf. And she wrote to me, *"the only one to whom I can be true, and tell all, without having to pretend, feign a cheerfulness I don't feel, or try to keep alive the hope that is fast dying inside my heart."* She sent me great, long, rambling letters, pages and pages, weeks in the making, thick as books sometimes, wherein she set down her every thought and deed, giving me a window into her life through which I could see her so achingly clearly as though I were right there at Gosfield Hall standing outside her window looking in.

In a strange way, I felt closer to my sister than I ever had before in all the years when I saw her almost daily. At any given hour of the day or night, I could picture her and feel the sorrow weighing her down, and I tried, so hard, to send my strength across the distance, to will her to fight this pain that held her more a prisoner than the Queen's commandment. I even sent her a new petticoat, embroidered around the hem with healing herbs—white-petaled chamomile with cheery yellow suns at each flower's center to calm and soothe her, delicate pink and white clusters of valerian for the banishing of nightmares and to give her restful sleep, pale purple thyme to give peace to a troubled mind, and yellow St. John's wort to fight the melancholy, lift her spirits, and restore good cheer.

"Your life isn't over, Kate, even if your life with Ned is," I wrote her, even though I knew these words would hurt her and make her heart bleed anew, but she needed to face the truth and accept and learn to live with it. If she continued to live in this constant, unrealistic hope of a reunion, the wound would never heal; it would bleed and fester and spread a poison that would kill her in the end.

Lady Wentworth, such a kind soul, also took it upon herself to write to me about how "our Kate" fared. She was alarmed by the way the flesh was falling from Kate's bones and was determined to save her. Resorting to what she called "sweet temptation," she set about feeding Kate mint, lilac, and rose jellies, spooning these, and rich, creamy custards, or compotes of summer fruits and berries, into her mouth like a mother feeding a balky babe. She tempted her with dainty cakes too pretty to resist, moist golden cakes iced with rich cream, crowned with sugar-crusted violets and heart's ease pansies, their vibrant colors sparkling through the sugar crystals, "like blossoms fallen on snow not yet wilted or withered by the frost," she said, writing words worthy of Father.

She would rush in excitedly with the first strawberries of the season, or all manner of berries baked into tarts. She dosed her every day with thyme and St. John's wort and gave her a draught of valerian and chamomile every night. She stirred spoonfuls of sugar into Kate's milk and made her drink wines of honeysuckle, dandelions, cherry, and elderberry. She would, in time, succeed in luring Kate out of her bed, on the pretext that her rooms must be "aired, swept, and sweetened," to help make meadowsweet beer, coaxing her out to gather the foamy white flowers, which the country folk called "kiss-me-quick" or "courtship and matrimony," and the dandelions and stalks of starry yellow agrimony, then into the kitchen to boil and mix these blossoms with lemons, sugar, honey, and yeast.

When I heard this news I smiled and hoped it would remind Kate of the time we made gillyflower wine for Jane and Guildford at Chelsea. I could still see my Kate in the meadow that day, smiling at me over the rim of her cup as she sipped the sweet, syrupy golden "wine of love" we, acting as Cupid's emissaries, had made.

Lady Wentworth kept Kate's rooms, clothes, and person sweet and fragrant with rosemary, lavender, chamomile, and rose petals. Even as Kate winced and turned away, burrowing deeper into the bedclothes and hiding her head beneath the pillows, she would throw the windows wide and welcome the sunshine in. She refused to let Kate languish and lie about unwashed. She would pull her up, out of bed, and undress her as though she were a living doll, stripping off "that rank black rag," and sending it off to the laundress for a good scrubbing, then roll up her sleeves, and plunge Kate into the tub. "I will not let you go, my lady, even if you would let yourself go," she said as she scrubbed the stink and sweat, oil and grime, from my sister's body and hair, bemoaning that it was "a sad and sorry sight to see so beautiful a lady mired so deep in the black mud of misery."

Each and every week without fail, she washed Kate's hair, which had darkened with her pregnancies, with chamomile and lemon juice to lighten it, and vigorously toweled it dry with silk to restore its shine and luster. She simply would not give up on her; she fought for Kate just as I would have, even when it meant actually fighting Kate herself, and for that I bless and thank Anne Wentworth every day.

After that first outing, to make meadowsweet beer, Kate began to slowly step outside her self-imposed solitude. Security at Gosfield Hall was lax, and she might wander where she wished as long as she did not venture beyond the estate's boundaries.

Sometimes she was seen to sit listlessly by the fishpond. But instead of delighting in the golden carp and feeding them breadcrumbs, she would create a little flotilla of leaves, bidding them "sail away, little boats, and carry my love to Ned and my sweet boys." Other times she would be seen in the vegetable garden behind the kitchen, kneeling in the dirt, covering her face with her hands and weeping, for the sight of the tender new green shoots emerging from the earth reminded her of the joy she had experienced carrying and giving birth to her children, of seeing a new life come out of the red darkness of her womb into the light of the world. It made her even more aware that her sons were growing up without her. Even the sight of the fruit-laden trees in the orchard made her cry, for they reminded her that she would spend the rest of her life bereft and barren, she who loved being pregnant and longed to swell with the promise of new life and proof of the love she lived for. She would return from these excursions and fall weeping onto her bed, crying out, "What a life this is to me, to live thus in the Queen's displeasure; but for my Sweet Ned, and our boys, I would to God I were dead and buried!"

The sight of little boys, the tenants' sons and peasant lads, tugged and tore at her heart and made it bleed. Yet she would call them over to her and ask them questions, just to see what her sons might be like at that age. She took an avid interest in the servants' sons, explaining that she had never had brothers, so she did not know what boys were like, and would beg them to tell her all about their boys, anything and everything, good and bad, funny and sad; her thirst for this knowledge was unquenchable. "The years go by," she said sadly, as she watched the children of others playing and changing, growing up every day before her eyes. "You cannot get them back."

There would be small glimmers of hope that Kate's spirit was fighting back, endeavoring to slay the dragon called melancholy, but then they would of a sudden disappear, and the light would go out. Even after a year, then two, and three with the Wentworths her letters were filled with a deep and alarming sadness that made me fear for my sister's life.

> *Although there is sunshine and roses outside, it is raining, cold and barren, in my heart. And all that grows are thorns that pierce my heart and make it bleed anew every time I think of Ned and our boys going on with their lives without me, mayhap even forgetting me.*
>
> *Once I was filled with love, now loneliness has taken its place. It presses on me like a great, heavy stone upon my breast, when my husband, the only lover I long for, should lie on me instead, filling me with warmth, joy, and life."*

"How do you go on living when your heart has been cut out?" she demanded of me in angry, anguished words writ so hard the pen tore through the paper and tears blotched and blurred the black ink.

> *The grief gnaws at me so sharply I feel like I am weeping blood! I've shed so much, why have I not yet bled to death? My heart is shackled and weighed down by sorrow, and I know now that I shall never be free of it. Why does my life endure when its ending would be far kinder? Why has life, which should be God's greatest gift, become a burden, curse, and torment, why does He punish me when all I did I did for love, sweet love?*
>
> *How do I stop wanting what I cannot have? How do I make peace with it? How do I make the pain stop? Everywhere I look I see love—but not for me! If I go outdoors, I see animals mating, mother hens tending their chicks, ducks and ducklings, geese and goslings, cows and calves, dogs and puppies, cats and kittens,*

> *even squirming pink piglets glad and greedy at the teat! And everywhere I see people, I see couples courting, stealing a kiss when they think no one is looking, or husbands and wives, mothers and children, brothers and sisters! I wish I could cut out my heart. I can think of no other way but dying to make the pain stop! I've tried everything else. I cannot close my heart, harden or freeze it! I just don't know how to make my heart stop feeling, far easier if it would just stop beating!*
>
> *There is an emptiness inside me where all my love, hopes, and joy used to be. It is like a bottomless night-black pit, only it is not truly empty for it is filled with pain, like an unbearable well of loneliness, ever replenishing, day by day, so that it never runs dry. I try, I try, and try, and try again, and I keep trying to find something to fill it with, to drive out all that darkness, and cold and black pain, but I cannot! I have failed, but not from lack of trying. I tried so hard, with all my heart, I tried.*

Sometimes for days on end she sat in darkness refusing all sustenance, even water. I was sorely worried about her and wished I could go to her. But Lady Wentworth knew what to do. She was willing to put her own life, and all that she and her husband possessed, in peril, to risk the Queen's wrath, in order to save my sister. *Oh, Kate, you were loved more than you ever realized! So many people tried to save you from your own sorrowing self! Sometimes you helped them and fought back against that crushing, stifling sorrow, sometimes you just went along docile as a milk cow, and other times you fought and resisted everything and everyone that might have saved you. You were, like me, a study in contradictions.*

Lady Wentworth knew that Kate could never find peace anywhere in the world, whether it be palace, prison, or paradise, unless she first found peace within herself. In order to do that, she had to take the risk, she had to let Kate run, to let Kate find out that there was nothing left to run to, what she wanted most was already lost and gone forever. She had to trust that once Kate found out, she would come back, because there was nowhere else to go, and her disappearance would bring destruction crashing down on the heads of those who had tried to help her.

They made it easy for her, and even used a servant girl, sent to tidy the room while Kate lay listless in her bed, both body and sheets rank and in need of washing, to put the idea in her head. The windows were thrown wide to air the room, and the guards, usually stationed outside, were called away. Kate leapt ravenously at the opportunity and ran, through the dust and mud, wind and rain, scorching sun and cool moonlight of that tempestuous summer, tearing fruit and nuts from the trees or berries from the brambles whenever she was hungry, drinking milk from the teats of cows she passed, or cupping water from passing streams, all the way to Middlesex, to Hanworth. She never stopped, fearing if she did, she would be caught and all would be for naught.

By cover of darkness, she crept to a window and saw, framed by that window, the picture of a perfect, happy family—Ned in evergreen velvet, seated by the fire, with little Neddy laughing on his knee, brandishing a wooden toy cow, part of a set of wooden animals that lay scattered on the floor. Ned was smiling at the young woman in plain and prim brown velvet seated opposite him, the dark red of her hair, coiled neatly at the nape of her neck beneath her hood, shining in the firelight as she bent over little Thomas, smiling and waving a pink wooden pig on her own lap. Who was she? The governess? A daughter of a neighboring family? A cousin perhaps? Who was she? Why was she here? Why was she so familiar and seemingly dear to Kate's husband and sons? Had she replaced Kate in their hearts? In Ned's bed? Was my sister now, to them, a dying, best forgotten memory not worth even trying to keep alive? Convenient and easy always trumps distance and difficulty.

Kate later wrote me:

> *My children will grow up without me, they will forget all about me, if they have not done so already. Ned's mother will see to that. She will raise them to believe I was a brazen strumpet who tried to lure and trap her son into marriage, or else lusty youth led him into a make-believe marriage simply to bed a beautiful girl*

> *who had taken his fancy. I know the Duchess of Somerset, and she shall work to restore her son's reputation, a day will come when he is welcomed back at court, and he will marry again as soon as a suitable bride is found. Their lives will go on without me. I have become an inconvenience, an embarrassment, a disgrace to those I love most dearly!*

And she was right.

"I marvel that they did not hear my heart breaking as I stood and watched outside that window," Kate wrote me afterward.

In quiet defeat, she crept away and took to the road again, returning to Gosfield Hall because there was nowhere else to go. The house that was her prison was in truth the only safe haven. There was no one who had the power to defy the Queen and shelter and protect her. She had no money of her own, and no home. She arrived after dark and staggered into the courtyard during a violent downpour. Lady Wentworth found her collapsed and weeping, kneeling in a puddle as the rain, like a punishment, hammered down upon "this poor young woman who was already beaten down as much as a body could bear without dying."

Kate looked up at her, the tears streaming from her eyes mingling with the pouring rain. "I was hurt by love, yet I went back for more," she said, and fell, fainting, into the arms of Lady Wentworth.

For a fortnight the fever burned her. She didn't fight; and everyone feared this was the end, she had lost all will to live, the hope that had been keeping her alive was dead, and Lady Wentworth feared that in trying to help Kate she had made a grave mistake. In a moment of rare consciousness, when Lady Wentworth said, "You must try to get better, dear," Kate looked at her, in full and knowing seriousness, and said, "I don't want to," before she shut her eyes and fell into oblivion again. But, just as suddenly as the fever had come, it was gone. Kate opened her eyes, as though waking from an ordinary sleep, and sat up and said, "I would like a bath, please."

She truly began to try then, striving to find a purpose, *something* to go on for, to give her life meaning. Though the wound dealt her heart would never truly heal, the effort still was valiant. She began to assist the local midwife, delivering the tenants' babies. In this work she found a kind of peace, but also a quiet torment. *"Every time I hold a new baby, my heart mends and at the same time breaks,"* she wrote me. Yet she fought relentlessly for each little life, never giving up even on the most difficult deliveries; when even the old midwife shook her head and said it was all in God's hands, Kate persevered. "I can't let another mother lose her child, or a baby lose its mother!" she would cry as she fought to keep Death away and save both mother and child. Sometimes she succeeded in cheating Death, other times He won, and Kate took each triumph and failure to heart.

An unexpected glimmer of romance came again into Kate's life in the person of the Wentworths' new steward—Mr. Roke-Green. He was a handsome, clever, kind, dark-haired, and bearded young man in his early thirties, half English, half French, who had married early in his impetuous youth, and lost his French wife in the birthing of their sixth child. With his black-haired brood of three boys and three girls, he had come to Gosfield Hall to start a new life. He fell in love with Kate at first sight.

At first, she tried to fight it, making excuses to avoid his company, as her hope of being reunited with Ned and their boys, like the most stubborn, hard to kill weed, tried to revive itself, but then she would remember the red-haired girl she had seen through the window at Hanworth and remind herself that Ned had already moved on. And Mr. Roke-Green was tenacious; like the Wentworths, he simply would not give up on Kate. Rather than see her sink like a stone, he would teach her to swim again. He had a habit of appearing seemingly out of nowhere to walk beside her. When the maids came to tidy and freshen her rooms, he would appear to take Kate's arm and lead her out to walk in the gardens, observing, "You need a little color in your cheeks. You've been hiding indoors far too long, Mistress Kate. The sun has grown lonesome for sight of you, as I have too." He would appear to accompany her to and from the birthings she attended, even at dusk or dawn or any hour in between, falling seamlessly into step with her. She tried to discourage him with brooding silence, by refusing to talk except in clipped and rude monosyllables, but he had a knack for drawing her out. I think, knowing my sister as I do, deep down she was truly flattered to have the attention of a man again; she had always been a pert, pretty flirt, and I'm certain, even if she pretended otherwise, that she missed it.

Soon he began to bring her books, and for the first time in her life, Kate, always an indifferent, bored, and easily distracted student, became a reader. She found that she enjoyed, and even looked forward to, the discussions she would have with Mr. Roke-Green about the volumes he lent her. He took her home, to his comfortable cottage on the grounds of Gosfield Hall, to meet his children. Soon Kate was there every night, laughing and smiling, enjoying the company of them all, as she prepared their evening meal. She learned to cook, simple country fare, and became quite good at it. When Mr. Roke-Green protested that she would ruin her hands and should leave such things to the housekeeper, Kate laughed and said, "Things like soft, ladylike, lily-white hands have no place in my life anymore." With her swain at her side, insisting that he must be allowed to help, the better to be close to her, the two would stand side by side in the little kitchen and chop chunks of beef or lamb and slice carrots and onions to make a stew. Sometimes one or the other would steal a kiss. And they would each take a sip of red wine from the bottle before Kate carefully poured it into the pot to thicken the gravy.

But Kate, no matter how hard she tried, could never truly banish her melancholy. It was *always* there, lurking just below the surface, ready to seize just the right moment and come bursting forth like a crocodile to bite and rend her heart again and drag it down to drown. When Kate would stand, watching the stew pot and the bay leaves she had just added bobbing like little boats atop the bubbling brown brew, she would remember the little leaf boats she used to float upon the fishpond, to carry her love to Ned and her boys, and tears would fill her eyes, though she would always whisk them away and claim it was only the onions that made her cry.

Then a night came when she stood naked in a pool of silver white moonlight pouring in through her open window, a gentle breeze stirring the curtains. She was still very beautiful despite her sorrow; everyone said so. Nervously, she daubed rosewater behind her ears and on her throat, breasts, and wrists. She pulled on her purple wool stockings, and with trembling hands tied the violet-embroidered nightcap over her hair and took a deep breath, opened her arms, and let Mr. Roke-Green in. It was the first time she had known a man's touch in five years.

The next morning she awakened to find Lady Wentworth standing smiling beside her bed with a cup of pennyroyal tea to guard against conception. She was not going to make the same mistake as the gaolers in the Tower had. Each morning, after Kate and Mr. Roke-Green had passed a passionate night in her bed, Lady Wentworth was always there with a cup of pennyroyal tea, to make sure Kate drank every drop. There would be no "little accidents" on Lady Wentworth's watch. "Must I?" Kate would always ask, even though she knew she must, though she *longed* to feel a new life growing inside her, fluttering like a beautiful butterfly in her belly and making her feel alive, giving her sweet proof that God truly was giving her a fresh start. But it could not be, and as she obediently drank the pennyroyal tea, Lady Wentworth would put an arm around Kate's shoulders, kiss the tousled flame of her hair, and say, "Don't think about it, my dear. It will only take another bite out of your heart. Best to enjoy what you *can* have, and not brood and dwell on what you cannot." Sage advice. If only Kate's mind could have imbibed that wisdom the way her body did the pennyroyal tea.

19

Though I was now Kate's confidante, more than I had ever been before, I kept my own life a close-guarded secret. Grown even more self-interested in her sorrow, Kate never asked about me. Perhaps she thought she was being kind? That to ask would only remind me just how little I had to hope for and look forward to? Maybe her own loneliness made her more conscious of mine? After all, dwarves have never been deemed desirable paramours, and there was little else to recommend me and encourage a suitor's interest. All I had now was the trickle of Tudor blood in my veins, my yearly stipend from my service at court, and a small annuity. All the Greys' wealth had been squandered, gambled, or frittered away, and even Bradgate was no longer ours; after our lady-mother died it went, with all the rest of her remaining property, to her second husband, Adrian Stokes. The once lowly Master of the Horse had certainly done well by us; he had risen in the world, going from groom to master, and was now the proud owner of the estate where he had come to work as a stable boy. For him, playing stallion to our lady-mother's mare and suffering the bite of her riding crop on his buttocks and haunches had proved most profitable. Mayhap, as with her own daughters, she left him with a few scars to remember her by? But by saying this I really do not mean to be unkind. I saw him occasionally at court, and he always had a shy smile for me and looked as though he wanted to tarry and talk with me but was too bashful to try. I did not encourage him, especially after I realized, to my horror, after bolting up in bed in a sweat with his image still hovering naked above me, how much I wished he would, and that I liked Master Stokes's shy smiles and quiet ways a little *too* well, much more than was seemly for a maid to like the man who was her stepfather. And I shoved Master Stokes out of my mind.

I was four-and-twenty and I had a beau now. Kate never knew. No one did. The laughter would have been too loud to contain if they had. I myself blushed to even think it, and could not bear to actually say the words acknowledging it, lest bad luck come and snatch him away and give him to another. He was the most unlikely mate for me anyone could have imagined, the tallest man in London, as big as I was small, and when he stood beside me it was like a great oak towering over a tiny acorn far down below on the ground. I hadn't grown even half an inch since I was five, and he was but a smidgen under seven feet. He had been offered vast sums to tour the provinces and show himself at fairs, or to take up residence in the curiosity cabinets of royalty avid for human oddities, but he chose instead to serve his queen as sergeant porter, guarding the gate at Whitehall Palace, turning out the troublemakers and keeping the undesirables out. He quelled the drunken quarrels, arguments over dice and cards, and even lovers' spats when fists were raised and claws came out. His name was Thomas Keyes. And I loved him.

He'd been there all along, guarding the gate at Whitehall, but strange as it may sound, especially when speaking of a giant, and one with a taste for showy garb at that, I never noticed him until after Kate was gone, when I was alone . . . and in need of a friend. He knew what it was like to be different and lonely too. Our differences, though great to the world around us, made us alike in a way that no one else could see. Though he was tall and I was small, my birth was high and his was low, his years were well seasoned and mine were tender and raw, he was a widower with six children and I was a virgin spinster, we both knew what it was like to be set apart, shunned, laughed at, and to feel alone even in the midst of a crowd. He sent me a tiny sparrow, an exquisite little bird carved out of a walnut shell. Then, a few days later, he sent me a mate for her, slightly larger than herself, so that when they were put together, her head nestled comfortably in the crook of his neck, and it was as though he were sheltering and protecting the one he loved most. A week later, he sent me a nest for them, woven out of straw. Then came three little speckled stones shaped like eggs. I have them still, now as they were then, perched upon my dressing table, on a little ledge above the mirror. Later, he would give me a little mother-of-pearl bottle on a golden chain. Filled with some of Kate's cinnamon rose perfume that I kept, it still hangs between my breasts.

We began to talk. I was little and no one noticed me going to and from his rooms above the water gate at night after our duties were done for the day. He was ever the perfect gentleman, and we only met privily to spare ourselves the deep belly laughs, pointing fingers, and jests our tender companionship was certain to inspire. We tried to pretend that we wanted only friendship, and he was supremely and humbly conscious of my royal blood, saying I was "too high a star for me ever to aspire to." If a giant has ever spoken more ironic words to a dwarf I have never heard them. But did it truly matter? I thought the Tudor blood in my veins an irrelevant nuisance. None had ever come to me whispering conspiratorially about the Crown, imagining a day when I, Mary Grey, would be queen.

Pause a moment and imagine me as queen, and I dare you not to laugh. Not to let your mind conjure up lively pictures of dwarfish jesters with tin crowns and bell-spangled scepters. If I ever sat upon the throne, I would turn the monarchy into a monumental jest, and everyone would keep expecting me to spring up and dance or do acrobatic tricks, boggle my eyes, and put out my tongue, and make funny faces and jokes at my courtiers' expense with the freedom that is allotted only to the royal fool. Just think if I were mated with my Mr. Keyes as my king, what a freak show we would make. People would gladly pay a penny to come into the presence chamber to gawk and gape at us. I was no threat to Elizabeth! None at all! Suddenly things like the Queen's permission, and all the counsel I had given Kate against marrying Ned Seymour, didn't seem so important anymore. Why should I not follow in Kate's footsteps and listen to my heart and go where it led me? I knew it was leading me straight into the arms of my Thomas.

One night, after the Queen had been put to bed, I went to him, still in my black velvet and silver tinsel-cloth court finery, with a diamond star pinned to the top of my high-piled hair. He was sitting by the fire with a book when I came in. Boldly, I clambered up onto his lap, and, planting one silver-shod foot on each of his thighs, I stood up straight. Even though my hair was only barely above his salt-and-pepper stubbled pate—that was why I had piled it as high as I could even though it strained and pulled at the roots and made my head ache—it was enough for me to make my point. I pulled the diamond star free and let the scarlet-sheened sable tumble down to caress his face and curtain my own as I kissed him. It was the first time I had ever kissed a man's mouth.

"What a bold one you are, Mary Grey!" he beamed, his eyes twinkling like stars, as his broad hands grasped and encircled my thick tree-trunk waist, making it feel all of a sudden tiny as Kate's seductive hourglass shape. He kissed me back. He held me close, I clung to him, and we kissed again and again until I quite lost count. I only know that when we stopped the stars had left the sky and the sun had come out.

20

But just as love, and life, I felt, was beginning for me, for Kate it was all about to end. The brief, bright candle of her life was about to burn out, and I didn't even know it.

One winter's day, when she was out playing in the snow with Mr. Roke-Green's three daughters, a milk cow wandered past, dragging a frayed rope and crying to be milked, her angry pink udders swollen and swaying. Kate's mind was instantly catapulted back in time, to that February day, so long ago, when we three sisters had our syllabub before our lives changed forever. Looking at her suitor's three girls, she must have seen us. Perhaps she was driven to try to recapture the joy of that day, the last day when we were truly little girls, to remind herself of her youth and zest for life, to prove to herself that it was still there, that she could be that Kate again if she really tried.

"A syllabub! We shall have a syllabub! A sweet, sweet syllabub!" my Kate impulsively cried, echoing her long ago girlhood self.

I can see her now, in the black gown I had made with the row of buckram stiffened bows on the bodice, its skirt trailing listlessly, like a wilted black tail, behind her in the snow, and her hair, now faded to peaches and cream, either streaming free in a mass of wilted ringlets or braided into a coronet perched high atop her head, a coiffure made in mockery of the Crown she never coveted but had nonetheless cast such a giant shadow over her life. She sent Mr. Roke-Green's three little girls scurrying off to fetch sugar, cinnamon, wine, honey, and a long-handled spoon, while she fetched a three-legged milking stool and a pail from the barn and sat down to milk the cow.

But when it was ready, everything changed suddenly, and she could not partake of it, not even one sip. She just suddenly seemed to lose interest.

"I thought I wanted it," she said apologetically, and walked away, black skirt trailing through the snow. She took to her bed again and sank deep down, back into the black mud of melancholy, and this time nothing and no one could pull her back out. All the fight had gone out of her; she simply gave up. A part of her died that day.

She was still abed, in the same black gown, a few weeks later, staring at the rose-patterned spice-orange damask canopy above her head, refusing all sustenance, complaining that everything tasted burnt and bitter, as though her mouth were full of ashes, when the Wentworths died, one after the other. A trifling cough and fever of the kind common in winter had proved deadly for the elderly couple, and it had flooded their lungs and drowned out their lives.

Mr. Roke-Green decided to write to the Queen, to ask her permission to marry Kate. Since her union with Ned had been adjudged a "pretend marriage" this should prove no barrier, he reasoned, and, by taking a husband of lower birth, as her own mother and grandmother had done before her, she would be proving, once and for all, that she lacked any royal pretensions. For good measure, he promised that he would assure the Queen that Kate was willing to make a public renunciation as well as a written declaration, barring herself and any children born of her body from the succession permanently and forever. Kate stood beside his desk and watched him eagerly sign and seal the letter. Then, without a word, she took it from his hand and held it unwaveringly into the candle's bright flame and watched it burn until its scorching tongue lapped her fingertips. After that she walked away, without a word of explanation. Why did she do it? She never told me. But it is my belief that Kate chose to destroy her own happiness rather than give Elizabeth another chance to. Or mayhap she did it for her boys? Every mother wants the best for her children, and perhaps she did not think she had the right to deny them any hope of England's throne? Or maybe it was simply that she still loved Ned and could not envision herself with any husband but him? I do not know.

Shortly afterward, she was removed to what would be her final prison, Cockfield Hall in Yoxford, a bleak, gray, ramshackle manor in Suffolk, surrounded by a cluster of dilapidated cottages and a church falling fast into ruin.

Too weak to walk, Kate was carried upstairs to her bed by Sir Owen Hopton, her new gaoler. She never left it. Though when she was first laid down, she raised her head and laughed when she saw that the walls were hung with a series of tapestries depicting the tale of the prodigal son. She pointed feebly to the one showing him being welcomed home, back into his father's loving embrace. "Would that were me, being forgiven by Elizabeth!" She sighed. "But I know now I shall never lie in my husband's arms again or hold and play with my sweet little boys. They are growing up now—seven and six, Sir Owen! My how the time flies! The years go by without me, and I cannot get them back!"

She fell to weeping piteously into her pillows.

At midnight on January 26, 1568, I awoke, or thought I did, to the touch of a hand, a gentle caress, upon my cheek. I found Kate sitting beside me, smiling down at me, pale as a white rose lightly blushed with pink. She was wearing the black gown with the ladder of bows on the bodice, the last I had made for her, and her peaches and cream hair was a mass of shining ringlets that seemed to have captured the sun in their curls. The storms of anguished torment that had filled her blue gray eyes had all blown out, leaving only peace and tranquility behind. She was glowing, radiant, and I knew instinctively that the last faint ember of her life had finally burned out; there was nothing left in this world that she could hope to have that would make her shine so.

"Live for love, Mary, *all for love!*" she said to me with urgent, loving tenderness—the Kate I had known and loved restored to me for one brief, shining instant.

She pointed out my window, and I saw a star fall, like a diamond dropped down into dark water, and when I looked back, she was gone. "Going toward God, as fast as I can!" a faint voice whispered with a hopeful smile I heard but couldn't see, then silence, sad but sacred silence that told me that my Kate was at long last at peace.

I sat in the darkness, hugging my knees, and wept for my sister, then I got up and did what I knew she would want me to do.

I threw a dark cloak over my shift, and, without even bothering to put on my slippers, I went to my Thomas's rooms above the water gate.

Fearlessly, I let my cloak fall, and wriggled out of my shift. Naked as a babe, unashamed, for the first time in my life, of my squat, gnarled, thick goblin's body, I crawled into his bed and kissed him awake and told him yes, I would marry him, and felt his arms close about me and his lips upon mine.

When the messenger finally came, he didn't have to tell me she was gone; Kate had already told me herself. All he could give me were the details, how Kate had entrusted three rings to Sir Owen Hopton, asking him to see them safely delivered to her husband—her sky blue diamond betrothal ring, the five-banded gold puzzle ring he had put on her finger the day they were wed, and, lastly, a silver skull, an ornately wrought death's head set with sapphire eyes, its band engraved inside with the words *While I Lived, Yours*. Then, seemingly content, she folded her arms across her breast, shut her eyes, and prayed, "O Lord, for Thy many mercies, blot out of Thy book my many sins."

Alarmed, Sir Owen sent a maid running to the nearby church, to ask that the bells be rung, calling all to pray for the departing soul of one, though not acknowledged, they considered a princess.

"Yes, good Sir Owen"—Kate smiled without opening her eyes—"let it be so."

Sensing Death's approach, Kate sat up, for the first time in many days, "jubilant and radiant as I had never seen her before," Sir Owen reported. She rejoiced to see her fingernails turning blue. "Look you, here He comes!" she cried eagerly, excitedly holding out her hand for those about her—the maids, doctor, priest, and Sir Owen and his wife—to see. "For all the world like a girl happily displaying her betrothal ring to her dearest friends," Sir Owen would say after. Then she flung wide her arms, "like a woman welcoming her lover," and cried out, *"Welcome, Death!"* and fell back, eyes closed, lips parted as if in ecstasy, like a woman surrendering to the most passionate embrace.

So died the broken spirit that was once my sunshine girl, my lovely, lively Kate. She was only twenty-eight.

I didn't go to Yoxford to see her buried; I wanted to remember her as I saw her last, beautiful and radiant, and blissfully at peace. But I sent a gown of soft orange silk, to complement her sorrow-bleached hair, since I couldn't bear the thought of Kate being buried in black, and a wreath of gilded laurel leaves for her hair, to show all who looked upon her that she had won her battle with life.

21

We were married by candlelight in his quarters at Whitehall on July 16 by a silver-haired priest, with Thomas's eldest son and his wife as our witnesses. A pair of pipers played for us, and the feast that followed was fine but small, with the table laid with fruits, cheeses, meats, and a golden cake baked full of red currants and raisins. It was a brief repast. We were impatient to be alone together. When I appeared in my black and yellow gown, he called me his "bumblebee bride." That night was the first and only time, since I was a child, that I dared dance before others. Then everyone was gone and we were all alone. I unlaced his leather doublet and he opened my gown. He said my breasts were like little pears and kissed and nibbled them as I laughed and cried at this most exquisite pleasure.

The first time we made love I lost myself. Me—that was the first thing to go, even before my virginity. I forgot all about my stunted, little misshapen lump of a body, my crooked spine, and the face and figure that made people recoil and call me "goblin," "gargoyle," "changeling," and "Satan's imp." As his lips devoured me and his hands caressed me, gently probing my secret depths where no one, not even myself, had ever dared explore, I felt no shame; I experienced only pleasure. It was as though I was climbing out of myself, going higher and higher, to the top of the world's tallest mountain, and then, with a breathless gasp of wonder, I jumped, I fell and floated down, in lovely terror, only I did not crash and impale myself on the jagged rocks below, for my Thomas caught me and held me close and kissed me. Soon I was ready to scale the heights again.

A month of love was all we had, a four-week feast of passion before we had to pay the penalty for that pleasure and the ring of gold that my Thomas had put upon my tiny finger. We were abed, after midnight, by candlelight, when the door crashed down and the guards came pouring in. A full dozen of them surrounded our bed, gaping at our nakedness, eyes bulging wide with astonishment at the odd and indecent sight spread before them.

In the golden flattery of the candlelight, and the shadows cast by the dark red curtain of my hair, I must have looked like a child, instead of a woman—a *passionate* woman—my legs stretched like a wishbone about to break as I straddled my husband. His cock must have loomed large, like the most threatening battering ram, poised and ready to assault an innocent child.

"For shame!" one of the guards cried as he reached out and plucked me off my Thomas, and out of, what he must have thought, was harm's way. He bundled me in a cloak, as if I were his own little girl, and carried me out, even as I shamelessly bawled and cried and reached out over his shoulder for my Thomas, my lover, my husband.

Like Philistines surrounding Samson, they fell upon my Mr. Keyes, and bound him in chains. I never saw him alive again. They took him to the Tower and stuffed and crammed his giant's body into the tiniest cell, crushing his bones and causing his joints to cramp and swell. The gaoler was cruel and sometimes denied him food, causing my tenderhearted Thomas, who loved all creatures great and small, to have to resort to killing with his bare hands the birds that sometimes perched upon his windowsill. He ate them raw since he had no means to cook them. When his children found out and went to plead before Sir William Cecil, begging him to remedy and ease their father's plight, the gaoler retaliated by feeding my love rotten meat that had been dropped into the poison used to treat the mange that afflicted his dogs. When they finally let him out of that "noisome and narrow cell," it was too late; he was broken and crippled beyond repair and soon died. My only consolation was that he was allowed to go home to his cottage in Kent, the one we had dreamed of retiring to, to die surrounded by his many children and grandchildren, with birds singing and the roses he loved blooming outside his window.

As for myself, Elizabeth sent me under house arrest to Chequers, the sumptuous country house of Sir William Hawtrey, the high sheriff of Buckinghamshire. It was a sprawling estate, adorned with stately elms and several pleasure gardens, each of which had been given a name evocative of its particular theme. I had a fine view of the ones called "Silver Spring" and "Velvet Lawn" from my window, but I didn't care.

Our married life was passed in separate prisons, with no hope of a reunion. Still my heart dreamed of the two of us and that little cottage in Kent he had told me about, even though my head knew better. *Annul me, divorce me, I don't care, only let my love go free!* I said, it was cruel to keep him so confined. I had been a fool to think Elizabeth would discount me as a danger because I was a dwarf—royal blood was royal blood.

When I heard that he was dead, I lost my mind. The hair began to fall from my head, like the tears from my eyes, until I hacked it off. Bald and naked, keening out my grief, I drew pictures on the white plastered walls, with my own blood and feces when they saw what mischief I was about and took away my ink. Over and over again, I drew my Thomas sprouting wings and flying free. I wished him Godspeed and told him he was well rid of me, for loving me had brought him nothing but misfortune.

I felt blasted, bitter, and blighted, the ache inside me was at once bloody red and raw, dry as if scorched by desert suns, and wet as though drowned in a salty ocean that burned my nose, throat, and eyes. Pain filled my lungs like water, and the weight dragged me down into darkness so deep I feared I would never see the light again. I had lost the one person who truly saw and loved *me.* I was his Mary, not one of Mother Nature's mistakes, to toss a penny and shout, "Dance, dwarf, dance; make me laugh!" He never saw me that way. He loved *me,* the *real me!*

In this way five years of my life slipped past. "The years go by," as Kate said. "You cannot get them back." I fell—but there was no one there to catch me, and I shattered. I was supposed to be the strong one, practical and pragmatic. I was the one who had kept pushing Kate in the same circumstances to fight, to not give in to the darkness that would swallow up her soul if she let it. But I didn't fight it, I was weak; I failed to practice what I preached, and there was no one to push and bolster me. Madness and melancholy took me as their whore and did whatever they wanted to with me. Even now when I think about it, I still disgust, and disappoint, myself.

In 1573, when Elizabeth finally set me free, I made a pilgrimage to Kent, and in the gray gold light of dawn, I planted raspberries and rosemary, for remorse and remembrance, on my beloved's grave and watered them with my tears. I sat with him, my hand atop the soil that covered him like a brown velvet blanket, and imagined him holding my hand as we watched the sun rise together, though in truth he should have crushed it with anger for what I did to him. Had I not been as rash and foolish as I once chided Kate for being, I would not have brought destruction crashing down like the jawbone of an ass upon his head. I lay on his grave, as I used to lie with my head upon his shoulder, listening to his heartbeat, but that heart had been stilled forever while mine went on beating knowing that I was responsible for the stopping of his. Then I slunk away, too cowardly to face his children, fearing that they would hate and blame me, even though I well deserved it.

I returned to London and took lodgings in the cheapest inn I could find. I hadn't a friend in the world and did not know what would become of me. I had little money, and as small as a child myself, I knew I would not present a very imposing figure as a nursery governess.

My stepfather, Adrian Stokes, came to my rescue. He insisted on settling a sum of money on me and offered me a home at Bradgate: "For it *is* your home, Mary, and always will be." When I refused, wanting something new in reckless defiance of my strained circumstances, he helped me find and buy my little house in St. Botolph's-Without-Aldgate. He even planted with his own hands a little garden of raspberries and rosemary for me, yet when I was not looking he added purple hyacinths for forgiveness. "Because you *must* forgive yourself, Mary. Thomas Keyes married you because he loved you, and if he had the chance, he would do it all the same again. Don't dishonor your marriage by regretting it, Mary, he never did, nor would I if . . ." He left the words unspoken and hung his head, as a crimson blush spread across his lean and handsome face, still boyish even at forty with a few skeins of silver snaking through his black hair. He had dared to almost say the words that should never be spoken, yet they hung in the air between us, like a specter, the ghost of a dream that could never be more than a dream.

I was astonished. How could he want *me?* A handsome man who could have his pick of women, like flowers from a garden. But I couldn't let myself even consider, I couldn't let myself desire or even dream, I knew that part of me that longed for love and its carnal expression had to die forever lest it lead another to disaster.

I let him kiss me, just once—I promised myself—just one first and last sweet kiss in the little garden he had made for me, knowing it really would be my last.

With a shaky hand. I caressed his cheek as I breathed out a long, trembling sigh. Then I sent him away, because I had to, for his sake, and my own.

"I will ever love and protect you, Mary," he said as he closed the garden gate behind him, just as my heart closed the door upon love. But I was weak. Even though in my heart it was still Thomas I pined for, that long ago stifled and denied attraction was still there. I kicked that closing door back open again. "Adrian—wait! Come back!" I cried. And he did. He swept me up into his arms and held me close against his heart and kissed me as I thought I would never be kissed again.

Sometimes there are no second chances, but sometimes there are.

As we knelt together on my bed, pausing to kiss the flesh as we bared it, he told me he had always loved me, even when he knew he shouldn't on account of my high and his humble birth. When he had finally, after our string of misfortunes and I had been forsaken by Lord Wilton, worked up the courage to ask my lady-mother for my hand, she flew into a terrifying riding-crop-swinging, screaming rage, "madder than any woman I ever saw." " 'Twas rather bewildering," he confessed. "I still can't make sense of it all—one moment I was asking for you, and the next I was standing before the priest with her with my ear bleeding and feeling like nails were being driven into my arm the way she held it, and between the two there was a red and raging storm that left me sorely battered and my soul feeling all tired out and wrung dry."

"Aye"—I nodded as I kissed his throat—"I understand full well—such was my lady-mother."

But I was older and wiser now; I didn't let him ruin his life because of me. I chose to be a mistress rather than a wife. As I was his stepdaughter none ever suspected. Why ever would they? How could it ever be anything but innocent? In fairy tales the handsome prince never woos, weds, or beds a troll or goblin. I made him marry, and I even helped him choose a bride, a sweet, sensible widow with several children. Her name was Anne Carew, and if she ever knew of the delightful afternoons, and occasional nights, he spent in my bed, she was too well-bred to mention it and never gave a sign. She had the security of marriage; I had someone who was both a lover and a friend to keep the sharp teeth of loneliness from biting too deep. Sometimes one must compromise and bargain to get the best out of life.

To my surprise, Elizabeth summoned me to Hampton Court to attend the New Year's celebrations. Though it taxed my meager funds considerably, I knew I could not arrive without a suitable offering for my sovereign. I bought her a set of four dozen gold floral buttons, each one studded with a pearl at its center, and a pair of sweet-scented buff-colored leather gloves sewn with seed pearls and gold embroidery in a floral pattern.

I put on the finest gown I had, my gold-lace-garnished, black velvet wedding gown and my black-and-yellow-striped "bumblebee" kirtle. Though it was a few years out of fashion, I didn't care; it meant more to me to be once again my Thomas's "bumblebee bride." Beneath it, I wore once again my red silk petticoat embroidered with three golden butterflies for three sisters, two dead, one living, and around my solid, tree trunk waist the girdle of fine goldsmith's work, pearls, and red orange jacinth stones Adrian had given me as a New Year's gift. I felt the little mother-of-pearl bottle hanging between my breasts, cool against my hot skin, and lifted it to inhale the spicy-sweet cinnamon rose of Kate's perfume, and any fear I felt melted from me; I knew, in spirit, my love was with me, as were my sisters. *Nothing is ever truly lost,* I told myself as I straightened the mound of gaudy pearl-impaled sable red curls atop my head, *certainly not true love, like that betwixt sisters, or that which I gave to and received from my Thomas.* As I left my little house, to climb into the coach Adrian had so thoughtfully provided, I felt my sisters walking alongside me, their hands reaching out to hold mine, and the protective presence of my Thomas hovering, like a great oak, mighty and sheltering, high above me. I walked in love and knew I would never walk alone.

Now past her child-bearing years, her face an inscrutable white-marble mask beneath the flaming red of her pearl-encrusted wig, Elizabeth, "The Virgin Queen," sat on her throne resplendent in a gown of olive green and yellow satin embroidered with olive branches and wheat stalks to symbolize peace and plenty, the two things she wanted most for her beloved people.

Everyone turned and stared in stunned silence when they saw bold black-and-yellow-clad me standing in the wide doorway of the presence chamber.

The chamberlain banged his staff upon the marbled floor and announced—"Lady Mary Grey!"

But I shook my head, and instead of approaching the Queen, I went to him and tugged sharply at the hem of his doublet to get his attention.

"Mrs. Thomas Keyes!" I insisted in a voice clear and steady that carried throughout the cavernous chamber.

Across that great, wide room that intimidated so many, an amused and approving gleam lit Elizabeth's dark eyes, and she gave an imperceptible nod as a smile twitched at her taut bloodred rouged lips. But it was enough. I could tell that she approved of me. My audacity had not offended the Queen's Majesty, though in truth I wouldn't have cared if it had.

She gave a quick nod to the chamberlain, and the staff pounded the floor again as his voice rang out, announcing—"Mrs. Thomas Keyes!"

Proudly, with head held high, like a little queen, I approached the dais and made my curtsy to my cousin, the Queen.

POSTSCRIPT

Lady Mary Grey died alone in her little house in St. Botolph's-Without-Aldgate in April 1578, her constitution fatally weakened by the plague that had visited London that winter. The "mystic ruby," crystallized, legend claimed, from a drop of blood at the base of a unicorn's horn, believed to protect the wearer from plague, that Thomas Keyes had given her, was still on her finger. She was thirty-four years old. Her small, child-sized coffin was entombed with her mother in Westminster Abbey. No plaque or monument marks her grave.

Kate's "Sweet Ned," Edward Seymour, Earl of Hertford, went on to marry twice more—first to Lady Frances Howard, his mistress of many years, and after her death in 1598, a wealthy wine merchant's widow, Frances Prannell.

In 1608, the validity of his marriage to Lady Katherine Grey was at long last proven when the red-bearded priest, now old, stoop-backed, and gray, and sworn off strong drink, emerged from the obscurity of a sleepy little country parish. Though forty years had passed since her death, Katherine's body was exhumed and laid to her second rest beneath a beautiful white marble effigy with all honors due her as the rightful Countess of Hertford in Salisbury Cathedral, where Ned would come to sleep beside her when he died in 1621 at the age of 83, having outlived both their sons.

Kate's "sweet little boys" grew to manhood, dabbling in romance and royal intrigue. Thomas died with the new century in 1600; his elder brother, Edward, Viscount Beauchamp, outlived him by a dozen years, dying in 1612.

FURTHER READING

For those interested in a factual account of the lives of the Grey sisters, I recommend *The Sisters Who Would Be Queen* by Leanda de Lisle.

A READING GROUP GUIDE

THE QUEEN'S RIVALS

Brandy Purdy

About this Guide

The suggested questions are included to enhance your group's reading of Brandy Purdy's ***The Queen's Rivals.***

DISCUSSION QUESTIONS

1. Discuss the personalities of the three sisters—Jane, Kate, and Mary. Which do you like best and why?

2. The Grey sisters have a little ritual in which they stand before the mirror and identify themselves as "the brilliant one," "the beautiful one," and "the beastly little one," poking fun at the way other people see them. Discuss the outside world's perceptions of the three sisters and how they see themselves. Discuss their relationship with each other. If they weren't united by blood and family ties, would these three girls have been friends?

3. Because of Jane's confession to Roger Ascham, history remembers her mother, Frances Grey, the Duchess of Suffolk, as a ruthless, ambitious, child-beating monster. The modern concept of child abuse was nonexistent in Tudor times, and what we would today consider harsh punishments were not uncommon. What do you think about this? Was Frances Grey typical and merely a product of the time she lived in or did she cross the line?

4. Discuss the girls' father, Henry Grey, Duke of Suffolk. In this book, he's depicted as a weak-willed man of many vices and addictions—gambling, sweets, and Guildford Dudley. Compared to his wife, is he the good, fun parent? Discuss his influence on his daughters. Is it good or bad? Would their lives, or the course of the story, have been different if he had been a stronger or wiser man? Discuss his relationship with Guildford Dudley. Do you believe the two were lovers in the full physical sense or was it just an innocent infatuation that was really all talk and no substance?

5. In this novel, Lady Jane Grey deplores anything that even hints of sex and romance, urging those who are weak, or might be tempted, to fight against lust and "despise the flesh." Why is she so vehemently opposed to what others consider a natural part of life? Does she really, as some sus-

pect, secretly desire her handsome young husband but fight against a desire she loathes discovering inside herself, or does she really hate him? And is Guildford really as stupid and conceited as people think?

6. Do you agree with Mary Grey that her eldest sister, Jane, chose and embraced the role of martyr and victim? If so, why do you think Jane did this? If you disagree, why do you think Mary thought this? And how do you see Jane?

7. Mary says that "all for love" should have been Kate's motto. Is this true? If so, is it a good or a bad thing? Love definitely played a starring role in Katherine Grey's life and death. Do you agree or disagree with the choices she made? Discuss her relationships with the various men in her life—her father, her two husbands, her father-in-law, and the minor dalliances and flirtations. How did they affect, mold, and shape her? Why does she risk her life to save her father's head from London Bridge? Did she really love her first husband, or was she, as Mary thought, simply in love with love? Should she have married Ned Seymour? Is his love for her sincere or does her royal blood play a role in his decision to secretly marry her? Does it stand the test of time even when they are separated?

8. Discuss Frances Grey's marriage to Adrian Stokes. Why does she *really* marry him? Throughout history, and even in the modern day, men routinely date and marry women considerably younger than themselves, but an older woman with a much younger man still invites comment, sometimes even jokes and laughter. What do you think of this? In this novel, her surviving daughters are clearly appalled by her actions, and Frances herself realizes that she is likely to become a laughingstock at court. Do you think this is justified?

9. After she becomes friends with Lady Jane Seymour, Kate begins to neglect and ignore Mary. They no longer share a room and drift apart until they are more like casual acquaintances than sisters. Why do you think this happened? How

would you have reacted if you were in Mary's shoes? Kate seems to dance in and out of Mary's life at her own convenience, as it suits her, when she wants new clothes, and, after Lady Jane dies, when she has no one else to turn to. Even when Kate is in prison and makes Mary her confidante, it is still all about Kate, and she never asks about Mary. Do you think Kate uses or takes advantage of Mary? How does this make you feel about Kate?

10. Why does Kate give up? Why does she stop fighting? Why does she burn Mr. Roke-Green's letter to Queen Elizabeth before he has a chance to send it? She died at only twenty-eight after losing a long battle with depression. Could this have been avoided? Could she have won this battle? What, if anything, could Kate have done to ensure a happier or longer life for herself?

11. Why does Mary, the practical and pragmatic one who should have known better, follow in Kate's footsteps when she knows the danger that comes with marrying secretly, without the Queen's consent? Discuss her relationship with Thomas Keyes. Why do they fall in love? And is it really love? During her sister's imprisonment, Mary was constantly pushing Kate to fight and not give in to her depression, to find a way to go on with her life, yet, as Mary freely admits, when she is in the same position, she does not practice what she preached and actually goes mad for a time. How does this make you feel about Mary? Does it make her more human, or a more or less sympathetic character? What do you think of our little narrator? Discuss what life must have been like for someone who was physically different or challenged in Tudor England. Did the difficulties and disappointments she faced make Mary a stronger or wiser person?

12. Discuss Mary's life after she is released from prison. Even though she still mourns her husband and has already made the decision to shut love out of her life, she spontaneously begins a secret affair with her stepfather, Adrian Stokes.

Why does she do this? Is it a good or bad decision? And, why, when she is received back at court, does she insist on calling herself "Mrs. Thomas Keyes"? Is this an act of pride, insolence, and defiance, or her way of honoring the memory of the man she truly loved?